ALSO BY E.E.

THE WORLD OF THE GATEWAY

The Gateway Trilogy (Series 1)
Spirit Legacy: Book 1 of The Gateway Trilogy
Spirit Prophecy: Book 2 of The Gateway Trilogy
Spirit Ascendancy: Book 3 of The Gateway Trilogy

The Gateway Trackers (Series 2)
Whispers of the Walker: The Gateway Trackers Book 1
Plague of the Shattered: The Gateway Trackers Book 2
Awakening of the Seer: The Gateway Trackers Book 3
Portraits of the Forsaken: The Gateway Trackers Book 4
Heart of the Rebellion: The Gateway Trackers Book 5
Soul of the Sentinel: The Gateway Trackers Book 6
Gift of the Darkness: The Gateway Trackers Book 7

PORTRAITS OF THE FORSAKEN

PORTRAITS OF THE FORSAKEN

The Gateway Trackers Book 4

E.E. HOLMES

Lily Faire Publishing

Lily Faire Publishing
Townsend, MA

www.lilyfairepublishing.com

ISBN 978-0-9984762-5-4 (Print edition)

ISBN 978-0-9984762-6-1 (Digital edition)

Publisher's note: This is a work of fiction. Names, characters, places and incidents are either the product of the author's imagination or are used fictitiously.

Cover design by James T. Egan of Bookfly Design LLC
Author photography by Cydney Scott Photography

This one is for my always fascinating girls at Table 9.

"We have scotch'd the snake, not kill'd it:
She'll close and be herself, whilst our poor malice
Remains in danger of her former tooth.
But let the frame of things disjoint, both the
worlds suffer,
Ere we will eat our meal in fear and sleep
In the affliction of these terrible dreams
That shake us nightly: better be with the dead,
Whom we, to gain our peace, have sent to peace,
Than on the torture of the mind to lie
In restless ecstasy."

—William Shakespeare

"Macbeth"

CONTENTS

GHOSTS ON THE UNDERGROUND

T HERE IS SOMETHING BOTH INTIMATE and exhilarating about exploring a new city on your own. Getting to know its curves and angles, its sights and smells. Stepping into the light from the darkened entrance to the underground and realizing that you know where you are, and how to get where you're going next. It's like any relationship, really. There's the initial trepidation, the hesitancy to even find the courage to introduce yourself. Then there's the awkward question phase, an interrogation of sorts, when you're trying to establish your suitability to each other. And then finally, the conversations flow easily and the smiles come naturally.

And so it was with me and London that spring—comfortable at last.

Yes, London and I were finally getting to know each other and, truth be told, we were getting along just fine. But there were two Londons to explore when you were a Durupinen: the London of the living, and the London of the dead. Today, it was the London of the dead that had my full attention.

The barista behind the counter of the café, for example, was dead. There was no doubt about that.

I watched her covertly as I sipped my tea, unwilling to draw attention to myself until I got a sense of her mental state.

She was young and beautiful, with a smile that kept faltering as she tried to go through the motions of a life she was no longer connected to. Through the warm haze of steam rising from my mug, I watched as she reached for an apron hanging on a hook, only to realize that she was already wearing one. She stared down at it, and I knew she was trying to remember when she had put it on. Then, shrugging off her confusion, she approached the counter and beamed politely at the elderly customer who waited there.

"What can I get for you today, love?" she asked brightly. Her smile faded into a frown of puzzlement when the old man did not acknowledge her, but gave his order instead to the young man at the other register.

The young man shouted the order over his shoulder, and the spirit sprang into action, purpose clear and determined on her face. But after a few moments, she was wandering amongst the equipment, unable to remember what it was she was supposed to be doing. Her eyes filled with tears as she watched another barista plunk the old man's coffee down on the counter with a cheery, "Enjoy your day!" Then she spotted the aprons hanging on the wall and started the whole routine over again.

For me, these were always the saddest spirit encounters. It was heartbreaking to see the mixture of bewilderment and hope in their eyes as they poked and prodded at the new boundaries of their existence, fighting valiantly against a realization too awful to face.

I looked away from the spirit of the barista and down at a copy of that morning's edition of The Sun under my saucer. The same beautiful face smiled up at me from a photo on the front page. The headline read, "Woman Found Murdered in South Kensington Flat, Boyfriend in Custody."

I waited for an hour or so, watching surreptitiously as the young woman struggled to find her bearings, but she just wasn't ready.

It was easy to tell when they were ready. A spirit would stop trying to force herself into a living role, and grow still, and quiet. She would look—really *look*—around herself for the first time. She would sense the distance that had sprung up between herself and the material world. And only in that stillness would she be able to sense the presence of the Gateway.

The Gateway was the doorway from the world of the living to the world of the dead. Most spirits passed through it right at the moment of death, but others, for reasons as varied as the spirits themselves, remained behind. But when those spirits were ready to Cross, they would seek out the Durupinen, the ancient sisterhood of women who acted as the gatekeepers, opening the Gateways and allowing trapped spirits to move beyond.

I swigged the last of my tea and stood up, throwing my bag over my shoulder. I would try again tomorrow. By then, perhaps, the spirit may have come to terms with her new state of being. It was always best to try to catch them early in that realization, before they started panicking and scaring the shit out of the surrounding living people by slamming doors and causing the lights to flicker.

I turned with the cup in my hand, ready to deposit it into a tray of dirty dishes, when a figure outside the window caught my eye. The man was tall and broad-shouldered, with shaggy dark hair that obscured his face as he strode by on the opposite sidewalk.

I gasped. The teacup slipped from my fingers and shattered all over the tile floor.

Everyone turned to stare at me, including the spirit behind the counter. Without intending to, I caught her eye.

"You can see me!" she cried.

I looked swiftly away, trying to pretend that I could not hear her. Mumbling a rapid apology to the still gawking staff, I bent and scooped up the shards of the cup and threw them unceremoniously into the trash bin. I bolted for the door, my heart hammering.

I skidded to a halt on the pavement and scanned the milling crowd on the opposite side of the road. I spotted him almost at once, overtaking a group of tourists huddled around a map.

"Finn!" I shouted.

He did not look up, or even break his stride. Cursing under my breath, I broke into a run.

"Hey! Come back! You can see me!" The barista had followed me out of the café and was gliding along beside me, her face stricken.

I ignored her, pushing my way past a man taking a selfie with a red phone booth. I had to get to the corner, where I could cross the street. I had to keep him in my sights or I would lose him in the bustle of the morning crowds.

The spirit was not fooled. "Answer me! I'm not crazy! You looked right at me! I saw you!" the girl shrieked at me. She planted herself in front of me, but I barreled right through her, shivering violently at the bone-deep cold that only contact with a spirit could produce.

She screamed in terror. I swallowed back a wave of guilt. It was a shitty thing to do to a girl who didn't yet realize she was dead. I would find a way to make it up to her, but not now. I reached the corner and jammed my finger at the walk button. Five months in this city and I couldn't get used to the way the cars zipped past me from the opposite direction than I was expecting. Even the warnings spray painted onto the street, reminding me to "Look Right!" weren't much of a help.

"You have to talk to me! You have to tell me what's going on!" the

3

spirit screamed. Her energy rose to an unbearable pitch, vibrating inside my head so that my vision blurred. The bulb in the traffic light beside us flickered, buzzed, and then exploded in a shower of sparks.

Unable to ignore her any longer, I turned on the girl and hissed, "Yes! Yes, I can see you! And I'm very, very sorry, but I cannot help you right now."

"But what's happening?" she sobbed. "I can't remember what I've been doing, or where I've been. I don't know how I got to work this morning. Why isn't anyone answering me? And I feel so... so strange. So strange and numb."

I took advantage of the motorists' confusion over the traffic light to dart across the street. Undaunted, the spirit followed me, continuing to shout at increasing levels of shrillness. I blocked her out and focused all my energy on shoving through the pedestrians blocking my way. Twenty yards ahead of me, I could still see the dark head of hair bobbing through the sea of people.

"Finn!" I cried again, but the sounds of the crowds and the traffic swallowed my voice. "Damn it. Excuse me, please. Excuse me!" I said over and over again as I shoved and pushed and elbowed without mercy. Why the hell didn't people know how to *move!*

If I lost him...

"Please, I'm begging you!" the spirit was sobbing now. "Is this a dream? Am I stuck in some kind of a dream? I can't touch anything! I can't feel anything!"

But I had frozen in a moment of panic. The head of hair, that familiar loping stride, was vanishing from view down into the Tube station entrance.

I tore after him, leaving a woman laden with shopping bags sprawled on the ground behind me. I took the steps two at a time, digging desperately into my bag for my wallet, trying to locate and extract my Oyster card with trembling fingers. The rumble of the approaching train muffled the cries of the pursuing spirit.

I slammed the Oyster card into the sensor panel and the gate slid open. I pounded forward the last few steps and caught his shoulder just as the train ground to a stop in front of us.

"Finn!" I gasped as I spun him around.

He turned, blinking down at me in surprise with a pair of bright green eyes I did not know. He pulled an earbud out of one ear. "What's that, then?" he asked.

4

I jumped back, releasing my grip on his jacket. "I... I'm sorry. I thought you were someone else."

The young man smiled at me, revealing slightly crooked teeth and a dimple in one unshaven cheek. "Who do you want me to be, darl?" he asked, winking. "I'm sure I could give it a go."

I tried to return his smile. "Sorry. You'll miss your train."

The man chuckled, shrugged, and popped his earbud back into his ear. Then he turned and slid deftly into the train car even as the doors began to close.

I stood motionless, watching him take a seat as the train picked up speed and trundled off into the yawning mouth of the tunnel.

I hovered on the verge of tears for a moment, then laughed bitterly at myself.

"You are losing it, Jess. You are officially losing it," I whispered.

In the hollow, ringing emptiness left behind in the absence of the train, the spirit was still pleading and begging with me to help her. I took a long, shuddering breath and slammed the lid on the Pandora's Box of emotions threatening to spill out of me. What a fool I was to dare flirt with a remorseless bastard like hope.

I turned to the spirit and held up a hand. She became utterly still in the shock of finally being acknowledged.

"I'm sorry," I said. "I didn't mean to ignore you. I've been looking for someone and I had to know if that was him."

The girl didn't answer. She seemed afraid to interrupt me now that I'd decided to start talking to her.

"I know you're confused," I said. "And I know you're frightened. You don't yet understand what's happened to you, and that's got to be terrifying."

The girl nodded her head, unblinking.

"I can tell you what happened, if you'd like, but it's going to be difficult to hear."

Her wide eyes filled with the glimmer of tears, and she swallowed hard. "I... think I must know it, but... I can't remember it clearly."

"That's just your mind protecting itself," I told her, as gently as I could. "When something traumatic happens, our memories blur it out sometimes, so that we don't have to suffer the pain of remembering it over and over again. Does it seem hazy and unclear?"

"Yes." The girl's mouth moved, but she made no sound.

I nodded. "It will become clearer, if you concentrate on it. You've been too distracted and too confused to really focus. Go back to the last thing you remember clearly and try to move your mind past it to what happened next."

I stood and waited as she closed her eyes and reached back into the depths of her living memory. I didn't watch her do it; I had long since learned to put some distance between myself and the raw pain of spirits, simply to protect myself. I tuned her out, focusing instead on the saxophone music drifting over from the far end of the Tube station. Reginald was in rare form today. I let the music wash over me, let it mask the gasps and sobs and utterances of disbelief now tumbling out of the spirit as she allowed herself to remember the unbearable end of things. Finally, when she had quieted and addressed me directly once more, I tuned back in.

"I'm dead," she said. It wasn't a question. She understood now.

"Yes. I'm sorry."

"So, I'm... what? A ghost?" The last word was a horrified squeak, an acknowledgement of a thing she had never believed to be real. I felt the echo of it in my own memory—that first moment I came up against the harsh, undeniable truth of what once was fiction.

"Yes," I told her.

"Why... why is it that you can see me?" she asked. "Why are you different?"

I laughed out loud and immediately stifled it. "Sorry. That's just... *such* a loaded question."

"What?"

"Never mind. You know the answer to this question, too. If you focus in on my energy, I think you'll be able to see why we're drawn to each other," I said.

The spirit frowned, looking wary, but after a moment she closed her eyes and became very still again. I focused as well, making sure that I wasn't working to mask the presence of the Gateway, as I often did when trying to avoid detection. I felt it happen, the moment the Gateway tugged at her, waking her up to its irresistible pull.

As we looked into each other's eyes again, all the fear was gone from her face. It had been replaced with a raw, unfiltered wonder, and I smiled gently at her.

"You see?" I asked.

"Yes," she breathed. "It's so... can I go now?"

"There is a sort of... ceremony. And I need someone to help me, but, yes. You can go as soon as you wish. But first I must ask you if there's anything you want me to do for you?"

Her face darkened like a storm cloud. "Will... will you make sure they all know what he did to me? I want them all to know."

"I can't promise what the outcome will be, but it sounds to me like they already do," I said.

She nodded grimly, her fists opening and closing by her sides. Then she seemed to droop. "My parents. We weren't speaking. I can't go without telling them I'm sorry."

"We'll find a way," I promised her. "We can talk about it on the way. Will you come with me?"

She took a deep, steadying breath. "Yes. Yes, I'll come with you."

Together, we headed for the Tube station entrance. She floated along beside me, gazing around herself rather wistfully now, as though she realized that the world around her was already fading away, or rather, that she was fading from it.

I paused for a moment as Reginald finished out a long, complicated riff, and then applauded. "Beautiful, as always."

"Cheers, duck," Reginald said, with a tip of his hat. "Found yourself a taker today, did you?" He winked at the spirit of the young woman, whose mouth fell open.

"Yep," I said. "You sure you don't want to join us? You'll have company for the journey."

Reginald threw his head back and laughed. I could see the gold fillings in all of his molars. "Are you mad? I can play all day and night, and ain't no one trying to stop me. I ain't giving up this spot for nothing. Best gig I ever had."

"Isn't it tough, playing for an audience who can't hear you?" I asked, smiling at him.

He leaned forward and winked conspiratorially. "Oh, they can't hear me, duck, but they can feel me, believe you me. A busker should be so lucky."

"Suit yourself. See you around," I said. And, even though I knew that some stranger would just pick it up, I tossed a pound onto the ground into the specter of his instrument case before I walked away.

"Him, too?" the spirit of the young woman asked me.

"Yes," I said. "If you stuck around among the living for a bit longer, you'd see that the world is full of spirits who have stayed behind, especially in a city like this. So old. So much painful history."

"But... why do they stay? Don't they realize..." She gestured to me, lacking the words to express what she sensed within me.

"Some of them do, like Reginald. Others can't accept what has happened to them. There are so many reasons to stay, but don't be fooled. None of them are as important as the reason to go."

"And what is the reason to go?" the girl asked me, a little desperately.

"You felt it, didn't you?" I asked her.

She nodded.

"That's the reason," I said. "What you felt... that sense of... home. Peace. Belonging. You will never have that here, no matter how long you stay."

She sniffed. She was crying again.

"Everything will be okay," I told her, regretting that I could not give her the hug she needed. "I'm probably the only person alive who can tell you that with certainty."

"How do you know? How can you be so sure about where I'm going now?"

"Because," I said, smiling gently. "I've been there."

2

SPOTLIGHT

"**T**ÉIGH ANONN. TÉIGH ANONN. TÉIGH ANONN."

Hannah's hand was clutched tightly in mine. In a vibrant, speeding barrage of images, the young woman's life flashed through our connected consciousness. It used to be disorientating, this aspect of Crossings, but I'd learned to detach myself from my senses, to usher the memories onward instead of getting caught up in their details. They slipped smoothly past, like water through cupped hands.

A line of uniformed young girls marching into a brick building, tripping on a stone and scattering my books everywhere as the others giggled.

A stolen kiss under a footbridge, a hand that wandered deliciously along my back.

A spotlight blinding me, a trembling page of Shakespearean verse clutched in my sweaty hand.

A drunken young man rampaging through my flat, shouting and throwing things as I desperately tried to barricade a door.

And then a feeling like sighing—a release—and finally, the familiar and satisfying closing of the Gateway, like a door deep inside my mind.

Hannah gave my hand a little squeeze and then let it go. I sighed deeply and opened my eyes. She was already leaning across the summoning circle to blow out the candles.

"Well. That went more smoothly than I would have thought," she said, smiling in a contented sort of way, as though a shared feeling of peace with the young woman still lingered. "You thought she was going to take longer to convince, didn't you?"

"Yeah," I said. "I was just going to wait, but... well, she spotted me sooner than expected." *Because I chased a stranger through the streets of London like an unhinged paparazzo without a camera,* I added silently.

Hannah turned to our Caomhnóir who stood hulking in the doorway. "Thank you, Ambrose. We're finished now."

"I'll be next door. How many guests you expecting, then?" he grunted.

"Two. Savannah Todd and her mother. And Tia will be home around the same time as well," Hannah told him.

"And could you hold on to this, please," I added, pulling a folded-up letter from my back pocket and handing it to Ambrose. "Someone from the Trackers' office will be coming by to pick it up."

"What is it?" Ambrose asked, turning it over suspiciously in his hands, as though he had never seen an envelope before.

"It's a letter from the spirit we just Crossed. We need to get it into her possessions somewhere her parents will find it. I called in the request and Catriona said one of the other Trackers could take care of it for us," I said.

Ambrose narrowed his eyes at me, as though he didn't believe a word of what I was saying.

"Look, if you want to steam the damn thing open and check, be my guest," I snapped at him. "But you'll have to figure out how to seal it back up and forge the handwriting on the envelope, because the spirit has Crossed and I can't write it over again without her."

Ambrose pulled his eyebrows together in a single, furry, judgmental clump. He snorted at me, stuffed the letter in his pocket, and shuffled out the door, closing it behind him.

"He's a laugh a minute, isn't he?" I said to Hannah. "What a charmer."

Together, Hannah and I gathered up the smoking candle stubs, removed them from their holders, and returned them to the wooden box on the mantelpiece where we kept them in pride of place, the way other people might display family photographs. Then we unrolled the area rug back over the summoning circle we had painted onto the floorboards. It was so much easier than drawing a new one every time we needed to perform a Crossing, particularly because they sometimes needed to be performed in a hurry, depending on the mental state of the spirit in question. We straightened out the rug and stepped back to admire our handiwork. All hint of Durupinen ceremony gone.

"There. It almost looks like normal people live here," I said.

The words still hung in the air between us as Milo Chang, our Spirit Guide, came sailing through the wall and began swooping around the room like an oversized, agitated bat.

"Almost," Hannah said with a laugh.

"Yeah, spoke too soon on that one," I agreed.

Milo was making a constant, high-pitched squealing noise that sounded something like, "*Ohmygodohmygodohmygodohmygodohmygodohmygod.*"

"Milo, you have *got* to calm down," Hannah said soothingly to him as he zoomed past. "If you keep expending energy like this, you'll have nothing left to manifest by the time the show comes on."

Milo continued his panicked circling, a spirit aircraft unable to land due to chronic malfunction.

Normally, I would rag on Milo for acting so erratically, but I couldn't bring myself to do it this time, since it was basically my fault he was in this state. Nearly five months ago, we'd launched a style blog for him as a surprise Christmas gift. We wanted to give him a place to show the world all of his brilliant fashion designs, and he'd leapt at the chance. Using my Muse talents to sketch the designs, and Savvy's mother's seamstress skills to create them, Milo had shared his vision and quickly amassed a small but ardent internet following of his work. The pièce de résistance of the gift, however, was far better than a little social media buzz. The previous year, I'd helped a world-famous actress find closure with her deceased fiancée, and I'd called in a little favor. I'd hoped she might just wear one of his accessories to a minor event, but she took one look at Milo's work and fell in love with it. So tonight, Talia Simms was going to wear a Milo Chang original down the red carpet at the Cannes Film Festival for the premiere of her newest film, and hence Milo was in imminent danger of exploding.

"Has he been like this all day?" I asked Hannah quietly.

"And night, I expect," Hannah said, rolling her eyes. "Savvy couldn't take it anymore. I thought she was going lose her shit and Cage him. I convinced her to go for a walk and have a cigarette instead."

"At least she *could* go have a cigarette!" Milo hissed, coming to a stop beside us, but still vibrating so intensely that his entire outline was blurred. "If I had a body, at least I could use it to harness some of this in! I could have a cigarette, or a drink. I could go for a run, or scream into a pillow or punch something! I don't have an outlet! I have no tools! I can't cope! I'M A BASKETCASE WITHOUT THE BASKET!!!!"

"We could still try that containment Casting, if you want," Hannah said gently. "It might help."

"Or it might leave me too zoned out to focus on the television!" Milo snapped. "I already told you no! I can't risk it!" He ran both of his hands through the specter of his shaggy black hair and then took several long, deep breaths. "I'm sorry. I'm sorry I keep yelling, I just…"

"You don't need to apologize, Milo," Hannah said. "We get it. This is a big deal. We're all excited, too."

"Big deal? Only the biggest deal of my life!" Milo babbled.

"Well, afterlife," I pointed out.

He glared at me, and I mimed zipping my lips.

"You know what I mean. I've been waiting my entire li—*existence* for this," Milo corrected himself before I could tease him again. "If this doesn't go well… If they don't like it…"

"Everyone is going to love it," I said. "You're brilliant. We know it, and now the world will know it."

Milo squealed in horror, threw his arms up over his face and started rocketing around the room again.

"Did I say the world?" I amended myself quickly as Hannah glared at me. "I meant only the five or six people who even bother to watch this kind of thing. I mean, honestly, I'm surprised they're even bothering to put it on television. Lowest ratings ever." I gave him two enthusiastic thumbs down, but Milo was not even pretending to listen to me.

"It's not about who watches, it's about who's there. And everyone who matters will be there! *Everyone!*" He dissolved into incomprehensible squeaking.

I gave up and turned back to Hannah. "Tia knows what time it starts, right?"

Hannah nodded. "Yes. Milo reminded her five times before she left. She promised she'd be back in plenty of time."

"And did I hear you tell Ambrose that Alice is coming, too?"

Hannah grinned. "She'll be here. And she's bringing enough food to feed a small army, according to Savvy." Evidently, Savvy's mom was incapable of cooking for fewer than ten people on any given occasion.

I flopped onto the couch and stared out the window. The intermittent spring sunshine of only an hour before was already losing its battle with a rolling bank of gray clouds. It would be drizzling again before long. I was finding London weather to be an excellent meteorological metaphor for my state of mind these days.

As Milo continued to flit around over our heads like a trapped bird, Hannah sat down beside me.

"Are you okay, Jess? You seem... I don't know... troubled."

"I'm good," I said, pulling out my phone and pretending to check notifications.

I avoided her gaze, but I could feel her eyes on me, burrowing through my defenses, revealing all the things I'd prefer to keep hidden.

"You're doing it again. You're giving me that look," I told her.

"What look?" she asked, a little too innocently.

"That look that says you're calling my bluff. The look that leaves no stone unturned until I've spilled my guts," I told her, tossing the phone aside with a sigh of resignation.

Her mouth puckered defensively. "I just asked if you were okay. You don't have to talk if you don't want to."

I laughed. "What's the point? Whether I talk now or later, you'll weasel it out of me eventually. Might as well get it over with."

Hannah scowled. "I don't *weasel* things—"

"I thought I saw Finn today."

The words stopped her like a slap in the face. She clapped a hand over her mouth with a gasp, and when she spoke it was in a whisper from between her fingers. "You saw him? Where? When?"

"No, I said, I *thought* I saw him," I corrected her, and then watched as her face fell.

"It wasn't him?"

"Nope. In fact, once I got up close to him, it didn't even remotely look like him. But that didn't stop me from dodging cabs across the street, man-handling pedestrians for several blocks, and then almost tackling him before he got on the Tube," I replied with a sardonic smile.

"Oh, Jess."

"I know. This is a whole new level of pathetic, even for me," I said.

The sudden absence of hysterical muttering made me glance up to the ceiling. Milo had stopped his frantic circling and was staring down at me with a face full of pity, leaving me feeling even more ashamed than I had a moment before.

Damn it, floors never just opened up and swallowed you whole when you wanted them to, did they?

"Who was it?" Milo asked in a soft voice.

"Nobody. Just some guy who took advantage of my momentary confusion to hit on me, and then went on his merry way," I said with a casual shrug that fooled no one. "It's okay, you can say it. I'm pitiful."

But neither of them would say something like that, even if they were thinking it. They'd been nothing but supportive since the day this past January when I'd stepped into Celeste's chamber and learned that Ileana, High Priestess of the Traveler Clans, had betrayed evidence of Finn's and my illicit relationship to the new High Priestess of the Northern Clans, Celeste. Celeste would have been well within her rights to drag both Finn and me before the Council for a hearing, exposing us both to public ridicule and shame. But instead, she'd quietly had Finn reassigned somewhere far from Fairhaven, so that our transgression could be swept surreptitiously under the rug, saving Clan Sassanaigh from yet another scandal. I knew that, somewhere inside me, I was supposed to be grateful that Celeste had spared us in this manner, but the only feeling I could summon when I thought of her was a sense of deep, bitter anger. In fact, I hadn't set foot back in Fairhaven since we had moved out because I was afraid of what I might say or do if I saw her.

Finn.

We hadn't even had a chance to say goodbye to each other, and now I had no idea where he was. The only thing I could be sure of was that, wherever he had been stationed, it was far enough from me that there was no chance of ever running into him by accident in my own city. No, wherever Celeste and the Caomhnóir had sent him, they would be sure it was far beyond my reach. And there was no way to track him down without drawing attention to my search. The only resources I had were Durupinen resources, and anyway, whatever my morning's actions suggested to the contrary, I wasn't an idiot. I knew that Seamus and the rest of the Caomhnóir would be watching me closely, on high alert for any sign that I was attempting to find Finn. Celeste had probably given them specific instructions to do so, and politically, it made perfect sense. She had just become High Priestess, and had to establish herself as such. Though Hannah had won with considerable support from lesser clans, the more powerful clans were quietly mutinous about her presence amongst them on the Council, and Celeste did not need to heap another reason to mistrust us onto the already festering pile. Hannah's struggle to gain respect within the Council itself was already an uphill battle. I didn't doubt, though, that if I made any attempts to find Finn, Celeste would not hesitate to air this particular dirty laundry in full view of the Northern Clans. She could not show this kind of mercy twice, or she would be viewed as weak. And I knew she thought of it as mercy—a laughable thought really, considering how her actions had seemed to have ripped my heart right out of my chest.

Distrust of me was one of the reasons, no doubt, that our new Caomhnóir, Ambrose, was so frustratingly, constantly *present*. It was like having a great, hulking shadow that smelled like beef jerky and whistled through its nose when it breathed. If I strained my ears, I could hear him through the wall in the adjoining flat, where he spent his time skulking and lifting weights while chain-smoking menthol cigarettes.

The front door banged open, making all three of us jump.

"Yes, it's us, you stupid great prat. I practically live here, don't I? Go drink a protein shake or something and sod all the way off," Savvy shouted over her shoulder in the direction of Ambrose's flat. I heard his door slam shut.

"Oi there, you three. All right?" Savvy asked as she staggered through the door under the weight of three casserole dishes with a paper shopping bag teetering on top. Hannah hurried forward to help her, snatching the paper bag just before it toppled over.

"Hi, Sav. Hey, Alice," I said, jogging over to the table and clearing a space so Savvy could put down the food. "Thanks for the spread! It looks incredible."

"Just a little something I knocked up, me lovies," Alice said, grinning broadly. Looking at Alice was like jumping in a time machine and running into Savvy thirty years in the future. Her thick red hair was shot through with gray, and her boisterous voice was hoarse with several more decades of smoking, but the broad nose, freckled face, and toothy smile were all nearly identical. She scanned the room eagerly with her eyes and boomed, "Milo, love, you here?"

"He's dead, not deaf, you mad old cow," Savvy grumbled. "Get your arse over here, so Hannah can do that Melding thing, will you?"

Alice hurried over to Hannah, who sat her down at the table and quickly performed the Casting that would allow Alice to temporarily see and hear Milo. We'd had to do it several times before so that Alice and Milo could discuss the details of Milo's designs together.

"There you are, then!" Alice said, looking up and immediately spotting Milo hovering near the television, staring at a commercial for chocolate biscuits as though it were the most important moment in televised history. She glanced uneasily at Hannah. "Can... can't he hear me?"

Hannah smiled reassuringly. "The Casting works fine. He's just a bit distracted right now. Nerves."

"Oh, right," Alice said, her expression clearing at once. "Well, cheer up there, love. Ain't no one who wore something I made what didn't love it, and no mistake. You just settle down now. That dress is flawless."

Milo might have been trying to smile, but the effect was more of a grimace of intense pain. He didn't seem able to find the words to respond. He dropped his eyes back to the TV and began biting ferociously at a fingernail, a habit that couldn't possibly bring relief to someone with no actual fingers.

"Is this your steak and ale pie?" I asked weakly, pulling a sheet of tinfoil off the first casserole dish and inhaling the mouthwatering aroma.

"That's right," Alice said. "And that there's the roast potatoes, the meat and veg pasties, the cheese platter, the rolls, the crisps, the trifle, and the banoffee pie." She pointed to each container in turn, and then nodded in a satisfied way. "That ought to hold us through the evening."

"Through the evening?" I said, laughing. "Alice, this will hold us through the end of next month!"

"All the better, then," she said with a shrug. "I've seen you, walking out your door with a black coffee and calling it breakfast. You're wasting away, you are. This way, I can be sure you're being fed up, good and proper."

I helped Alice and Savvy set out all the food, trying not to drool over it as I did, while Hannah pulled glasses and plates out of the cabinets. Milo, unable to physically manipulate objects without draining his energy, concentrated on having a mental health crisis in front of the television instead.

"Hey, Jess?" Hannah called, sounding stern.

"I'm sorry, I couldn't wait. This one has pulled pork in it!" I said guiltily through a mouthful of pasty.

"No, not that," Hannah said impatiently. "This."

I walked over to the fridge to see what she was pointing at. Her finger was tapping against a wedding invitation stuck to the door with a magnet.

"Oh. Right."

"We have to RSVP before the end of the week," Hannah reminded me.

"Yeah," I said. "Yeah, we should do that."

I'd been avoiding even looking at that wedding invitation for the last three weeks, since it arrived in the mail in a shimmering white envelope covered in calligraphy. When I'd opened it, unsure of what it was, literal gold confetti hearts fell out of it and fluttered to the floor. After I recovered from the shock of being glitter-bombed, I'd unfolded it and realized that Róisín Lightfoot had invited us to her wedding.

Ugh.

It wasn't that I hated weddings on principle. Weddings were great, in theory. Like, on TV, they looked just adorable. I mean, food, dancing, live music, happy people—what's not to love? And Róisín's family was mind-numbingly rich, so her wedding was sure to be worth the trip just for the passed hors-de-oeuvres alone. Even I could be convinced to socialize if someone was handing me things wrapped in bacon. Unfortunately, none of that could outweigh my disgust for scouting.

Scouting was a Durupinen practice not unlike matchmaking, where young Durupinen would be set up with pre-approved young men in an effort to establish marriages with the best possible connections, advantages, and—most horrifying of all—best chance of producing the next generation of Durupinen. It wasn't that I was naïve—I knew that these types of practices were common in cultures all over the world. But the idea that I was now part of one of those cultures was enough to make me want to toss that invitation into the nearest available shredder and then light the shredder itself on fire.

Róisín wasn't exactly a friend, but she was an acquaintance that I had grown to like, and I wasn't jazzed about the idea of watching her walk into the arms of an arranged marriage at twenty-two years old, however willingly.

"You don't want to go, do you?" Hannah said. I hadn't realized that she was still watching me.

"What makes you say that?" I said, pulling open the fridge and pulling out a bottle of malt vinegar.

"Oh, I don't know. Probably just the way you were staring at that invitation like it was a portal to hell," Hannah said, smirking.

"Are you suggesting that's not what it is?" I muttered.

"We really should go. It was nice of her to invite us," Hannah said.

I snorted. "Hannah, it wasn't nice. It was politics. We're a Council Clan now, remember? I bet there's some ancient rule somewhere that says Róisín's marriage isn't valid unless the entire Council is in attendance, or something."

Tiny frown lines creased Hannah's brow. "I hadn't considered that."

It wasn't all that surprising that Hannah hadn't considered the invite a political move. We'd only been involved in politics for a few months, since Hannah won a seat on the Durupinen Council in a shocking, landslide victory. She's been attending weekly meetings and learning the ropes, but it was all still very new, and we hadn't really had time to process the implications yet.

"Well, no matter why she invited us," Hannah went on, "I still think we should go. I don't want it to seem like a slight on her or her clan if we don't show up. At the very least, I'm going to have to go to represent us, and I'd rather not go by myself. Just think about it for another couple of days."

"Fine," I muttered, sounding like a sulky teenager. "Just send it back and tell her we're coming. And every single freaking particle of food better be wrapped in bacon."

The door banged open a second time, this time revealing a breathless, pink-cheeked Tia Vezga pulling off her raincoat and staring around wildly.

"Did I miss it? It hasn't started yet, has it?"

"No, no, you're good. Still a few minutes until they start airing the red carpet," Hannah told her.

"Oh, thank goodness! We got chatting and I lost track of time,"

Tia sighed, hastening to hang her coat and umbrella in the hall closet. "Hi, Savannah! Hi, Alice!"

"Wotcha, Ti," Savvy called from the couch, where she was already tucking in to a heaping pile of her mom's cooking.

"Hello, lovie," Alice said. "Come make a plate."

Tia looked up and caught my eye, spotted my grin, and immediately looked away, rolling her eyes as she did so.

"So, lost track of time, huh? That's a good sign," I said.

Tia pointedly ignored me, choosing instead to pick up a plate and start filling it with food.

"I mean, that's what you want on a first date, right?" I pressed, grabbing a plate and trailing behind her. "For the conversation to be so good that you forget what else is going on around you?"

"It was not a date, Jess," Tia said loftily, thrusting her hand into a crisps bag. "How many times do I have to tell you? We are just friends. It was just a cup of coffee. That's all."

"Does Charlie know that?" I teased.

"What's this, now?" Alice asked, twisting around in her chair, her expression perking up with interest. "Who's Charlie?"

Tia narrowed her eyes at me and then turned back to Alice, smiling politely. "His name is Charlie Wright. He goes to school with me. We were paired up as lab partners and we got to talking. He asked me out for a cup of coffee as friends to discuss our next project. It's really not a big deal, even though Jess insists on making it sound like one."

I dropped the subject, but Tia didn't fool me for a second. It was a big deal, and we both knew it. Tia and I were in the same proverbial boat: the S.S. Emotional Shitstorm. On the very same day Celeste sent Finn away, Tia had her own heart broken when her boyfriend of more than three years, Sam, broke up with her. Rather than allowing her to wallow in misery halfway across the world, I'd encouraged her to come to England and, to my absolute shock, she'd done the most un-Tia-like thing she'd ever done in her life and spontaneously bought a plane ticket. And thank God she did, because I'd never needed my best friend more than I'd needed her over the past few months. Misery loves company, right?

"Hey, Milo," Tia called, "I bumped into Flavia on campus this morning. She said she's going to dismiss her class a few minutes early so that she can catch the live stream of the red carpet, and she wanted me to wish you luck."

I chuckled, shaking my head. "It's so weird that you know Flavia," I said to Tia. "My worlds are colliding." Flavia was a friend of mine, a Traveler Durupinen and a recent London transplant who was finishing up her doctorate at the same college Tia now attended. She and I had bonded even more now that we lived within a few miles of each other, each healing from recent rifts in our lives—my separation from Finn and her separation from her entire clan, who refused to speak to her since she had chosen to move away from the isolation of the Traveler camp and into the city. It was quite the makeshift little family of misfits we had created, banding together as we attempted to build lives for ourselves in a new place.

"Oh, God. OH, GOD!" Milo's voice rose to a pitch that threatened to shatter the window panes. He pointed a violently trembling finger at the television. "It's starting!"

My heart leapt into my throat. I snatched another pasty off the plate as I bolted past the table and flung myself onto the couch between Hannah and Savvy.

"I can't do it. I can't watch it. Someone just Cross me right now and pluck me out of the Aether when it's over," Milo squealed.

"Milo, I will seriously Cage you if you don't sit down and shut up!" I yelled. "You are going to miss it if you don't stop freaking out!"

"Shhh!" Hannah hissed, flapping her hands frantically to shush us all, before snatching up the remote and turning up the volume. We all leaned forward as one, eyes glued to the screen as a parade of A-list celebrities began to strut their way up the red carpet.

"Thank you for joining us for our live coverage of the Cannes Film Festival red carpet where it could not be clearer that the glitz and glamour are in full effect tonight," gushed a waifish young reporter clutching a microphone. "I can't remember the last time I saw so many statement necklaces, can you, Todd?"

"No, Valerie. It is truly blinding!" chuckled a flamboyant older man beside her, clad in a navy-blue velvet tuxedo. "I hadn't realized I'd need my sunglasses to conduct these interviews tonight!"

"Nor I," Valerie giggled. "But avert your eyes because here comes one of our night's big stars."

One of Talia's co-stars slunk over to the reporters, her neck encased in a stunning network of gemstones. She flashed a smile and struck a pose as they thrust their microphones in her face and began peppering her with questions, none of which we could hear because Milo was shrieking again.

"I knew it. I *knew* we should have gone with the black! I've seen three women go by in black already!"

"Yeah, but you don't want her to blend in, do you?" Tia said soothingly. "You want her to stand out. What's the point of getting lost in a sea of black dresses?"

"Oh, sure, sure, there's rising to the top, but then there's sticking out like a sore thumb!" Milo snapped. "I don't want her to do that either!"

"She's not going to!" Hannah said. "She looked stunning, Milo. The dress is a knock-out."

"It fit her like a glove," Alice added. "I made sure of that. *I still can't believe I met her!*" she added in a hiss to Savvy, who rolled her eyes.

"Get a grip, Mum," she muttered.

"I should have had her accessorize more," Milo wailed.

"No way," Savvy said through a mouthful of crisps. "That would have been over-the-top."

"But if the trend du jour is big jewelry..."

"Screw the trend!" I said. "You're setting your own trend!"

"You did pick out that gold cuff," Hannah added quickly, as Milo swelled with an angry retort. "The dress didn't need more than that."

The reporters were now interviewing a dapper young man in a classic black tux. Hannah's leg was bouncing up and down so hard she was making the entire couch vibrate.

"Men have it so easy at these things," I remarked, to break the tension. "I mean, any one of these women would be crucified if she wore the same dress more than once, and these guys can just dust off the same tired old suit for every single red carpet event they ever have to attend, and they'll always be praised for looking 'classic.'"

"Yeah, not to mention the work it takes to get into some of them dresses," Savvy agreed, cocking her head to the side and examining another woman as she walked by. "I mean, it defies physics, dunnit? She must have three yards of tape holding all them bits of dress where they need to go. Imagine someone like me trying to cram me girls into a frock like that. No wonder they all live on kale juice, them Hollywood types."

"I think... is that... yes! Here she comes!" Hannah cried.

In the corner of the camera shot, a tall, willowy young woman was emerging from a limousine, swaths of red and gold fabric flowing around her like rippling water. Even slightly out of focus in the background, we could already tell. She was stunning.

We all started clapping and shouting at once, so that Hannah had to shush us all again as the reporters realized that Talia had arrived.

"And I think I see... yes, the star of tonight's premiere *Bridge Between Two Hearts*, the lovely Talia Simms has indeed arrived on the red carpet this evening," Todd said. "Let's see if we can get a word with her here. Talia, good evening!"

Talia seemed to glide over to the two reporters. She had always been a bit of an introvert given her chosen profession in the spotlight, but nevertheless, she smiled politely and took her place between the microphones to be interviewed. She was clad in a red chiffon confection that Milo had dreamed up, with a high neckline, an open draped back, and a magnificent gold fabric flower at the collarbone. It clung tightly to her hips and then pooled around her feet where the red of the fabric seemed to melt into a deeper, richer plum color. She had worn her hair natural, with a plum-colored fabric flower, edged in gold, nestled in the halo of tight black curls. Milo had thrown his hands up over his face and was now watching through the cracks between his fingers.

"Talia, I must say, you look absolutely stunning this evening!" Valerie gushed, and we all broke out into a chorus of cheers again. "I just finished telling Todd that this evening was all about the jewelry, but I think I'm about to eat my words! What a knock-out this dress is!"

Talia smiled graciously. Milo, meanwhile, had gone so still he might have been turned to ice. His eyes, from what we could see of them between his fingers, were wide.

"Thank you very much," Talia said.

"I must say, I agree," Todd chimed in, stepping back to take in the full effect of Talia's ensemble. "No need for statement jewelry when the dress is such a statement on its own. Who are you wearing this evening?"

We all held our breath.

"A brilliant new designer, Milo Chang," Talia said, running a hand along the curve of her hip and executing a turn to show off the back detailing. "Gorgeous, isn't it? And if the next piece he makes for me is this comfortable, I might just have to wear him exclusively."

Alice stood up and whooped. Savvy and Tia cheered and clapped, while Hannah laughed and sobbed simultaneously. Milo still hadn't moved. Could ghosts go into shock?

"Well, it is just breath-taking," Valerie cooed. "As is your turn in this film. Tell us about the process of working with..."

I didn't listen to another word of the interview. Nor could I clearly see Talia anymore through a haze of happy tears. I turned to Milo.

"You did it," I whispered.

"I did it," he repeated, as though they were words in a foreign language, and he was simply trying them out in his mouth to see what they felt like.

"Congratulations," I said.

He dropped his hands. His lips were trembling. He gave me just the smallest suggestion of a smile, and then he burst into a stormy, uncontrollable mess of sobbing, every tear of which he deserved to cry without interruption.

3

AT THE MARKET

"WE'RE HEADING DOWN to the market, Milo!" Hannah called.

"Hang on, hang on! I want to come!" Milo called back, lingering in front of the laptop, where he'd spent the majority of the last few days.

"You're going to come? The great Milo Chang is going to grace the bourgeoisie with his presence and walk amongst us like a mere mortal?" I gasped.

Milo winked. "You should be so lucky, peasant."

The three days following Milo's red carpet debut had been complete pandemonium. Milo's blog had exploded, and there had been numerous requests for interviews, articles, and podcast appearances. It was immediately apparent that Talia had single-handedly launched Milo's fashion career, which was ever so slightly complicated by the fact that he was dead. Luckily, in the age of technology, aided by a few smoke and mirrors courtesy of Durupinen Castings, we'd been able to field most of the interview requests without Milo having to promise any public appearances. Best of all, several prominent actresses were now sending requests via assistants to see some of his other pieces. Once the initial panic wore off, Milo snapped into mogul-mode, and now it was clear that he was in his element.

"I want to see if I can find a cool tea set. Like, a vintage one," Hannah said eagerly.

"Planning on hosting some tea parties?" I sniggered.

"Hey, we're proper Brits now. I'm pretty sure you have to acquire one within six months of becoming a citizen or they deport you. Besides, teapots are so cute," Hannah replied.

"I'll go get Tia," I said, walking down the hall.

"Is she up?" Hannah asked. "Don't wake her if she's not up."

I snorted. "Is she up? She already went for a run, took a shower, made breakfast, and has been studying for two hours." I knocked softly on the door.

"Come in," came Tia's voice.

"Hey, Ti," I said, poking my head around the door to see her curled up in an armchair, buried in her customary exoskeleton of textbooks. "Fancy a break? We're headed out to the Portobello Market to buy more junk we don't need."

"Yeah, sounds great," Tia said, smiling gratefully. "My head is crammed full of as many bacterial infections as it can remember right now."

"Gross," I said, smiling.

"Oh, you know what I mean," Tia said, extricating herself from the books and slipping on her sandals and peering out the window at the cloudless sky. "It's a beautiful day out today."

"Yeah, it is. Let's enjoy the sunshine while we can," I agreed.

A buzzing sound made us both reach automatically for our phones.

"Not mine," I said, checking it.

"Mine!" Tia said, digging through the books until she found it buried at the bottom of the pile. She glanced down at the notification and her face dropped. "Oh."

"What's wrong? Your mom again?" I asked her. Tia's mom had been waging a constant battle to get Tia to come back home, and was forever barraging her with guilt trips, bribes, and links to applications for American medical programs. Tia took it much more good-naturedly than I would have, of course.

"No, it's... um... well, it's Charlie," she said, still staring down at the phone screen.

"Is he dead?" I asked.

Tia's head shot up. "What? No! Of course not!"

"Great! Then that makes whatever he texted you only half as weird as all of the communication I've had this morning!" I said, smiling brightly. "So, what's up?"

"He... well, he says he's working his boss's booth at the market this morning and wants me to stop by," Tia said reluctantly.

"Oooookay," I said slowly. "So, why exactly do you look so horrified?"

Tia smiled sheepishly. "It's just... I'm still... I don't really know what this is." She gestured down to the phone.

"It's a phone," I replied helpfully.

She nearly threw said phone at my head, which frankly, I deserved. "You know what I mean, Jess! I know we're friends, and I really like him, but I'm just... I don't know where my head is at right now, and I just... I don't want to be pressured into anything when I'm still pretty messed up from the break-up, you know?"

"Is he pressuring you?" I asked, suddenly serious.

"No, but it kind of feels like you are," Tia muttered to her feet.

"Oh, Ti, no!" I jogged, half-groaning, half-laughing, across the room and gave her a squeeze around the shoulders. "You know me, I just like to tease people. But jokes aren't funny unless everyone is laughing, and you aren't laughing. I'm really sorry."

Tia shrugged, betraying a smile. "It's okay."

"No, it's not. I was just excited for you, that you might have found someone to make you happy," I told her.

"I am happy," she said.

"I know," I said quickly. "You don't need a guy for that. I just meant... you know what I mean."

"Yeah, I do. And I think I'm just scared to start down that road again. I still haven't recovered from the last trip," Tia said. I couldn't see her eyes, but her voice had tears in it.

"Hey, I get it. And I should think before I open my big mouth," I said.

"Charlie's really sweet. And he hasn't even suggested dating, or anything like that. But I *think* maybe he likes me. I think he would ask me, if I hinted that I was open to it. But..." She shrugged helplessly.

"You're not there yet," I finished for her.

"No, I'm not."

"Then I'm not going to say another word about it," I said. "Cross my heart."

"Really?"

"Yes. Really."

Tia smiled. "Okay, then. So, if I take you over to his booth at the market, you'll behave yourself?"

"Or may I never eat Nutella crepes from the street vendors again," I said, with an elaborate salute.

This was an oath of the highest order. Those crepes were freaking magical.

§

The Saturday morning bustle of Notting Hill greeted us like a familiar song. I loved living in this neighborhood. I loved the colorful buildings, all cozied up next to each other. I loved the quirky shops and steady trickle of musicians and street artists. It was a vibrant, living, breathing place, which was exactly what I needed to counterbalance the constant presence of the dead. I didn't understand how any Durupinen could live anywhere quiet. I needed to be able to tune out.

Our flat, courtesy of the elaborate network of Durupinen connections, was nestled on Lonsdale Road, right off the main thoroughfare of Portobello Road. If I could have picked any building on the street, I would have picked the one we lived in. It was painted a creamy white, like most of the buildings on the street, but with a slightly rebellious tangle of ivy growing up its front and a front door painted a bright, robin's egg blue. The tiny front garden was divided from the street by a quaint black wrought iron gate, and it was through that little gate that Hannah, Milo, Tia, and myself set out to lose ourselves in the hectic beauty of the Portobello Market.

We'd come to the market almost every Saturday since we'd moved in, and though it was packed full of tourists, the novelty still hadn't worn off. The market was over a mile long, and always changing, with something new to see every time we went. Street musicians added their melodies to the joyful cacophony on every corner, and the smells of the street food were intoxicating.

The first stretch of the market stalls was crammed with antiques, everything from furniture, to knick-knacks, to paintings, and every other bizarre old contraption anyone ever unearthed from their grandparents' attic. Of course, with so many old items came a fair share of spirit activity as well. I spotted several spirits almost immediately; a young woman in a hippie dress, screaming at an old man about daring to sell her guitar. A small figure dressed all in black, face covered in a mourning veil, crouching over an old trunk. An elderly gentleman in a Fair Isle sweater vest, circling a woman's display of antique typewriters and pointing out the ones she had priced too low. A pair of women haggling over the price of long-gone wares. They were just part of the fabric of the market, as natural a fixture of the street as the living people. I breathed it all in.

Within a few minutes, a delighted Hannah found a vendor offering a vast collection of quaint old tea sets and Milo floated off in search of design inspiration amongst the vintage clothing. Tia and I meandered the stalls, examining the various curiosities. But the further we traveled along the road, the more a peculiar feeling began to creep over me.

"Huh," I said to myself, as a chill that had nothing to do with the pleasant spring breeze sent a shiver through me.

"What is it?" Tia asked, frowning at me.

"It's just kind of... uh... crowded today," I said.

"What are you talking about?" Tia asked, laughing. "It's Saturday at Portobello Market. It's crowded every time we come here."

"No, that's not what I mean," I said, dropping my voice. "I mean it's *crowded*." I raised my eyebrows at her until she let out a little gasp of understanding.

"Oh!" she exclaimed. "How can you tell? Can you see a lot of them?"

I shook my head. "No. I see the usual number of them. It's just this feeling. The energy feels very concentrated today."

"Why today?" Tia asked, sounding a little nervous now.

I stopped scanning the crowd and looked over at her. When I spotted the anxious look on her face, I broke into an easy laugh. "Oh, don't worry about it. I'm sure it's just the usual ghostly comings and goings. Or maybe word is finally getting around that there's a Gateway in the area."

I pretended to be interested in a display of Doctor Who memorabilia from the '70s until Tia resumed her browsing. Poor Tia. So much of the paranormal had simply become normal since she met me, but I tried not to frighten her with anything too para-paranormal if I could help it. The truth was, though, that I did not like the feeling I was getting at the market that morning. I didn't like it at all.

As though my thought had escaped my own head and slipped right through our connection, I could suddenly hear Hannah in my head. "Jess, do you feel..."

"Yup," I replied. "I have no idea what's causing it though. Keep those Durupinen tentacles out and keep me posted if you find anything."

"Tentacles? Really? Is that the best metaphor you could come up with? Aren't we freakish enough without comparing ourselves to sea monsters?" Hannah grumbled.

"Okay, feelers, then. Spidey-sense. Whatever, just pay attention," I snapped and closed the connection with a sharper-than-necessary twang.

"Wow, look at these!" Tia exclaimed. I looked over to see her bent over a box of old Victorian brooches. "Accessories were so much cooler back then, weren't they?"

I joined her and picked up one of the brooches tentatively—I never knew if an object was connected to a spirit and therefore if it might spark a Visitation. The one I had selected felt marvelously ordinary and un-haunted in my palm, thank goodness. It had a carved ivory likeness of a young woman in the center. She looked like a Greek goddess with laurel in her curls. I held it up to my jacket and looked in the mirror, admiring the quirky effect of Victorian jewelry against distressed gray denim. "Yeah, they were. Of course, the tradeoff was that you also had to squeeze your organs into a corset," I pointed out.

Tia's laugh turned into a shriek as she dropped one of the brooches on the table.

"Careful there, love, them pins is sharp," the old woman behind the table said.

"No, it's not that, it's... that one has... has *hair* in it!" answered Tia in a horrified whisper.

"That's right!" the old woman said brightly, scooping the brooch back up and holding it out for us to see. We bent over it. Instead of a carving or a painting, this brooch had a little compartment in the center. Behind its tiny, dusty glass window lay a dry, curled lock of blondish hair. "They was tokens of remembrance, see? When your sweetheart died, you kept a lock of their hair inside it, so as to always keep 'em close to your heart. Romantic, eh?" She grinned enthusiastically at us, revealing several missing teeth.

"If by romantic you mean creepy as hell, then yes, very romantic," I said with a shudder. "Do people actually buy century-old jewelry with mummified hair inside it?"

The old woman's grin vanished, and she shrugged loftily as she nestled the brooch carefully back amongst its fellows. "Some people appreciate the history."

I opened my mouth to retort, but Tia grabbed my arm, thanked the woman, and pulled me away from the table.

"Let's not spar with the street vendors today, okay, Jess?" Tia said. "It's not worth it."

The idea of being told by some morbid old hag that I didn't appreciate history when I was perpetually fending off ghosts from every time period of human history was beyond galling, but I let it go and placated myself with a Nutella crepe. But even the gooey hazelnut goodness could not completely distract me from the increasingly intense spirit presence, which grew stronger and stronger the further we walked along the market. I tried to shake it off, but it clung to me like a film of frost, chilling my bones and raising goosebumps beneath my jacket.

"So, you said Charlie is working a booth for his boss?" I asked, still licking my fingers.

"Yes. He texted me the intersection, so we could find it," Tia replied, squinting down at her phone in the bright sunlight.

"What kind of booth is it? I mean, where does he work?"

"It's this tiny old photography museum and shop tucked in the old City of London district called 'Pickwick's History of Photography,'" Tia replied.

I perked up at once. "A photography museum? That sounds so... cool!"

"I know! Charlie's invited me to stop by several times now, but I haven't been there yet. He says it's a really fascinating place to work," Tia said. "Okay, this should be it coming up on the right and I think... yes, that's their booth, right over there!"

Tia trotted ahead of me, raising a hand in greeting, but I stopped dead in my tracks, having run headlong into a concentration of spirit energy so strong, it felt like a brick wall. I gasped and shuddered. Then, as the shock wore off, I focused my gaze and found the source.

There, in front of me, was a quaint little booth with a red-and-white-striped awning atop what looked like a glass-topped display case on wheels. A banner hung across the front of it that read, "Pickwick's History of Photography" in carnival-style letters. Behind the booth, a handsome young man in his mid-twenties was polishing a picture frame and whistling to himself. And around him, on every side, crowding each other and floating over and

31

jostling past each other to get closer to him, was a crowd of at least fifty spirits.

"Holy shit," I muttered under my breath.

As though he had heard my almost silent exclamation, the young man looked up expectantly. His eyes fell not on me, however, but on Tia, and his amiable face split into a friendly smile.

"Tia! There you are! I'm chuffed you decided to come down!" he called, waving her over.

"Hey, Charlie," Tia said, her own face alight with the kind of smile I hadn't seen there in months. She stopped and turned, realizing I hadn't followed her.

"Jess? Come on, I want to introduce you," she said, her brow furrowed in puzzled amusement.

I hesitated for just a moment. I didn't know what would happen if I approached a group of spirits that large in broad daylight in a public place. Whatever happened, it would be sure to draw exactly the kind of attention I usually tried to avoid. On the other hand, the spirits seemed incredibly fixated on Charlie—almost hypnotized. And I could hardly just turn tail and run; he'd already seen me.

I hoisted a reluctant smile onto my face and closed the last few yards between myself and the Pickwick cart. Sure enough, as I planted myself in front of it, holding my breath, not a single spirit acknowledged my presence. I allowed myself to exhale.

"Charlie, I'd like you to meet my best friend Jess Ballard," Tia said, flushing just a little. "Jess, this is my classmate Charlie Wright."

Charlie grinned still more broadly. His eyes twinkled behind his wire-rimmed glasses as he carefully set down the frame, wiped his palms on his pants, and held out a hand. "Jess. A pleasure. I've heard quite a lot about you."

"Nice to meet you, Charlie," I said, taking his hand and giving it a hearty shake. I felt nothing unusual—no tingle of the kind that might indicate another sensitive. I looked up into his face, searching for any sign that he might be aware of his spirit entourage, but he simply smiled expectantly at me. He had a dimple in one cheek and a shock of brown hair that made him look as though he'd just rolled out of bed, but in a charming way, like a little kid.

"Lovely morning for the market," Charlie said, dropping the small frame into a cardboard box by his elbow and pulling a

32

handkerchief out of his pocket to wipe his brow. "Bit warmer than I expected. The sweater vest was a mistake, certainly. But my boss should be here soon. I'm only just covering for her for a bit this morning. Have you ladies found anything of interest?"

"You could say that," I said, more to myself than to Charlie.

"No, not really. We've just been browsing around," Tia said. "This all looks so interesting! What are you selling?"

"Well, to be honest, we're really just trying to plug the museum—encourage people to come down and have a look at the exhibits, you know," Charlie admitted. "There's not much in the collection that my boss would part with. But we've got a few things on offer." He pointed down into the case. "Some old frames and daguerreotypes. A couple of early Polaroids and 35 mm models, too."

I bent over the cart, pretending to examine the items as Charlie explained them. In actuality, I was trying to sneak glimpses of the jostling crowd of spirits. Every one of them had their eyes fixed on Charlie. Some looked fascinated, others wary, still others merely curious.

"Do you feel that, then?" the ghost of a woman in a long gown whispered to the man in the top hat beside her. "It's... dazzling!"

"I must confess I was drawn here as soon as he arrived," the man replied.

Their words sent a shiver down my spine. What about Charlie Wright could be so overpowering that spirits were drawn to him like a magnet? I had never seen anything like it. And how in the world could they fail to notice me, an actual Gateway, standing right in front of them?

"... don't you, Jess?" Tia voice broke into my musing, startling me.

"Sorry, I didn't catch that. Totally distracted. These are just so fascinating!" I said, pointing at random to a little portrait mounted in a gold box.

"I was just saying, Pickwick's would be right up your alley, what with your art history background," Tia said pointedly. She widened her eyes at me, like a parent trying to remind her kid to behave herself.

"Oh, yeah!" I said, straightening up and attempting to give my full attention to the conversation. "It sounds really cool. We'll definitely have to stop by."

"That would be brilliant!" Charlie said. "I'd be glad to give you the tour any time I'm on shift. If we can pull Tia away from her studies, of course."

"Always a challenge," I said, nudging Tia affectionately with my elbow. "But I'm sure we can manage it."

"Jess?"

I spun around to see Hannah standing several stalls away. She appeared unwilling to move any closer. Her eyes were round with shock and though she said nothing but my name out loud, through the connection she was asking, "What the hell is going on here?"

I widened my own eyes and shook my head a fraction of an inch from side to side before continuing in an easy voice, "Hannah, there you are! Come on over here and meet Charlie!"

"Charlie?" Hannah asked blankly, and then something clicked and she let out a little gasp. "Tia's Charlie?"

"Oh-ho!" Charlie said with a little chuckle. He turned to Tia. "So, I'm your Charlie, now, am I?"

Tia turned bright red, and started mumbling something, under cover of which I explained through the connection, "They're attracted to him for some reason. They haven't even noticed me. And he has no idea. I can't figure it out."

I had to hand it to Hannah. She pulled herself together more quickly than I ever would have thought possible. She smoothed out her face, relaxed it into a smile and strolled forward as though she couldn't clearly see a horde of spirits crowding the space.

"I just meant the Charlie that Tia mentioned from class," Hannah said, smiling and holding out her hand to Charlie. "I'm sorry, I didn't mean to imply anything. I'm Hannah, I'm one of Tia's flatmates."

Charlie took her hand and wrung it delightedly. "Charlie Wright, and please don't apologize. I'd never consider it anything but a compliment to be associated with Tia."

Tia blushed, if possible, still redder. I decided to change the subject before she reached full traffic light-status.

"Charlie invited us to stop by the museum for a tour," I said, gesturing to the sign on the wagon's striped awning. "Doesn't that sound fun?"

Hannah nodded vigorously. "Yes, absolutely!" I could see she was trying to steal glances at the crowd of spirits without drawing attention to herself.

"Great!" Tia said, grabbing my arm. "Well, it was nice seeing you, Charlie. Good luck with the stall. I'll see you in lecture on Monday?"

"I look forward to it," Charlie said with another disarming smile. "Brilliant meeting you both. I'll be at the museum Tuesdays, Thursdays, and most weekends, so do stop by."

"Sounds great! See you later, Charlie!" Tia called, actually shoving Hannah and me along in front of her.

As we passed the wagon, the spirit of a small girl in ragged clothing peered out from behind her mother's skirts to gawk at us. As I glanced toward the spirit crowd, I caught her gaze by accident, and the girl's eyes went as wide and round as coins.

"Mummy, she can see us," the little girl whispered. "Look, Mummy, there goes another one!"

But before the girl could get her mother's attention, Tia had pulled and yanked and prodded us down the road until the curve of the street swallowed Charlie and the Pickwick stall from view.

"I'm sorry," Tia said, and she was almost breathless, though we'd only been walking a few yards. "I had to get out of there. I was totally freaking out."

"I'm sorry I said that, about Charlie being your Charlie," Hannah said fretfully. "I really didn't mean to. It just came out."

"I know, I know," Tia said. "It's fine, it's just... let's go home, okay?"

"Sure," I told her, throwing one last look over my shoulder. "Sure, let's go home."

4

MAKING MISTAKES

WE ARRIVED BACK AT THE FLAT. Tia, murmuring that she needed to keep studying, scurried back into her bedroom, and shut the door. I knew I needed to check on her, to make sure she was okay, but there was a more pressing issue to deal with.

I followed Hannah into her room and shut the door.

"So, Tia's new boyfriend is hella haunted, huh?" I announced, sitting down on her bed beside her.

"That is one of the strangest things I've ever seen," Hannah said. "And you know I can't say something like that lightly. I contacted Milo on our way up here and told him to go check it out, see if he could discover anything."

"Good idea," I said, sighing with relief. "I tried to assess the situation as best I could, but I could hardly start questioning spirits with Charlie and Tia standing right there!"

"I know," Hannah said, biting at the fingernail on her pinky finger.

"They were drawn to him, but... I couldn't feel anything. Nothing unusual about him at all."

Hannah shook her head. "Me neither. I don't even think he was a sensitive."

"If he knew those spirits were there, he was doing a very good job of hiding it," I agreed, nodding. "Although, I suppose he could just be a really good actor."

"And did you hear what that child spirit said as we walked away?" Hannah asked.

"Yeah, I did," I said slowly. "I think she said, 'Look Mummy, there goes another one'."

Hannah bit her lip. "That's what I heard, too."

"Another one what?" I asked. "What do you think she was talking about?"

"Well... it's obvious, isn't it? Another Gateway."

I gaped at her. "Hannah, that's not possible."

"I know, but what else could she have meant?" Hannah asked, her voice shaking slightly. "The Gateway is what draws spirits to us. It's like a beacon—they feel it and they follow it. What could that girl have meant, other than the fact that she could sense the same thing in Charlie that she sensed in us?"

"But that doesn't make any sense!" I said in a calm, rational voice, as though I could force the situation to make sense just by speaking about it in the right tone. "Durupinen are only ever women. Spirits couldn't sense a Gateway in a man."

Hannah just looked at me.

I faltered. "Could they?"

Hannah shrugged. "I have no idea. There's still a lot about Durupinen culture that we don't understand."

"One aspect I think I've got a pretty good handle on is the gender aspect. Durupinen are women. Four years in, I think I've managed to grasp that much," I said.

"I don't understand it either," Hannah said. "But... I don't know. What about Dormants?"

"What do you mean?" I asked, starting to pace now. I could feel a headache coming on.

"Well, you know that Dormants exist," Hannah began.

I rolled my eyes. "Yes, of course I do." As our good friend Annabelle was a Dormant—and a powerful one at that—I wasn't likely to forget this particular tidbit about the Durupinen world.

"Well, we had no idea the Dormants could have any particular abilities, besides varying levels of sensitivity to spirits," she said slowly, as though she were writing the words out in the space inside her head so she could analyze the idea as it formed. "But Annabelle turned out to have Walker ability."

"So?" I failed to understand the connection.

"So, abilities in the Durupinen world clearly linger, even when the family is no longer an active Gateway," Hannah said. "Don't you think it's possible that male family members are susceptible to the same phenomenon?"

I blinked. "Oh."

Hannah nodded, seeing the understanding dawn in my eyes. "Maybe Charlie is part of a family with Durupinen or Caomhnóir blood. Maybe the connection to the Gateway is still there?"

"Do spirits sense the Gateway in Caomhnóir the same way they sense it in Durupinen?" I asked. I'd never considered this before.

Hannah frowned. "I don't know. They never really taught us very much about how the Caomhnóir are connected to the spirit world, did they?"

"Yeah, well, that's no big surprise, is it? Remember the Sanctity Line? They were much more concerned about keeping us separate than educating us about each other," I snorted.

"I wish Finn was here so that we could ask..." Hannah cut herself off abruptly in mid-thought and shot me an apologetic look.

My whole body had gone stiff at the sound of Finn's name, as though the word itself were a physical blow rather than just an emotional one. A muscle started jumping in my eyelid in anticipation of tears.

"Oh, God, I'm sorry, Jess. I wasn't thinking," Hannah whispered from behind her hands, which she had thrown up over her mouth in horror.

I swallowed. "Don't worry about it. It's fine. I'm fine," I said dully. "I can't just fall apart every time I hear his name, Hannah. We should all just get used to the fact that he's not here and talk about him normally. Like a Band-Aid, you know? Just rip it off and be done with it."

"Right. I mean, if that's what you want. Do... do you think we should just ask Ambrose?" Hannah asked, her voice still very small in her embarrassment.

I shrugged. "Be my guest. I should go talk to Tia."

"Good idea. Please apologize to her again for me," Hannah said. "Apparently, I've decided to just walk around with my foot in my mouth today."

I smiled at her. "Don't sweat it. I've been hopping around with my foot in my mouth for years. You'll get used to it."

Hannah returned the smile with a little sigh of relief and hopped up off the bed. "I'll go talk to Ambrose, then. I'll be right back."

I watched her walk out of the bedroom, across the flat, and out the front door. Then I continued to stare at the place she had vanished, allowing my eyes to go out of focus, my vision to blur with a film of tears, and the pain to wash over me.

These moments happened when I wasn't careful, so I tried to succumb to them only when I was alone and, even then, only briefly. The benefit of never dealing with your feelings is that you learn to appear like you are functioning normally. The façade becomes more and more lifelike. And since everyone around you wants you to be functioning normally, they happily buy into the illusion. And everyone wraps themselves in the lie and protects themselves with it.

Say what you will about lies, but they are damn comfortable sometimes. Downright snuggly, even.

But they vanish like smoke the moment they are tested, those lies, and then you're only left with what you have let fester behind them, the intensity of which can take your breath away. So, I sat in that absence of air, of protection, of lies, and let it all wash over me for an endless few moments. And then I stood up, bandaged myself back up in the lies, and went to check on my best friend, because dealing with her pain would help me to avoid my own, and that was totally healthy and absolutely would not bite me in the ass later.

Clearly, I was nailing this "adult" thing.

Tia answered my quiet knock right away. "Come in."

She was over at her desk now, bent over a stack of notecards, scribbling away on the topmost one.

"Hey, Jess."

"Hey. Just checking on you," I said. "But I can come back if you're in the flashcard zone." This comment might have sounded snarky, but it wasn't. The flashcard zone was an actual physical plane upon which Tia sometimes claimed to exist.

Tia sighed and put her pen down. "No, it's okay. I'm not in the zone."

"So... what happened in the market?"

Tia hoisted an innocent look onto her face. "What are you talking about?"

"I'm talking about you grabbing my arm and dragging Hannah and me away from Charlie as though he were juggling live grenades," I said.

Tia's face sagged. "You noticed, huh?"

"Noticed? I'm going to have a bruise on my arm for a week."

Tia narrowed her eyes at me. "Don't exaggerate, Jess," she said sternly, before widening her eyes in alarm. "Do you think Charlie noticed?"

"It might have caught his attention, yeah," I said with an incredulous laugh.

Tia groaned. "This is a disaster. I don't know what happened. I just... panicked!"

"Panicked about what?"

"About the fact that I really, really like this guy, and I don't think I realized just how much until I had to introduce you to each other today," Tia said. She was still looking down at the notecard, as though it were a cue card that she was reading her lines off of.

Uncharacteristically, I kept my mouth shut and waited until she was ready to keep talking. After a minute or so, she finally went on.

"I wasn't expecting it. I felt so... impenetrable. So, I don't think I recognized the warning signs before it was too late. You know me. When I want something, I just make it happen. I make it real. I didn't want to be susceptible to falling for someone, so I just... wasn't. So, it felt safe to talk to him, because I was so sure of myself. It felt safe to laugh with him. It felt safe to hang out with him. I should have realized it, Jess, because it's exactly what happened with Sam. I told myself I had no time or interest in boys because I had school to focus on. So, I let my guard down and then..."

"Boom," I said quietly.

"Boom," she agreed. "And it's like in medicine. You don't consider the ailments that don't fit the profile. You don't test for illnesses that don't match the presented symptoms. It's illogical."

"The problem, of course, being that love defies logic," I said with a chuckle.

"Precisely!" Tia said. "And I'm not usually one to make the same mistake twice, but here I am!"

"Hey," I said, pulling my chair over closer to her desk. "You know, it's not necessarily a mistake."

Tia made a sound that was halfway between a laugh and a stifled sob. She put her head down on her arms. "Of course, it's a mistake. What else could it be?"

"I'll grant you that it could be a mistake. Literally every decision we make in life can be a mistake. But if you think that way, you'll never make a decision again. You'll spend the rest of your life standing in front of a coffee shop menu, paralyzed by the implications of mocha instead of vanilla."

Tia made a little sound from behind her arms. It might have been a laugh. I took heart from it.

"But the truth is, that even if it is a mistake—even if taking a chance on Charlie turns out to be a huge mistake—mistakes are important. Mistakes teach us things. They help us grow into the people we're supposed to be."

"So, I'm supposed to be a person who is heart-broken and terrified of relationships? Awesome," Tia sighed.

"No, you're supposed to be someone who makes plans *and* takes chances. Before this break-up happened to you, you only ever made plans. And you probably missed out on opportunities because you didn't want to mess with your plans. I'm not saying plans are a bad thing," I added swiftly, for Tia showed every indication of protesting. "I could stand to make a plan once in a while instead of drifting around aimlessly. But the point is that you grew from this. You took a chance. You changed the plan and look what happened? You're independent. You're living abroad. You're fulfilling your dream of medical school and seeing the world, and you never would have done any of it if you hadn't had that heartbreak."

"That's true, I guess," Tia said.

"You guess? Come on, Tia. You are literally the smartest person I know. Give yourself the credit. You're not just surviving, you're thriving here. And once you get a little more distance from this, you'll realize it was the best thing that ever happened to you."

"Well, I don't know if I'd take it quite *that* far," Tia said, wiping a smudge of mascara-stained tears from her cheek. "But I get what you're saying, Jess, and I appreciate it. Thank you."

"You're welcome. And don't worry about Charlie. I don't think he'll care how you left today as long as you come back."

Tia grinned sheepishly, throwing her hands up in front of her face. "He's so cute, isn't he?"

"Very cute," I agreed. "And really nice, too. I can see why you like him."

"Do you want to come with me to the museum next week?" Tia asked.

"Absolutely," I said.

"So... so you really don't think pursuing this... whatever it is... with Charlie is a mistake?"

I considered, for the very briefest of moments, telling her that Charlie was probably the most severely haunted person I had ever encountered, but I couldn't bring myself to do it. She looked so hopeful, so happy for the first time in months. How could I ruin that for her? No, whatever was going on with Charlie and the spirits,

42

surely I could handle it without stamping out my best friend's first spark of romance since getting her heart broken.

"No. Definitely not a mistake," I said.

§

I left Tia to her studying and found Hannah sitting on the living room sofa, jiggling her foot impatiently.

"What's up?" I asked as she looked up at me.

"Ambrose was giving a report over the phone to Seamus. He told me to 'come back later,'" Hannah said, rolling her eyes. "And then he slammed the door in my face."

My whole body stiffened. "Come on," I said, and marched out the door.

I hammered on Ambrose's door. I heard a pause in the low murmuring of speech inside, then his heavy, shuffling footsteps crossing the room. He opened the door.

"We need to talk to you," I said without preamble. "Now."

"I'm giving a report to S—"

I reached out, pulled the phone out of his hand, and held it up to my ear. "Sorry, Seamus, Ambrose will have to call you back," I said, and ended the call.

Ambrose tried to grab the phone back from me, but I pocketed it. "Hey, what do you think you're—"

"I think I'm asking you to do your goddamn job and help us with something," I said, shoving past him into his flat. "You can send your little spy report to Seamus later."

"It's not a spy report," Ambrose grumbled, but I ignored him, stepping over a pile of magazines and an overflowing trashcan full of Chinese takeout containers toward the couch.

Honestly, I didn't understand how anyone could live like this. His apartment looked like the site of a perpetual FBI stake-out, if FBI stakeouts took place in locker rooms. The blinds were always drawn, and so the room was always in semi-darkness, except where light slipped through the bent places in the blinds where he habitually surveyed the comings and goings on the street below. The table was littered with protein bar wrappers and empty soda cans strewn over a bed of disheveled file folders and images of runes. A football match was playing on the television screen, but its sound was muted, so that it merely cast a flickering glow over the entire space. The sofa had been pushed back against the wall and the carpet rolled up to make room for a weight bench and all its bulky, sweat-scented accessories.

"What is it, then?"

"Did you follow us to the market this morning?" I asked bluntly.

It was hard to tell in the dim light, but I thought his face flushed a bit beneath his beard.

"I went for a bit, just to do a sweep," Ambrose mumbled.

"Oh, a sweep? Really? And did that sweep involve actual spiritual activity, or were you just making sure I wasn't attempting to make contact with Finn Carey?"

Ambrose did not reply.

"Because if you had been monitoring for unusual spiritual activity, which is, in fact, what your real job is supposed to be, you might have noticed a huge congregation of spirits about a third of the way along the market," I went on.

Ambrose raised his eyebrows but still seemed incapable of an intelligible reply.

"No? Did that escape your keen Caomhnóir senses? You're so busy playing detective you're going to get one of us killed. You want to spy on me? Fine. You want to steam open my mail, listen to my phone calls, or follow me like a testosterone-fueled shadow? Great. Knock yourself out. But if you can't find time to also be a Caomhnóir, resign and find someone who fucking can."

Hannah, still standing in the doorway, froze. For just a moment, Ambrose seemed to take up slightly less space than usual. Then he straightened up, puffed out his chest, and asked, "Where was this congregation of spirits?"

"On the corner of Portobello Road and Colville Terrace, grouped around a wagon stall for Pickwick's History of Photography," I told him. "It's a museum here in London. Ever heard of it?"

Ambrose shook his head.

"We couldn't investigate much, given all of the people around, but it seemed to us that the spirits were drawn to a young man who was working the stall," I said.

"This young man, he's someone you know?" Ambrose asked.

I narrowed my eyes at him, trying to decide if the question was sarcastic or not, but decided he generally operated below the level of achieving successful sarcasm. "No, but Tia does. I just met him for the first time today."

"So, he's a sensitive, then?" Ambrose asked.

"No, not that we could tell. He seemed genuinely not to realize the spirits were there," Hannah said, jumping in and taking control now that the confrontation appeared to have fizzled out. "The strange part was what the spirits said, though."

"Which was what, exactly?" Ambrose asked.

"Well, several of them spoke of being 'drawn to' the stall. The pull was so strong that none of the spirits even realized Jess and I were there at first."

Ambrose's usually dour expression lifted into one of surprise. "They didn't notice a fully intact Gateway standing right in front of them? That's... unusual."

"Yeah, that's what we thought, too," Hannah said. "Normally they can sense us immediately. But it took until we were walking away for one of the spirits to notice us, and when she did, she said something... odd."

Ambrose just waited, looking expectantly between us.

"She said to one of the other spirits, 'There goes another one,'" Hannah finished.

Ambrose scowled, which I could only assume meant he was thinking. "Another what?" he finally asked.

"We don't know. That's why we're asking you," I said. "How do spirits recognize Caomhnóir?"

"But you don't think he's a Caomh—"

"Just answer the question," I said impatiently. "What is it in a Caomhnóir that draws a spirit to him?"

"It's the proximity to the Gateway. Not the Gateway itself, of course. That's only in Durupinen. But our ability to see and sense spirits is a result of a shared bloodline with Durupinen. It's that connection that gives us our sight, and draws spirits to us."

"So, is it possible for someone—a man—to be a Dormant, like it is with Durupinen?" Hannah asked.

Ambrose nodded. "Yes. There are men born into inactive Durupinen bloodlines—lines that no longer have an open Gateway—who can be sensitives. It's not as common, but it happens."

"And is it possible that the spirits could have sensed that he was Dormant, and that was why they were drawn to him?" I followed up eagerly.

Ambrose looked skeptical. "It's possible," he said slowly, "but improbable. Caomhnóir are already a degree removed from the Gateway. A Dormant of the Caomhnóir bloodline would be even further removed. For his connection to the spirit world to mask yours... I would say it is very unlikely."

Hannah and I looked at each other, more confused than when we'd entered the room.

"Do you have any background on this man?" Ambrose asked, snapping into Caomhnóir business-mode.

"No, but that's simple enough to get," I muttered. Then when I saw Ambrose looking confused, I pointed to myself and said, "Tracker, remember?"

"Right, yeah," Ambrose grunted.

"Okay. Well, thanks, Ambrose. We'll... uh... see you, I guess," Hannah said, looking at me and cocking her head toward the door.

I stood up and tossed Ambrose's phone back to him. "Tell Seamus I said hi, and that I'm being a good little girl," I told him as I walked by him and out the door.

"Well, that didn't tell us much, did it?" Hannah said as we entered our flat again.

"Useless as usual," I agreed, pulling out my cell phone and hitting number eight on my speed dial.

"Who are you—" Hannah began, but the voice on the end of the line picked up almost immediately.

"Make it quick," said a bored voice.

"Hi Catriona," I said, endeavoring to sound polite. Since being a Tracker was as close as I had to a real job, Catriona was as close as I had to an actual boss, and so I had to at least feign a respectful tone. "How are you?"

"Busy," she replied. "What is it, Jessica?"

"I need a background check on someone," I said. "Can, uh... is that something one of the other Trackers could do for me?"

"Obviously," Catriona said. "But not simply for fun, Jessica. I need a valid reason to run a check."

"It's not for fun," I said through slightly gritted teeth. "I met someone today—a school friend of my roommate. His name is Charlie Wright and he was completely swarmed by spirits."

"Really?" Catriona said. "How fascinating. And why do I have to waste Tracker resources on this? Can't you just Cross the spirits and be done with it?"

46

"Did I mention the spirits were so interested in him that they didn't notice both Hannah and I standing right beside them?"

There was a pause. Then, "I'm listening. Tell me more."

As succinctly as I could, I told Catriona the rest of the story. When I had finished, she stayed silent a few moments, and then asked, "So, you want to know if he has any Durupinen connections."

"Yeah. We thought there was a chance he might be part of a Dormant line, or something like that," I explained.

"Hmm. Yes, it's possible. The name doesn't sound familiar, but if the line is long Dormant... very well. I'll run a check. Tell me what you know about him."

"I don't know a lot. He's a first-year medical student at the University of Central London. He works at Pickwick's History of Photography Museum in the old City of London district. Do you need me to find out more, or...?"

"No. That will be sufficient. Give me a day or two. I'll be back in touch," Catriona said, and hung up without saying goodbye.

"What did she say?" Hannah asked.

"Charming as ever," I muttered to myself, slipping the phone back into my pocket. Then I turned to Hannah and replied, "She's going to run the check."

At that moment, Milo sailed through the wall from outside.

"Any luck?" Hannah asked.

Milo shook his head ruefully. "I went straight over to the spot you mentioned, but Charlie wasn't there. There was a woman working the booth, and all the spirits had gone."

"You're kidding," I groaned. "You must have just missed him."

"Apparently. I did manage to find one of the spirits who had seen him, though," Milo added.

"Really?" Hannah asked excitedly. "What did you find out?"

"Well, he wasn't the most reliable of floaters," Milo said, and when we looked confused, he clarified, "In total denial. The longer they stay, the further out of touch with reality they become sometimes, you know that. But he said something pretty interesting."

"Yeah?" Hannah and I prompted at once.

"I asked him if he'd seen Charlie, and he said, 'Oh, I saw him, all right. He can't fool me with that nonsense. The others might be hoodwinked, but I know it's all a trap. I'm right where I want to be. I don't have any interest in leaving, thank you very much.'"

"Leaving?" Hannah gasped. "But that means..."

"The Gateway," I said. "It has to be. What else could he possibly be talking about?"

Hannah shrugged helplessly. Milo looked nervous.

"Okay," I said, beginning to pace. "Okay. So, for some reason, spirits think Tia's new boyfriend is a Gateway."

Milo gasped. "Boyfriend?! Did Tia say they were actually dating, or—"

"Milo, focus!" I snapped.

Milo grinned sheepishly. "Right. Focusing. Sorry."

"Thank you. Now, we need to figure out why that's happening," I said, trying to quell the uneasiness I felt by adopting a determinedly rational tone. "Catriona will look for a Durupinen or Caomhnóir connection somewhere in his background. And in the meantime, we should take him up on his invitation to tour the museum. The more time we spend around him, the better the chance that we can figure out exactly what's going on. I'm sure there's a reasonable explanation."

Hannah raised one skeptical eyebrow at me.

"Okay, fine, I'm not sure there's a reasonable explanation, but for Tia's sake, I'm going to attempt to find one," I said.

Milo sighed. "Leave it to Tia to fall for the most haunted guy in the city."

"Yeah," I said, more to myself than to anyone else. "My luck with relationships must be starting to rub off on her."

5

UNFINISHED BUSINESS

I STUMBLED INTO THE KITCHEN Tuesday morning, a study in the art of unsexy dishevelment, as usual. I yawned and dropped into the nearest chair. At the sound of my incoherent grunt, Hannah passed me a cup of black coffee and a platter of waffles. I chugged half the coffee, scalding my throat, and then speared two waffles at once and dropped them onto my plate, drowning them remorselessly in syrup.

"You look... tired," she said euphemistically.

"Thanks," I said.

"Rough night?"

I yawned again and reached into my bathrobe pocket, extracting a folded sheet of drawing paper. I tossed it across the table to Hannah, who unfolded it.

"Spirit drawing?" she asked.

"Yep," I replied. "Bastard woke me up three times in two hours."

Hannah grimaced down at the image of the man. He had an unshaven, dirty face, a newsboy cap, and a pair of dark, fingerless gloves. He carried a chimney sweep brush slung over his shoulder. "Gah. He looks a bit... scary."

"Yeah, he wasn't a pleasant face to wake up to, I'll give him that."

"Did he say what he wants?"

"He kept saying, 'I didn't kill my Rosie! I need them to know!' Sounds like an unsolved crime thing."

Hannah nodded. Our lives were strange enough by this point that this kind of thing was a fairly common occurrence. "Did you get a name?"

"No, but see at the bottom? That's the street."

She squinted down at the drawing of the narrow, cobblestoned alleyway, which looked like it had been plucked straight out of the pages of a Dickensian novel. A small square sign on one of the buildings said "Fleet Street."

"Looks creepy."

"I'm pretty sure all of Victorian London looked creepy, by our standards," I said.

"Does this street still exist?" she asked.

"No idea," I said. "But I thought I'd do a little research and see if I can find it." I looked down at the picture and then dropped my head onto my arms. "I'm going to spend my morning wandering a street that may or may not still exist, looking for an accused murderer ghost. Dear God, I need a real job."

I heard Milo snort-laughing from the living room, where he was watching a re-run of Project Runway.

"What's on tap for you today?" I asked Hannah, ignoring Milo.

Hannah held up a finger while chewing a bite of waffle, then swallowed. "I've got to go to Fairhaven, remember? It's committee day."

"Oh, yeah, that's right," I said. "Sorry, I swear I would have remembered that after I finished my coffee."

Hannah hesitated, then pulled a folder from the bag at her feet and slid it across the table to me. "I'm going to start floating this around today. I wanted to show it to you first."

I pulled the folder toward me, flipped it open, and read the heading on the top of a stack of papers. "Proposed Amendment to Clan Conduct Code Part III Subsection IV."

I scanned the first few sentences and my heart began to race. I looked up at her. "Is... is this..."

Hannah nodded. "Yes. The ban on relationships between Durupinen and Caomhnóir."

I swallowed back something that seemed to be half-waffle, half-sob. "Are you sure? This is the very first legislation you're proposing. It's going to get a lot of resistance."

"I know," Hannah said. "But let's face it, anything I try to do is going to be met with resistance because... well, it's *me*." She pushed back from the table and reached out for my mug. I drained the rest of the coffee in it and handed it to her. "Besides, I'm not proposing it. Not yet. First, I'm going to feel out a few of the friendlier Council members and see if I can find a couple of them to co-sponsor it with me."

"You don't think this is too transparent? I mean, most of the

Council doesn't know what happened with me and Finn, but Celeste…"

"Look, there's no way to address the law without… well, addressing it. Obviously, Celeste will know what part of the motivation is behind this. But, I think that's okay."

"Why would it be okay for her to see right through what you're doing? She's bound to call you out on it, isn't she?" I asked slowly.

Hannah put down her fork and sighed. "Look, I know you're angry at Celeste. We all are. But I don't think she did what she did because she agrees with the law. I think she did it because she has to uphold the law. If changes could be made, reasonably and with consensus, I think she'd be happy to implement them. She's not Marion, Jess. She's reasonable. And she has always supported us. I know it felt really personal when she sent Finn away, but I know that you know it's not true. She honestly thought she was saving you from a nasty, public scandal that would have ended the same way. And let's face it, she was probably right."

I didn't reply, choosing to violently spear three pieces of waffle and cram them into my mouth instead. I was not ready to concede anything about Celeste, not this early in the morning.

Hannah went on, "I think that, if we could find a way to make the Caomhnóir –Durupinen relationships function better, that would be good for everyone, not just you and Finn. The more I've looked into it, the more convinced I am that the whole system needs an overhaul."

"And we all know how much the Durupinen like change," I said, rolling my eyes.

"I think quite a few of them have realized that if we aren't willing to change and adjust, we are vulnerable," Hannah said firmly. "I'm not naïve, I know it will be an uphill battle. But we've got to start somewhere, and I'm not going to waste the chance to do something. This Council seat wasn't just a political stunt. I have things I want to accomplish."

In the hall, we heard a door open and shut, then Tia bounced into the kitchen, smiling.

"Good morning, everyone!" she said cheerily.

"How do you wake up like this? Don't you have an exam today?" I asked her.

"Yup," she said, pulling a carton of orange juice from the refrigerator and pouring a glass.

"Well, I'd like to make some comment about how you can't possibly be a normal human, but I spent half the night drawing Victorian-era ghost murderers in my sleep, so who the hell am I to talk?" I grumbled.

"Good luck on your exam," Hannah said. "What time do you need to leave?"

"Eight o'clock," Tia said, buttering herself a scone.

"Do you want a ride over to the college?" Hannah offered. "Ambrose is driving me out to Fairhaven today. It's right on the way."

Tia smiled even more brightly. "That would be great! I mean, if you really don't mind!"

Hannah smiled back. "Not at all. It'll be nice to have someone to talk to for a bit. Trying to have a conversation with Ambrose is about as productive and entertaining as chatting up a utility pole."

Milo sailed into the kitchen and settled in the only empty seat, completing our dysfunctional little makeshift family breakfast. "Did I hear something in here about murdering someone?"

"This guy," I said to Milo, pushing the sketch across the table. "I'm off to find him this morning. Any chance you want to come with me?"

Milo flared his nostrils as he looked down at the man's face. "Well, he looks just delightful. And why do you have to find him?"

"Three visits last night. Seems he was accused of a murder he didn't commit, or something."

Milo pouted. "Why don't you ever get visited by any ghosts I'd want to hang out with?"

I rolled my eyes. "I'll try to work on that, Milo. So, I take it you don't want to accompany me on this little excursion?"

Milo bit his lip. "I mean... I will if you need me to, obviously, but... well, the new Dolce and Gabbana collection is coming into Brown's this morning, and I want to scope it out before the real housewives of Holland Park descend and start clawing each other's eyes out over it."

"Never mind," I told him with a sigh.

"No, let's do the murderer chimney sweep thing, that sounds better," he said, looking down at the picture again.

I laughed. "No, forget it. You're off the hook for this one. But I reserve the right to call you away from the handbag display if he turns out to be more than I can handle, okay?"

Milo sighed with relief. "I'm just one blood-curdling scream away, I promise. Thanks, Jess."

Two hours and a very crowded Tube ride later, I was standing alone in a shadowy alley, trying not to look too conspicuous to passersby on the main road. Thanks to the deep and endless well of information known as the internet, I had been able not only to find the street that the spirit had named in his Visitation, but I discovered that it still existed, virtually untouched by the relentless development and reshaping of the city's features. It had also been featured in *Sweeney Todd*, a musical about a demon barber who slits people's throats while he shaves them, and then bakes them into meat pies, a tidbit of trivia that made me feel all the more warm and fuzzy about visiting the place. I took the Central line from Notting Hill Gate to Chancery Lane, walked several blocks through throngs of morning commuters, and found the place I was searching for at last, in the heart of the original City of London, one of the oldest developed areas of greater London, brimming with a quirky, anachronistic mix of old and new. Keeping my senses on high alert, I pulled the folded-up sketch out of my pocket and smoothed out its creases against a brick wall, so that I could focus my energy on the man's face, using my connection to the image to feel my way out into the space around me, searching for another signal from the unique energy that had helped me to create it.

I felt him a second before I heard him, and so I managed not to jump too badly as his gruff voice echoed down the alley.

"You came."

I turned, keeping my face a mask of calm. If I remained calm, I had found, the spirits I interacted with had a better chance of staying calm, too.

"Yes, I did. I could tell that you needed my help."

He stepped out of a shadow, taking form before my eyes. He was short but broad, with a torso like a whisky barrel and muscular arms. He was glaring suspiciously at me through one eye—the other one seemed to be swollen shut. "'Ow is it you can see me, then? Ain't never met no one what could see me before."

"It's my... talent. My gift," I said, knowing a true, detailed explanation would try this man's patience. "It's also my job, to help spirits such as yourself."

The man snorted. "Some job. 'Ow'd you get landed wif it, then, a little scrap of a thing like you?"

I smiled grimly. "Just lucky, I guess. Can you remember your name?"

"What you mean, then? O' course I can remember me own name! It's Albie Turner," the man said, thrusting his chest out in front of him and bellowed, "A name I intend to clear, you 'ear me?"

"Loud and clear, Mr. Turner," I said gently. "I'm glad to help with that. Why don't you tell me why you need your name to be cleared?"

"They think I killed me girl, Rosie, but I never. She never come back, see, from her shift at the factory. We looked for 'er all over, and couldn't find no trace of 'er." He swallowed hard, and his lips trembled. "I was lost without her. Then, she done washed up on the shores of the Thames. The coppers said some pigeon-livered scum strangled her and... and other things." He looked down at his own feet, breathing heavily, trying to master his anger. "They came down the Red Dragon to bring me in for questioning. I told 'em, I says, I ain't going nowhere with you. I ain't done nothing and I want to help find the monster what killed my Rosie."

"Then what happened?" I prompted, after a few moments of silence.

"I tried to run. I know it was stupid, but I was half-mad with grief and I'd drunk meself near under the table. I fell out into the street as a lorry was passin'. Killed on the spot, I was," Albie said quietly.

I waited a few moments to allow him to reflect as he needed to on his own demise. It couldn't be an easy thing to think about, even more than a hundred years later.

"What happened after that, Albie?" I asked.

"Got confused. Lost," Albie said, furrowing his brow like he had a hard time recalling the details. "Took me a while to get my head clear. When I managed it, all I wanted was to find my Rosie. I searched and searched, but I couldn't never find her. At last, I figured she'd gone on to 'eaven. She was always too good for me, too good for this world, and that's the God's honest truth. Why should she wait around for the likes of me?"

"So, why didn't you follow her?" I asked him. "Once you realized she was gone, didn't you want to go, too?"

Albie looked at me suspiciously. "I ain't spent as much time in a church as I ought, it's true, but I know a thing or two about good and bad. I done bad things in my life, and I ain't never made 'em right. I don't trust what's waitin' for me on the other side of that... that thing you're tempting me with."

"Well, if you don't want to Cross, how can I help you, Albie? Why did you reach out to me?"

Albie licked his lips and cleared his throat. "Well, now, like I said, I done some bad things in my life. I admit to it, and I'll accept what's comin' to me, whatever that might be. But I never done nothing so 'orrible as what they think I did to my Rosie, I swear to it. And I been trying for a while now to find a way to clear me name, see? But..." he looked around him, at a city he didn't know any more. "It's all so strange now... the places... everything looks different, and I don't reckon I know where to start."

"You came to me," I said, trying a tentative smile. "That was a good place to start."

Albie's face brightened at once. "You think you can help me?"

I nodded. "I've got an important tool you haven't got, Albie."

"What's that, then?" Albie asked.

I held up my phone. "The internet."

Albie looked mystified. "What the devil—"

"Your Rosie," I said, cutting him off before I had to launch into an explanation of modern technology, "Was her full name Rose Hathaway?"

Albie gasped. "That's right! 'Ow did you... I ain't never told you that!"

I tapped the phone screen. "God bless the British Library."

"What do you—"

"They've got a wonderful digital archive," I told him. "You can access it from almost anywhere." I saw the bewildered look on his face and adjusted a bit. "Sorry, I got ahead of you there. They have a collection of old newspapers. Do you remember Rosie's death being in the papers?"

Albie nodded. "It was awful, seeing her name over and over again like that."

"Well, Rosie's wasn't the only name in the paper at that time. Other women were attacked as well, three of them. Did you know that?" I asked him, holding up the phone screen so that he could see the image of the headline and article I had pulled up.

"No, I never 'eard," Albie said, eyes wide as he took in the words, then pointed to the phone. "What is that contraption, then? I seen people all over the city with them."

"Never mind that, it's not important," I said. "Now, it says here that Rosie's body was found on the 12th of May 1889, is that right?"

"Yeah. Yeah, that's right," Albie said.

"And you died... when?" I asked gently.

"Next day," Albie said. "May the 13th."

"Well, these three other women who were attacked, Mary Murray, Ann Gladstone, and Irene King—they were all killed after you died, from late May to early July, all strangled, and all dumped in the river, just like Rosie. Their killer was caught, tried, and convicted in December of that same year. His name was Edward Hobbs. They hanged him."

Albie blinked. "They... they caught him? The man what killed my Rosie?"

"Yes," I told him. "And executed him. He was found guilty of all four crimes."

Albie closed his eyes and mouthed silently to himself. Finally he whispered, "I prayed. I prayed so many times that he would rot for what he did. But then I thought, that's not a prayer that anyone's goin' to answer. It ain't right, praying for another man's destruction. But I did it. I did it every day."

"It's not wrong to want justice for Rosie," I told him gently. "And she got it, in the end."

Albie didn't seem able to speak. He just nodded and sniffed loudly, dragging the back of his hand across his face.

"So, now that you know that your name is clear, what do you think about... maybe... Crossing?" I asked him.

He looked wary again. "That... that's that feelin' I've got. That pull, then?"

"Yes," I told him. "It's how you found me, and it's how you'll find Rosie as well."

"Well," he said, sounding very nervous now. "Guess I ain't really got no reason to stay, now I know what you told me. But..."

"If the only thing holding you back is your fear, don't let it," I told him. "It's where you're meant to be, surely you can feel that."

"Aye, that I do, to be sure," Albie said, still sounding wary.

"Have you ever felt that sense of belonging before in life?" I ventured.

Albie's eyes began to sparkle. "Every time I was with Rosie," he murmured.

"Then why not go join her?" I asked him. "I'm sure she's been waiting on you."

Albie sniffed loudly. "Yeah. Yeah, I guess you're right. Ain't never regretted a moment I spent with her, even knowin' how it ended."

"I don't think you'll regret this either," I told him.

Albie took a slow, deep breath, and then blew it out. "All right then. I trust you. But is there any reason I should use this one?" Albie asked, pointing at me.

I frowned. "This one?"

"Well, yeah," Albie said. "I mean, I know you ain't the only one is town. There's another one right up the road 'ere." He cocked his thumb over his shoulder back toward the main road.

"Hold up," I said, laughing incredulously. "Another Gateway? On this *street?* You're joking, right?"

"Wouldn't joke about something like that," Albie said. "It's just there, at Pickwick's."

My heart skipped a beat, then pumped into overdrive. "Pickwick's? Are you talking about Pickwick's History of Photography? The museum?"

"That's the one, all right," Albie agreed. "Been feeling that pull for a bit now, but I ain't never been tempted."

I hesitated only a moment. I had promised Tia that we would visit the museum together, and I felt guilty going without her. At the same time, it was just too much of a coincidence to ignore that this spirit would lead me practically to its doorstep. How could I come this close and not at least get a peek? Charlie had said he was working Tuesday and Thursday, and I could just pretend I had just happened to be in the neighborhood... which was true, leaving out the bizarre circumstances that had brought me here. And I could always call on Milo if I wanted a second opinion or needed help. A tiny voice in the back of my head woke up and whispered, so quietly that I could almost pretend to ignore it, *"Finn would be so pissed if he knew you were going to this place alone."*

Finn's not here, I told the voice. *And he's not going to be, so we might as well stop waiting around for his permission. We're never going to get it.*

I turned back to Albie.

"Can you show me where it is?" I asked. "I just want to take a quick look around."

Albie looked surprised, but nodded. "'Appy to oblige. Least I can do, seeing as 'ow you 'elped me today."

Albie picked up his chimney sweeping brush, slung it over his shoulder, and set out in front of me, whistling a tune as he walked. He led me out of the alley and strolled along the main street, utterly at his ease amongst a throng of modern-day Londoners going about their digital, hashtagged existences.

Damn, being a ghost must be *really* weird sometimes.

We crossed Fleet Street and had followed two quieter side streets only a couple of blocks when Albie stopped, swung the chimney brush from his shoulder and pointed it down a side street.

"Right there on your left, duckie. Pickwick's History of Photography in Gough Square. 'Course, it was just a place to get your likeness taken back in my day. Never had two farthings to make a jingle in me pocket back then. Watch yourself," he added, his face suddenly grave. "They don't all take as kindly to living folk as I do, and you will certainly attract some attention."

"I'll be careful, thank you," I assured him. "And will you think about my offer? To Cross you over?"

He tipped his hat respectfully. "I will, at that," he said. "And if I decide to accept?"

"Just reach out and find me, like you did with the drawing. It should be a lot easier now, since we've spent a bit of time together. Any time you're ready, we can arrange it."

"Cheerio, then, miss," Albie said. "I won't never forget the help you gave me."

I watched as Albie turned on the spot and walked back the way we had come, his form fading with each step until he vanished altogether. I sighed, pushing away the sorrow of his story, forcing him to take it with him. I couldn't afford to have it clinging to me, weighing me down. I needed a clear head for what I was about to do. I turned and faced the building.

6

PICKWICK'S HISTORY OF PHOTOGRAPHY

PICKWICK'S HISTORY OF PHOTOGRAPHY looked like something straight out of a Dickensian fantasy, an impression that was only strengthened by the fact that I had followed behind an actual chimney sweep to get there. The building itself was so old that the bricks had a faded, rounded, crumbling look to them, and the whole structure seemed to lean slightly to one side, like a block tower a child might build. It seemed out of danger of tumbling over in the same manner as a block tower, though, due to the fact that it was wedged so tightly against the buildings on either side of it. The top two stories were brick, while the street level was paneled in shiny lacquered black wood set with a tall row of glass windows through which displays and glimpses of the museum itself might be gazed at. No one was gazing, however. People drifted by Pickwick's as though it were a ghost itself; old, forgotten, and practically invisible. Peeling, gilded gold letters were painted across the top of the lacquered panels: "Pickwick's History of Photography." The front door, with an ornate brass doorknob right in the center, was painted a bright lilac purple. And beside it, an old lamppost had been affixed to the wall, a sputtering gas flame burning inside it, even in daylight.

All of this would have been sufficient to pique my curiosity about the place. The chilling and overpowering aura of concentrated spirit energy was just the icing on this weird cake of a situation.

I approached carefully and peered into the first window. A length of red velvet had been draped across a multilevel display case, which showcased a number of dusty old cameras and other gadgets I could only assume were used with them, though what they were, I couldn't say. In front of each piece was a small, blue-lined notecard pinned to the fabric, on which someone had typed out the name of each device. The labels looked like they'd been typed on a vintage typewriter, because the letters had that slightly askew typeset quality to them. Although, I thought to myself, the labels looked so old, curled, and faded, that the typewriter used to create them might have been state-of-the-art at the time.

I skirted a large hanging basket of red geraniums and looked into the next window. Here, a wooden dummy of a woman in a high-necked Victorian gown sat on a wooden stool as though posing for a photograph. What could be seen of her faded, painted expression was somewhat dour. Before her, another dummy of a man in a jacket with coattails was bent over behind a camera on a tripod. The top half of his body was obscured beneath a black velvet cloth save for his left arm, which was raised above him holding a dented metal tray meant to hold flash powder. I recognized the setup from old movies, where the photographer would usually wind up disappearing behind a puff of smoke and emerge coughing with a blackened face and a singed moustache. I smirked and moved on. The third and final window display held a number of framed sepia-toned portraits suspended from fishing line, so that they seemed to float in the air behind the dusty glass. I was so engrossed in looking at them that I didn't notice the little boy with his face pressed to the glass of the front door.

"Oh!" I said in surprise when I looked down and saw his dirt-smudged face. "I'm sorry, I didn't notice..." But my voice trailed away. The boy wore a pageboy cap, fingerless gloves, and knickers, and the dirty little face that glared up at me had long since been buried.

"It's not what you think," he said to me, his little mouth puckered in an expression of extreme consternation.

"What's not what I think?" I asked him.

He pointed a filthy little finger at the glass door of the museum. "Don't let her fool you, that woman. It's not what you think."

"What are you...?" The end of my question was lost in a gasp as the tiny figure shot up from the ground so that his smudged and freckled nose was barely an inch from mine. His eyes were so dark they looked bottomless.

"*It's not real!*" he hissed at me, and then vanished.

I stood for a moment with my heart in my throat. Then I exhaled slowly, stepped forward, and placed my hand on the doorknob.

Typically, when the ghost of a Dickensian street urchin warns you against entering a place, you run screaming.

When you're me, you pop inside for a look around.

A friendly little bell jingled upon the opening of the door.

My first thought as I looked around Pickwick's History of Photography, was that I wasn't entirely sure it knew what it was supposed to be. The walls were covered in an ornate gold and green wallpaper. Gas lamps flickered in sconces at intervals along the walls. A chandelier hung from a medallion in the center of the ceiling, and a number of settees and fainting couches had been set along the walls. In this respect, it looked like a Victorian era parlor of some sort. But between the couches were tall glass cases full of an assortment of photography artifacts of various shapes and sizes, from tiny snippets of film negative and batteries, to what seemed to be an early movie camera on wheels. On the walls between the cases, velvet drapes hung in folds to the floor, swept back with gold-tasseled tie-backs to reveal not windows, but collections of framed photographs. Glass-topped display cases stood all around the center of the room, crammed full of still more artifacts, and from what I could see, the collection continued into two further rooms and partially up a narrow staircase. The air was thick with dust, mildew, and the chill of spirit presence.

"Um, hello?" I called.

"We're still closed!" called a woman's muffled voice from one of the back rooms.

"Oh, I'm sorry. The sign says ten o'clock."

"So, common sense should tell you to wait until ten o'clock before trying the door," the woman's aggravated voice replied.

"It's 10:07," I told her, checking my phone display.

"What?! Oh my... hang on, I'll be right with you!" I heard a series of bangs, a bit of cursing, and then a woman emerged from the far door, rubbing her hands on the pant legs of her jeans and wiping sweat from her brow with a white handkerchief. She was a tall, thin woman, probably in her mid-thirties, with thick, dark hair pinned up under a bandana and a deep olive complexion that was shining with sweat and sticky with dust. She looked up at the clock on the wall. It said 9:20. She looked down at her watch and swore again. Then she looked up and smiled a bit maniacally at me.

"My apologies for the delay. And my appearance. And the excessive cursing," she said with a note of desperation in her voice.

"For some reason, my watch and all three of the clocks in here stopped working at twenty-past nine, so rather than opening on time, I nearly turned away our first—and potentially only—customer of the day."

"That's okay, don't worry about it," I said, smiling. I extended my hand out to her. "My name is Jess Ballard."

The woman took my hand and grasped it firmly. "Shriya Brown, née Pickwick. I'm the proprietor of this fine establishment. Or at least, I'm trying to be. I inherited it a month ago from my grandfather and so I'm still trying to figure out how it all works."

A muffled crashing sound echoed from the back room.

"Damn it. Excuse me, for just a moment please," Shriya said, and disappeared into the back room again.

As I stood waiting for her, a pair of female spirits floated through the room, whispering to each other. They stared around the place, bewildered. One was clutching at her head. Then they disappeared up the staircase. They took no notice of me.

Shriya appeared again, rubbing one of her elbows and smiling ruefully. "Apologies again. I'm operating under the assumption that the storage room is trying to kill me."

"No problem. Do... do you want me to come back another time?" I asked.

"No! No, not at all!" Shriya cried, looking horrified. "Just... just give me a moment, please, and I'll be delighted to assist you."

I watched as Shriya scurried around, pulling up the shades, turning on the lights, and plugging in and powering on various items all over the room. Several costumed mannequins began jerking and swiveling. Sound effects of clicking, popping, and whirring started to play through little speakers set in the various displays. As she pulled a black fabric cover off an antique cash register, another spirit passed directly behind her. She shuddered violently and turned, staring wildly around, and then placed her hand along the sill of the nearby window, apparently convinced there had been a draft.

"So, did you say that you just inherited this museum?" I asked.

"Yeah, my grandfather used to run it," Shriya said as she fiddled with the cash register. "I used to come here all the time as a kid. I loved it, but I haven't been back in years. I'll let you in on a little secret," she leaned across the counter and said, in a stage whisper, "I don't really know what I'm doing."

I laughed. "I'm sure you'll get the hang of it."

"Can I ask you how you heard about the museum?" Shriya asked. "I'm trying to figure out how to market the place. My grandfather, bless him, didn't seem too fussed with letting people know the museum actually exists. I don't know how he's stayed open so long."

"I saw your booth at the Portobello Market this past weekend."

"Oh, did you? Excellent!" the woman said. "We've never done the market before. I was dubious about the value in it, but lo and behold, a real live customer!"

"Yeah, well, a friend of my roommate was working the booth for you. Charlie Wright?"

Shriya's face lit up. "Oh, you know Charlie!"

"Not really," I said. "I only just met him for the first time on Saturday. But he said I should stop by and check out the museum, so that's what I'm doing. He said he was working today."

"He would have been, but he's just phoned to say he's been taken ill," Shriya said. "Which is part of the reason I'm scrambling like this. Charlie worked for my grandfather before he passed away. He knows more about this place than I do. I'd be quite lost without him."

I nodded politely, but inside, my brain was whirring. So, if Charlie was the one who was supposed to be haunted, and Charlie wasn't here today... then what the hell was with all the ghosts? If he wasn't here, shouldn't they just be haunting him at his flat, or wherever else he happened to be? Why were they hanging around the museum, if the object of their fascination was elsewhere?

Curiouser and curiouser.

"... don't even know how to categorize all the artifacts in the back," Shriya was still chattering away. She sighed and gestured theatrically around her. "Anyway, enough about my general incompetence. We're up and running! Now what can I do for you?"

"I... uh... wanted to buy a ticket, please," I said, somewhat distracted by the spirits that kept wandering back and forth through the room. Each and every one of them had a mystified, almost entranced expression on their faces. Were they confused? Were they searching for Charlie?

"Brilliant. That will be five pounds please," Shriya said, prodding at the keys on the register, each of which made a hollow clunking noise. As I handed over my money, the drawer slid open with violent force, sending paper notes fluttering everywhere.

"Bollocks!" Shriya shouted. "I'm so sorry, I... I don't know what happened. I must say that about fifty times a day around here."

"No problem," I said. "Here let me help you." I dropped to the floor and started picking up money. A child's spirit giggled at me from beneath the counter.

"That wasn't very nice, you know," I whispered, staring the child right in the eye. He gasped at being discovered and vanished on the spot, leaving nothing but an icy draft in his wake.

"Here you go," I said to Shriya, straightening up and depositing the crumpled pile of money on the counter. "I think that's everything that fell on this side."

"Cheers," Shriya said, trying to organize the money with slightly trembling hands. "You must think I'm completely mad—can't open on time, can't work a cash register. Great first impression I'm making."

"Of course not," I said. "So... so Charlie isn't even here today?"

"That's right," Shriya said distractedly, trying to count. "Hope he's feeling better soon, or the place is likely to fall apart without him. Well, here you are." She handed me a large cardstock ticket that was designed to look like a ticket to a carnival or a sideshow. She took a large silver puncher and, with a flourish, punched a hole in my ticket the shape of a curled moustache. I looked down at it and chuckled.

"My grandfather was a quirky man," Shriya said, laughing along with me. "So, you can look at the exhibits in any order, but if you follow the footprints, they will lead you through the museum in chronological order."

"The footprints?" I asked, confused.

Shriya pointed down to the floor, where large, cartoonish white shoe prints had been painted onto the black floorboards. For the first time I noticed that they wandered all over the museum, as though an invisible clown were taking a tour.

"Oh, I see. Thank you," I said.

"Do you want me to show you around?" Shriya asked.

"No!" I said, a little too sharply. Shriya looked taken aback, but I quickly slapped on a smile and went on, "I'm perfectly content to just wander, thanks. Besides, it sounds like you've got a lot to do.

64

Why don't you take the opportunity to get a few things done before it gets too busy?"

Shriya smiled a little sadly. "It never gets busy. That's part of the problem." She stepped out from behind the counter. "If you have any questions, just give me a shout, yeah? I'll be right in the back room."

I think I made a generic reply, but my thoughts were racing ahead. Charlie wasn't here, and yet Pickwick's History of Photography was absolutely swarming with spirits. This made no sense. The spirits had been looking at him—following him with their eyes, and swarming around his body. He had been the focus of their obsession. Were all of these spirits perhaps just waiting for him to return? And if so, why?

I backtracked to the front door where the painted footsteps began. I worked my way slowly around the room, stopping dutifully at each display as though I was reading it, but really keeping my senses alert for further spirit encounters. The entire place was buzzing with the energy.

At the third display, the spirit of a young man was staring at a display of portraits on the wall, walking in circles, then returning to the portraits.

"Hello," I said to him. "Are you all right?"

He turned and looked at me. His gaze was completely unfocused. "I can't find it," he said, sounding a little desperate. "It's here, in this place, but I can't find it. It's like a bloody maze!"

"What are you—" I began, but the man gave a roar of frustration and vanished, appearing again on the other side of the room, where he continued to stare and pace and circle.

I moved a little further along. The spirit of an old woman sat at the foot of the staircase that led to the upper level. She was sobbing into her hands.

"What's wrong?" I asked her, but she didn't seem to even be able to hear me. Bending closer to her, I could make out some of the words buried in the fit of crying.

"I've waited too long," she was whispering. "I've waited too long and now I can't find it. I've lost the way. It won't let me through, not now, not ever."

I straightened up, a deep uneasiness growing in the pit of my stomach. In the back corner of the room, the ghost of a younger woman with long, braided hair was staring around her, as though looking for a street sign.

"Who are you looking for?" I asked her, after making sure that Shriya was still safely in the back room.

The girl seemed not even to realize where my voice had come from. Her eyes continued to dart around the room. "I... I can't get through," she was saying, over and over again. "It's here... but... where is it?"

I encountered at least a dozen other spirits in my self-guided tour, but not a single one of them seemed capable of speaking to me. Without exception they were confused, frustrated, and generally disoriented. I could not make sense of it, except for one, glaring fact.

It wasn't Charlie who was haunted at all. It was the museum itself.

§

I'd barely finished calling a hasty goodbye to Shriya and pulled the front door shut behind me, and my phone was already out of my pocket and up to my ear.

"Yes?" drawled the bored voice I expected on the other end.

"Hi, Catriona," I said. "How are you?"

"Just ducky," she said. I could practically hear her eyes rolling. "And you are calling because...?"

"You really have to stop sounding so happy to hear from me," I said. "Honestly, people will think there's something going on between us."

A moment of silence, and then, "And you are calling because...?"

"Did you have any luck with the background check on Charlie Wright?" I asked her.

"Wright, Wright," she said, and I could hear her flipping through papers on her desk. "Hang on, I think I saw something come through this morning, actually. Yes, here it is." I waited as she flipped through and scanned the report. "No, nothing here to tie him to any known active or Dormant clan."

I nodded. That, at least, made sense based on what I'd just witnessed. "Okay. So, my next question is, have you ever heard of a place called 'Pickwick's History of Photography?'"

"No," Catriona said. "Should I have?"

"Not necessarily, no. It's the museum where Charlie works. I just visited the place and it is swarming with spirits. Like, I've never seen so many ghosts outside of Fairhaven."

"Riveting," Catriona said blandly. "Why do I need to know this?"

"I think it's the building—or something housed inside it—that is drawing the spirits. Charlie hasn't been in today—he's called out sick—and the place is still crawling with ghosts. I can't figure it out."

"Any other people working there?" Catriona asked.

"The only one there today was the owner, Shriya Brown, but she doesn't seem to be a sensitive. I mean, she knows weird stuff is happening, but no more than any other normal person whose space is haunted," I said. "Here's the strange thing, though. The spirits there seem convinced they're being drawn to a Gateway, but then they wander around the museum all frustrated and confused, unable to Cross. I just can't make heads or tails of it."

"So, what do you want to do, then? Have a team come check the place out?" Catriona asked. "I don't really know who I can spare at the moment. We've got some high priority—"

"No, I was thinking that maybe I could take the case on myself. This seems like one of those situations where my team might be a good fit," I said hesitantly.

"Your team?" Catriona drawled.

"Yes, you know, the paranormal investigative team. The thing is, the owner of this place just inherited it, and she's trying to drum up publicity. The team recently started a web series about their investigations, and it's really popular. I think, if I offered for the museum to be featured on one of the episodes, Shriya might jump at the chance."

"Are you telling me," Catriona said with a snort, "that non-sensitives actually watch that nonsense?"

"Well, obviously someone like you wouldn't find it very interesting," I said, exerting serious effort now to keep the tone polite. "But non-sensitives find ghost hunting shows really entertaining."

"So, you use the investigation as the pretext to get in there and have a proper look around?" Catriona asked.

"Yes," I said. "I can't possibly do what I need to do if the place is full of customers. But if it's empty, and I have the run of the place, I might be able to figure out what the hell is going on."

Catriona was silent for a few moments, then said, "All right, then. I'll officially put it on your docket. Set it all up with the owner, call your team, and I'll take care of the travel arrangements and lodging. I'm also going to submit a research order into the history of the building and surrounding area, so that we can know if there is any history of spiritual disruption there."

I blinked. "Really? You're saying yes?"

"Yes," Catriona said, and then, almost grudgingly. "Good work."

"Uh, thanks," I said. "I'll uh... get going on those arrangements."

"Let me know when you've got commitments from the owner and your team," Catriona said.

"Will do," I said. She answered with a click as she hung up the phone.

Wow. "Good work." I might as well bask in the glory of that praise. It was likely to be the last I'd get from Catriona probably ever.

7

HALF-TRUTHS

"**L**ONDON? Are you freaking kidding me?"

Iggy's excited voice boomed through the phone speaker, so that I had to hold it a good foot from my ear to avoid eardrum damage.

"I am, indeed, *not* freaking kidding you," I told him, laughing. "Do you think the rest of the guys would go for it?"

"Of course!" Iggy said at once. "Damn, I've never been to England before. Neither has Dan. I think Oscar might have spent some time over there when he was in the Navy, but it's been years. What's the gig?"

"A haunted museum," I told him. "The owner just inherited it from her grandfather and it is swarming with spirit activity. It would make an incredible episode for the web series. And maybe you guys could line up some other stuff to investigate while you're here," I suggested.

"Yeah! Yeah, I mean, haunted London is just iconic, isn't it? So much history, so many beheadings!"

"Easy there, guy," I said. "I've got to get the owner to agree to the investigation first. And then we've got to figure out when you guys can get here, the sooner the better. Any ideas?"

"Well, we're filming another location this weekend, but our next big shoot isn't for another three weeks after that. It would put us behind on our editing, but I think we could squeeze it in. What do you think? How long do you think it would take to investigate the museum?"

"That would be amazing," I said gratefully. "It should only be a one-night job. It's not a big place, but it packs a serious spiritual punch. You will not be disappointed, I promise you."

"Aw, man, I can't wait to tell the guys. We'll have to budget it out, unless—" he trailed off hopefully, and I knew why.

"Don't worry about that. I can get your expenses covered," I assured him.

Iggy whooped and then chuckled. "I know I'm not supposed to know who you work for, but man, you have got the best bosses."

I thought of Catriona and smirked. "Yeah, they have their moments. So, round up the guys and let me know, okay?"

"You got it, Ghost Girl," Iggy said, using his affectionate nickname for me. "Man. Investigating London. Pierce would have freaking loved this."

I tried not to let my voice break as I replied. "Yeah. Yeah, he sure as hell would have."

Iggy sniffed loudly. "Well, we'll have to catch video of a full-body apparition just for him."

"That's the spirit," I said. "Pun absolutely intended."

"Take care, kid," Iggy said. "I'll call you back when I've talked to the team."

"Great. Talk soon," I said, and hung up. "Well, that was about as easy as I thought it would be," I said, pocketing the phone.

It had only been two days since my first trip to Pickwick's and already the pieces for the investigation were falling into place. Catriona had gotten a travel budget approved the previous day, and I knew that Iggy would have no problem convincing the rest of the team to agree to the trip. The final piece of the puzzle was getting Shriya to agree to the investigation, and as Hannah was reading up on Durupinen law at the library and Tia was in classes all day, this was the perfect opportunity for a trip over to Pickwick's. I wasn't entirely sure Shriya would be easy to convince, but luckily, I had a secret weapon to help persuade her.

"Milo, you ready?"

There was a brief stirring of energy, and then Milo popped into existence beside me. "You're done already?" he asked, looking surprised.

"Yup. They're on board. There's no way they're going to miss a chance like this," I told him.

"Great!" Milo said.

"Yeah, I know they're excited, but I owe them bigtime. Maybe you could come along to the investigation and make sure they get some good action?"

Milo arched one eyebrow. "What are you insinuating, madam?"

I rolled my eyes. "You know what I mean."

Milo chuckled. "Yes, I do, and I'd be happy to rattle some door knobs and levitate some candlesticks, or whatever. Just don't ask me to wear one of those white sheets. They clash with my aesthetic."

I snorted. "What's your aesthetic? Non-corporeal chic?"

"You know it, sweetness," Milo said with a little twirl. "And no one does it better than me."

"That's true," I said. "Well, let's get going, your Chic-ness."

"Hold up," Milo said, looking suddenly concerned. "I just thought of something. Charlie told you he works Thursdays, right? Aren't you afraid that we'll run into him?"

"Nope," I said confidently. "Tia told me last night that he's still sick. He told her he was staying home again today."

"Oh, good," Milo said. "I'd feel like shit if we scared him off before Tia even got to go on a date with him."

"I know, I thought about that, too," I said, biting my lip. "Obviously, he's going to find out about the investigation eventually, but I'd like to delay that as long as possible. It would be nice if he got to know us all a little better before he finds out what freaks we actually are."

Milo snorted. "A girl can dream. All right, then. Let's get this over with. Freak squad, OUT."

§

A short Tube ride later, Milo and I turned into the forgotten little anachronism that was Gough Square. It looked like a scene stolen from a Sherlock Holmes mystery, with the rain kicking up a misty fog that swirled around the block, covering everything in chilly condensation. It was easy to see why tourists and locals alike seemed not to know the museum existed—it was tucked away so securely from the foot traffic that, unless you set out specifically to find it, I couldn't see how a single customer would ever stumble upon it. As we approached Pickwick's, Milo sucked in a loud breath.

"You feel that?" I asked dryly.

"What the hell?" Milo whispered. "It's... damn, it feels like a Gateway but... different."

"Different, how?" I asked him.

Milo frowned, trying to find the right words. "It's... I mean, I can

71

feel the Aether, but... it's like it's twisted. Like, I'm sensing it on the other side of a funhouse mirror. Does that make sense?"

"Not even a little," I told him. "But none of this makes sense, so you're par for the course. That's why we need to get in here for a really good look around."

I peered in the window. The place was almost deserted. One elderly man was shuffling toward a display of film negatives in the back corner, but otherwise there seemed to be no other customers. I spotted Shriya over at the cash register, flipping through a newspaper and sipping a mug of tea. I could also see at least half a dozen ghosts floating around, drifting in and out of walls, all with that same mesmerized, disoriented look.

"Okay, let's do this," I said to Milo, who didn't reply right away. "Milo!" I snapped my fingers in front of his face and he shook his head.

"Sorry. Yeah, let's go," he said, a bit dazedly.

"Are you okay?" I asked him.

"Yeah," he said, shaking his head as though to clear it. "It's just... it feels really strange."

"Are you sure you can come in? I can do it myself if—"

Milo waved me off. "No, no, I'm fine. I can handle it."

I gave him one last, concerned look, but decided to take his word for it. I pushed the door open and felt his chilly presence follow behind me as we entered the lobby.

Shriya looked up hopefully from her newspaper at the sound of the bell. She smiled when she saw me.

"Well, hello, again," she said. "Back for more already?"

"Hi, Shriya," I said. "How's it going?"

She gestured around, smirking. "Packed to the rafters, as you can see. I'm beating the hordes back with sticks."

I walked up to the counter, throwing a glance over at the one living customer in the place, but he was not paying us the slightest attention. His Coke-bottle glasses were pressed to the glass top of a display of lens caps. "I actually wanted to talk to you about that. I've got an idea that might get some more people in here, but... well, it's a bit unorthodox."

Shriya sat up straighter on her stool. "Unorthodox is kind of what we do here," she said. "If you've got an idea, let's hear it. I'd be willing to try almost anything at this point."

"Well, before I tell you my idea, I have a question to ask you. It's going to sound odd, but just go with it, okay?" I said.

Shriya eyed me suspiciously, but flashed a quick smile all the same. "You're making me nervous now," she said. "All right, what's the question, then?"

I took a deep breath. "Do you believe in ghosts?"

Shriya blinked. "Sorry?"

"I said, do you believe in ghosts?" I repeated calmly.

"Yes, that's what I thought you said," Shriya said with a nervous half-smile. "I was rather hoping I'd misheard you."

"Sorry to just spring it on you," I said. "But I've asked people that question probably a thousand times. I promise you, no matter how gently I ease into it, it never seems to help. So, do you?" I asked again. "Believe in ghosts?"

Shriya gave a slightly hysterical laugh. She glanced around the room, not at her only living customer, but just into the space around her, as though trying to sense invisible eavesdroppers. "I... I never used to."

"Used to?"

"Before I inherited this place. I never was the kind of person to hear a strange noise and panic..."

"And now?" I prompted.

She bit her lip. "I... I've never told anyone this before, but... things have been happening here since I opened it back up... really strange things."

"What kinds of things?" I asked her.

She dropped her voice to a whisper. "Doors opening and closing. Coming in mornings and finding lights on, when I know I've turned them out. Footsteps. Putting things down in one place and finding them in another." She stopped and shook her head. "Listen to me, crying ghost when I know there could be a logical explanation for every one of those things. What must you think of me?"

"I don't think you're—"

"No, no, it's silly. Paranoid. It's an old building, full of noises, and I'm just being ridiculous."

I reached through the connection. "Milo? Give her a little something."

"You got it," Milo replied cheerily.

He floated over to the counter and, a moment later, as Shriya reached for her cup of tea, he gave a grunt of effort as he used his energy to slide the mug several inches across the counter, away from her outstretched hand as she made to close her fingers around the handle.

Shriya did not startle or scream. Indeed, she barely reacted at all, at first. She just stared down at the cup for a long, silent moment, her hand still hovering where the cup had been a few seconds before. Then she looked up at me, her eyes filling with tears.

"Did... did you see..." she whispered.

I nodded solemnly. "Yes, I did."

She dropped her face into her hands. "I've gone mad, haven't I?" she mumbled into her fingers. "I've actually gone mad now. This is just bloody brilliant."

"You're not mad," I said, reaching out and pulling her hands away from her face, so that she was forced to look at me. "In fact, you're likely to think I'm mad once I tell you why I've come here this morning."

Shriya began chewing nervously on a fingernail. "Why have you come here this morning?"

I pulled a nearby stool up to the counter and sat down so that just the counter separated us. "I'm a member of a paranormal investigative team. Have you ever heard of that before?"

Shriya narrowed her eyes. "They've got some on the telly, right? They're those nutters who spend the night in haunted places and video it, aren't they?"

"Guilty," I said, with a shrug. "We investigate locations that have a history of paranormal activity. We use all different kinds of equipment to try to gather evidence of the haunting."

Shriya was shaking her head like I'd just told her that I jumped out of airplanes without parachutes for fun. "How in the world did you get mixed up in something like that?"

I smiled grimly. "I didn't have a lot of choice, actually. That thing that happened just now, with the mug? That kind of stuff happens to me all the time. No matter where I go. I guess you could say I'm sensitive to it."

"So, you're like... a psychic?" Shriya asked.

"No," I said firmly. "I know the types you're talking about—the ones with hotlines who offer to communicate with your dead relatives and read your fortune for $5 a minute. I'm not involved in anything like that. I've just... experienced more than my fair share of what you're experiencing now, and it got me interested in getting to learn more about it."

Shriya's face betrayed both awe and horror. "You're pulling my leg, yeah?"

"I wish I were," I told her, smiling sadly.

"You... you think it's real, what's happening to me here?" Shriya asked.

"It's definitely real," I told her firmly. "You aren't mad and you aren't imagining things. The other day when I stopped in, I knew the place was haunted right from the moment I walked in. Remember the cash register?"

Shriya nodded, wide-eyed. "I... I told myself that was just because it was old. I've been telling myself a lot of things like that lately."

"And the clocks?" I reminded her.

"That wasn't the first time, either," Shriya said. "They've been going haywire since my first day here."

"And there were a few other little things that caught my attention while I was walking around the displays—"

"Excuse me."

Both of us whipped around, startled. The little old man who had been touring the museum was standing directly behind me. How a man with a cane and a distinct wheeze in his breathing had snuck up behind us, I had no idea.

"Yes, sir, how can I assist you?" Shriya asked.

"I'd like to see the displays upstairs. Have you a lift?" the man inquired politely.

"No, I'm sorry sir, there are no displays upstairs. The upper level is only used for storage," Shriya told him.

"Are you quite sure?" he asked, squinting at her.

Shriya darted a look at me and then, continuing to smile politely, said, "Yes, I am, sir. You see, I'm the owner and proprietor of the museum."

"Oh, I see," the old man said. "Well, then you ought to tell those children to come down."

Shriya's smile became very fixed on her face. "I'm sorry?"

The old man picked up his cane and pointed it toward the staircase. "Those two little whippers who just went upstairs. You'd best go and collect them."

At that moment, two sets of feet could be heard running around over our heads, followed by two giggling voices.

Shriya looked at me, her eyes wide, and then swallowed hard before turning back to the man. "Right you are. I'll do that, sir. Cheers."

The man nodded in a satisfied way, then shuffled over to the display of souvenirs to the right of the counter and selected a package of postcards. I took advantage of Shriya's momentary distraction as she rung him up to check in with Milo.

"Did you have anything to do with that?" I asked him through the connection.

His smugness wafted through like a strong perfume. "I may have encouraged it. Too much?"

"No, that was perfect. Thanks," I told him.

"No problem, sweetness. Do you think you could hurry up, though? I'm not sure how much longer I can stand to be in here," Milo said, and pulled out of the connection again, leaving my head clear to turn back to Shriya, who was just holding the door open for the man and bidding him a good afternoon.

She closed the door behind him, then put her back against it, looking horrified. "Those aren't real bloody children, are they?" she asked me in a hiss.

I shook my head solemnly. "Nope."

Shriya dropped her face into her hands again. "Blimey. What am I going to do? I can't keep this museum open if ghosts have the run of the place! They'll scare away the only customers I've managed to scrape together!"

"Don't panic, it's okay," I told her. "Come sit down. Remember we started this whole conversation because I had an idea that might help with that problem, remember?"

"Right. Right. Yeah, pull yourself together, Shriya," Shriya muttered to herself, wiping fiercely at her damp cheeks. She crossed back to the counter, sat down, and took a very shaky gulp of tea. "Okay, this idea, then. Let's hear it."

"Well, like I said, I'm part of a—" I began, but the tinkling of the bell interrupted me again.

"Hiya, Shriya. I know, I know. I'm not supposed to be in, but—oh!" Charlie Wright froze halfway through the door at the sight of me. He looked stunned for a moment, and then his face

76

broke into a wide, cheerful smile. "Jessica! What a pleasant surprise!"

"Oh, hey, Charlie," I said, trying to grin back.

Milo's panicked voice rang through the connection. "Charlie?! Oh shit!"

I tried to block Milo out, along with his sudden burst of nervous energy, as Charlie said, "I didn't expect... is Tia here?"

"Nope, just me, I'm afraid," I said, watching the expectant look slide adorably from his face.

"Of course, she's got class, hasn't she?" Charlie said, a bit sheepishly. "Did you come by for the tour? I'd be delighted to give you one, but I'm afraid I'm not on shift today. I just popped in to drop these boxes by for Shriya."

"No, actually, I took the tour Tuesday," I said. "I just happened to be in the area, so I figured, why not? Sorry I missed you. Shriya said you were sick. Are you feeling better?"

"Getting there," Charlie said with a shrug. He certainly looked ill. His complexion was chalky, and his eyes were bloodshot and ringed with deep purple circles, like he hadn't slept in days. He gestured to Shriya. "Well, I'd introduce you two, but clearly you've already met!"

"That's right," Shriya said "Yeah, we've just been having a nice chat."

"Well, don't let me interrupt," Charlie said with a little bow. "I'm just going to leave these for you." He placed a battered cardboard box on the counter. "It's the negatives from the Hamilton estate sale. I've finished organizing them."

"Oh, thanks, Charlie, you're a lifesaver," Shriya said, peering into the box. There were several large, neatly-lettered manila envelopes inside. "You didn't need to do all this when you were sick. It could have waited."

"Nah, I was glad of something to do. I've been terribly bored, holed up in my sickbed," Charlie said. "And now that it's sorted, we can get that new display started when I get back on Sunday."

"Yes, but why have you brought them all the way down here?" Shriya said, sounding for a moment more like Charlie's mother than his boss. "You're supposed to be in bed with your feet up, remember? Doctor's orders."

Charlie hung his head a little sheepishly. "I meant to be, but... well, it's a bit embarrassing, but I got all the way to the druggist last night and I realized I didn't have my wallet. I've torn my flat apart, but it's not there. I thought I might have left it behind when I closed up on Sunday. I just wanted to pop into the back and see if I can find it."

"Yes, of course, go right ahead," Shriya told him, gesturing over her shoulder to the door that led to the storage areas and office. "I don't remember seeing it, but have a look-see."

"Thanks," Charlie said, and headed back through the door.

Shriya and I sat in silence for a few minutes, until we heard Charlie's voice call out, "Found it!" Then he emerged from the back room, shaking his head and laughing. "Up on the shelf next to the lens polishers. Must have set it down when I was cleaning."

"Glad you found it," Shriya said.

"Me, too," Charlie said, swinging his backpack around so that he could deposit the wallet into the front zippered pocket. Then he swung it back onto his shoulders and looked pleasantly between the two of us. "So, Jessica, what do you think of the place? Didn't I tell you it was great?"

"Yeah, it's... unique," I hedged, looking at Shriya for some hint as to what to do. I wasn't sure if she wanted me to say anything to Charlie about why I was really there. I wasn't sure I wanted to either, but it seemed I may not have a choice.

Shriya drained her tea and turned to Charlie. "Actually, Jess was just about to tell me a marketing idea she had for the museum."

Charlie raised his eyebrows, looking between the two of us. "Really! Brilliant! I think we need all the help we can get, frankly. What's the idea, then?"

Damn it. Poor Tia was just getting to know this guy and I was going to scare him off with my paranormal proclivities before they could even go to dinner. I should be quarantined—I screwed up other people's relationships just by being around them.

Shriya and Charlie were both looking at me expectantly. What could I do? If Shriya agreed to the investigation, Charlie would find out about it anyway. I sighed.

"Well, see, I'm part of this paranormal investigative team, as a sort of hobby. Just for fun, you know. And we do a web series about haunted locations. I thought maybe we could feature the museum."

Charlie blinked. He looked at Shriya, and then back at me. "Haunted?"

"Yeah," I said.

"Charlie haven't you ever noticed anything... unusual about this place?" Shriya asked.

Charlie opened and closed his mouth a few times, like he was utterly lost for what to say. Then he seemed to slump, letting out a huge sigh and laughing.

"I'm so glad you said it before I did," he said, still laughing.

Shriya sagged with relief. "You've noticed it, too?"

"I wasn't going to say anything to you, because you'd just inherited the place, and I didn't want to scare you off, but... well, I've heard and seen a few things that have left me scratching my head," Charlie said. "I'm not... that is to say, I'm not one to believe in this sort of thing, but... it does make one wonder."

"Yeah, it bloody well does!" Shriya muttered, glancing around the room.

Charlie grinned sheepishly. "I'm sorry I never mentioned it. I didn't want you to think I was a nutter."

"Which is the very same reason I never mentioned it to you," Shriya said. "Not a great way to keep employees, scaring them off with talk of spirits and spooks."

"Not that I'm saying I necessarily believe that's what's going on," Charlie said, stoutly, straightening up.

"Nor am I, necessarily," said Shriya quickly. "But it might be nice to have a professional come in and give us an answer either way."

"Right," said Charlie. Then he turned to me, grinning. "And you're a professional, eh? Tia never told me her friends were quite so... interesting."

"That's a euphemism if ever I heard one, but I'll take it," I said, smiling at last. Maybe I hadn't completely scared him off after all.

"So, explain to me how this investigation could help the museum?" Shriya asked, sounding a bit more eager, now that she realized Charlie was on board.

"Well, the web series has millions of viewers—it's really popular. And a lot of those viewers love to frequent the locations we feature. Not only would it publicize that the museum exists, but it would popularize it with a large segment of the population who are fascinated with haunted places. I think it would send visitor numbers through the roof, honestly."

A slow smile was blooming on Shriya's face. "That would be absolutely brilliant. You really think it would work?"

"I really do," I said.

"I think she's got something there," Charlie added thoughtfully. "Just think about tourism in London. How many haunted walking tours are there? How many Jack the Ripper displays? How many famously haunted castles and pubs? People come from all over the world to see things like that. Adding Pickwick's to the list of haunted London destinations might be just the ticket."

Shriya turned back to me. "Right, then. Sign us up! How soon can you do it?"

"Let me check in with the team, but within a few weeks, I think," I said, smiling.

"Brilliant!" Shriya said. "You're hired! Wait... um... how much is this investigation going to set me back?"

"Nothing!" I said quickly. "All we ask is unrestricted access to the building overnight."

"Why overnight?" Shriya asked.

"Two reasons, really. The first is because we don't want to interrupt one of your business days—the point is to help your business, not hurt it. And secondly, investigating at night is much better for evidence collection. Most of what we capture is either on audio or video equipment, and there is a lot less contamination when the streets aren't bustling with people." I gestured toward the front windows, where even at that moment, a knot of three women was passing. Their voices carried easily into the museum.

"Oh, I see. Yeah, that makes sense," Shriya said, nodding.

"And one other thing," I added. "Can you make sure not to move anything out of the museum between now and then?"

Shriya frowned. "Why?"

"Well, there's always the possibility that it's the building itself that's attracting the spirits. But it could also be artifacts in the building that are the real attraction. I mean, you've got lots of very old stuff in here."

"Oh, right," Shriya said, and now she was scanning the room wide-eyed, as though the object causing the haunting would suddenly have a bright, blinking arrow hanging over it. "No problem. We won't touch anything, will we, Charlie?"

Charlie crossed his heart solemnly. "Not a speck of dust."

Shriya gave a great sigh of relief. "Well, all right then. Let's do it."

"Great!" I said. "I'll talk to my team and we can coordinate a date and time." As I stood up to go, I looked over at Charlie, who was chuckling and shaking his head. "What's so funny?" I asked him.

"Well, well, well, Jessica," he said. "You are just full of surprises, aren't you?"

Wasn't that the goddamn truth.

8

UNEXPECTED ALLY

"ARE YOU MAD AT ME? Please tell me you aren't mad at me."

It was Friday afternoon. I was standing in front of Tia like a convict about to be sentenced. I bounced nervously on the balls of my feet. She'd stayed so late studying at the library on Thursday night that I was asleep when she got home, and she was out the door again in the morning before I could drag my lazy ass out of bed. With Hannah gone at a Council meeting all day, and Milo with her for moral support, I had no one to distract me from my own fear that Charlie would tell Tia about our run-in at the museum before I would get a chance to do it. The moment she had walked in the door from school that afternoon, I had accosted her, sat her down, and told her everything about Charlie, the museum, and the investigation. She'd now been silent for at least a full minute, and I was starting to think she might have gone into shock.

"Tia? Say something. Are you mad at me?" I repeated.

"I don't know yet," Tia said dazedly. "I'm still trying to process what you just said to me."

"I know. Sorry. That was a lot to drop on you in one fell swoop," I said with a grimace.

Tia shook her head a little, like she had water in her ears. "So... so that first morning when you met Charlie, you thought he was haunted?"

I nodded. "Yup. Most haunted person I'd ever seen."

"And why exactly didn't you tell me that right away?" Tia asked, starting to sound severe now that she was getting over her initial shock.

"Because you were already freaking out, remember?" I reminded her. "I didn't want to scare you away from him, not until I understood a little better what was going on. I was going to tell you yesterday, but this is the first time I've seen you."

"I can't believe this," Tia muttered.

"Neither could I, which is why Hannah and I decided to look into it right away," I said.

"Hannah knew, too?" Tia gasped.

I gave a guilty grimace. "Well, yeah. There was a massive crowd of ghosts. It was... kind of impossible to miss."

"Unless you're me," Tia grumbled.

"You mean, unless you're normal," I corrected her. "Which you are. And so is Charlie! See? Match made in heaven."

"So, then why were all those ghosts hanging around him in the market when it's the museum that's haunted?" Tia asked, a note of hysteria just creeping into her voice. I attempted to stamp it out at once.

"It wasn't him at all," I said. "They were attracted to something—or maybe everything—in that display cart."

"But why?" Tia asked.

"That's what we're trying to find out. Look, I'd love to just let it go, but it has something to do with a Gateway, so I really can't just ignore it," I said.

"I know, I know," Tia said. "And... and you're sure that Charlie didn't seem freaked out or anything?"

"No," I said quickly. "Honestly, Tia, he seemed kind of fascinated. He even said himself that he'd seen and heard things in the museum that he couldn't explain."

Tia exhaled slowly. "Okay. Okay. He didn't run screaming. That's good."

"He told me I was 'full of surprises,'" I said, flashing her a winning smile.

Tia allowed herself a nervous little laugh. "Well, he's not wrong about that, is he?"

"I'm really sorry, Tia," I said seriously, folding myself onto the couch cushion beside her. "I didn't want to tell you until I had a better understanding of what the hell was going on. There was no point in scaring you away from Charlie over what might turn out to be nothing. You were finally healing, and I didn't want to ruin that."

Tia narrowed her eyes at me. "Well, I'm still a little aggravated that you weren't honest with me, but... I understand that you were just trying to protect me."

"I was, I promise. I still am," I told her. "Forgive me?"

Tia's arms were still folded across her chest, and she wasn't looking at me anymore, but I thought I saw the corner of her mouth twitching upward. "I haven't decided yet. I think I'm going to hold it over your head for a while."

"Fair enough. I deserve it," I said. Hanging my head contritely, I put my hand into my cardigan pocket and pulled out a king-sized bag of Skittles. "Here, have some of this shameless bribery candy to help you make up your mind. I know they don't taste exactly like the American ones, but they're still pretty good."

Tia was definitely fighting a smile now. "I cannot be bribed."

"If you say so," I said, plunking the bag of candy down onto the coffee table before heading off to raid the fridge.

I'd barely made it into the kitchen when Tia called out, "What was Charlie doing at the museum anyway? I thought he was sick?"

"He is," I told her. "But he left his wallet there on Sunday, and couldn't pick up his meds."

"Oh," Tia said. "I... I got nervous for a second that..."

"What? That he lied to you about being sick? Why would he do that?" I asked.

"I don't know." Tia sighed, tearing into the Skittles package. "I'm just being paranoid. It's what I do now."

"Well, don't," I said firmly. "He looked awful—like he hadn't slept at all. And besides, the first thing he did when he saw me in the museum was ask for you."

Tia sat up, looking at me eagerly. "He did?"

"Yup. And you should have seen the sad little look on his face when I told him it was just me." I stuck my lip out in an exaggerated pout.

Tia blushed and giggled as she popped a handful of candy into her mouth. "Yeah, right."

Our buzzer sounded loudly, making both of us jump.

"You expecting anyone?" I asked Tia. She shook her head.

I jammed my finger against the silver button on the speaker by the door and spoke into it. "Who is it?"

"It's Fiona," barked a familiar voice. "Open the door, would you? It's coming down in buckets out here."

I pressed the door release, wondering, as I did so, what in the world Fiona was doing here. She'd never come to our flat before.

Hell, I could hardly remember her ever coming out of the castle grounds before.

I opened the door to find Ambrose poking his head out of his flat like a rat scenting garbage. He caught my eye and jutted out his chin defiantly.

"Who is it, then?" he asked.

"Fiona," I told him.

He frowned. "What's she doing here? You expecting her?"

"I have no idea why she's here. Ask her yourself," I replied.

At that moment, Fiona's kerchiefed head appeared at the top of the staircase. She was panting slightly and carrying a large portfolio under her arm.

"Hey, Fiona," I said.

"Hey, yourself. Couldn't do me a brew, could you?" she asked.

"Sure. Come on in," I said, stepping aside so she could walk through.

She crossed to the doorway but paused when she caught sight of Ambrose staring at her.

"What do you want, then?" she barked at him.

For all of his usually persistent attitude, he quailed under the stare of a senior Council member. "Just keeping an eye on things," he mumbled, inclining his head.

"Well, go keep an eye on something else," Fiona snapped. "I'm here on Council business and I'd like to get to it without being gawked at like an animal at the bloody zoo."

Ambrose ducked back into his flat and shut the door. Fiona threw one last disgusted look at the place where he had stood, then shuffled through the door, thrusting the portfolio into my arms as she came.

"Bugger those stairs!" she cursed, hobbling over to the sofa and collapsing upon it.

"It's only one flight," I said. "Don't you live at the top of a tower?"

"Eh, my knees are acting up again. Spent the whole week restoring the artwork on the Léarscáil map. Four days of kneeling on stone, and I'm about ready to chop my legs off and have done with it." She grunted as she pulled off her shoes and began massaging her kneecaps.

"Do you want ice or something?" I asked as I set the portfolio down on the table.

"No, no, just the tea," Fiona snapped. "If... if you would," she added in an attempt at sounding polite. She looked over and saw Tia still sitting on the couch, clutching her Skittles and looking alarmed.

"Who are you, then?" Fiona asked bluntly.

"I... uh..." Tia stammered.

"Stumped you with that one, have I?" Fiona asked, rolling her eyes.

I stepped in quickly, tea kettle in hand. "Fiona, this is my roommate Tia Vezga. Tia, this is my... art instructor, Fiona."

Fiona scoffed at being introduced as such, but held out her hand grudgingly. Tia took it, shook it quickly, and murmured, "Nice to meet you."

Fiona grunted. This was meant as a pleasantry, evidently.

"Well, I've, uh... got some work to catch up on," Tia said, rising from the couch. This was a lie, obviously, as Tia had never been behind on work in her life. "I'll let you two chat." Tia nodded once at Fiona, waved a hand at me, and disappeared into her room.

"I don't know how you do it," Fiona grumbled, shaking her head.

"How I do what?" I asked, setting the teapot to boil.

"Keep up the charades," Fiona said. "I haven't the stomach for that nonsense."

"Well, we're supposed to," I said, shrugging. "Besides, Tia actually knows a lot about the Durupinen. We had to get permission to fill her in when she had to go into hiding to protect her from the Necromancers. I just don't... overburden her with stuff she doesn't need to know."

"Bah," Fiona said, picking absently at a bit of plaster stuck under her fingernail. "I've never had the patience for it. All this secrecy. It's bollocks. Tell 'em all what we do and let them bloody well deal with it. All this tip-toeing around, dealing in half-truths. That's why I don't have outside friends. Not worth the bother."

I could think of about a hundred reasons that Fiona didn't have outside friends—her propensity for hurling furniture at people who mildly annoyed her, for example. But I decided to bite back the urge to tell her this; whatever she was here for, it would be much easier not to send her into a temper, and anyway, we didn't have much in the way of expendable furniture to spare.

"I'm glad to see you. Milk or sugar in this?"

"Two sugars, cheers," Fiona said.

I prepared the tea, put the cup on a saucer, and carried it carefully over to Fiona, who took it and then tutted loudly at me.

"You've left the teabag in! Were you raised by wolves?" she snapped, fishing it out.

"No, Americans," I said. "Same difference, apparently, when it comes to tea etiquette."

Fiona smirked just slightly, then gulped her tea noisily.

"So, what can I do for you this afternoon, Fiona?" I asked. "Besides the tea, I mean?"

"I can't stay long. Just wanted to drop your latest batch of work off to you. I've been through it all," Fiona said in an overly loud voice.

I frowned at her. "Why didn't you just give it to Hannah at the meeting today? You didn't need to come all the way out here."

"I wasn't at the meeting today," Fiona said, nearly shouting. "I had business in London, so I decided to drop by. Not a crime, is it?"

"No, of course not," I said with a chuckle. "Why are you—"

But Fiona was shaking her head and jerking a thumb toward the far wall. I opened my mouth to ask what the hell she was doing, but then the proverbial lightbulb went on. Ambrose's flat was on the other side of that wall. She was staging this conversation for his benefit. What I didn't understand was why.

"Well, thanks," I said, raising my own voice as well. "Thanks for dropping it by."

Fiona gave me a wink and a nod, to acknowledge my participation in... whatever this was. "Don't expect me to make a habit of it. I can't be expected to be making house calls on the regular. I'm too bloody busy up at the castle."

"No problem," I said. "So..." I widened my eyes at her, looking for some kind of direction. "Any feedback?"

"I've left it all here for you, in the notes," Fiona said, opening up the portfolio and tapping the stack of paper she'd tucked inside on top of my spirit drawings. "I've got suggestions in there for you on clarifying spirit intent, so be sure to read it carefully." She widened her eyes at me again.

"Okay, I will. Thanks," I said.

"All of it, now. No skimming," she added, quietly.

"Every word," I promised, wondering as I did so, why the hell she was being so cryptic. I could feel my nerves beginning to tense.

"Right. And don't bring me any more of your work until you've

88

implemented that advice," Fiona barked, standing up suddenly and knocking back the rest of her tea like it was a shot of something much stiffer. "I don't want to suffer through another load of tosh like that."

"Are you leaving already?" I asked, standing up as well, and knocking my portfolio to the floor in my haste. "You just got here."

"I'm not here for a cozy catch up, Jess," Fiona cried. "Didn't you hear me say I'm busy?"

I just stood there, waiting for her to give me something—anything—that would clue me in as to what the hell this was all about, but she just rubbed at her knees a bit, hobbled over to the door and said. "I'll see you 'round, then. Stay out of trouble, now."

I followed her to the door mumbling words of goodbye. Just as I opened the door for her, she reached down and grabbed a blue umbrella that was leaning against the wall. She leaned her face in close to me and whispered. "Read it all. And then destroy it."

I stared at her, too stunned even to stop her from stealing my only umbrella as she turned and stomped down the stairs. Feeling as though I were floating through a kind of waking dream, I shut the door and stood with my back to it. My eyes found the portfolio where it lay on the floor and I stared at it, as though it were going to jump up from the floor and finally give me an explanation.

It didn't.

I listened carefully for any sound from the flat next door. All I could hear was the television blaring dully in the background. Not willing to take any chances, I crossed the room, scooped the portfolio up off the floor, and carried it with me into my room, closing the door behind me.

I attempted to take a deep breath, but my lungs didn't cooperate, so I gave it up. I cursed Fiona under my breath as I picked at the knot in the ribbon—no matter how many times I sent it over to her tied in a bow, she always sent it back tied in the kind of knot that suggested she never wanted the contents to see the light of day again. Finally, after several minutes of muttering obscenities at my shaking fingers, I managed to pull the two pieces of ribbon apart and lay the portfolio open. Meticulously, I pulled each sheet of paper out of the pockets and laid them out across the floor of my room. Each drawing had several sticky notes taped to it—every time

I told her that sticky notes didn't need tape, Fiona just used more tape.

I felt into the corners of the portfolio's pockets, then tossed it aside, turning my attention to Fiona's nearly illegible scrawlings. Drawing by drawing, I read carefully through the notes, finding absolutely nothing unusual. This was the same kind of feedback Fiona always provided: critiques of perspective, suggestions for shadow work, telling me over and over again to think about the "movement" inherent in a still image, blah, blah, blah. Was I supposed to be finding some kind of hidden message in these perfectly ordinary comments? Mystified, I picked up the fifth sketch and gasped.

I hadn't drawn it. But I knew who it was.

The figure in the picture was in midstride, walking away from the artist. The broad shoulders were slightly hunched, as though the figure were leaning forward as he walked. The hands were thrust into the pockets, balled up into fists, so that they tugged the coat away from the body with the force of them. The long, dark hair was tied back into a ponytail, secured with a length of worn leather cord. I could see just the merest suggestion of a strong, square jawline...

Finn.

All the air seemed to have left the room. I stared hungrily down at him, as though the force of my gaze could pull him from the paper and into reality beside me, or, at the very least, make him turn, just so I could see his face. Then, I was overtaken by a violent wave of molten fear. Was this a spirit drawing? Was it possible... could Finn be...

I blinked away a film of tears that was clouding my view, and my eyes fell on the single sticky note taped to the image. It contained only seven words.

He is posted at the Skye Príosún.

I read them over and over again, letting wave after wave of relief wash over me. I couldn't say for sure why relief was the strongest emotion. After all, the Skye Príosún was hundreds of miles away, as remote a location as I could imagine, meaning that Finn was just as unreachable in reality as I had feared he was in my nightmares. But at least I knew where he was. At last, after months of wondering, I finally knew where he was. Perhaps now I could stop accosting random strangers on the street in the vain, desperate hope of running into him.

Skye Príosún. What did I know about it? Not much, admittedly. I knew that it was where the most dangerous criminals of the Durupinen world were housed. Lucida was imprisoned there, as were the Necromancers who had survived the siege of Fairhaven. Mackie had also told me once that the place had cells that were specially Warded to contain spirits instead.

"We trap spirits on earth?" I had asked, horrified. "Isn't that... like... against everything we stand for?"

"Don't forget that we can only Cross willing spirits," Mackie had reminded me. "We can't force a spirit to Cross, no matter what kind of havoc they are wreaking in the living world. That's why some spirits have to be trapped and contained, until such time as they can be convinced to Cross."

"And if they can't be convinced to Cross?" I had asked.

She had shrugged and grimaced. "Wards have no expiration date. If they so choose, they can remain imprisoned indefinitely."

The thought at the time had sent a shiver down my spine, but the harsh reality of it hadn't set in until I had met Eleanora Larkin, the Shattered spirit who had unknowingly wreaked such havoc at Fairhaven the previous year. Eleanora had been imprisoned while she was still alive for the crime of daring to be born a Caller. The bone-deep terror that all Durupinen harbored for Callers meant that she was not only locked away like the very worst of criminals, but she was also left to die when the *príosún* had burned nearly to the ground. And then, as if her fate hadn't been harsh enough, her spirit couldn't escape the *príosún* even after her body had perished. It was not until Lucida managed to Call her out of her bonds more than a hundred years later that Eleanora was able to break free of the *príosún* at last, only to be Shattered when Lucida tricked her into thinking she could Cross. Hearing her harrowing story had long given me a strange, creeping feeling any time I thought about the *príosún* and the prisoners—both living and dead—who were held there.

And now, I would be forced to imagine Finn among them, standing guard in such a dark and lonely place. I sucked in a long, shuddering gasp. Here I was, comfortable in a cozy flat in the center of bustling London, allowed to carry on with my life, free to go where I pleased and choose my own path, while he was forced into a thankless post in the middle of nowhere.

For the first time since we'd been separated, I considered the possibility that he might hate me. I wouldn't blame him. I hated myself for daring to complain.

I stared down at the drawing again, suddenly glad his figure wasn't looking at me, dreading what I might see in his eyes and expression. My thoughts turned to Fiona. I had never once spoken to her about Finn being reassigned. I mean, she could hardly fail to notice that I had a new Caomhnóir, but I had never once, in all the time I'd known her, confided anything about our relationship to her. So how, then, did she know? Had Celeste told her? That seemed unlikely, unless Celeste had hoped to enlist her help in keeping an eye on me, to ensure that I wasn't trying to get back in touch with Finn. Perhaps Fiona, like Milo and Hannah, had simply been more observant than I had given her credit for, and had figured it out for herself that Finn and I were in love with each other. In either case, she had risked a great deal to pass this information along to me. She obviously knew that Ambrose couldn't be trusted, and she didn't want to risk trying to speak to me about it when we were both at Fairhaven.

I wondered how she had found out where Finn was. It was possible she had just overheard the information, but somehow I didn't think so. She had gone to such extraordinary lengths to get the information to me, that I couldn't help but think that she had actively sought the information out in the first place. It was unlikely that I'd have much of chance to ask her any of these questions, and, knowing Fiona, she'd be unlikely to answer them. She probably wouldn't even accept a thank you.

Now, what did I do with this knowledge? Was there anything I *could* do? I knew where Finn was now, but I was not any closer to finding my way back to him. I couldn't very well go anywhere near the place without a valid reason, and getting arrested and thrown in jail was not exactly in my game plan. I could try to find out what I could about the *príosún*, but even with more details, what could I actually do? I was grateful to Fiona for letting me know, at last, where he was, but all she had done was assign a latitude and longitude to my loneliness. Now I could fixate my heartbreak onto a spot on the map, instead of scattering it aimlessly wherever I went. I didn't know if this was better or worse, but for the moment,

I was just relieved that at least one of so many questions had been answered.

On sudden inspiration, I closed my eyes and felt my way out into my connection with Milo.

"Milo? You there?"

A snap, a pop of familiar, crackling energy. "What kind of question is that, sweetness? Where else would I..." He stopped suddenly as my energy mingled with his; I wasn't doing a very good job of suppressing the avalanche of emotions I'd just experienced. "Hey, are you okay? What's going on?"

"I'm fine," I said. I felt his skepticism skipping over the top of our blending energy, like a flat stone on a smooth lake. "Honestly. I'll tell you all about it when you and Hannah get back."

"Do you need me to come back now?" Milo asked. "Hannah's still finishing up her committee junk, but I could—"

"No, no, seriously. It can wait. But I do need you to do something for me while you're still at Fairhaven."

"Are you finally going to let me tell off Celeste?" Milo asked eagerly.

"No," I said firmly. "Don't go anywhere near Celeste. In fact, make sure no one but Hannah knows about this request."

Milo sighed sulkily. "Fine, what is it?"

"Ask Hannah to find out everything she can about the Skye Príosún," I said. "I don't want her to ask Council members or Caomhnóir—that would raise too much suspicion."

"Too much suspicion about what?" Milo asked, but I cut him off.

"Just have her check it out in the library. The Scribes must have documentation that can shed some light on the place. It might not hurt to ask some of the spirits around Fairhaven, too. Some of them might have had firsthand experience."

"Yeah, but why—"

"Just ask her, Milo, okay? I promise I'll tell you guys everything when you get home," I said.

"I... okay, fine. I'll let Hannah know, and we'll see you tonight," Milo said recognizing defeat and giving up with a sigh.

"What time do you think you'll be back?" I asked.

"Not sure. Probably not before nine or ten, I'd say. These meetings are brutally long."

"Right. Well, let me know when you're on your way. And tell Hannah I'm ordering Indian food, so I'll save some for her."

"You got it, sweetness," Milo said, and popped out of the connection.

I sighed and looked down at the drawing again with a pang of regret. It would be incredibly foolish of me not to destroy this drawing immediately, along with the Post-it Note. The only problem was that the thought of doing so made me feel like there was a boulder on my chest, pressing all the air out of my lungs.

At that moment, as though to knock some much-needed sense into me, Ambrose gave a loud, hacking cough from next door, which penetrated all the way through the walls and through my emotional fog. I couldn't keep the drawing. Not only would it get me and Finn into trouble if anyone ever found it, but it could mean trouble for Fiona as well and I couldn't do that to her, not when she'd gone to such lengths to help me. Before the sight of him could change my mind, I crumpled up the sketch of Finn into a tight ball and jumped to my feet. I marched straight to the kitchen, pulled out a frying pan and lid, and plunked it onto the stove. I put the ball of paper in the pan, turned on the burner, pulled a match from the drawer, lit it from the open flame, and dropped it into the pan. I watched with grim determination as the paper quickly caught fire. There was a brief moment, as the paper unfurled and burned, that the fire illuminated the curve of Finn's cheek and neck, but then it was gone, consumed by the hungry little leaping flames. Within moments, the entire sketch had crumbled to ash. Quickly, before the smoke could spread, I smothered the little bonfire with the cover to the pan. A little while later, when the ashes had gone cold, I would wash them down the sink and smile good-naturedly through Tia's joking comments about my pathetic attempts at cooking.

"No offense, Jess, but haven't you resigned yourself to a life of take-out yet?" Tia laughed.

I watched the ashes turn the water gray and swirl away down the drain.

"I know, right? When will I learn?" I said quietly.

9

TWISTED

HANNAH AND MILO were later than they had expected. I was dozing on the couch in front of a re-run of "Fawlty Towers" when they came in the door at last.

"Sorry!" Hannah said, as I jerked myself awake and stared around confusedly. "I texted to let you know we were going to be late."

"That's okay," I said, squinting down at my phone. It was after midnight, and I did indeed have a message from Hannah waiting for me, along with a couple of missed calls from Flavia. I tossed the phone aside and yawned widely. "How did it all go?"

Hannah frowned thoughtfully. "Good, I think. Well, we got through our entire agenda, which, as Siobhán says, is a miracle in itself." She stopped and sniffed the air. "Did you try to cook something again?"

The acrid smell of smoke still lingered beneath the scent of curry. "Yeah, it ended badly. There's Indian take-out in the fridge," I told her.

Hannah groaned. "Excellent, I'm starving." She tossed her coat and bag onto the table and began poking around in the take-out containers in the fridge.

"So, what took so long?" I asked her.

"We voted to stay and get it all done rather than reconvene for another session tomorrow," Hannah said. "Not everyone was thrilled, but majority carried. I didn't want to spend half my weekend in meetings."

"Thank goodness," Milo said, drifting down onto the couch as though the meetings had left him physically exhausted despite the absence of a body. "The Fairhaven floaters are très dull. I can seriously only take them in small doses."

"Really?" I said. "I feel like you used to like hanging out with them."

"That was before I got to know the London deadside," Milo sighed, gesturing wistfully toward the window. "It's just a cornucopia of weird and quirky fabulousness out there. No wonder so many floaters hang around for so long."

"I stopped by the library for you on my dinner break," Hannah said, "I found a few books on—"

I flapped my arms at her and put my finger to my lips. She froze, eyes wide.

"What's wrong?" she mouthed.

I pointed to Milo, to indicate we should use the connection to talk. Luckily, she caught on almost immediately. I opened up the connection and felt them both there, like a floodgate of confusion let loose inside my own head.

"What is going on?" their simultaneous question hit me like a slap directly to the gray matter. I winced a little.

"Easy there," I told them. "It's crowded in here."

"Sorry, sorry," Hannah said, and I felt her energy shift, felt her rein back her anxiousness. "I just hate all the cryptic stuff."

"Did Ambrose hear you come in?" I asked.

"Of course," Hannah said, and I could feel her aggravation blending with my own. "You know how he is when one of us is out, even when another Caomhnóir is with us. I saw him at the window when we pulled up, and he watched us come in."

"I don't want him to hear any part of this conversation," I said.

"I don't think the walls are that thin, Jess," Hannah said.

"I'm not taking any chances," I insisted.

"But why?" Milo asked. "Just tell us what's up!"

And so, I did. In the quiet of the connection, I told them about Fiona's unexpected visit to the flat and what she had brought for me inside the portfolio. Both Hannah and Milo were as shocked to hear about the sketch as I had been to see it.

"How did she find out?" Hannah asked.

"I have no idea. I didn't have a chance to ask, and even if I did, I doubt she would tell me," I said.

"So, that's why you wanted the information on the Skye Príosún," Hannah said. "When you asked, I thought maybe it had something to do with Lucida."

"And that should probably be your cover, if anyone happens to notice you've checked that stuff out," I said. "No one would fault you for wanting to know a little more about how the Durupinen plan to keep her locked up."

"That's true," Hannah said. "But... what do you want the information for?"

I frowned. "What do you mean, what do I want it for?" I asked.

Hannah looked nervous. "Jess, I know you want to see him, but..."

"Look, I'm not planning on breaking into the place to rescue him, if that's what you're worried about," I said, more angrily than I intended. I saw both of them wince as my energy sharpened. "I just... I want to know more about... about where he is."

Milo's energy was gentle. "Jess, that makes sense, but... don't torture yourself."

"I'm not trying to," I grumbled. "I just think it will be easier if I can picture where he is."

"Or it might be harder," Milo said.

If we'd been having the conversation out loud, I could have refrained from speaking my next thought aloud, but as we were inside the connection, it came tumbling across before I could stop it. "If it is harder, I deserve it."

A solid few seconds of radio silence followed this thought.

"No. No, you don't," Hannah said.

"The last thing you deserve is for any of this to be harder," Milo said.

I couldn't agree with them, so I said nothing.

"Well, anyway, the books are there in my bag," Hannah said. "Read them or don't, but just remember that we're working on this, Jess. I gave my proposed amendment to Kiera today to take a look at."

I looked up at her, startled. In the craziness of the day's events, I had forgotten all about Hannah's amendment. "Why Kiera?"

"I was going through some old minutes, just to see what kind of precedent there might be for this kind of proposed change. And I came across an old proposal from about fifteen years ago. Keira helped to write it, and it was a proposal to overhaul the Caomhnóir-Durupinen dynamic."

"You're kidding!" I said. "Someone has tried this before?"

"I bet if I went far enough back, I'd find other attempts as well," Hannah said. "The arrangements between the Durupinen and Caomhnóir have caused all kinds of tension since it began, you know that. Keira's amendment wasn't exactly the same thing—from what I've read, it focused more on training protocols and overhauling communication, but it seemed to acknowledge many of the same problems that my amendment addresses. Anyway, since Keira has worked on a similar proposal before, I thought she might be a good place to start. She seemed really interested, and promised to give it a thorough reading so we could discuss it the next time we meet."

It was maddening to think of my chances of seeing Finn again going through a long, arduous bureaucratic process—that our lives were reduced to legal jargon and votes tallied—but I pushed the feeling away. It was the only chance we had right now. I had to be grateful for it, and for a sister who was willing to do the kind of work it took to change things for me.

"Thank you, Hannah," I told her. I walked into the kitchen where she stood by the microwave, waiting for her chicken Bhuna to warm through. I wrapped my arms around her, and dropped my head onto her shoulder. She laughed in surprise, but wriggled her arms out from under mine so that she could hug me back.

"We're going to figure it out, Jess," she whispered into my ear rather than through the connection. "We'll get him back."

"Yeah. If anyone can do it, you can," I told her. "I mean, it was more satisfying when you just unleashed spirit armies on people, but I'm sure this legislative process is cool, too."

Hannah tried to smile at the joke for my sake, but I knew it wasn't funny.

"Sorry," I whispered. "Just kidding."

The harsh metallic buzzing of the doorbell broke us apart.

"Who the hell could that be?" I asked, glancing at the clock on the microwave. "It's past 12:30!"

Hannah, who had a hand pressed over her heart, shook her head. "Savvy, maybe? She's crashed after a night at the pub before."

Figuring this was the most likely explanation, I walked over to the buzzer and pressed the intercom button. "Sav, is that you?"

"Is this Jessica? Jessica Ballard?"

The voice was out-of-breath, tearful, and approaching hysteria.

"Yeah, this is Jessica Ballard, who is this?"

"Oh, thank God," the voice sobbed. "It's Jeta Loveridge. Do you remember me? We met at the Traveler camp?"

"Jeta! Yes, of course I remember—"

"Please," she gasped, and I thought I could hear another voice behind hers, moaning and muttering. "Please, I need your help. It's Flavia, she's been attacked. I don't know where else to go, please."

I stared at Hannah, who shook her head in bewildered fear. Without a word, Milo blinked out of existence, and I knew he was going down to see what was going on.

"Attacked? Attacked by who?" I asked.

"I don't know!" Jeta cried, Flavia's voice rising behind her. "Please! Please, I need to get her help! I don't know what to—"

At that moment, Milo's voice rang through the connection.

"Open the door and get down here, now!"

I shook away my shock, jammed the door-release button with the heel of my hand and flung the door open, Hannah right on my heels.

"Get Ambrose," I told her, but she was already banging on his door.

I flew down the stairs and found Jeta at the bottom, trying to ease Flavia through the door. She had flung Flavia's arm over her shoulder, but it was clear that Flavia could barely stand. She sagged against Jeta's body, her head lolling back and forth on her neck. I would have thought she was unconscious except that she was groaning and muttering unintelligibly. I reached for her other arm, meaning to put it around my shoulders and take some of her weight, but as I did so, I got a clearer view of her and let out a horrified gasp.

Her eyes were closed—one of them looked like it was swollen shut. There were several cuts on her face that were bleeding freely, and bruises on her face and arms. Her shirt was torn and smeared with blood, and someone had inked runes onto her skin.

"Jesus! What happened to her?" I cried.

Jeta's voice was thick with tears. "I don't know. I found her like this outside her flat."

Ambrose came thundering down the stairs two at a time. Swiftly, he assessed Flavia, then in one fluid motion he swept her up into his arms and carried her up the stairs. It seemed he had his uses after all.

We followed him into our flat, where he laid Flavia on the sofa, cradling her head in his hand as he slid a pillow beneath it, displaying more gentleness that I would have thought him capable of. He felt her pulse, timing it against his watch. We all stood in tense silence as he did this. Beside me, Milo was actually blurring at the edges, his nerves were so wound up.

"Pulse is strong but rapid," Ambrose said curtly. "She seems in no immediate danger."

"Did you say your name was Jeta?" Hannah asked tentatively, touching Jeta's arm. Despite the gentleness of the touch, Jeta leapt back as though burned.

"Y-yeah," she said.

"Tell us what happened," Hannah said.

Jeta took a deep, shaky breath. "Flavia has been living in London. Since Irina's trial, she—"

"I know," I told her quickly. "We've been in touch since she got here."

"I haven't seen her since she left, and she's been begging me to visit. I... I avoided it at first. Flavia has fallen out of the Council's favor. She's been cast out, ever since she defied their order and moved to the city. I... it was shitty, but I didn't want to get in trouble."

"It's okay, Jeta, we get it," I said a little impatiently. "Nobody wants to piss off the Council if they can help it. But what happened tonight?"

Jeta stifled a sob. "She was supposed to meet me at the train station, but she never showed up, and she wasn't answering her phone. Eventually, I just hailed a cab and he took me to her building, but I couldn't get in, so I waited again. Finally, the girl who lived in the flat downstairs got home and took pity on me and let me in so I wouldn't have to wait in the rain. I went up and knocked, but no one answered. Then I found an extra key hidden up under her mailbox, so I just used it to let myself in."

From the couch, Flavia gave a low moan. One of her hands was twitching.

"I waited a couple more hours. I started looking around the place for a clue about where she might have gone, but there was nothing—no note, nothing on her calendar," Jeta said, her voice nearly unintelligible now as the sobs overwhelmed her. "I was debating whether I should head back home when I heard screeching tires outside. I ran to the window just in time to see a dark car peeling away from the sidewalk and... and... Flavia was just lying in a crumpled heap on the ground."

"So, whoever was in the car just... dumped her there?" Hannah asked, throwing a hand up over her mouth in horror.

"I think so," Jeta said.

"Did you get a good look at the car?" I asked.

Jeta shook her head. "It was raining really hard, so everything was very blurred. I just know it was big and dark—probably an SUV, but I couldn't swear to it. I might not have even seen her on the ground if it hadn't been for the hair color." We all looked over at Flavia, whose hair had been dyed a deep magenta color since I had last seen her.

"So, what happened next?" Milo prompted.

"I ran outside and brought her in," Jeta said. She crossed over to Flavia, knelt beside her, and started stroking her head. "She was shaking like mad, and bleeding everywhere. I tried to get her to speak to me, but she hardly seemed to realize I was there. It's almost like she's dreaming, though, because she seems to be reacting to things I can't see."

We all followed her gaze to Flavia again. It was true. Her lips were moving, and she appeared to be carrying on a fractured, frantic conversation with someone... or something. Her hands were twitching, and her fingers were tracing shapes in the air. Her head was also jerking around as though she were trying to follow the progress of something invisible that was moving ceaselessly around the room, though her eyes were still closed.

"Where is her Caomhnóir?" Ambrose barked. "Why has she been left unprotected?"

"Traveler Durupinen forfeit their protection if they leave the camp without permission," Jeta said. "Flavia has had no Caomhnóir for several months."

"That's bullshit," Ambrose hissed through clenched teeth.

"Why didn't you call an ambulance?" Hannah asked.

Jeta glared at her as though she'd just suggested calling the Buckingham Guard. "We don't trust hospitals. Or law enforcement."

"We don't like to get them involved either, if we can avoid it, but in some instances..." Hannah murmured, gesturing to Flavia.

"And what would they have thought, with these runes drawn all over her?" Jeta snapped, finding her anger amidst the wash of fear and sadness. "I'd have been hauled in and hammered with ignorant questions about voodoo and satanic rituals. Then some trashy tabloid would have gotten wind of it and splashed it all over the bloody country."

"She's right," Ambrose grunted. "We cannot involve the authorities. It would be a disaster for the code of secrecy."

"I can't bring her back to the Traveler camp. They'll refuse to help her, she's betrayed the bloodlines, and anyway, how could I possibly get her there without being stopped and questioned?" Jeta asked. "I knew you were in the city. I found Flavia's phone on the sidewalk, searched through her contacts, and found your number. When you didn't answer, I searched your address, and here we are. There was nowhere else to go. The cabbie looked suspicious, but I told him she was on some drugs, and I think he bought it."

"No, it's okay," I told Jeta, placing a tentative hand on her shoulder and then giving it a squeeze when she didn't shrug it off. "You absolutely should have brought her here. That was the right thing to do."

"I just don't understand who would do something like this to her," Jeta said.

"Did she have any enemies that you know of?" Ambrose asked.

Jeta shook her head. "She's so quiet. Such an introvert, you know?"

"You do not believe, then, that the Traveler Durupinen had anything to do with this attack?" Ambrose asked, scowling at her.

Jeta looked affronted. "Of course we didn't," she spat at him.

Ambrose crossed his arms truculently. "You just said she had been banished from—"

"Banishment and physical torture are not the same thing!" Jeta hissed at him. "I realize our ways and laws are not yours, Northerner, but we are not savages, whatever you may believe in your ignorance. We do not inflict physical punishment on members who simply choose to leave the protection of our camp. She may not be welcomed back, but no one from our camp would ever attack her. It is not in our code."

"Codes can be broken," Ambrose said stubbornly.

"Not where I come from," Jeta shot back. "Honor counts for something there."

Ambrose snorted, as though the idea of Travelers and honor had little to do with each other. Jeta opened her mouth to retort, but Flavia groaned loudly at that moment, thrusting a trembling hand into the air as though pointing to something and then letting it fall again.

I took advantage of the distraction to intervene before they could argue again. "What about the attack itself? Do you have any idea what the nature of it was? What the attacker was trying to do?"

Jeta shook her head, looking tearful again. "I don't recognize the placement or combination of runes. It's not any Casting I know."

"Nor do I," Hannah said, stepping forward for a closer look. "It seems to be... pretty crudely done."

Ambrose stepped forward, pulling his phone from his pocket and holding it up. "I'm going to document them," he said, his tone wavering somewhere between hostility and asking for permission.

No one objected, and so he began taking photos like a crime scene investigator, walking around the couch and making careful adjustments to Flavia's limbs so that he could get clearer shots.

As he worked, I knelt down beside Flavia and caressed her forehead with the back of my fingers. Her skin was cool to the touch, though she looked flushed and feverish. "Hey, Flavia. Hey, it's Jess. You know, Northern Girl. Can you hear me?"

Flavia just continued moaning and muttering, making no sign she knew I was there.

Brushing her sweaty hair back from her cheeks, I took a closer look at the runes. Very carefully, I reached out and touched one with the tip of my finger. It smudged easily, leaving a gray sooty residue on my fingertip.

"Is that... charcoal?" Hannah asked tentatively.

I lifted the finger to my nose and sniffed. "Ash," I said. "From a fire."

"Ash?" Jeta repeated.

"Yeah," I said. "You can see the rain has washed it away in places. And see the skin here?" I pointed to her right cheekbone, where the skin beneath the rune was red and a little blistered. "The ash was hot when they put it on her face."

"That's just sick," Milo muttered, squirming uncomfortably.

At the sound of Milo's voice, Flavia's eyes fluttered open and I fell back into the coffee table, gasping in shock. Flavia's eyes, once dark and full of sparkling wit, were a milky, silvery color. They darted around in their sockets, as though following the rapid process of something that only she could see as her eyelids twitched.

"What the... what the hell happened to her *eyes*?" I breathed.

Hannah squeaked with fear. Jeta let out a cry of terror. Milo swore quietly under his breath. Ambrose leaned forward and snapped a photo.

"Her eyes do not typically look like this?" he asked matter-of-factly, staring down at the screen to make sure he had gotten a clear image.

"No, of course they don't!" I snapped at him. "Who the fuck's eyes typically look like that?"

Ambrose shrugged, unconcerned.

"I know," Milo said quietly.

I looked over at him. "What did you say?"

He hesitated, his form crackling with an anxiety so powerful that it seemed to chill the entire room. "I know whose eyes look like that. And you do, too."

"Milo, what are you..." But it hit me like a sledgehammer mid-thought.

I *had* seen eyes like these before.

We all had. Many of them. A virtual army of them.

But only one pair in particular really stood out in my mind. One pair that had burned though me, that had torn my life apart, that had nearly destroyed all I had held dear.

Those eyes had stared out of the face of Neil Caddigan.

I looked up at Ambrose, who looked mystified by our sudden understanding.

"Bring the car around. We need to get her to Fairhaven. Now."

10

BLINDED

B Y THE TIME WE REACHED FAIRHAVEN, the worst of the rain had passed, and the castle loomed up at us out of a thick white fog that rolled and swirled like a sentient creature stalking rays of moonlight through the grounds. They were waiting for us, lined up along the drive, holding torches aloft, like living candles. Ambrose had called ahead to warn Seamus that we were coming, and to ask him to alert the Council members on site and Mrs. Mistlemoore, who ran the hospital ward.

The SUV crunched through the gravel and came to a stop. No one had spoken much during the drive, except to ask periodically how Flavia was doing. She lay across the back seat now, her head in Jeta's lap, as seemingly oblivious to our arrival at Fairhaven as she was to any of our presences.

With almost creepy efficiency, the Caomhnóir descended on the car, opening all four doors simultaneously. Mrs. Mistlemoore hurried forward, saying briskly, "Let me give her a quick look, and then I will need you to help her onto the stretcher and inside."

Two Caomhnóir stepped forward alongside her, ready to carry out these instructions.

Mrs. Mistlemoore's hands flew expertly over Flavia, from her pulse in her neck, to her temples, to her chest. She lifted an eyelid and muttered what sounded like a curse under her breath. She looked up at Jeta, her face unreadable but her voice gentle. "You are the one who found her?"

Jeta nodded, lips pressed together against another onslaught of tears.

"What's your name, love?"

"Jeta Loveridge," she managed to choke out.

"Very well, Jeta. I would like you to come with me into the ward, so that I may ask you some questions. Can you manage that?"

Again, Jeta nodded.

"Very well. Gentlemen, if you would move her. *Carefully,* please, and especially mind her head and face."

The Caomhnóir smoothly transferred Flavia from the back seat to the stretcher and marched her into the castle, followed immediately by Mrs. Mistlemoore and Jeta jogging along in their wake. Hannah and I clambered out of the car, followed by Milo, and found ourselves facing a row of grim-faced Council members.

Siobhán stepped forward, nodding respectfully to each of us. "I've been instructed to take you up to the High Priestess' office," she said.

I had been expecting it, but that didn't lessen the dread I felt as we followed Siobhán into the castle, through the corridors, and up the winding staircases, tight as corkscrews, to the tower room. Even if I hadn't been out of breath from the stairs, I knew I would find it hard to breathe if ever I entered this room again. Hannah reached out and pulled my hand into hers, squeezing it tightly. Behind us, Milo pressed the reassuring coolness of his energy against us, a hand on each of our shoulders, and a supportive whisper in our ears.

"You've got this. I'm right behind you."

The door opened and we stepped through. The contents of the room had been greatly changed since we had last stood inside it, but I could still see the old furnishings in my mind's eye, haunting the space like the abundant spirits within the castle walls. I could still see the bed in the corner, Finvarra's wracked and battered body beneath the sheets. I could still see the scattering of medical equipment—the pill bottles, the silenced machines, rendered useless after her passing. But more clearly than all of this, I could still see, in breathtaking detail, the form of my father, lingering just this side of the Gateway, clinging to the living world by the very tips of his fingers just to say goodbye to us.

"Jessica. Hannah. Thank you for coming."

I jumped, startled, at the sound of Celeste's voice, though she was clearly seated behind the desk, waiting for us. Hannah recovered herself first.

"Hello, High Priestess. We apologize for the late hour," she said.

I stiffened beside her. Speak for yourself. I'm not apologizing for anything.

As though my thought had materialized in front of Milo for him to read, he sent a response through the connection. "Deep breath, sweetness. Picking a fight with the High Priestess isn't going to help Flavia."

"Why do you have to be so reasonable when I want to light shit on fire?" I asked him.

"It's part of my charm?" Milo suggested. "Just keep it together. Repeat to yourself: we are here for Flavia."

I repeated it under my breath like a mantra, keeping my temper under control.

Celeste waved Hannah's apology away. "No apologies, please. This was an emergency, and you were right to bring her here." She turned and looked at me, and I could have sworn, for just a moment, there was a flicker of guilt in her eyes.

"Jess. Nice to see you again. I trust you are well?" she asked delicately.

Other than the fact that I want to dive across that desk and tackle you, and rage and storm and scream at you until you beg me to let you restore the normalcy of my life and bring back the one person who makes me feel like I'm worth a damn? "I'm fine," I muttered, looking anywhere but at her.

"So, please," Celeste said, gesturing to two chairs in front of her desk. "Tell me what happened tonight."

I remained stubbornly on my feet. With an uneasy glance at me, Hannah perched herself on the edge of the offered chair and explained, in as much detail as she could, about how Jeta and Flavia had arrived at our flat, and everything that Jeta had told us when we questioned her. Celeste listened intently. A long wavy tendril of black hair had escaped from her braid, and she was twisting it unconsciously around her finger.

"This girl, Flavia," she said at last. "What do you know of her?"

"I don't actually know her very well," Hannah said, looking to me for assistance. "It was Jess who—"

"I met her in the Traveler camp when I hid there from the Necromancers four years ago. We became friends," I said, keeping my eyes fixed deliberately on a blue glass paperweight on the desk near Celeste's right hand.

"And why didn't her friend—Jeta, you said her name was?—why didn't she return Flavia to the Traveler camp?" Celeste asked.

"Flavia has broken with their traditions and chosen to live outside of the confines of the camp," I replied. "Jeta can explain it better, but it's my understanding that, because of that decision, Flavia has forfeited the right to protection and aid from the Traveler Clans. Jeta was afraid that if she brought Flavia there, they might refuse to help her."

Celeste knitted her eyebrows together. "Yes, that is possible. I understand that the Traveler Clans have very strict guidelines, particularly when it comes to their borders. I would not be surprised if they had been turned away. Why did Flavia choose to leave?"

"To further her education," I said. "She was—is—a doctoral student at a university in London. She wants to be a professor."

Celeste tapped a finger thoughtfully against her lips. "And you know of no reason why someone would want to harm her?"

I hesitated a moment, thinking back to the way that Flavia had helped Irina to escape. If the Traveler Council had found out about her role in that plan, might they not seek some kind of revenge? But I couldn't risk telling Celeste any of that. I didn't see how that information could help Flavia now, but it could certainly hurt her if it got back to the ears of the Traveler Council.

"No," I said. "And Jeta didn't either, but... well..." I looked at Milo, who nodded encouragingly. "We noticed something strange about Flavia."

Celeste fixed me with a serious look. "Go on."

"It was her eyes. Did... has anyone told you about her eyes?" I asked, hesitantly.

Celeste shook her head. "No. I was told she was attacked, and that there were physical injuries and runes involved. That is all I know at this point."

"Well, she opened her eyes and they looked... different."

"Different in what way?" Celeste asked, the slightest bite of impatience in her voice.

"They used to be dark brown—almost black. But now they're this milky silvery-white color and she can't seem to see anyone."

Celeste's own dark eyes became very wide in her shock. "She's gone blind?"

I shrugged. "I'm not sure. She doesn't seem to be able to see any of us, even when her eyes are open, though she does seem to be looking at something, because her eyes are moving around."

"That is... very disturbing," Celeste said.

"You haven't even heard the disturbing part yet," I said.

Celeste raised an eyebrow. "Enlighten me."

"I—that is to say, *we*—have seen eyes like hers before," I said.

Celeste looked from Milo to Hannah to me, still mystified. "Am I supposed to know where?" she asked at last.

"Right here," I said. "At Fairhaven. An army of them. The Necromancers—at least, the ones I saw up close—had eyes that looked just like Flavia's."

For a moment, Celeste did not respond. In fact, she gave no indication that she had heard me at all. Then something in her brain seemed to snap into place and she started toward us so quickly that all three of us jumped back in surprise.

"You are sure of this? You are absolutely sure?"

"Yes," I said.

"Do you know the significance of it? That is to say, was it ever made clear to you why the Necromancers' eyes looked the way they did?"

I shook my head. "No. I remember thinking that they looked creepy, but... well, they *were* creepy, so I didn't really stop to consider it. Not to mention the fact that we were running for our lives at the time."

Celeste turned her laser-focused gaze on Hannah. "Hannah, you spent more time amongst them than any of us, as their captive. Did any of them ever do or say anything that might shed some light on this?"

Hannah shook her head, but said nothing. I knew she was doing her best to hold it together at the mention of her time with the Necromancers. Though she was doing much better at not blaming herself, there was still a lot of lingering guilt there. I jumped in, to give her a chance to recover herself.

"It just seems like too much of a coincidence that a Durupinen would be attacked using runes, and that afterwards her eyes would resemble those of a Necromancer, doesn't it?"

Celeste bit on her lip, staring off into the middle distance, considering my words. "Yes," she said at last. "Yes, it does." And again, with a swiftness that startled us, she spun around to face the door where her Caomhnóir stood like a statue. I hadn't even realized he was there.

"Did you hear all of that, Colin?" she asked.

"Yes, High Priestess, I did indeed," Colin replied stiffly.

"Please alert the Council that there will be a meeting in the morning. Nine o'clock. I want every Council member there, no exceptions. Have the Trackers send word to Catriona that I need her back here, and to make whatever arrangements she must in order to make that happen."

Celeste whirled back around and asked, "You will stay and tell the Council what you have just told me?"

I glanced at Hannah, startled. "I... sure, if you want us to."

"I do."

Hannah nodded grimly. "Then, we'll be there, of course."

"Very good," Celeste said, and then turned back to Colin. "When you have done that, please have Mrs. Mistlemoore come here to give me an update on the young woman's status."

"It shall be done at once, High Priestess," Colin said, and backed out the door with a respectful bow.

"Thank you for telling me all of this," Celeste said to us, once Colin had closed the door. "If you'd like, I can have someone prepare your clan's room, and you can get some sleep? Surely you must be exhausted."

"I don't think I could sleep, do you?" Hannah asked, turning to me.

I shook my head. "No way. Not until we hear something about Flavia, and even then..." I shuddered, remembering the emptiness of her eyes.

Celeste held up a hand. "I understand. Of course, it is all very traumatizing. I shall prepare the room anyway, and have some tea and sandwiches sent down. You can wait there until an update is available, and rest if you so choose."

Hannah nodded gratefully. "Yes. Thank you."

I nodded as well. As far as I was concerned, I could not get out of this room fast enough.

Celeste used an intercom I had never noticed before to call for assistance, and then ushered us out the door. We began the long walk down to our old clan digs on the second floor. In the time it took us to reach the familiar corridor, the beds had been turned down, the lights turned on, the fire in the grate lit, and a full tea service set up on the coffee table.

"Impressive," Milo said, examining the three-tiered serving tray of sandwiches. "They've even cut the sandwiches into cute little shapes."

I couldn't say how long we sat, staring into the fire, cramming tiny sandwiches into our mouths just for something to do. I think I might have dozed off at one point, although I couldn't say for sure; everything was just a tired, jittery haze. Sometimes, I would check the clock, sure hours had gone by, and five minutes had barely passed. At other times, I would look at the clock, convinced I had only just glanced at it, and a whole hour had slipped by unnoticed. It was disorienting. Finally, when it seemed I would go insane from the anticipation, a gentle knock sounded on our door.

"Come in," Hannah called, her voice cracked from hours of silence.

Mrs. Mistlemoore poked her head inside the door. Jeta stood beside her.

"Your friend is resting comfortably now," Mrs. Mistlemoore said. "We've sedated her and treated all her wounds. Her wrist and three fingers sustained fractures, and her clavicle is broken as well."

"Jesus," Milo muttered.

"Come sit, Jeta. You look exhausted. Do you want something to eat?" Hannah asked, waving Jeta into the room. "Mrs. Mistlemoore, do you want some tea?"

"No, thank you," Mrs. Mistlemoore said, with the air of a person who had never taken a break when there was an opportunity to keep working.

"I don't think I can eat anything," Jeta said. "But... would you mind... could I lie down?"

"Of course you can!" Hannah said. "Take my bed, it's the one right over there."

Jeta stumbled over to it, sat on the edge, and began removing her shoes. She still had on her raincoat and her hair had dried into a mass of untamable curls.

"Can you tell us anything else?" I asked her. "About her attack?"

"She isn't speaking yet, so I haven't been able to question her," Mrs. Mistlemoore said. "It is hard to be certain whether she is in shock, or if the Casting has rendered her incapable of communicating clearly."

"So, she has definitely been placed under a Casting?" I asked, my heart speeding up inside my chest.

"Almost certainly," Mrs. Mistlemoore said. "Someone has at least attempted a Casting. What it was, and whether it was properly done, I cannot say. The placement and combination of the runes is unfamiliar to me, and many were smudged and washed away by the rain. We have been able to identify lavender, sage, and copper dust on her body as well. She also bears marks that she may have been bound at the wrists and ankles. I have the Scribes looking at her now, and they will research meticulously to try to interpret the meaning."

"And what's wrong with... I mean, do you know what's happened with... with her eyes?" Milo asked, barely able to get the question out over the power of his revulsion.

For the first time, Mrs. Mistlemoore looked disturbed. "I cannot say how, or why, but... it is her Spirit Sight. It has been... altered."

A ringing silence met these words. For a few moments, no one seemed to breathe. Then Hannah asked, in a squeak of a voice. "Altered? What do you mean?"

"It... I have never seen anything like it, so I cannot be sure, but... her Spirit Sight appears to be... twisted. Turned inward."

"I don't understand," I said in a whisper.

"Our gift has imbued us with Spirit Sight. We can see spirits in the world around us. But something—a perversion of a Casting, it seems—has turned Flavia's Spirit Sight inward on herself. Rather than seeing spirits around her, the sight has been... twisted, and she is being forced to stare at her own spirit."

"Is... that bad?" I asked. "Looking at your own spirit?"

Mrs. Mistlemoore seemed to be choosing her words very carefully. "It is... disorienting. Possibly maddening. We are not aware, in life, of our spirit's wish to be free of our mortal shells and seek the Aether. But Flavia is being forced to confront that need while being trapped inside her own body."

"Is that why she kept clawing at herself? At her clothes and her skin? We thought she was in pain, or... or feverish... but she felt so cold!" Jeta's voice was shaking so badly that it was hard to understand her.

"Yes, I think so," Mrs. Mistlemoore said. "Her body feels unnatural now that she is seeing her spirit for the first time in its true form."

A pall of horror fell over the entire room like a cloak. We were all wrapped in it. But Mrs. Mistlemoore's words had stirred something besides my horror: a memory. My mind, reeling, traveled back to the first time I'd ever met my grandfather.

"What you're saying... it made me think of someone else. Our grandfather... did you ever hear what happened to him?" I asked Mrs. Mistlemoore.

She looked a little taken aback by the turn the conversation had taken. "Your grandfather? No, I... I don't think I know what you're referring to."

"He walked in on our mother and Karen in the middle of a Crossing. He entered the summoning circle and tried to pull their hands apart."

Mrs. Mistlemoore closed her eyes, as though that could somehow lessen the horror of what she had understood. From the corner of Hannah's bed, Jeta let out a horrified gasp.

I went on, "He didn't die, but Karen told me his spirit was pulled partially from his body before they could end the Crossing. Since then, he has lived in a state of desperation, obsessed with a constant, all-consuming desire to be sent back to the Aether, because, now that he's seen it, he can't bear to remain trapped in his body. It has driven him mad."

Mrs. Mistlemoore's eyes remained closed, but she nodded. "So that's the truth of it, then. I often wondered, but your grandmother did not want the details made public. I think it was only ever the Council who knew the whole story. It is terrible, what your grandfather has suffered. The soul cannot rest within the confines of the living body once it has glimpsed the Aether."

"Mine did," I pointed out.

She opened her eyes. "Yours is different."

"Because I'm a Durupinen?" I asked.

"In part, yes, but also because you are a Walker. Your soul did indeed traverse into the realm of the Aether, but it remained tied to your body and your living consciousness. It had to be, or it could not have made the journey back."

"Flavia's soul hasn't left her body. It hasn't entered the Aether, and yet what you're saying sounds a lot like what Karen explained about my grandfather. Is it really as bad as all of that?"

Mrs. Mistlemoore shook her head sadly. "I cannot say. I have never seen anything like it. I cannot imagine what bizarre bastardization of a Casting this young woman has undergone, to be found in such a state. I have never seen the Spirit Sight perverted in this way. All I know is that this perversion could drive her mad, if we do not find a way to reverse it."

"So... can you reverse it?" Hannah asked. "Is there a way?"

Mrs. Mistlemoore shrugged. "We cannot reverse what we do not understand. I don't know why someone would have done this to her. It is cruel and unusual to the highest degree."

I looked questioningly over at Hannah. She nodded, understanding my hesitancy. Mrs. Mistlemoore should know what we told Celeste about the Necromancers, but it was not our place to share the information.

"Mrs. Mistlemoore, did... that is, have you spoken with the High Priestess? Or with her Caomhnóir?"

Mrs. Mistlemoore nodded again. "Yes. She's told me what you confided in her—about the Necromancers."

"And?" Hannah prompted.

"I... cannot say for sure whether the conditions are related. Necromancers, of course, have no Spirit Sight. It would not be prudent to say more on the subject at this time, not until the Council has met to discuss it."

I bit my lip. Weren't we wasting precious time, allowing Flavia to suffer while waiting for the Council to "discuss it?"

"I encourage you all to get a bit of sleep. There are a few hours yet before the meeting. There's nothing you can do for Flavia, who I assure you is resting quite comfortably now. I suggest you do the same," Mrs. Mistlemoore said, with a return to her usual brusque and efficient manner.

"Will you... that is to say, if anything changes..." Jeta sniffed, but Mrs. Mistlemoore waved away the end of the question.

"I will have someone fetch you immediately if there is any change in her condition," she assured us. "Rest yourselves, now."

11

THE MANY-HEADED MONSTER

A S WAS NOW A LONGSTANDING TRADITION when I was before the Durupinen Council, they were all staring at me with a mixture of fear and horror on their faces. I actually experienced a moment of nostalgia, thinking of all the other instances they had looked at me, just like that.

Good times.

On this occasion, at least, I was not really the subject of their shock and horror—I was merely the harbinger of the shocking and horrifying news. Jeta had stumbled her way through an explanation of how she had found Flavia, and then Mrs. Mistlemoore had struck them all dumb with an explanation of what had happened to Flavia's Spirit Sight. Finally, I had followed up by detailing the connection I had made between Flavia's condition and what I had observed of the Necromancers' appearances when last we had seen them. It felt like a very long time before anyone could get beyond their initial surprise to respond.

"High Priestess, do you... can you... confirm what she says? About the Necromancers?" Kiera finally stammered.

"I remember it," Siobhán piped up, her tone one of utter disgust. "I was out in the entrance hall when they arrived to storm the castle. One of them grabbed me and forced me into this room. I pulled his mask from his face in the struggle. I will never forget looking up into his face and seeing those eyes."

"And it was all of them? Every single one?" Patricia Lightfoot asked.

"Who can possibly say for sure?" another Council member said. "The vast majority of them were masked."

"And no one ever looked into this? No one ever stopped to investigate what it might have meant?" Kiera asked.

"No," Celeste said. "Those still living were rounded up and

imprisoned, but I don't remember any inquiries of that sort being made. We were simply interested in capturing them, making sure they were locked away."

Siobhán turned to Catriona, who was sitting in the back row, poker-straight and looking incredibly tense. "Catriona, what of the Trackers? They surely would have handled any investigations of this nature. Do you remember anything coming across your desk about this?"

Catriona shook her head stiffly. "No, nothing. As Celeste said, our priority was to capture and contain."

"Nothing in the interrogations?" Patricia pressed.

"No," Catriona asserted. "I can check all the transcripts, if you like, but I can't recall a single instance of this being investigated. And as most of you know, Necromancers are not known to be forthcoming when questioned."

"We were reeling," Fiona piped up from where she slouched in the back row. "I don't think anyone was much fussed with the details. What did wonky eye color matter in the scope of what had happened? We were in self-preservation mode. Capture, kill, imprison, and contain the damage. That was all we were interested in."

The Council sat in silence for a moment, some looking defensive, others incredulous that such a detail could have escaped investigation. Then Hannah stood up in the second row, looking nervous but determined.

"Please, if I may," she began. "We aren't going to get anywhere looking backward. Perhaps it ought to have been looked into, but it wasn't. There were so many more life-or-death details to contend with. We have the chance to look into it now. Let's take that chance."

There were several nods and murmurs of assent amongst the group. Then Patricia Lightfoot flicked a finger into the air to signal she meant to speak.

"Are we even sure there is any relevance here? That is to say, are we even sure that this girl's condition and the Necromancers' condition were the same?"

"A valid question," Celeste said. She turned to Mrs. Mistlemoore, who was sitting in a chair to the side of the platform, a stack of medical notes clutched in her hands. "Mrs. Mistlemoore? Can you speak to this? Do you think there is a connection?"

Mrs. Mistlemoore stood up. "They may look similar, but I would have to examine a Necromancer with the condition in order to have a clearer idea. Certainly, none of the Necromancers that came to Fairhaven suffered from their condition the way that Flavia does."

"How do you mean?" Celeste asked. "Can you clarify?"

"The Necromancers were fully functional. They undertook a complicated and multi-pronged attack on the castle while dealing with whatever condition gave them that appearance. Flavia has been rendered incapacitated. She can neither see outside of her own body, nor speak coherently to answer questions."

"There you are," Patricia said, as though this settled the matter. "You see? How can these two details be related if the symptoms are so different? It makes no sense."

"It would surprise me if the two were related, but I would still recommend looking into it," Mrs. Mistlemoore said.

"But why would we...?" Patricia began, but I cut her off.

"Why wouldn't we? I mean, if there's the slightest chance that Flavia's condition is related to the Necromancers, why wouldn't we try to rule that out?" I asked.

"And how do you propose to do that?" Patricia asked, a definite sneer in her voice.

Mrs. Mistlemoore answered before I could retort, which was probably lucky, as I was fairly sure that nothing polite was going to come out of my mouth. "I will likely have to make a trip to the Isle of Skye, to the *príosún* there," she said, her voice dripping with distaste. "The surviving Necromancers—those who weren't killed in the attack on the castle—are all being held there."

My heart seemed to skip a beat. I chanced a glance at Fiona, who was looking determinedly at her feet. I quickly did the same.

"And some of those Necromancers have this... condition?" Patricia asked.

"It would take only a phone call to confirm it," Mrs. Mistlemoore said.

"High Priestess," Siobhán said quickly, holding up a hand to silence the half-dozen voices now trying to weigh in on the matter. "How do you wish to proceed?"

Celeste was not looking at anyone, but staring thoughtfully at her own clasped hands. Finally, without looking up, she said, more to herself than to anyone else, "Never let it be said of me that

I repeated the sins of the past by shrugging off the threat of an enemy to revel instead in the glow of our own superiority."

"I'm sorry?" Siobhán asked.

Celeste looked up, her face calm and determined. "We will investigate the Necromancer connection. If this event is in any way related to Necromancer activity, we must know, and we must act upon that information quickly and decisively. I will not allow another Necromancer uprising to gain a hold while this Council and these clans are under my watch."

Patricia made an incredulous noise through her nose. "High Priestess, even Mrs. Mistlemoore has said that the chances are very remote—"

"Let them be remote. I care not," Celeste said quellingly. "What purpose does it serve to ignore those chances, remote or otherwise? We all thought the fulfillment of the Prophecy was an impossibility and here we are, four years later and still reeling from its consequences. No more."

She turned with a forcefulness of purpose so powerful that I was reminded overwhelmingly of Finvarra, who, despite her failings, never wavered in her surety. "Mrs. Mistlemoore, we will arrange for you to leave for Skye Príosún as soon as possible. Catriona, you will coordinate with the Tracker office to launch a new investigation into this issue. I will speak to the Caomhnóir and ensure that security is taken care of. If there is any chance this attack is connected to the Necromancers, I want it to be thoroughly disproven before we lay it to rest."

"Yes, High Priestess," Mrs. Mistlemoore said, Catriona's voice a murmuring echo of the same words.

"Now," Celeste said, seeming to choose her words carefully. "I have a few more questions for you, Jeta, if you would be so kind."

"I will answer them if I can, High Priestess," Jeta said, her voice still thick with repressed tears.

"You mentioned that Flavia was living in London outside of the boundaries of Traveler protection, which was why she did not have a Caomhnóir. Can you elaborate on that?"

Jeta shifted uncomfortably from one foot to the other. "I don't like to discuss Traveler business with outsiders."

"The High Priestess of the Northern Clans is hardly some riffraff outsider," Siobhán cried out, practically swelling with indignation.

Celeste held up a hand, and Siobhán fell silent. "Nor am I a

Traveler. I understand the close-knit nature of your clans, Jeta, and I respect your secrecy. However, you brought Flavia here rather than to your own Council, and I therefore must infer one of two things. Either you thought the distance to the Traveler camp too far to travel with her in this condition, or else, you thought that she would not get the help she needed if you brought her back there. Which is it?"

Jeta swallowed hard. "I... I was not sure if they would help her."

"And for the Traveler Durupinen to ignore the duty to serve and protect one of their own bloodline, there must have been a truly unforgivable transgression committed," Celeste went on.

Jeta's face spasmed with pain. "It... it shouldn't have been unforgivable."

"Tell us what happened," Celeste said. "Please. It will be important in deciding what to do going forward."

Jeta dissolved into tears again, and I put an arm around her shoulders. "Can I tell them?" I asked her quietly.

She looked up, sniffling.

"If I tell them, then you won't have betrayed anyone's trust. I've got no Traveler trust to lose, not anymore," I said. I looked up and caught Celeste in a fierce gaze. Her eyes darted quickly to Jeta instead.

Jeta, who had taken the moment to consider the matter, nodded her head gratefully.

Giving her shoulders a reassuring squeeze, I looked up at the expectant Council and said, "Flavia is a friend of mine. She has been my friend since she helped me survive the Necromancer attack on the Traveler camp four years ago. She is a Scribe, a very good one, but her love of books and learning goes far beyond Durupinen history. She chose, against Council wishes, to break with tradition and move away from the encampment. In giving up her role in the camp, she gave up their protection as well. They no longer acknowledge her as a member of their clans."

The Council members' faces were all frozen in various attitudes of shock, disgust, and incredulity. It was Kiera who broke the silence at last.

"They've withdrawn her protection... simply for living outside of the boundaries?" she asked.

"That's right," I said.

"That's absurd," Siobhán declared.

"That's tradition." Celeste said firmly. "Need I remind you all that we have many traditions of our own that would seem incomprehensible to outsiders?"

I couldn't help it. I let out a snort of laughter, which I quickly stifled behind my hand, though not before I earned several dirty looks from the Council benches.

"Is it fair to say, Jeta, that there are those amongst the Travelers who are unhappy—even angry—with Flavia?" Celeste asked.

Jeta hesitated, then nodded.

"Then there is a second possibility that must be investigated," Catriona said, "and that is Traveler Durupinen involvement in the attack."

I felt Jeta stiffen beside me. Out of the corner of my eye, I saw Milo reach out toward her, trying to reassure her with the immediacy of his presence and a few whispered words.

Celeste seemed to realize that her statement had offended Jeta, because she addressed her next words to her rather than to the Council. "It is critical to examine every possibility, no matter how remote. I do not wish to cast doubt on the suitability or methods of the Traveler justice system. Your laws are your laws, and they have always, in my experience, been carried out fairly."

It took every fiber of my strength not to laugh at the top of my lungs until my laughter turned to screams that shredded my throat raw. I clenched my fists, bit down on my tongue and prayed for self-control.

"But there is always the possibility," Celeste went on, "that unofficial justice was carried out in some way, or else that someone from the Traveler Clans may have information pertaining to this attack. For that reason, I ask you, Catriona, to launch an investigation into this possibility as well."

Jeta threw out her chest. "The Traveler Council will not take kindly to this, ma'am," she said, respect and defiance mingled in her tone. "But I trust you already know that."

"I do," said Celeste and her tone was gentle, even comforting. "But we have been put into an awkward position here. We are, in essence, harboring a fugitive. We are glad to do this," she added quickly, for both Jeta and I had opened our mouths angrily. "You were right to bring her to us, and we will do all we can, both to heal and protect her. But therefore, we must be fully aware of what we have undertaken. If we are acting against the wishes of the Traveler

Council, we must know it. If we are reversing a punishment they have deemed appropriate, we must know that, too. Much of how we proceed with Flavia's care will be informed by this information."

Jeta scowled, but she did not seem able to find any sort of argument against what Celeste had proposed; there was too much common sense in it to reasonably ignore.

"In the meantime, our Scribes and Mrs. Mistlemoore are doing everything they can to discover the nature of Flavia's condition and reverse it. We must put our hope, for now, in their admirable skill. With that, if there are no further questions for her, I would like to excuse Mrs. Mistlemoore so that she can go attend to her patient."

No one offered any objections, and so Mrs. Mistlemoore stood again, bowed stiffly, and hurried down off the platform and out the side door.

"I would also like to thank you, Jeta, for your courage, and for trusting us with the care of your friend. We will do our utmost to prove that your trust has not been misplaced. You are welcome to stay here at Fairhaven for as long as you wish during Flavia's recovery. We can provide you accommodations, if that is your wish."

Jeta's mouth twisted as several emotions battled for dominance, but in the end, she nodded and mumbled, "Thank you, High Priestess. I would like to stay until she is well."

"I only ask," Celeste said, "that you delay contacting the rest of the Travelers until such time as we can ascertain their involvement in Flavia's attack. Can you do this?"

Jeta nodded. "I will need to check in with my mother and sister to let them know I'm well, but I can do that without letting them know what's happened. But if the full moon arrives and we still have no answers, I will have to return home for the lunar Crossing, and once I do, I cannot see how I can hide the truth from them."

Celeste nodded approvingly. "A more than fair window for the Trackers to make their investigations, wouldn't you say, Catriona?"

Catriona forced her face into something resembling a smile. "Piece of cake," she said dryly.

"Very well, then. If there are no further details to discuss, I suggest we adjourn and allow Jessica, Hannah, and Jeta to get some much-needed sleep," Celeste said, rising from her throne beside the podium. "I can't imagine that any of you were able to rest much last night."

None of us felt the need to reply. Nor did any of the other Council members, who began to mill about, gathering their things and murmuring quietly to each other. None of them acknowledged us as they walked out except for Fiona, whose pointed effort to give us a wide berth on the way out could be construed as acknowledgment.

We waited as Hannah descended the benches, and then began the walk back to the entrance hall. Somehow, now that the details of Flavia's stay had been settled, a bubble of adrenaline inside of me seemed to have burst, and in its place was a bone-deep exhaustion. I needed a big breakfast and a long nap. I was about to tell Hannah this when I noticed her eyes were glimmering with tears.

"Hey, what's going on? Are you okay?" I asked her.

She started to nod, but couldn't force herself to do it, and dropped her head into her hands. "I can't believe this is happening again," came her muffled voice from between her fingers.

"What do you mean, 'Can't believe this is happening again'?" I asked her, wrapping an arm around her just as Milo turned and saw what was happening and swooped over to comfort her.

"Sweetness, what is it? Did one of those Council bitches say something to you?" Milo asked, craning his neck as though the culprit would have a neon sign over her head.

"No, no, it's not the Council. It's just... the Necromancers... I can't believe we're facing a threat from them again," Hannah said, her face still hidden.

"Hey, hey, let's not get ahead of ourselves," I told her, catching Milo's eye and silently asking for back up. "You heard Mrs. Mistlemoore. She said the chances were remote."

"But the chance is there," Hannah said, her voice rising with barely controlled panic. "They're like that many-headed monster in Greek mythology. You know, the one where you cut off its head, but there are always more heads, ready to attack. How do you defeat something like that?"

"You're right. The chance has always been there," Milo said bluntly. We both stared at him. If he'd had a corporeal foot, I would have stomped on it: this was not the reassuring back up I had been hoping for.

"Real talk, sweetness," Milo said sternly. "You keep me around to guide you, so here's some guidance. The Necromancers aren't going anywhere, okay? They never were. Even for the centuries the

Durupinen insisted they were gone, they were right there in the shadows, growing like a cancer. Do you know why?"

"N-no," Hannah stammered.

"Because the patriarchy cannot handle a sisterhood like the Durupinen. As long as women are dominating a realm they can neither control nor exploit, the men's heads will continue to explode all over everything forever."

I stared at Milo, mouth agape. To be honest, it was an angle I hadn't considered much before. It was amazing how a battle between the worlds of the living and the dead could overshadow a classic case of gender politics, but there it was. A moment after feeling surprised, I wondered how I ever could have missed it.

Milo gave us a moment for it to sink in, and then he went on, "I know Celeste is on our shit list right now, but in this case, she's right. This is the way to deal with them. Every hint, track it down. Even a whiff of a Necromancer, and we pounce. We never let them grow unchecked again. We can't let fear or denial feed their fire. We snuff those fuckers out at every glimpse of a spark."

Hannah sniffed, but she nodded. "You're right, Milo."

"At some point we are going to have to address the fact that you always sound surprised when you say that. But for today, I'm feeling generous, so I'm going to let it slide," Milo said with a wink.

"I'm just... I'm letting my fear take over. That's how they manipulated me in the first place—by stoking my fears."

"That's right," Milo said soothingly. "So, now we make damn sure that they're the ones who are running scared."

I grinned. "I like that plan."

Hannah managed a small smile as well. "Me, too."

"Fabulous. We agree, then," Milo said. "Agenda: Kick ass first, take names later, and always in the least sensible shoes we can possibly walk in."

We were so busy laughing at his subsequent strut to the doors that we were completely surprised as Ambrose swung out from around the threshold, stepping into our path.

"Jesus!" I cried, putting a hand to my heart. "What is wrong with you? Can't you just clear your throat and announce yourself like a civilized person?"

Ambrose cleared his throat in response. "I just wanted to find out when you wanted to head back to London."

"And you felt the best way to get an answer was to scare the shit out of us?" I asked.

"Not until this afternoon," Hannah said quickly, ever the peacemaker. "We need to eat and take a rest. We didn't sleep much at all last night. Why? Do you need to get back sooner?"

Ambrose shrugged indifferently. "I just want to plan ahead."

"Let's plan for three o'clock," Hannah said, turning to me with raised eyebrows that were clearly begging me not to make a scene in the entrance hall. "Does that sound okay to you, Jess?"

I rolled my eyes at her but decided I was too tired to start real trouble anyway, even for my own amusement. "Whatever."

"See? Jess is on board," Hannah told Ambrose. "We'll see you at three o'clock in the front drive."

Ambrose looked for a moment like he wanted to argue—maybe he thought he should spend the intervening time hulking outside our bedroom door. Whatever his hesitation, he let it go and instead stalked off toward the front entrance and out into the grounds. We watched him meet up with several other Caomhnóir before the massive doors swung shut, ending our view of what appeared to be a contest to see who could thrust his chest out the furthest.

"Jess."

I turned to see Fiona standing on the staircase. My pulse quickened at once.

"Hey, Fiona," I said, offhandedly.

"I need a word," she said.

"Okay, sure," I said. I nodded to Hannah whose eyes had gone wide, and made my way up to the first landing of the grand staircase, where Fiona was slouching, arms crossed.

"You go through my notes on your artwork?" she asked without preamble.

"Uh, yeah, I did," I said. "All of them."

She nodded curtly and turned to go.

"No wait!" I called. She turned back to me, her eyes sparking with a warning, which I ignored.

I looked quickly around the entrance hall, but Hannah, Milo, and Jeta were the only ones present. Hannah, catching my eye, quickly started pointing to a tapestry over the fireplace and drawing Jeta's attention onto it.

"How did you know?" I asked Fiona. "How did you find out?"

Fiona pursed her lip into a tight knot, and for a moment I thought she might not answer me. Finally, after looking around herself to confirm that there was no chance of anyone hearing us, she muttered. "Went to visit my mother there. Saw him on duty."

I was momentarily distracted. "Your mother? What was she doing there?"

"Serving a sentence for her attack on you," Fiona said in an indifferent voice.

My mouth fell open. "They sent her to the *príosún* for *that*?"

Fiona snorted. "I'm not quite sure how this escaped your keen notice, but it was, in fact, attempted murder."

I scowled. "I know that, but... well, you said it yourself. She's not right. I mean, they can't actually hold her responsible for her actions!"

Fiona scratched at her chin, which had a smudge of charcoal on it. "The Council didn't agree with you. Not that they've actually convicted her, mind. They just sent her there for 'observation,' whatever that means."

"Oh, my God," I muttered, feeling utterly ashamed of myself. "I had no idea. I would've... I'm so sorry, Fiona."

"Nothing for you to apologize for," Fiona said with a snap in her voice, which I knew meant she was fighting against experiencing an actual feeling. "You didn't ship her up there, did you?"

"No, but still... I would have said something—told them not to punish her like that," I said.

Fiona shrugged. "Wouldn't have made a difference, I reckon. Anyway, she'll be out in a few weeks. They've all but determined that she's not a threat to herself or others anymore, as long as my sister agrees to keep her well away from Fairhaven."

I didn't know what else to say. She wasn't going to let me console her, and I wasn't fool enough to try it. We both stood in silence for a few moments until the question that I was trying to avoid asking burst from me before I could stop it.

"Did... did you speak to him?"

"No."

I felt a lump rise in my throat and the corners of my eyes began to sting, but I smiled and nodded at her. "Okay."

Fiona's face was twisted with an odd combination of pity for me and distaste for my display of emotions. She jiggled her leg agitatedly for a moment and then said, apologetically, "I couldn't, all right? There were too many people around, and he was on duty. But he... he looks... fine."

I nodded my head, grateful for the information, sparse though it was.

"We shouldn't speak about it here. Or anywhere, for that matter. Don't ask me again, you hear?" Fiona hissed.

"I know. I'm sorry."

"And the sketch? The note?" she asked, eyeing me shrewdly.

"Destroyed. I promise," I told her. Even as I did so, I was visited by the agonizing thought that, if I'd just been careful enough to destroy the sketch I'd done of Finn at the Traveler camp, we wouldn't have been in this mess in the first place. The more I thought about it, the angrier I became.

How stupid we'd been. How stupid and reckless and foolish.

"Good," Fiona said with a grunt. "Let's hear no more of it, then."

There was a look in her eyes, a look that suggested that she might try to console me if only she knew how. But she didn't. So, she turned and stomped away from me up the stairs and out of sight.

12

SETTING THE STAGE

W E WERE ALL STILL SO EXHAUSTED when we got home that afternoon that I fell into bed almost as soon as we walked in the door, and didn't wake up until the next morning. I should have felt fantastic after nearly fourteen hours of sleep, but I didn't. It had been an unsettled, restless kind of night, punctuated with disturbing dreams about Flavia. Try as I may to reassure myself that the Trackers would discover what had happened to her, I couldn't stop my imagination from hypothesizing on the worst possible scenarios. My sleep had been full of masked, cloaked figures, all with mammoth builds and bright, silvery eyes, leaping out from shadowy corners and snatching people one by one.

I also replayed my last visit to Flavia over and over again. We'd stopped by the hospital ward to see her before we left, and though I knew it was the right thing to do, I selfishly wished we hadn't. It was so disturbing to see her lying there, eyes wide and staring, darting around in their sockets, focused on things she was never meant to see. Her face haunted me more than any faceless fear ever could.

"Wow, you look terrible!" Tia announced as I shuffled into the living room. Hannah and Milo were already there, grouped around the kitchen table.

"Good morning to you, too, Ti," I grumbled.

"Sorry," she said. "Can I make it up to you with a cup of coffee?"

"How about a vat of coffee?" I suggested, stifling a yawn.

"Hannah told me about what happened to your friend," Tia said. "That's so awful. How scary."

As I struggled to respond, Milo's voice drifted through the connection. "We told her about the attack, but not the possible Necromancer involvement. No reason to scare her to death."

I threw him a grateful nod, then accepted an oversized mug from Tia. "Yeah, it was pretty frightening. She'll be okay though. The staff at Fairhaven are great. They know what they're doing." I said the words as much to reassure myself as anyone else. I wish I felt as confident as I sounded.

I knocked back half the mug of coffee in several long swigs and then said, "So what are you up to today?"

"Actually, that depends on you," Tia said, grinning shiftily. "Are you free?"

"Uh... yes?" I said uncertainly. "Unless your idea of plans means me quizzing you for hours on communicable diseases, in which case, gee, I'm suddenly all booked up."

"No, no, I have no intention of torturing you. Besides, we're done with communicable diseases. We've moved on to bacterial and fungal infections!" Tia said brightly.

"Joy."

"No, I wanted to ask you... well, first let me show you this. I took a message for you, from Charlie's boss Shriya, at the photography museum."

"Oh!" I said. Flavia's attack had driven everything else completely out of my mind, including the fact that I was supposed to be coordinating a paranormal investigation across two continents. "What did she say?"

"She said that she hoped it wasn't too late, but she just got an invitation to a photographer's estate sale and auction out of town in three weeks, and she would have to close the museum for at least three days. She thought maybe, if it worked for your team, it might be the perfect time to have the investigation. They can take their time setting up, stay multiple nights—they would have full access and it wouldn't even interrupt business time. What do you think?"

"I think that would be perfect, if I can get the team organized that quickly!" I said.

Hannah sat up at the table. "Wait, what are the dates?" she asked.

"I've got them here," Tia said, handing me a pink Post-it Note in the shape of a flower.

I glanced down at her inhumanly neat penmanship. "June 26–28th," I read aloud. "Hey, that's your birthday weekend!" I said to Tia.

"I know!" she said, "but if you're thinking of a ghost-hunt-themed party for me, I'm not interested."

"You spoil everything," I said, pouting at her.

Hannah, meanwhile, had gotten up from the table and was looking at the calendar on the fridge. "Oh, good. That's the weekend after the wedding."

I groaned. "We aren't still planning to go to that, are we?"

"Yes, we most certainly are," Hannah said in a scolding tone that made me feel instantly five years old. "We RSVP'd, and it would be rude not to show up."

"Yeah, well, most of those people already think I'm rude, so..."

Hannah held up an admonitory finger to silence me. "We already had this discussion."

I was smart enough to recognize a brick wall before I started banging my head against it. I turned my back on Hannah and told Tia, "I'll get the team on the phone and see if we can make those dates work. Did Shriya say anything else?"

Tia smirked. "Before she hung up, she invited me down to the museum today for a visit. Any chance you'd like to come with me?"

I eyed her suspiciously. "Any chance a certain bespectacled young man is on duty today?"

Tia grinned. "Maybe. He usually is on Sundays, and he was finally starting to feel better when I talked to him yesterday."

I grinned back, happy to find that I had both a reason and the ability to smile. "Let's do it. Hannah still hasn't seen the place. Hannah? Field trip?"

"Sounds great!" Hannah said eagerly. "I've been dying to check the museum out since Jess told me about it! Milo, what do you say?"

"Huh?' Milo looked up from a newspaper article on a fashion show. It seemed he'd only been half-listening to the conversation.

"Pickwick's Photography Museum. Do you want to go with us this afternoon?" Hannah repeated.

Milo hesitated. "That place was kind of... disorienting. I'll come, but I might have to check out for a bit."

Hannah frowned, looking concerned. "You don't have to come at all if—"

"No," Milo said firmly. "I'm coming. But I might step out, that's all."

Hannah bit her lip but didn't argue. She was as protective of Milo as Milo was of her.

"I'd love to be able to make some phone calls, to see if I can hammer out the details with the team first," I told Tia. "Can we wait a couple of hours? It's only," I checked my phone, "seven o'clock in the morning over there."

"Sure!" Tia said. "Charlie is working until five."

Milo perked up. "Ooh, checking out the boy toy again, are we? I may not blink out after all."

§

Three hours, several phone calls, and one long, hot shower later, I was almost ready to make the trip over to Pickwick's. Iggy had assured me that the entire team would make the trip their top priority, Dan had talked my ear off for nearly twenty minutes about a new kind of light spectrum camera he couldn't wait to test out, and Oscar had read me a long list of other locations he wanted to investigate while they were in London. I then left a message for Catriona, asking if the Tracker office could please handle the travel arrangements and accommodations.

After I hung up on Catriona's voicemail, I stared down at my phone, taking a long, deep breath. I had one last phone call to make, and I absolutely did not want to make it. I stared down at the name in my contacts for a full minute before I summoned the courage to pull the trigger.

The voice on the other end had a spooky, mystical edge to it.

"Madame Rabinski's Mystical Oddities welcomes your call. How can we help you reach out into the unknown?"

"Oh God," I snorted. "Do you really answer the phone like that every time now, or am I just special?"

Annabelle dropped her air of mystery at once. "It's a new thing we're trying. The patrons get a kick out of it."

"Your patrons must be idiots," I said.

"Almost exclusively," Annabelle said, and I heard a smile in her voice. "It's good to hear from you, Jess. How's London life?"

"Weirder than usual, actually," I told her and, without further hesitation, launched into the full story of Pickwick's History of Photography.

"So now, Catriona's opened a Tracker investigation into the

130

place, and I've got the boys lined up for a trip across the pond to investigate," I finished.

"Oh my God," Annabelle laughed. "Iggy and Oscar are going to lose their minds."

"Already gone, I'm fairly confident," I told her. "We've set an investigation date for three weeks from now."

"Wow," Annabelle said with a deep breath. "That's soon. I'll have to see if I can get coverage for the shop while I—"

"Annabelle, no," I said, cutting her off. "That's what I'm calling to tell you. I don't want you to come."

Annabelle laughed. "What? Why not?"

"I should rephrase that," I said. "Of course, I want you to come. It would be wonderful to see you and we can always use your help, but... well, something else has happened that has made life in London not just stranger, but scarier, too."

Annabelle's voice was wary now. "Okay, I'm listening. Let's hear the worst."

I told her the worst. I spared no awful detail. There were probably a dozen kinder ways to tell Annabelle what happened to Flavia, but I didn't want to be kind. I wanted to scare her away from London for the foreseeable future. When I had finished, she was silent for so long that I wondered if I had dropped the call.

"Annabelle? Are you still there?" I asked.

She cleared her throat, but her voice was still hoarse. "Yes. Yes, I'm here."

"So, you see, that's why I don't want you to come. Not this time. What if the Travelers somehow figured out that Flavia helped Irina escape? If the attack on Flavia was retribution, it's not safe for you to be here. If they know Flavia is involved, they will surely know that you had a hand in it, too."

Annabelle's voice shook, though with fear or fury, I couldn't be sure. "And if the Necromancers are responsible?"

"I'd want you here even less," I said firmly. "You've had one run-in with the Necromancers already. I think we can both agree that once was more than enough."

"If they really are back... if they really are growing stronger again..."

"Then it's best to stay far out of their way. You know what they're capable of," I said. I promised myself I would only invoke David Pierce's name if it was absolutely necessary—to use it felt like a low blow to someone I only wanted to protect. Luckily, just the suggestion of him seemed to do it.

"Okay. Okay, I'll make an excuse," Annabelle said, an audible tremor in her voice. "I'll tell them I can't leave the shop. I'll think of something."

"Thank you," I told her. "I don't think I could handle the worry or the guilt if something happened to you in the midst of this mess—whoever is causing it."

Annabelle made a noise that sounded like a swallowed sob. "Promise me you'll look after yourself."

"Without a doubt," I said.

"And that if it is the Necromancers... that you'll tell me and... and..."

"And let you throat punch one if we catch him?" I suggested.

Annabelle actually managed a laugh. "I was thinking somewhere a bit further south, but yes. That will do."

"It's a deal," I said. "And I also promise that if there's anything you can do... if I need another Walker... you're my first call."

"I'm your only call," she pointed out. This touch of her trademark attitude eased my conscience just a bit.

"Fair point," I said. "I'll call you soon and let you know what's going on as soon as we know more."

"You'd better," she said, and hung up.

There. One tiny drop of the worry and anxiety now building inside me had drained away. I allowed myself to feel the relief of it, small though it was. Then I stood up and poked my head out into the sitting room.

"Ready when you all are!" I announced.

§

"Tia! You came!" Charlie looked up from his book at the sound of the bell, grinning from ear to ear at the sight of Tia. "Brilliant! And hello, again, Jess. Hannah."

We both greeted Charlie as well. I tried to catch Hannah's eye and grin as Charlie smoothed his hair and fumbled awkwardly with the little swinging door that would release him from behind the counter, but she was completely distracted. Her eyes were wide, staring around the place at the pervasive spirit energy, which I knew would feel even more intense to her than it did to me. Even as we entered, several spirits passed through the space, each with the same dazed, fascinated expression on his face.

At the sound of Charlie's greetings, Shriya emerged from the back room, smiling. Charlie quickly made the introductions, under cover of which Milo faded away to do a bit more exploring. Hannah pulled herself together, smiling at Shriya and shaking her hand.

"Would you like the tour?" Charlie asked us.

"Sure!" Tia said eagerly.

"That would be great, thank you," said Hannah.

"I've already had it, so I'm going to chat with Shriya," I told them. "You all go ahead."

"I'll take you back to the office," Shriya said, gesturing for me to follow her.

We headed for the back room she had just exited. Behind us, I could hear Charlie trying to convince Tia and Hannah to let him use his employee discount for their tickets, which they were firmly refusing to do.

"So, you got my message, then?" Shriya said eagerly, when we had wedged our way into the cramped office space. She moved a box full of camera parts to clear a chair for me to sit on, and then perched herself on the corner of the desk. "What do you think?"

"It's perfect," I told her. "I've already been in touch with the team and they are making the necessary arrangements."

Shriya sighed, looking relieved. "I'm so glad to hear it. I... this is going to sound crazy, but..."

"Shriya, I'm just gonna go ahead and stop you right there. Nothing that could possibly come out of your mouth at this point would sound crazy, especially to me," I told her.

Shriya smiled nervously. "Right. Well, it's just... it feels like the—incidents, activity, whatever you want to call it—has gotten worse since you were here. Is that... normal?"

"Well, none of this is normal, strictly speaking," I reminded her. "But, yes, that's a common phenomenon. Before yesterday, you spent all your time consciously and unconsciously convincing yourself that what you were experiencing wasn't real, like just about any reasonable person in your position would do. But now you've accepted what's happening. You've acknowledged it. You're bound to be hyperaware of it now."

"But you don't think I've... I don't know... angered something by agreeing to let you come investigate here?" She had lowered her voice to a whisper.

"Let me ask you this. Does the energy feel different? Angrier?"

Shriya pondered this for a moment. "No, I don't think so."

"Has the kind of activity changed? Is it more aggressive? Has anything tried to hurt you?"

This time she was quicker to answer. "No. It's the usual stuff—bangs and flickering lights. Objects appearing in odd places. That sort of thing. But... I think... I think I've actually heard some voices in here."

"Like I said, you've acknowledged them now. I bet you've heard voices before, but you chalked them up to other sounds, or else dismissed them entirely. Denial can be a strong defense, even against the evidence of your own senses. I've done this a lot, and I promise you, the energy in here today feels just the same as it did yesterday. I sense a lot of interest and curiosity, but no hostility. Believe me, if something in here were angry, you would know it without having to ask my opinion."

Shriya's features relaxed. "Right. Okay. Yeah, I'm just freaking myself out now."

"Look, if it will make you feel better, why don't you let me have a quick look around? The team has given me a list of things to check, regarding the electrical and stuff, to make it easier for them to figure out what to bring for equipment. I could go down their list and check for angry spirits at the same time."

Shriya stared at me. "You can just... sense them, yeah?"

I shrugged. "Yup. Someone once told me that it's like an antenna. Everyone's got one. Mine just picks up a few extra channels. And yes, it's pretty much as terrible as it sounds."

Shriya laughed. "Right, then. Can I see that list?"

I handed it to her and she scanned down it quickly. "I can help you with all of this. Let's start with the electrical panel."

We headed for the basement door, listening to Charlie's voice drift down the hallway. He was chatting enthusiastically about the "innovation of the film negative." I grinned, and Shriya caught my eye.

"He really likes your friend. Tia, is it?"

"Yeah."

"It's nice to see him socializing a bit. I don't get the sense he has much of a social life," she said. "Shame, really, because he's such a nice kid."

"Tia's the same way," I said. "Sometimes people get so wrapped up in their studies that they miss those opportunities. I'm glad Tia is starting to take them."

"That's nice, isn't it?" Shriya said. "All right, here we are. Mind your step. These stairs are a right deathtrap."

We moved slowly, feeling the rickety old boards sinking under our weight. I reached for the railing and then quickly pulled my hand back, rubbing away a film of cobwebs. A single bare lightbulb swung from the ceiling, the pull chain clinking against it. The walls were rough unfinished stone, and the floorboards at the base of the stairs had rotted down to the dirt beneath.

"I'd be freaked out to run this place even if it wasn't haunted," I told Shriya, and she chuckled.

"My grandfather never saw the use in updating anything around here that he deemed 'functional,' let alone parts of the building that the public would never see," she said. She reached up into the gloom above her head, groped around for a moment, and then a second bulb flared to life above us. I swore quietly under my breath.

"Here's the electrical panel," Shriya said, "I don't know that I can tell you much about it, except that it's bloody ancient. You reckon your team can work with this?"

I pulled out my phone and snapped a photo of it. "I'll send it to Dan. He's pretty much a miracle worker when it comes to electrical stuff. And if it's a problem, they'll just bring a ton of batteries. Plenty of the places they've investigated don't even have electricity, and they always find a way to make it work."

"Oh, yeah. Yeah, I didn't think of that. I watched their YouTube channel last night, by the way," Shriya said.

"Did you? What did you think?" I asked.

"I think they're all stark raving mad, doing what they do," she laughed.

"Can't argue with you there," I said, laughing too. "Ghost hunting is not for the faint of heart... or sound of mind, some would argue."

"But I was impressed. They're very... methodical. Careful, like. And they don't make something out of nothing, you know?" Shriya said. "Like, they're not going to call a place haunted just because the door squeaks."

I smiled a little sadly. "It's all about the science. They learned from the best, believe me."

As we walked back up the stairs, we passed a door on the right. It was heavily locked up.

"What's in there?" I asked.

"Couldn't tell you. I'm not allowed to open it."

I stopped short. "You're not allowed to open a door in your own building?"

Shriya shook her head. "It's been sealed off. See?" She pointed to the tape that ran all along the edge of the doorway. "Black mold. It was all in the paperwork when I finally got the deed to the place. City health inspector would have to shut us down if we broke the seal. That stuff can kill you."

I shuddered. "Okay, yeah, let's definitely keep that closed, then. I'll make a note to tell the boys to steer clear of it."

"Shriya?" Charlie's voice called down the stairs.

"On our way up, Charlie!" Shriya called back, but Charlie was already descending the stairs, looking slightly panicked. He stopped several steps from the bottom.

"Do you need help?" he asked, a little breathlessly.

"No, we're fine. Just showing Jess where the electrical is, in case they need to access it for the investigation next month."

"Oh, I see," Charlie said. "I just wanted to make sure no one tried to open... did you tell her about the mold?"

"Of course I did!" Shriya said, laughing. "What am I, a fool?"

Charlie smiled sheepishly, his expression clearing. "No, of course not. Sorry, I just... we're studying that sort of thing in class at the moment. It's got me rather on edge, knowing it's in the building. Did you know it can actually kill you?"

"Not when it's been treated and sealed up, like this has been," Shriya said calmly. "The womenfolk can handle themselves down here, Charlie, all right? Now go on back up there and finish your tour. We're right behind you."

We emerged from the dankness into the corridor above, which seemed downright cheerful now that I'd seen the horror-movie set that was the basement, and made our way out to the main display area.

"So, you've settled on a time for this investigation, have you?" Charlie asked.

"That's right, last weekend in June. I've got to close anyway, for the estate sale, so it's perfect timing, really," Shriya said.

"Excellent," Charlie said. "Well, listen, I'm on hand if you need anything, Jess. Happy to help in any way I can."

"Thanks, Charlie," I said, smiling at him. "It would probably be good to have you on call, in case we have any questions, or can't find something."

"No trouble at all," Charlie said. "Right, well, I'll leave you to it, then." He inclined his head toward me and then crossed the room to join Hannah and Tia, who were taking turns looking through the lens of some kind of projector.

Shriya and I spent the next half hour walking the perimeter of the museum, counting outlets and making note of where all the switches were. As we walked, I made note of the spirits hanging around the place, trying to determine, as I had on my first visit, if they seemed to be gravitating toward anything in particular. And just like on my first visit, I had no luck. They seemed too disoriented by the energy of the place to find the source of their fascination. They drifted aimlessly through walls, circled room after room—some just stood still, staring blankly off into space. There also seemed to be a steady stream of spirits who wandered the sidewalks outside the museum, intrigued but too wary to enter. Among them, I spotted Milo. He caught my eye and spoke through the connection, "Sorry, sweetness. I've had all I can handle of that place."

When we had finished, I gave Shriya Dan's email address, and told her he would follow up with a few more details in the upcoming weeks.

"Thanks again for this, Jess," Shriya said. "Truly, I appreciate your help."

"No problem," I told her. "And try not to be too freaked out. I didn't sense a single angry spirit vibe in the whole place."

Shriya laughed. "I'm right relieved to hear it."

"I'll be in touch, okay?" I told her, just as Hannah walked over to join us.

"How about you, then?" Shriya asked, smiling at Hannah. "You enjoy all of this mad ghost hunting stuff as well?"

"Who me?" Hannah asked, wide-eyed. "Goodness, no. We might be twins, but I leave the investigating to my sister."

"Did you finish your tour?" I asked.

Hannah nodded. "This place is really fascinating. I hope you're able to bring business in."

"So do I," Shriya said. "Here's hoping, eh?"

I looked over to the other side of the room. Tia and Charlie were still deep in conversation. Charlie was gesticulating enthusiastically while Tia nodded her head, her chin resting on her hand. I had the feeling that the rest of the museum could have gone up in literal flames around them and they wouldn't have noticed unless they were forced to look away from each other.

"Hey, Tia," I called over to her. "We're going to head out."

Tia looked up, seemingly startled to be reminded that there were other people in the room. "Huh? Already?"

"I've got a few more phone calls to make," I told her, "But you should totally stay. I don't want to cut your tour short, just for me."

Tia widened her eyes at me. The message was clear: "Do not abandon me here by myself or I will hop a plane back across the ocean and never speak to you again."

Luckily for me, Charlie spotted his chance and leapt upon it with gusto. "If you'd like to stay for a bit, Tia, I can finish up my shift and we could get a bite to eat. There's an excellent spot right across the way," he suggested, reddening adorably on the tops of his ears.

Shriya, clearly a sucker for young love, jumped in for the assist. "Finish your shift? What for? Go on with you, now. There's not another soul coming here before we close, and you bloody well know it. Take off early, and get your bite to eat now."

Charlie's face, glowing with the embarrassment of having asked Tia out in front of all of us, broke into a relieved smile. He nodded gratefully at Shriya and then turned back to Tia. "What do you think, then?" he asked.

I watched, elated, as Tia swallowed back five months' worth of heartache and fear. "That sounds great," she said, attempting a casual smile that dissolved into a giddy sort of grin.

"That's sorted, then," Shriya said. "Sod off, the lot of you, and leave me here alone with my new ghost friends. If this place isn't going to close after all, we may as well get chummy."

Yes, I thought, as Tia gave me an excited little wave and followed Charlie out the door. It appeared that "getting chummy" was now going to be on a few people's schedules for the afternoon.

The thought itself had just a touch of a bitter aftertaste, which I pointedly ignored. I refused to feel anything but joy for Tia in that moment because she deserved nothing less, selfish emotional impulses be damned. Besides, I knew that, if I had been the one walking out that door with a chance at happiness in my grasp, she would have felt nothing but joy for me.

13

HAPPILY EVER AFTER

"**I** CAN'T BELIEVE I let you talk me into this."

"Yes, you can," Milo replied. "I can talk anyone into anything. It's a gift. Now, hold still."

"I'm itchy."

"You'll live."

"I can't breathe."

"Neither can I."

"Milo! I'm serious!"

"Ugh, will you stop complaining? You're gorgeous."

"What's the point of being gorgeous if you can't breathe?"

"Suffer, sweetness," Milo cried dramatically. "You must suffer for your art!"

"This isn't my art!" I whined.

"Okay, fine. Suffer for *my* art, then," Milo said with a roll of his eyes. "Just hold still so Hannah can take the damn picture already. And try not to look so miserable."

I shifted slightly. "Milo, you just told me to suffer, but not be miserable. Do you even listen to yourself when you talk, or do the words just fall out of your mouth in a random order like sassy fridge poetry?"

"You know what I mean!" Milo cried, exasperated. "Models manage to suffer without looking miserable!"

I laughed, which was a mistake because it made my pose even more uncomfortable. "Milo, Mr. Fashion Designer Extraordinaire, have you ever even looked at a fashion magazine? They all look miserable. Every single one of them! All. The. Time."

"That's not misery, that's smolder. You're not smoldering enough."

I dropped my arms to my sides and sighed. "And how exactly does one 'smolder,' pray tell?"

Milo groaned. "I don't know how to explain it. It's a kind of pout, but with sexy eyes. Like this." He instantly struck a pose, pursing his lips and staring at me intensely.

I blinked, momentarily dropping my attitude in surprise. "Wow, actually, yeah. That's pretty smolder-y."

Milo flipped his hair. "I know. Now, just do what I just did."

I stuck my tongue out at him and tried again. "I feel like a jackass. An itchy jackass."

Milo cocked his head to the side and looked at me appraisingly. "Yeah, you look like one, too. Smoldering is not in your repertoire, sweetness. Just scowl a little, you're good at that."

I obliged with gusto.

Hannah snapped a few more photos quickly, then checked them on the screen, presumably to make sure I hadn't blinked. "Okay, we've got some good ones. We need to go, or we'll miss the ceremony."

I slouched and sighed with relief, immediately kicking off the high-heeled ankle boots and slipping my feet into slightly faded black suede flats. Milo raised a critical eyebrow at me. "For the car ride, okay? I'll put the torture devices back on when we get there."

"I need to get at least a few photos of you in the full outfit at the venue, so don't forget to bring them!" he demanded. "I saw that," he added, as I mimed chucking the boots into the trashcan before stowing them in a bag.

"Wait, wait, there's one more thing!" Milo said. He pointed to a stack of round boxes on the coffee table.

"What are these?" Hannah asked, picking up the top box and pulling off the cover to peek inside.

"They're fascinators," Milo said.

"What the hell are fascinators?" I asked.

Milo stared at me as though I'd just revealed to him that I didn't know what a purse was. "Are you kidding me? This is England. We're going to a ritzy wedding. Everyone will be wearing fascinators."

"Really?" Hannah asked skeptically. She pulled the fascinator out of the box and held it up. It looked like a tiny cushion of satin, with peacock feathers and puffs of tulle fabric fluttering off of it at unlikely angles. She held it up to the front of her dress, looking utterly bewildered. "Where... does it go?"

Milo looked like his head might explode. "It's a hat! It goes on your head! Am I the only one here who took copious notes during the royal wedding?"

"Yes," Hannah and I said together.

"Oi, you lot, let's get a move on, then, or all the good champagne will have disappeared down someone else's gullet," Savvy called from the front door. She was a much better sport than I was about her Milo Chang original, having gladly slipped into the jade green satin that so perfectly set off her creamy, freckled skin and red hair, which she wore in rippling waves over one shoulder like Veronica Lake—if Veronica Lake could drink your Irish uncle under the table.

"I don't think they run out of champagne at things like this," Hannah said.

"I'm not running any risks on that score, thank you," Savvy said, winking. Then she spotted the fascinator in Hannah's hands and gasped, evidently delighted. "Blimey! I've always wanted to wear one of these!" She opened another box and found the one that matched her gown. She perched it on her hair at an almost comical angle and grinned at us. "How do I look, then? Like one of the swells?"

"Like the Duchess of the House of Excessive Cleavage," I said sarcastically.

"Brilliant!" Savvy replied. "Pop 'em on, and let's go."

Hannah clipped hers dutifully onto her head, but I flat-out refused. Milo insisted on bringing the hatbox with us "in case I changed my mind," and we argued about it all the way down the stairs and out to the waiting car.

We piled into the Caomhnóir SUV that Ambrose had borrowed for the occasion, leaving the seat beside him in the front empty. He glowered at us in the rearview mirror like the babysitter from hell until he heard the click of all our seatbelts, and then pulled away from the curb and set off through the streets of London. I would have preferred to call an Uber, but was informed that all of the Caomhnóir were required to be present for vague "security purposes."

"Some of them will even be posing as waitstaff and dates," Hannah had informed me. "I guess they do that whenever there's a large event that involves Durupinen out in public like this."

As the car started and stopped in the congestion of the city traffic, Savvy, Milo, and Hannah began chatting about the final touches on the next post for Milo's Closet, but I didn't feel much like joining in, choosing instead to stare out the window and sulk like the mature adult I was.

It had been a miserable two weeks. Though I called every day for updates, there had been no change in Flavia's condition, and the Scribes had still been unable to determine what Casting had been attempted on her that had caused such appalling damage to her Spirit Sight. I had distracted myself as best I could by throwing myself whole-heartedly into the arrangements for the paranormal investigation at Pickwick's. Catriona had been unable to uncover anything unusual in the history of the building—no trace of Durupinen connections or proximity to abandoned Geatgrimas, or anything like that. It seemed likely, then, that whatever was causing the haunting was something that had been brought into the building, and so the investigation would go forward with the goal of locating whatever that object or objects might be. I was looking forward to finally getting some time inside the building without Shriya and Charlie, so that I could openly speak with the spirits there and start getting some questions answered. Yes, the investigation was a welcome distraction. This wedding, on the other hand, was a very unwelcome one.

I still wasn't entirely sure how I had been talked into attending, except that Hannah waited until I was half asleep and used lots of words like "responsibility" and "clan representation" and rounded it all off with a generous helping of guilt until I agreed just to shut her up. To be fair, I don't think she actually wanted to go either—she was too much of an introvert to enjoy big crowds, and I'm sure the idea of organized dancing probably gave her night terrors. But she had taken up the mantle of our clan's Council seat with almost obsessive enthusiasm, and she saw this wedding as a responsibility that must be upheld if she was going to be taken seriously in her new role as Council member, which she was bound and determined to be.

I, on the other hand, felt my palms begin to sweat as I ran through the litany of people I was absolutely dreading having to face, and wondering if it was possible, if I found a dark corner near the cheese display, that I might be able to avoid direct contact with most of them. Hannah had warned me that the entire Council would be there, including Celeste, whom I had seen only that once—in her office on the night of Flavia's attack—since the day she had torn the better part of my heart out of my chest.

Okay, that was a bit over-the-top, but Milo had dressed me up like a heroine in a telenovela, so I would allow myself the corresponding level of drama. The fact remained that Celeste was the reason that Finn and I were likely never to see each other again, and I didn't think I would ever be able to forgive her for that. I knew she hadn't done it to be malicious. In fact, as Hannah repeatedly tried to remind me, she had done it in the least public, least damaging way she could possibly have managed, saving our clan from yet another public bombshell of a scandal. But I couldn't force any of that information to penetrate the violent fury I'd constructed around the very thought of her. The encounter at Fairhaven had hardly been a time for discussing any of these events. We had had one urgent purpose—to uncover what had happened to Flavia. There had been no opportunity to address or even brood much upon Celeste's role in separating Finn and me. But this was a wedding, a venue made for small talk and forced social interaction. And without the barrier of a life-or-death emergency between us, amidst a sea of lovey-dovey couples twirling on the dance floor, I didn't want to have to face Celeste Morgan.

From our very first day at Fairhaven, Celeste had been an ally. She'd welcomed us when most others had turned their backs, and she did all she could to shield us from the nasty intimidation tactics of the other clans. She stood up for us in the face of the Council and had nearly always given us the benefit of the doubt. She was one of the last people within Fairhaven that I would have ever expected to strike such a blow to me, which was probably one of the reasons it hurt so profoundly.

But worse than all of that, was the fact that Celeste knew the awful, irreversible consequences our family had faced as a result of that law. That law had destroyed our mother. That law had kept our own father a stranger to us. And though many would argue stubbornly that the law would have prevented the rise of the Prophecy had it not been broken, there was a much stronger argument to be made for the fact that the law itself was the Prophecy's single greatest catalyst. And now, because Celeste chose to enforce it, that rule had torn Finn right out of my life by the roots, erasing him as though he had never been there, but for the gaping, suffocating absence of him.

So, what was I supposed to do today? Give a little bow and smile serenely as she made her rounds amongst the guests? Nod and clap along to whatever toast she offered to the bride and groom.

Not fucking likely.

And then, of course, there were the rest of the guests. I'd spent enough time at Fairhaven now to be on fairly friendly terms with many of the clans, but the glaring exception was Clan Gonachd, which I was sure would be prominently and abundantly represented. Patricia Lightfoot was very good friends with Marion Worthington, whose attempted coup over our former High Priestess had led to her expulsion from the Council. Marion had schemed against us from the moment we set foot in Fairhaven, and though she had fallen from grace and Hannah now occupied her Council seat, I was not foolish enough to believe she was no longer a danger to us.

And then there was Marion's daughter, Peyton. Blessed with the same charm and warmth as her mother, Peyton had done all she could to make our lives hell during our first few months at Fairhaven, including one particularly memorable evening when she kidnapped us and left us to the mercy of the Elemental. Peyton, and her cousin Olivia, were two of Róisín Lightfoot's best friends, which meant their entire pack of fem-bots would be in attendance.

And finally, as if all of this wouldn't be awkward and miserable enough, Olivia just happened to be Finn's sister. I had no idea if they were in touch with Finn, or how much they suspected, if anything, about our relationship.

In conclusion, I could think of several forms of torture that I would prefer over the cruel and unusual punishment that would surely await me at Róisín Lightfoot's wedding.

"You look nervous."

Milo's voice thrummed through our connection, startling me. I turned to see him frowning at me in an uncharacteristically serious way.

"Do I?"

"You know you do," Milo said. "As badly as you suck at having feelings, you suck even worse at hiding them."

"Not as badly as you suck at cheering people up," I told him.

He sighed. "Look, I'm sorry I made you wear the dress. And the shoes."

"And the torture bra?"

"And the torture bra," Milo amended. "I just wanted you to look fabulous."

"I'm not upset about the torture bra. Or any of the rest of it," I told him, still silently.

"You're not?"

"Nope. Well, not at the moment, anyway. It might be a different story after I wear the shoes for four hours."

"So, what's up, then?" Milo asked.

I only hesitated a moment. Gone were the glorious days when Milo and I could pretend our bond was constructed entirely of snark. Now, he was as much a confidante and friend as he was a pain in my ass. Maybe even more.

"I'm really dreading seeing... well, basically everyone at this wedding, but most of all, Finn's family," I admitted.

Milo sighed. "Oh, my God. I am such a jerk. I didn't even think... I mean, I should have realized right away, but..."

"It's okay," I said.

"No, it's not," Milo said. "I'm supposed to be the Spirit Guide, and I haven't done much guiding lately. The whole red carpet thing has kind of gone to my head."

"This wasn't supposed to be a criticism of you, Milo," I said. "I know how excited you are about your line. We all are."

"I know, I know, but that's not the most important thing right now," Milo said. "You have been going through some serious shit and I haven't been helping at all. I'm sorry, sweetness."

I managed a small smile. "It's okay. You have to screw up once in a while, so I have something to hold over your head."

"Happy to oblige," Milo said, smiling back. "So, talk to me, then. I mean, if you want to. Or not. Does Hannah know how nervous you are?"

"She knows I don't want to go," I said. "But she's got Council stuff to worry about. It's important for her to be there, I know that."

"She could go without you," Milo pointed out.

"Sure, and spend the whole night fielding questions about where I was and why I hadn't come," I said. "I didn't want to do that to her. This is the first major social event they've held since she became a Council member. I didn't want to screw it up for her."

"Okay, so you haven't really talked to her about it. So, talk to me," Milo said. "What's got you worried?"

I sighed. "What if they know?"

"Know what?"

"What if they know that I'm the reason Finn was sent away? What if they hate me for it?"

Milo considered this. "Well... and this isn't me being sassy, I promise, but... they already hate you, don't they?"

I almost laughed out loud, but stopped myself. "Yeah, I guess so."

"So, then... what's the problem, exactly?"

"What if someone makes a scene about it? What if one of them confronts me?"

Milo looked skeptical. "Is that likely? I mean, this is a huge social event, and these people are all about keeping up appearances. I'd be really surprised if any of them caused a scene with the entire Council there. Not to mention all of the guests on the groom's side, who don't know about the Durupinen. Plus, Finn's reassignment is as much of a potential scandal for Clan Gonachd as it is for you. They aren't going to want to draw unnecessary attention to it, not if they can help it. The whole clan is trying to save face anyway, after all the shit that Marion pulled."

I felt one of the knots in my stomach loosen slightly at this burst of logic. "That's... true."

"And anyway, Finn distanced himself from them. He didn't want to be associated with Marion or any of his clan, really. I don't think he'd be confiding in any of them about what happened, do you?"

"No, I don't," I said. "But that doesn't mean they couldn't still find out what happened."

"True, but whatever they found out would be speculation. I know you're pissed at Celeste—I am too, believe me—but I don't think she'd ever tell anyone why Finn was reassigned. I mean, that was kind of the whole point, wasn't it? She was trying to stop people from finding out about you two."

"I know, I just... I'm not looking forward to spending the night in a room full of people who despise me as much as I despise them," I said. My voice inside the connection vibrated with a sadness that surprised even me.

"Well, there is one good thing about it," Milo said, a laugh in his voice.

"Oh really?" I asked skeptically. "And what's that?"

"If there's one thing a roomful of catty women hate, it's one of their enemies showing up looking fabulous," Milo said. I looked up at him to see him winking. "And sweetness, thanks to yours truly, you look utterly beyond fabulous."

I felt my lips twitching into a smile in spite of myself. "You really think so? Think they'll hate it?"

"Oh, honey, they will loathe it. Cross my non-corporeal little heart," And he drew a long, slender finger over the specter of his chest, now grinning broadly.

I laughed, out loud this time.

Hannah and Savvy both turned. "What's so funny?" Hannah asked, eyes narrowed, looking back and forth between Milo and me. "What are you two up to over there?"

"Nothing," Milo and I said together.

§

An hour later we pulled up to the sprawling manor house where the wedding was being held. I gasped at the sight of it as we rounded the bend in the drive. Well, I would have gasped, if I could have drawn enough breath in that straightjacket of a dress. It was like pulling onto the set of a lavishly produced Jane Austen mini-series. The house loomed over perfectly manicured lawns and gardens, four floors of stately stonework and softly glowing windows. There were even white-gloved servants opening car doors for guests as their cars crunched to a stop on the gravel in front of the massive front doors. I sighed and slipped Milo's chosen shoes back onto my already protesting feet.

In an effort to blend in with the other wedding guests, the Caomhnóir in attendance were all dressed in tuxes rather than their traditional uniforms and boots. Ambrose looked as horribly uncomfortable in his tux as I felt in my dress, which lessened my misery just a bit. I watched with a smirk on my face as he inserted a finger under his collar, tugging and grumbling to himself. He caught my eye and glared at me before dropping the car keys in the valet's hands and stalking off toward the front doors.

Ambrose wasn't the only one uncomfortable with the surroundings. As I joined Hannah, Savvy, and Milo in front of the entrance, I noticed Savvy staring up at the grand façade of the building with definite trepidation. All her usual swagger seemed to have drained out of her.

"What's up, Sav?" I asked her.

She looked over at me, and tried to grin, but her facial muscles wouldn't cooperate. She leaned over and whispered. "Blimey, I knew they had money, but I didn't realize it was going to be so..." She gestured helplessly at the building, unable to retrieve the right word. I tried to help.

"Grand? Over-the-top? Aristocratic?"

"Yeah, all of that," Savvy said. "It's a bit much for a girl from the East End."

"I didn't think there was anything that was a bit much for you, Sav," I said, nudging her with my elbow. "Usually you're the one who's a bit much for everyone else."

Savvy winked. "Truer words were never spoken. Still..." She glanced up again.

"Savvy, listen to me," I said, taking her by the shoulders and turning her fully around to face me. Her feathers danced around on her head. "I'm going to be honest with you. I'm barely convincing myself to walk through those doors. There's a good chance I'm going to hide under the first tablecloth I find. I don't know if I can do this. So, I'm going to need every ounce of your too-muchness, do you hear me? I need your too-muchness to overflow and fill me up, too, because I honestly can't do this without you."

Savvy blinked once, as though shocked, then slowly, a grin spread over her face. Her cheeks flushed and her eyes sparkled with more than just her quintessential impishness.

"For you, mate, I will be the very Savviest of Savvies," she said, clapping me on the back so that I stumbled forward.

"I knew I could count on you," I told her. "Now, let's get this over with."

We followed a group of chattering young women in evening gowns into a cavernous grand foyer. A grand staircase swept down into the room, its elaborate railings and wide landings festooned with garlands of white blossoms. Over our heads, glittering crystal chandeliers hung suspended from the gold-gilded ceiling, and elegantly clad people strolled the balconies, the light glinting off of their champagne flutes and opulent jewelry. We'd barely cleared the threshold of the door when two waiters descended upon us, thrusting glasses of champagne into our hands.

"Drinking before the ceremony has even begun," Savvy said with a sigh of satisfaction. "I take it all back. This is my kind of party, after all."

I didn't reply, but took a sip of champagne instead. The bubbles leapt at my nose, tickling the tip and leaving their heady fragrance lingering in my nostrils. It wasn't unpleasant.

"What did I tell you about the fascinators!" Milo hissed at me, stamping his foot in frustration. "I told you you should have worn it! Everyone's wearing them!"

"I wasn't going to wear that stupid thing on my head!" I grumbled back at him. "It looked like a bird's nest!"

A bird's nest that would have blended right into a sea of unusual headwear, it seemed. Everywhere I looked, feathers and tulle sprouted from heads like plants out of a garden.

"Come on," Milo whined. "It's right in the car, we can still go and get it..."

"No!"

A flock of women scurried past us, laughs tinkling like expensive cutlery. I didn't recognize any of them. Each of them wore an almost bored expression, as though they regularly circulated in atmospheres of such lavishness.

"The Lightfoots... they don't actually live here, do they?" Milo whispered to us as he took it all in.

"No," Hannah said, and she almost sounded relieved. "It used to be a private home to a Lord or an Earl, but nobody lives here anymore. It's open for tours, and you can rent it for events, if you have enough money."

"Yeah, and you could probably let our flat for the next five years for what it cost them to use the place for a single night," I pointed out.

The crowd seemed to be slowly making its way through to a room at the far end of the entrance hall. The doors had been thrown wide and a pair of young girls, no older than ten or twelve, by the look of them, were handing out silver-tasseled program booklets from the baskets that dangled on their arms.

"Here's a wedding program for you, bride's side on the left, please," the girl said, beaming toothily up at me.

I smiled at her, wondering, as I did so, how she knew whether we were there for the bride or the groom. Then I saw her give half a glance and a slight nod to Milo, and it dawned on me: this girl was a future Durupinen, probably a relation of Róisín's, and so the presence of a ghost in our party was a dead giveaway—pun intended.

We filed into seats near the back of the room—Hannah wanted to sit closer to the front, because she saw a number of other Council members seated there, but I dragged her toward the back, preferring to skulk as much as was possible in such public circumstances. I tried not to gawk at the opulence of the space, but failed that particular challenge. My mouth hung open as I marveled over the arched windows, the painted frescos, and the flower-draped canopy under which Róisín and her fiancé would shortly tie the knot. As I turned to take my seat, I caught a glimpse of myself in the mirrored panel on the back wall and experienced a moment of shock.

I hadn't bothered to pay much attention when Milo and Savvy were experimenting on me like a make-up lab rat—preferring to close my eyes and go to my happy place—and so I hadn't experienced the full effect of my new look until that very moment. I looked... well, pretty damn glamorous, minus the dumbfounded expression on my face. My hair had definitely never looked so silky or my curls so tamed. Milo had Savvy do something to my face called contouring, which I didn't understand but, from the look of it, was a form of black magic performed with foundation that gave you someone else's face. And while I still hated the torture bra and the shoes for the little sartorial sadists they were, I had to grudgingly admit, Milo was right: I looked damn good.

Slowly, the room filled up with guests, all murmuring quietly to each other behind their programs, waiting for the ceremony to begin. We saw Siobhán walk in, accompanied by a woman I didn't know, but who looked so much like her that I knew it must be her sister. Close behind her, Seamus on her arm, was Celeste. She swept the room with her eyes, nodding graciously at the many guests who sought to greet her. As she turned to shake hands with an older woman, her eyes drifted over the heads of the assembled guests and landed on me.

I froze. So did she. I might have imagined it, because I was so hyper-sensitive to seeing her, but I could have sworn that Celeste's cheeks flushed slightly as she blinked and looked away. There was no doubt how quickly she broke eye contact, or that she pointedly avoided looking in our direction again. So maybe there was a bit of guilt there, after all. I squeezed a tiny drop of pleasure from that possibility and chased it with another sip of champagne.

Somewhere in one of the balconies above us, a string quartet began to play, and the remaining guests who were still milling around took it as a cue to hurry into their seats. The doors at the back of the hall had been pulled closed, and six men in tuxedos with tails walked in a line from a side door up onto the platform at the front of the room. The man at the front was tall and handsome, though with a definite air of snobbery that I could scent even from the back row. He looked down his nose at the crowd, a satisfied smile on his face as though he was being presented with some kind of prize.

I supposed, depending on how you looked at the whole marriage thing, he was.

The music swelled, and the doors at the back of the room opened. A woman in an elegant blue suit and matching fascinator was escorted up the aisle first—I could only assume it was the groom's mother. Next, Patricia Lightfoot, all smiles and nods, swept up the aisle on the arm of a barrel-chested young man I thought might be a Caomhnóir. Behind her, a pair of dark-haired girls, no more than five or six years old, floated past in dresses that looked like puffy little clouds, dropping fistfuls of bruised flower petals along the pale pink runner that covered the floor. Then a parade of bridesmaids processed past in blush-colored dresses, clutching their bouquets and smiling ingratiatingly at the upturned faces. I recognized every one of them from my Apprenticeship days at Fairhaven, including Olivia and Peyton.

The last of the bridesmaids to saunter up the aisle was Róisín's twin sister Riley, whose dress was a deeper shade of pink than the others. As she took her place at the corner of the canopy, all heads turned to the back of the room once more, where, to the sweeping melody of the quartet, Róisín appeared framed in the doorway.

A collective gasp rose up, and it was plain to see why. Róisín, a very pretty girl on a normal day, was a flawlessly airbrushed bridal magazine advertisement come to blushing, beaming life. The delicate lace of her dress clung to her body like a second skin and trailed out behind her in a long, sweeping train. Her inky curls were frosted over with a lace-edged veil that brushed her bare shoulders and cascaded to the floor behind her. She clutched the arm of a rather diminutive man with a black goatee and a reserved expression, whom I could only assume was her father.

Her form dissipated into a blur as tears filled my eyes and refused to be blinked away. They were tears that I would not properly be able to explain to myself in that or any moment, born of grief and longing, of fear and jealousy for things I had never wanted and yet somehow wanted desperately, all crashing together inside of me in a storm I was not sure I could weather. I took my seat, tears still falling, smiling politely on the outside as, on the inside, I battled the very real possibility that I would simply wreck and sink into the depths.

14

STOLEN MOMENT

"**Y**OU RECKON I COULD FIT this whole cheese display in my purse?" Savvy asked, with every indication that she intended to try, regardless of my answer.

"Not unless your purse is secretly the TARDIS," I told her.

She snorted appreciatively and loaded up her plate again. "Listen to you, dropping Doctor Who references like a proper Brit. Blimey, they could at least make these plates a bit bigger. I mean, bloody hell, I'll have to make twenty trips up to this table before they bring out the salad."

I snatched a piece of puff pastry off a passing tray and popped it into my mouth. It was full of melted brie and some kind of jam. I watched longingly as the tray bobbed away through the crowd, strongly considering tackling the waiter carrying it.

"Yeah, this food is incredible," I agreed. "Should we find our table so people can bring us more of it?" I was feeling antsy, lest someone mistake our standing around as an invitation for mingling or—God forbid—dancing.

I scanned the crowd as we walked, looking for the peacock feather on the top of Hannah's head. I spotted her near a grand piano, nodding earnestly along to whatever Siobhán was saying to a small knot of listeners. She looked so poised and professional, such a far cry from the girl I met four years ago—a girl so battered and bruised by her gift that she had endeavored to make herself all but invisible. Everything—*everything* we had been through up until this point was worth it just to see her grow and bloom even from the very ashes.

"You know what's weird?" I said.

"Reckon I know plenty things that are weird," Savvy replied.

"I haven't seen Marion anywhere, have you?" I asked.

Savvy froze mid-bite as this realization hit her. I watched as her eyes raked the sea of chattering faces, watched as she, too, came up empty.

"Huh," Savvy said and gave a large swallow. "What do you suppose that's about, then?"

"I have no idea," I said slowly. "I figured this would be exactly the kind of event she'd love to be at. Seated prominently, so she could lord it over people."

"Yeah, me too," Savvy agreed. "You reckon she wasn't invited?"

I shook my head. "No way. Peyton's a bridesmaid. Patricia is Marion's best friend. There's no way she wasn't invited."

"Huh," Savvy said again. "Well, I'm stumped."

So was I. It just seemed inconceivable that Marion wouldn't be present. As unpleasant as it would have been to see her, it gave me a jumpy, nervous feeling *not* to see her, like she was absent only so she could appear suddenly. I half-expected her to jump out of the wedding cake, dripping from head to toe with frosting and smugness.

My eyes wandered from the wedding cake to Róisín, who was floating around the middle of the dance floor with her new husband like a feather on the breeze. They looked like a Hallmark commercial, gazing sappily into each other's eyes and kissing repeatedly as the photographer bobbed and weaved around them, clicking and flashing madly for the perfect timeless image.

"I'm about to go into sugar shock over here," Savvy said, as though reading my mind.

"Yeah. The schmaltz levels are reaching maximum capacity," I agreed. "I'm kind of glad, though. Like, at least they look genuinely in love with each other. I had my doubts, because of the whole Scouting thing, but..." I shrugged.

"Yeah. I dunno, I might give it a try myself," Savvy said thoughtfully, popping an olive into her mouth.

I nearly choked on a cheese puff. "You want to *what?!*" I sputtered.

Savvy shrugged. "I dunno, mate. Have you seen the men I date?"

"Not often, no," I said. "You don't usually... well, they don't last long, do they?" I said awkwardly.

"Too right they don't," Savvy agreed. "If London were a barrel, I'd be scraping the dried-up dregs from the bottom and trying to mold them into a half-decent bloke."

"Yeah, well, wandering into pubs at one o'clock yields a lot of dregs," I said. "Why don't you try a dating app or something, if you want to meet someone?"

Savvy glared at me as though I'd said something offensive. "Not bloody likely. I like to see the goods before I sample them, thanks very much."

"Well, I'd trust my cell phone before I trusted Scouting," I said.

"Yeah, maybe you're right. 'Sides, I don't reckon anyone on their eligible bachelors list is any match for Savannah Todd, even on her best behavior," Savvy said, suppressing a burp and cracking her knuckles loudly. "Fancy a drink?"

"No, I'm good," I said.

"See you in a bit, then," she replied, and marched straight for the bar, where a small knot of men fell over themselves scattering to make room for her.

I watched her for a moment, chuckling as she knocked back a whiskey like it was water, and then turned, meaning to fill my plate again. My elbow caught someone's shoulder and I dropped my plate to the floor with a resounding clatter.

"Oh, shit," I muttered, stooping quickly to pick it up and straightening again. "I'm so sorry about—"

It was Peyton, with three other bridesmaids all trailing behind her like a flock of sour-faced flamingos. Olivia was among them as well, though she was looking determinedly at her shoes.

"—about that," I finished in a murmur. The crash of my plate seemed to reverberate four years into that past to the very first time I'd interacted with Peyton Worthington—also, coincidentally, in front of a food display.

"Watch where you're go—oh!" Her expression morphed from annoyance to shock as she met my gaze. It was clear that she hadn't recognized me until that moment. She took me in from head to toe, her mouth agape in unflattering disbelief.

"Jessica, I... I didn't recognize you," she gasped.

"Uh, yeah. Milo did it," I said awkwardly, my hand flicking in Milo's general direction where he hovered near the dance floor, basking in the glow of expensive fabrics on display. I couldn't be sure whether he'd heard his name or simply felt the surge of my nervous energy through our connection, but his head snapped up like a shark scenting blood. He appeared at my side before I could even register his disappearance from the dance floor.

"I felt a compliment coming on, so I came to take full credit,"

Milo said tossing a protective arm around me, calming my nerves with a wave of cool, unruffled energy.

Peyton blinked and recovered herself, hoisting an ingratiating smile onto her face. "Yes, well, kudos to you, Milo. You truly are a miracle worker."

I swallowed a nasty retort. It did not go down easily. I forced a smile. "Yes, he's very talented. Róisín told me that you got married last summer. Congratulations."

Peyton's smile widened, and she shrugged. "Thank you. It's been an—um—*eventful* year." She dropped her hands to rest on her abdomen and I saw, with a start of surprise, something I had not noticed when she had glided down the aisle, for her elaborate cluster of hydrangeas had concealed it. Beneath the delicate swath of peachy-pink fabric of her dress, a tell-tale curve and swelling of her belly—

"Holy shit!" I said again, and then pulled myself together. "I... wow, I... had no idea... uh, congratulations... again," I stammered.

She looked deeply satisfied, as though we were looking at each other across a chess board and she had just achieved a checkmate. Behind her, the other girls were mirror images of her smug expression—all but Olivia, who was still looking anywhere but at me. "How kind of you," she fluttered, then went on with a note of steel in her voice. "I must say, I'm surprised that you had the nerve to show up here today, but impressed as well. I'm glad you're able to enjoy this moment for the brief victory it is. Your clan had been wallowing in disgrace for so long, after all. But the tide of politics is fleeting. It ebbs and flows, and it can bury you in an instant. You mustn't get too comfortable."

I felt my smile turn to stone on my face, and had to grit my teeth to get my response out. "That sounds like advice your mother could have used a few months ago. You really ought to be saving some of these pearls of wisdom for her, you know. Then she might be able to show her face at some of these functions."

"Oh, yeah, about that," Milo said, chiming in with a simpering smile on his face. "Word on the dance floor is that Patricia asked your mother not to come, as a favor to Róisín. Seems like Patricia was afraid that your mother's propensity for scandal might upstage the bride."

I feigned a devastated expression. "Damn. And I was saving my first slow dance for her. Guess I'll have to clear my dance card."

Peyton's face had gone pink with humiliation. "My mother plays the long game, Jessica," she said in a dangerously quiet hiss. "Do you honestly believe that knocking a few stones from the top of the tower will have a lasting effect on the foundations our clan has built? How very droll."

She took a step closer to me. I did not back away.

"Our clan is old. It is strong. We look to the past and the future, and we shape our own destiny. Each of us knows what she must do to maintain our legacy, our power, and our longevity in the Durupinen world. This stunt you and your sister have pulled is just that: a stunt, quickly forgotten in the long march of power for which you have neither the stamina nor the ambition. Enjoy yourself. Have some champagne. You may even be able to scrounge someone up to dance with you while you look like that. And remember it all, when you look back at it from the gutters where you belong."

And placing a hand imperiously upon her belly, she lifted her chin into the air and strode away, the girls behind her all but holding up her skirt for her.

I stood for a moment, speechless, staring after her. Then Milo leaned in and whispered to me. "It's nice to know we can all mature and leave the petty disagreements of girlhood behind us, isn't it?"

I actually managed a laugh, though it wavered a bit. "Yeah, she's matured so nicely, that one. And to think we used to dislike each other."

Milo snorted then narrowed his eyes at me, I could feel him probing into the connection, assessing the moods and flashes he found there. "You okay?"

"Peachy."

"Mm-hmm," he said, popping an eyebrow like a champagne cork and pursing his lips at me.

Peyton sat beside a man I could only assume was her husband. He was at least ten years older than her, and he had clearly had too much to drink. He was laughing raucously with the man sitting on his other side, sharing in what I imagined, for my own satisfaction, was a crude joke. Her own flute of champagne stood untouched, naturally, until her husband reached across her, snatched it up, and drained it in a single gulp. A brief shadow passed over her face as she watched him do this, then she turned away and leaned across to another bridesmaid, who was already chattering away to her.

"She's just going to sacrifice herself to this, isn't she?" I said aloud, though more to myself than to Milo.

"Who? Peyton?" Milo asked.

"Yeah."

"Sacrifice herself to what?" Milo asked.

"To this," I said, gesturing around. "To the family name. To the right house in the right neighborhood. To the husband with the best resume, and the race to produce the next Gateway. It's horrifying."

"Yeah, well she's pretty horrifying. Maybe this really is what she wants," Milo suggested without any real conviction.

"She's never given a single goddamn thought to what she wants. Not really," I murmured. "It was eyes on the prize since she was old enough to walk. I mean, my God, imagine growing up with Marion for a mother."

"I'd rather not, thank you," Milo said.

"And now Peyton's just turning into her. Treating a baby like some kind of trophy instead of an impending human being. Imagine having to live as that kid when they find out she doesn't have the Gift. Or even worse, imagine having to live as that kid when they find out she *does* have it. From rosy-cheeked baby to pawn in the political game, just like that." I snapped my fingers.

Milo let out a low whistle. "And I thought my family was bad."

"She thinks everyone in this room envies her, but actually... I don't think I've ever felt sorrier for anyone in my entire life," I said.

Hannah appeared at my side, looking anxious. "Are you okay? I saw Peyton talking to you. She looked... well, like Peyton."

I laughed again, and was glad to hear that the tremble had gone out of it. "Oh, it was a delightful little chat. She's a charmer, as you know."

"I'm sorry I wasn't here with you," Hannah said, biting at her lip guiltily.

"No worries," I told her. "You had schmoozing to do. Besides, Milo scented the drama a mile away, and swooped in to save me."

"It's true, my drama-sensors are on constant high alert," Milo agreed.

"What... did she say?" Hannah asked. It couldn't have been plainer from her expression that she didn't really want to know, so I decided to gloss the whole thing over. After all, my skin was fake, my hair was fake, my cleavage was fake—half the people in this room were only pretending to enjoy each other's company. So, I smiled right along with them.

Just get through the night, Jess.

"Nothing," I told Hannah, shrugging dismissively. "Honestly, nothing worth a second more of your time or mine." I stuck out my arm and within seconds the passing waiter had thrust a glass of something into my hand. "Cheers," I said, and knocked it back.

Hannah frowned. "You don't usually drink much," she said. "Are you sure you're okay?"

"I will be once I stuff my face full of five courses of dinner," I assured her.

"Luckily, I think they're starting to serve dinner, now; look," Hannah said, pointing to the head table, where the bridal party were taking their seats. A line of waiters stood along the wall nearby, trays perched on white-gloved hands, ready to serve small plates of salad. I recognized Bertie, Savvy's Caomhnóir, among them. I watched as he readjusted his tray precariously so that he could wave to her as she strode across the room from the bar. She threw him one disgusted look and stalked toward us, looking bad-tempered.

"They put Bertie on kitchen duty, huh?" I asked, smirking at her as we made our way to our table.

She rolled her eyes. "Of course they bloody did. What else could they do with him? No one would believe he was security, and I sure as shit wasn't going to hang off his arm and pretend to dance with him. And even at this he's bloody useless. He's supposed to be undercover, so what the buggery bollocks is he doing waving at me, the great prat."

We made our way to table number nine, which was located near the fireplace and which bore our name cards. I'd half expected to be seated at a table crammed into a broom closet, but Hannah's recently elevated rank had evidently been enough to earn us seats near the dance floor. A quick scan of the tables revealed that Celeste was sitting on the opposite side of the room. I heaved a sigh of relief, before lapsing into silence with everyone else as Riley stood up and gushed her way through her maid-of-honor speech. At long last, after much toasting and polite clapping, the waiters began circulating amongst the tables.

I was gazing around the room, people watching, when my salad arrived, so I could not say for sure how the note got under it, but as I looked down in anticipation of spring greens and a fancy vinaigrette, there it was: a piece of paper wedged beneath the edge of my plate. I stared at it curiously for a moment, then looked around for our waiter, who had already vanished from the vicinity and could easily have been any one of a dozen now striding amongst the other tables.

For reasons I could not quite explain to myself, my heart began to hammer. Fingers trembling slightly, and looking around to make sure no one was watching me, I eased the paper out from beneath the china and transferred it to my lap. Then, under cover of unfolding my napkin and arranging it in my lap, I looked down and read the words scrawled upon the paper.

Come to the powder room in the entrance hall.
Come now, alone.
Please.

I closed my hand over the note, crumpling it into a tight ball. The palm in which it was clutched was beginning to sweat. I stared around the room again, searching in vain for an answering stare, a nod, any signal that might clue me in as to who had sent me the message. I picked up my fork, speared a cucumber, and put it in my mouth, thinking furiously.

I did not recognize the handwriting on the note and had no idea who sent it. As I saw it, I had two options. I knew how to find the powder room referenced in the message—I had waited outside it for Savvy between the ceremony and the reception. I could excuse myself, go to the powder room, and find out what this was all about. There were at least a dozen people in this room that I did not trust, but I couldn't see how the situation could be dangerous. The mansion was swarming with Caomhnóir and Milo was a single silent summons away. My other option was to ignore the message and eat my food. What could be so secretive or urgent that anyone in this room couldn't just approach me themselves?

What, indeed. Okay, there was really only one option.

Maybe it was the uncharacteristically large amount of alcohol in my bloodstream, but I was feeling bold and maybe even a little reckless. I stood up, placing my napkin on the table and grabbing for my clutch.

"Ladies room," I told Hannah when she looked up at me inquiringly.

"Do you want me to come—" she began, but I waved her off.

"No, no, eat your salad," I said. "I'll be right back."

I kept to the perimeter of the room, hoping to be noticed by as few people as possible. Luckily the long-awaited arrival of the food was as good a distraction as I could have hoped for. I opened up my clutch and pretended to be digging around in it as I walked; hopefully anyone who saw me would think I was simply going to touch up my lipstick or some bullshit like that.

The lobby was nearly empty, with the exception of two passing waiters and a young woman having a loud, tearful argument via cell phone in the shadow of the grand staircase. The doors into the grounds were opened wide, and I could see two Caomhnóir stationed beside them, staring stone-faced and motionless out into the twilight, like Buckingham Palace guards, but without the impressive hats.

I crossed the room casually, still digging in my purse to avoid eye contact with anyone, and eased open the door beneath an elegantly scripted sign that read "Powder Room."

My first frantic thought was that I had walked into the wrong place, despite the clearly labeled door. The room in which I found myself was not a bathroom, but some kind of elaborate parlor, full of settees and end tables and presided over by a massive crystal chandelier. I spun on the spot and stifled a scream at the sudden appearance of a woman on the far side of the room, then cursed my own stupidity as I realized it was merely my own reflection in a full-length mirror. The room was full of them, I realized now, for the purposes of primping and reapplying. As I looked at my own wide-eyed reflection, the sudden appearance of another figure just behind me sent my heart into my mouth for the second time in half a minute.

"Olivia!" I gasped. "You... uh... surprised me," I said, with a failed attempt at a smile. "Sorry, I should be better at handling sudden appearances at this point in my life."

Olivia barely seemed to register my babbling. She was scanning the room nervously. "Did you come alone?" she asked.

I stared at her, hardly able to believe my ears. "Did I...?"

"I said, did you come alone?" Olivia snapped, ducking into the adjoining room and checking under all of the bathroom stalls for feet.

"I... yeah," I said. This didn't make sense. What the hell would

Olivia want to see me for? Was this her way of confronting me without making a scene? "So you sent me that note?"

She looked at me, her face completely unreadable. "Yes."

"And have you arranged this little rendezvous to verbally assault me on behalf of Clan Gonachd? Because if you have, I should remind you that Peyton and I already had a delightful chat. So, if you're worried that I don't already know exactly how much your whole clan despises me, I assure you, I do," I said.

Olivia just stared at me, as though unsure of what she should say or do next.

I snorted and turned for the door. "Right, well, if that's it, I'm just going to head back to the—"

"Our whole clan doesn't despise you," Olivia hissed.

I spun around. "I'm sorry?"

She bit her lip and looked down at the floor, where the hem of her gown skimmed the polished floorboards with a soft swishing sound. "We... we don't all hate you."

"You've got a really funny way of showing it," I said.

Olivia wrung her hands together, glancing nervously at the door again. "It's complicated. Look, delving into all of that... that's not why I asked you here, and there's no time, anyway. I need you to... to come with me."

I stared again. "Come with you where?"

"Upstairs."

"And why the hell would I do that?" I asked. "The last time I went somewhere with you, I was blindfolded and left in the woods to be tortured."

"I know... I'm... I'm really sorry about that, now," Olivia said, bouncing on the balls of her feet, twisting her hands together agitatedly. "But times change... people change. Things aren't the way they were, and... and anyway this isn't about me. I just need you to come with me. Please."

Something in her expression gave me pause. "I can call my Spirit Guide and have him here in a second," I warned her.

"I know. Please, we don't have much time," she said.

I hesitated just one more moment. I must have lost my goddamned mind. "Okay. Let's go."

She sighed with relief and turned without another word toward the adjoining room with the bathroom stalls. But instead of entering one of them, she turned the corner and pressed on a panel in the wall. It sprang open with a creak, revealing a narrow, tightly spiraled staircase.

"Servant's staircase," she whispered in reply to my wary look. "Follow me. And take your shoes off. They'll make too much noise." She was already sliding her feet out of hers.

I followed her up the staircase, careful to keep my feet clear of the trailing hem of her gown, and silently rejoicing at every step that I was temporarily free of my torturous footwear. At last we arrived on a narrow landing. I struggled to catch my breath while Olivia eased the door open and peered around it. I stole a glance out of the narrow window in the wall beside it. We were three floors up from the ground now.

"It's all clear, come on. Quickly, now," Olivia said, and slipped out into the corridor beyond.

We emerged into a hallway that seemed to belong to another house altogether. The carpets were faded, the walls were dark paneled and dull. The light fixtures were dusty and the doors that led off the hallway were set with dull brass plates and knobs.

"These are the servants' quarters," Olivia whispered, in answer to my evident confusion. "At least, they were, when this house had a full-time live-in staff."

"Olivia, what are we doing up here?" I whispered.

"You'll see in a moment. Just hurry up," she replied over her shoulder as she set off down the hallway.

We crept along until we arrived in front of a door at the very end of the hallway that said, "Footman's quarters." Olivia turned to face me. Her cheeks were flushed.

"Go ahead in. I'll wait out here for you. We only have a few minutes."

"Olivia, what in the hell—"

"Just go, will you?! You're wasting time!" she cried, looking quite desperate.

Too alarmed to argue with her, I turned the knob and pushed the door open. The room beyond was dark and musty; the only light was that of the dying sun, which spilled in a golden orange patch through an arched window set up in the eaves.

I peered around the gloom, afraid to step forward, unsure of what was waiting for me. Every Durupinen sense I had was on high alert for the presence of a spirit. This was exactly the kind of room that should be haunted; the clatter and murmurs of living people felt as distant up here as though they were echoing up from another world altogether. It was no surprise, then, that when he stepped forward out of the shadows of the far corner, I was sure he was a spirit. I tensed, defenses on high alert, ready to fly or to fight. Then he spoke.

"Jess."

My heart stopped. *I knew that voice. Oh God, I knew that voice.*

"Jess, it's okay."

The question that escaped me was more of a sob than a whisper. I didn't dare trust myself, in my half-mad longing to see him again, to hear that voice again.

"Finn? Is that you?"

In answer, he took another step out of the corner, so that the fiery light splashed across his features, throwing into sharp relief every feature I so longed to see—his broad shoulders; his square jaw, clenched tight with emotion; the sweep of his hair tucked behind his ears where it had escaped his ponytail. And his eyes, alight with every fierce thing that was threatening to overwhelm me.

"Don't be frightened. It's only me," he said, his voice low and hoarse.

A sound escaped me, a wild half-laughing sob. "Only you? *Only you?*"

I dropped my shoes to the floor and stumbled forward just as he strode forward, closing the last of that terrible distance between us. I flung myself into his arms, arms that enveloped me, lifted me from the ground as though I were nothing, and enfolded me. He let out a ragged gasp into my hair. I reached up with both trembling hands and found his face, running my fingers over it as though I could memorize every plane of it with my hands, burn it into my fingertips so that I could trace him into existence whenever I wanted. His eyes fluttered closed at my touch, as though he were memorizing the feel of me in return. Then he reached down and pressed his lips to mine.

It was dizzying—the longing, the shock, the taste of passion and salty tears, all tangled up together in this one, stolen moment in the fiery light of the dying sun.

"I'm sorry. I'm so sorry," he whispered against my lips.

"Don't," I breathed, kissing him again.

He pulled away just enough to speak, our lips still touching.

"But it was my fault. The notebook. I'm such a bloody fool," he murmured. "How could I have been so—"

"It's not your fault. They found the sketch, too. The one I did of you in the Traveler wagon," I told him. "Wasn't it only a matter of time?"

"I suppose. But I'm just so sorry—"

"Don't you dare apologize to me," I told him, pulling back enough to look into his eyes. "Don't you apologize for loving me. I don't want to hear those words come out of your mouth. Ever. I'm the one who should be apologizing to you."

"You? Apologize? But whatever for?" Finn asked.

"They sent you to that *príosún* in the middle of nowhere!" I whispered. "Fiona saw you there, and she told me," I added in answer to the question in his eyes. "You're practically in exile, and here I am living in London, free to do what I want. You must despise me."

He grabbed my chin between his thumb and forefinger and forced it up so that I had no choice but to stare into his eyes. "I could never despise you. Never. Remove that thought from your head. It is an impossibility."

I gasped in relief and kissed him again. "I miss you."

"I miss you. So much. I'm ashamed to say I didn't even realize how bad it would be. How consuming," he said.

"But how? How did you do this? How did you get here?" I asked.

"With so many Durupinen in one place for this wedding, they needed all hands on deck for security. I volunteered, hoping there might be the slightest chance you would be here. Then I enlisted Olivia's help."

"But why in the world would Olivia want to help us?" I asked. "I mean, I know she's your sister, but..." I let the end of the sentence trail away. I didn't know what to think anymore.

"Olivia has been a fool, there's no denying that. She's been swallowing our clan's poisonous thinking for years. Hell, I swallowed it for years, until I met you." He paused, leaning forward to plant a gentle kiss on each of my eyelids. I shivered. "But recent events have really opened her eyes. She watched Marion's machinations collapse, watched as it nearly destroyed everything. She was there when the Necromancers descended upon the castle. And she has had to endure the days since—our diminished status, the censure, the consequences. And while Peyton and Marion have grown bitter and entrenched, Olivia has been changed by what she's seen."

"I had no idea. I half-expected to find the Elemental up here waiting for me," I said.

"Yes, well, she's not likely to parade this particular change of heart. But it was enough for her to reach out to her big brother and make amends, for which I was grateful. And after today, I will owe her more than I can ever repay," Finn said, running a finger along the length of my jaw.

"So will I," I admitted. "How much time do we have?"

"Only a few minutes. I'm on a break before my shift change, and I cannot afford to draw attention to myself by being late."

I could feel the tears instantly beginning to well. "Hannah is already doing all she can to have the law struck down by the Council. But if it doesn't work…"

"Shhh," Finn said, placing a gentle thumb against my lips, and then sealing them with another kiss. "It will work. It has to work. But there's another reason I had to meet you, Jess, and it's crucial that I tell you before we run out of time."

Something in his eyes, something behind the love and the longing, jolted me out of my self-pity. "What? What is it?"

"Something… strange is happening at the Skye Príosún," Finn said, glancing down at his watch.

"What do you mean? Strange how?" I asked.

"Well, first, you should know that all the Caomhnóir who work at the *príosún* have been censured in some way. It's as much a punishment as it is an assignment, which, of course, is why I'm there."

"Is it horrible there?" I asked him. "This is such bullshit. I'm just living my life and you're stuck in some hellhole."

But Finn waved an impatient hand. "Don't worry about that. I can handle that place, that's not the point. The point is, that there's something going on with some of the Caomhnóir there… something I can't quite put my finger on. There's always been a bit of discord in the ranks—that's to be expected, given the circumstances. But lately it's gotten out of control."

"Out of control how?"

"It's… odd. People are trading shifts without notice, covering up for each other, taking unscheduled breaks, leaving the barracks in the middle of the night. They used to complain a lot, but they followed the rules. Now, it's as though they just don't care. Like they've collectively decided to just quietly ignore orders."

"That is strange," I said. I had never met a Northern Clan Caomhnóir who didn't adhere to rules with military rigidity. They wore their duty like a crown, every single one of them. The thought of a Caomhnóir bucking orders was just... antithetical.

"Too right it is," Finn said. "And then, last week, I stumbled across something I'm sure I wasn't supposed to see. On my way back to the barracks from a late shift in the spirit cells, I saw a Caomhnóir going through a door. I wouldn't have looked twice except that when the door opened, I could see a circle of other Caomhnóir inside, as well as some sort of Casting set up—candles had been lit around the room, and there was a smell of sage. Before I could get more than a glimpse, though, the door had shut, but even just that glimpse was enough to convince me that something wasn't right. Then, when I got back to the barracks, there were seven bunks empty that ought to have been occupied."

"Couldn't there have been a logical explanation?" I asked him.

"I considered that," Finn said. "Mostly because I wanted my instinct to be wrong. I checked the official schedule and the logs from the previous night when I was signing in for my next shift. There were no meetings, rituals, or gatherings of any kind in the official log book. And the Caomhnóir I saw entering the room had been officially documented as having been a shift manager in the living cells unit at the time I saw him entering that basement room."

"Well, why don't you tell one of your superiors?" I said. "Report it. Surely they can do something about it."

"I've done that," Finn said, his face twisting into a bitter grimace. "The leadership there are just as resentful as the underlings, and they... ah... don't take kindly to criticism of the way they run things. I told them about what I saw, and they essentially said I was a liar. They insisted that all Caomhnóir were accounted for at that time. I asked if that included in the barracks, and they said yes. That was the moment I realized that someone on the supervisor's level had to be involved, because they are the only ones allowed to take and handle such records. But I didn't dare point that out. I was reprimanded and ignored, and then shoved unceremoniously onto the nightshift for good measure."

"But why wouldn't they want to know if something bad was going on? That's just ridiculous!"

"Don't you remember how the Council reacted when you warned them about the Necromancers four years ago? The Caomhnóir have the same blinders on when it comes to their own vulnerabilities," Finn said.

"But—"

A sharp knock, three times on the door made us both jump.

"That's Olivia," Finn said. "She's letting us know that time's nearly up."

"Already?" Even in the emotion of the moment I hated the sound of my own voice. So small. So hurt. So not the hardened survivor I determinedly told myself I was.

"I know. I'm sorry. I thought... I just had to see you. I hope... I didn't want to hurt you more..." He passed a hand over his face, shielding me from whatever the pain was doing to his features.

"No! Oh my God, no!" I said, pulling the hand from his eyes and placing it on my cheek. "I'd rather say goodbye a hundred times than not be able to say anything to you at all," I said, swallowing a sob.

His lips were pressed together, his eyes squeezed shut as he mastered himself. Then he let out a long breath he'd been holding and said, "What I just told you... about the Skye Príosún..."

It was hard to pull my mind out of the yawning abyss of the goodbye, but I managed it. "Yes? What about it?"

"I need you to help me. Something is not right there, I feel it in my bones. But if the Caomhnóir there won't do anything to investigate it, then I need you to help me."

I blinked, pulled momentarily up out of the depths of my mourning. "Of course, I'll do anything I can to help you, Finn, but... what is it you think I can do?"

"Find someone amongst the Caomhnóir at Fairhaven—or one of the Trackers, maybe—who can look into it from the outside."

"But who?" I asked, my tone a bit frantic as he looked at his watch again. "Who can I trust? And how can I get someone to help me without admitting I've seen you? They're going to want to know how I got wind of this situation."

"I don't know, Jess. But I'm counting on you to figure it out," Finn said.

Another sharp rap on the door.

"Please. Please just promise me you'll try," he said urgently.

"I will," I said hastily, prompted by an unprecedented note of hysteria in his voice. "I promise. I'll find a way."

"Thank you," he said. Then he wrapped his arms around me and enveloped me in a kiss that seemed to empty the entire room of air. I reeled as he pulled away and breathed the next words against my cheek. "I don't know how, but we will get through this."

"Of course, we will," I gasped, the tears coming now, try as I may to stop them. I faked an offhanded chuckle. "You think a little thing like a few hundred miles, an ancient law, and the entire clan power structure will stop us? Oh, ye of little faith."

He didn't even pretend to smile. What was the point? "I love you," he said.

"I love you, too."

"Keep fighting."

"Always."

He kissed me one last time, a kiss that tasted like the brine of bitter tears, and then he turned for the door. I don't know whether he looked back or not. I didn't watch him go. I stood in the deepening darkness of the room, eyes closed, burning the feeling of his lips on mine into my memory, carving the details afresh, greedily hoarding away the sensations like the treasures they were.

After a few moments, having given me all the time she could stand to waste, Olivia said, sharply, "Jessica. We need to get back downstairs before anyone notices we've gone."

I opened my eyes. "Yes. I'm coming."

15

FLIGHT OR FIGHT

O LIVIA AND I HAD TO WAIT at the bottom of the servant staircase for several long, tense minutes before the bathroom beyond was quiet and empty. Then we slipped through the door, shutting it behind us and heaving identical sighs of relief. We looked up at each other. It was a strange moment.

"Thank you," I said softly. "You could have gotten in a lot of trouble for doing that. I know you didn't do it for me, but thank you."

Olivia nodded brusquely. She walked past me, then stopped and turned back to me abruptly. "I'm sorry. I'm sorry for... well, I'm sorry for a lot of things, but mostly I'm sorry this happened. It's not right."

"Thank you," I said.

"My brother and I haven't always gotten along, but if I know him like I think I do, this won't stand. He'll find a way, somehow. He'll find a way back to you."

I fought back a fresh round of tears. I opened my mouth to reply, but no words would come out.

Olivia sniffed and peered into a nearby mirror, dabbing at the corners of her eyes and ensuring her makeup remained flawlessly intact. "This never happened. If you tell anyone, I will deny it. We have not spoken tonight," she said curtly.

"Right," I said hoarsely.

"You'd best see to your eye makeup or people will know you've been crying," she advised before flouncing out the door. Within seconds, I heard her in the entrance hall beyond, greeting someone in a loud, laughing voice.

Back in the reception, the waiters were clearing salads and soup bowls away from the tables and bringing plates of roasted duck.

"There you are!" Hannah exclaimed as I sat back down. "I almost went in after you. Are you all right?"

"I'm fine," I said. "I got a little distracted, checking out the paintings and stuff."

"Oh," Hannah said with a shrug. "Here. I let them take your salad, but I saved the soup for you, because it is delicious! I thought you'd want to—Jess, are you okay?" She was looking into my face now for the first time, and reading it as only she could.

"I'm good," I said. She showed every indication of arguing with me, so I fixed her with a direct, quelling sort of look and said, "We'll talk about it when we get home, okay?"

She bit her lip, but nodded. "We'll get out of here as soon as the dancing starts," she whispered.

I nodded. "Yeah. Good idea."

As the intensified emotions seeped through the connection, Milo looked up from across the room where he was chatting with a young gaggle of Durupinen.

"Later." I shot the word through the connection like a projectile and watched him as he flinched, nodded, and returned to his conversation.

I spent the rest of dinner trying to respond normally to questions, swallow food that tasted like nothing, and fighting off a near constant urge to cross the room and flip the wedding cake table.

At long last, the tables were cleared and the dance floor filled with people. We managed to extract Savvy from a loud knot of men at the bar, all cursing and cheering at a football match that someone was streaming on their phone.

"Get stuffed, you wanker!" she called over her shoulder as we pulled her away from the bar. "Oi, I can't go yet, I've got a bet on that match!"

"You can send him a check in the mail," I said, tugging her toward the door.

"Like hell I will. The way West Ham is playing, I'm going to bleed him dry!" Savvy said. "Come on, I never get to have a flutter on a game anymore, the boys at home all know better!"

"Come on, Savvy," I said. "Please."

She stopped and squinted at me, and even a few drinks in, I saw that keen nosiness light up in her eyes as she interpreted whatever she saw in my face and heard in my voice. "Yeah, all right, then. You okay? I mean... you seem... yeah, let's be off."

"Let's go," I said, turning for the doors. Savvy offered no more resistance.

I don't remember much about the ride back to London, except for the almost oppressive silence and the hypnotic way the lights flashed past the car on the highway. I knew they were all staring at me, silently asking each other what was wrong with me, but I couldn't bring myself to care.

"Ambrose, can you drop us at Savvy's place?" I asked suddenly.

"What?" Ambrose grunted.

"Huh?" Savvy and Milo asked simultaneously.

"Savvy's place," I said in an exaggeratedly slow voice. "We're crashing there tonight."

Ambrose just stared at me in the rearview.

"We aren't done partying," I told him. "We're still hungry, and we haven't been food shopping yet."

"You're hungry? But didn't you just eat a whole—" Ambrose began.

"Starving," I insisted. "There's nothing in the house. Savvy's got food and booze, right, Sav?"

"Uh... yeah," Savvy said, frowning at me, but going right along with me like a champ. "Yeah, me mum's done a whole roast, and there's all sorts in the fridge."

"Great," I told her. "She won't mind if we crash, will she?"

"The more the merrier at Chez Todd, you know that," Savvy said with a nod.

"Excellent," I said, clapping my hands together. "Let's keep the party going!"

Everyone was looking at me like I was insane, not least because I'd stared out the car window in silence the entire ride—not exactly like someone who wanted to party all night long. I didn't care, though. All I wanted was to get somewhere away from Ambrose, somewhere where I could get the terrible weight of my encounter with Finn off my chest.

At last, after thirty minutes of Ambrose quietly cursing the "character" of the neighborhood, the car pulled along the curb in front of Savvy's apartment building. We all piled out. Ambrose made to get out of the car, but Savvy pushed his door closed with her foot.

"No worries, mate," she said, grinning broadly. "We've got our own Caomhnóir on the premises, remember? So, you go have yourself a little fun, eh? You're off duty tonight."

And with a salacious wink, she turned and pointed to the front door. "We ride!"

We all followed her in. I was relieved to watch the SUV pull away as Hannah tugged the door shut behind us.

We trudged up three flights of stairs, too breathless even to curse the lack of elevator. At last, we stumbled through the door and into Savvy's tiny sitting room.

We had been to Savvy's flat several times now. I still remembered how I'd felt the first time I'd seen it, amazed that so many people could live crammed into such a tiny, dingy space: six people in a two-bedroom flat. Savvy had three half-sisters. The elder two, Emma and Lottie, who were both eleven, shared a room with her. Somehow, they had managed to cram a set of bunkbeds and a single bed, along with a single dresser, into a space not much bigger than the average bathroom. The youngest sister, Maisie, slept on a mattress on the floor in Savvy's mother's room, which Savvy's stepfather also occupied on the rare occasion that he felt the need to make a cameo in their lives. A chronic gambler and con man, Savvy had zero patience for him, and roared him out of the house any time she saw him, which was why he had taken to only returning in the dead of night when everyone was asleep.

Alice, in an attempt to detract from the bleakness of it all, had forced cheerfulness into every depressing corner of that flat. Photos of babies dressed up like flowers hung on the walls, and brightly colored knitted quilts and shams covered every available surface. The fridge door was hidden behind a mass of inspirational sayings, cut out of magazines and scribbled on Post-it Notes, each one designed to draw the eye away from everything in the place that was falling apart.

I had lived in too many shitty apartments with my mom to feel much shock over Savvy's living conditions. I knew what it was like to kill cockroaches and hear mice scurrying around in my walls, or to live off microwaved food because we didn't have a working stove. But for all of the challenges that Savvy's family faced, that flat was always full of the two most important things: good food, and loud, boisterous laughter.

Alice peeked her head out of the bedroom when she heard us

come in. She was wearing a voluminous nightgown covered in garish tropical flowers and a hairnet over foam curlers. "Oh, hello, loves," she said, as though it did not surprise her in the least to see us all standing in her sitting room dressed to the nines.

"Hey, Alice," we all said, including Milo.

Alice brightened at the sight of him. "Hey there, lamb! My Melding is still working from yesterday, look at that!" she said, waving her wrist around. I could just make out the faded mark of the runes we'd drawn there so that she and Milo could work together on his latest design.

"Hey, sweetness," Milo said, blowing her a kiss. "You are rocking that South Sea tropical look, let me tell you."

Alice grinned. "Oh, stop it," she said, though it couldn't have been clearer that she was pleased. "Well, you all look right dapper, don't you? You lot all right? You want me to knock you up something real quick?"

"Nah, we got leftovers, Mum," Savvy said. "Did Phoebe get in all right?"

Phoebe was Savvy's country bumpkin cousin and the other half of her Gateway. Savvy couldn't stand her, but was forced to see her out of the necessity of performing Crossings together, as well as other clan business. They were the first in their family to become Durupinen, and so they had none of the traditions but all the same responsibilities. They also lived several hours apart, but as Savvy point-blank refused to travel out into what she called "that godforsaken sheep-infested no-man's land," Phoebe traveled into the city whenever they had to briefly tolerate each other's company.

Alice frowned. "Phoebe? You expecting her again, love?"

Savvy rolled her eyes. "It's nearly the full moon, mum. She's coming in for the Crossing, remember?"

"Oh, that's right. Sorry, love, I keep forgetting," Alice said, slapping herself enthusiastically in the forehead. "All this moon cycle nonsense. Why don't you all just use calendars like normal folks?"

"I dunno, do I? It ain't my decision, that's for bloody sure. She was supposed to come in on the five o'clock train from Paddington. You sure she didn't come by for dinner?" Savvy asked.

"I think I'd notice if there were an extra person sitting at the table," Alice scoffed.

"Wouldn't count on it," Savvy muttered under her breath, then added, so that Alice could hear her, "Get yourself back to bed, we're all right."

"All right, all right," Alice said, turning back to her room. "You lot help yourselves to whatever you like and mind you don't wake your sisters, Sav."

She shut the door with a little wave. Savvy rolled her eyes.

"What you going on about that bloody stupid nightgown for?" she asked Milo grumpily as she pulled open the fridge door. "I've been trying to get her to bin it for ages."

Milo beamed. "Alice is my girl. I like to keep my favorite seamstress happy."

I flopped onto the couch and gently eased the shoes off my swollen feet. A blister was starting on my heel. Savvy tossed a few sodas across to us and then tiptoed over to her bedroom door, making sure her sisters were asleep and pulling it fully closed before sitting down beside me.

"Right," she said, uncharacteristically serious. "What's this all about, then? Because I know you ain't hungry."

She, Hannah, and Milo were all looking at me in tense, expectant silence.

"I didn't want there to be any chance that Ambrose would hear what I'm about to tell you," I said. "Bertie's not back, is he?"

"Nah, he was still on duty at the wedding when we left," Savvy said.

"What's going on, Jess?" Hannah prompted.

I inhaled deeply. "I saw Finn."

"What!?" all three of their voices cried out together.

"How? When?" Hannah sputtered.

"At the wedding. He was there on the grounds, providing extra security," I said.

"When were you on the—" Milo gasped.

"I wasn't," I said. "One of the Caomhnóir passed me an anonymous note with my food, telling me to go to the powder room in the lobby. When I got there, Olivia was waiting for me."

"Olivia? Olivia?!" Milo voice was rising in pitch so fast that only dogs would be able to hear it.

"Yes," I said. "I was shocked, too. I thought for sure I was about to be kidnapped and hazed again, but instead she took me up a hidden servants' staircase to the top floor. Finn was waiting for me up there."

"Blimey," Savvy whispered.

Hannah's hands were pressed to her cheeks. She looked like she was about to cry.

"What... what happened?" Milo asked tentatively, and without a single trace of his usual thirst for gossip.

The details were not hard to recall. If anything, it felt like my mind was clinging to them so tightly that it was hard to loosen the grip. But I told them everything, sharing all of it. Because maybe if they all knew it, kept it in their memories, too, it would be even more real. Even more lasting.

No one spoke at first. Hannah crawled up onto the couch and curled up against me like a cat. On my other side, Savvy stroked my hair. Milo, who had settled on the floor at my feet, rested his cool energy against my legs.

I sniffed. "If you guys could all stay just like this forever, that would be great," I said. Savvy chuckled softly. Hannah tucked the top of her head even more securely against my neck.

"I'm sorry," she said.

"I know," I told her.

"This is bollocks," Savvy added.

"It is, indeed," I said, with a nod.

More sniffing. More silence. More hugs. The hugs were helping.

"What... what are you going to do? About what he told you about the Caomhnóir at the *príosún*?" Milo asked finally.

"I don't know," I said with a helpless shrug. "It definitely sounds weird. He was really freaked out. I know he can overreact sometimes—read into stuff too much—but this was different. He was disturbed about it. If there's one thing Finn knows, it's how Caomhnóir are supposed to act, and this isn't it."

"And why's he telling you?" Savvy asked. "I get that he trusts you, but you're not exactly in a position to act, are you?"

"Exactly. Why couldn't he have told one of the other Caomhnóir while he was at the wedding? Plenty of the Caomhnóir from Fairhaven were on duty," Milo said.

I shook my head. "You know them, they're all obsessed with procedure. They'd likely just tell him to inform a superior, or else, just to let the superiors handle it. Besides, he's nervous. He doesn't know who he can trust, apart from me."

"There's got to be a way to get the message back to Seamus and the other Caomhnóir leadership without tipping them off that you and Finn have spoken," Hannah said, looking pensive.

"If there is, I haven't thought of it," I said. "How could I possibly give Seamus that information? I can't admit I've talked to Finn, and Finn is the only possible source."

"But *you're* not the only possible person he could have told," Savvy said slowly.

"What do you—" I began.

"Bertie!" Savvy said, throwing her hands up into the air like they were full of confetti. "Get him to help you!"

"How?" I asked.

"Tell him what Finn told you. He's been loyal to Finn ever since Finn rescued him on the Fairhaven grounds during the Necromancer invasion. He absolutely bloody worships him, do anything for him, I'd bet my life. All you'd need to do is tell him that Finn needs his help, and he'd be on board, no questions asked."

I was still skeptical, but Hannah was nodding slowly. "Yeah. Yeah, that might work," she muttered.

"What's this 'might work' nonsense? It's brilliant!" Savvy said defensively. "Listen, Bertie and Finn were both at that wedding, yeah? They could have talked then, couldn't they? It's the perfect cover to explain how Bertie got the information. And then Bertie can go to Seamus and report it."

Milo did not look convinced. "But, isn't Bertie kind of... well..."

"A useless prat?" Savvy supplied helpfully. "Well, yeah, but, like I said, he thinks the sun shines exclusively out of Finn Carey's arse. There's nothing he won't do to pay him back. 'A debt of honor,' I've heard him call it. You leave it to me, all right? Bertie and me, we'll get it sorted good and proper."

Savvy looked so utterly sure of herself that I felt the last of my reservations drain away. "Okay," I told her. "To be honest, I think it's the best chance we've got. Thanks, Sav."

"Don't mention it," she said, then dropped the smile. "Been feeling like shite about the Finn situation for ages, so I'm glad there's something I can do." She jumped up from the couch. "Actually, two things I can do."

"Two things?" I asked, frowning.

"Well, yeah. I mean, we never did get to have any of that wedding cake, did we?" she said as she began pulling plate after tin-foil-covered plate out of the fridge. It was like watching Mary Poppins pull floor lamps and potted plants out of her carpet bag—impossibly, they just kept coming.

"Scones, strawberries, clotted cream, treacle tart, custard pie, and half a trifle," she announced. "Let's help Jess eat her feelings, shall we?"

I managed to laugh. She handed me a spoon.

Feelings, it turned out, were delicious with clotted cream.

§

After a cramped night's sleep on Savvy's sofa, we arrived back at our flat the next day around noon, still slightly hungover and stuffed full of custard. Part of me wanted to fall into bed and stay there for several days, but the universe had other plans.

And by the universe, I actually meant Tia.

"Hey! How was the wedding?" she asked.

The answer to that question was so complicated that I decided to avoid it completely. "Never let Milo pick my shoes again," I replied.

"I saw the pictures on the blog. You all looked gorgeous!" Tia said.

I turned to Milo. "How did you find time to get pictures up on the blog already?" I asked incredulously.

Milo shrugged. "I have my ways," he said cryptically.

"He made you do it during dinner, didn't he?" I asked, turning to Hannah.

She smiled sheepishly. "He kept guilting me by reminding me that he couldn't eat."

"I never posed for any more pictures at the venue," I pointed out.

"Candids," Milo beamed.

"Did you get any shots where I didn't have my mouth full of cheese?" I grumbled.

"It was a challenge, but yes," Milo said. "And they are getting a lot of internet love, particularly you, I might add," Milo said. He was already hovering over the open laptop, which was permanently open to his blog home screen so he could keep tabs on it.

"Yeah, right," I scoffed.

"Yeah. Right," Milo said pointedly. "Turns out you've got some smolder after all."

"Shut up."

Tia laughed. "Did you guys decide to stay over?"

"Yeah," I said, without specifying where, and quickly changed the subject. "So, anything exciting going on here? Did you and Charlie hang out last night?"

Charlie and Tia had been seeing rather a lot of each other since Charlie's invitation to "grab a quick bite" after the museum tour had turned into a three-hour dinner, a trip to the movies, and then dessert and coffee into the wee small hours of the morning.

"No, he couldn't last night. He needed to study for a test," Tia said, and though she sounded reasonable enough, I caught an edge of disappointment in her voice.

"Maybe you should start dating slackers so this kind of thing doesn't happen," I suggested.

"Oh, yeah, who wants to get stuck with a future doctor?" Milo interrupted.

"What does it matter? She's going to be a doctor herself," Hannah pointed out. "It's not like she needs to land a rich or successful husband, Milo. This is the 21st century."

Milo sighed. "You're all missing the point. God, I would have been *such* a great trophy wife."

"Anyway," Tia said, with the air of someone trying to force the conversation back onto the tracks before it derailed completely, "he said he'd call me later today. It was a blessing in disguise, actually. I finished my paper on bacterial meningitis."

She looked so delighted with herself that I didn't even have the heart to make a snarky comment. I really must have been tired. "Well, since I don't have to write any papers about bacteria, I think I'll go lie down," I said.

"O-okay," she said, and I could hear the hesitation and concern in her voice that meant I wasn't doing a very good job of concealing my mood. Rather than give her the chance to ask me what was wrong, though, I avoided her eyes and made a beeline for my bedroom, closing the door quickly behind me.

I didn't bother to turn on my bedroom light or pull the blinds. If I was going to have a good, long, heartsick cry, I was going to do it old school—in the dark, snotting into a pillow, maybe with some really emo music blasting from my headphones until I gave myself the mother of all headaches.

I wriggled out of Milo's dress and left it in a wrinkled heap on my floor, where it joined several other items of clothing. I flung the torture bra directly into the trashcan where it belonged and dug my oldest, rattiest, and most comfortable sweatpants and sweatshirt out of my drawer. I had very nearly completed the cocooning process, and was just about to pull my blankets up over my head when I caught sight of a stack of books perched on the corner of my nightstand.

They were the books that Hannah had brought home for me from the library at Fairhaven—the ones I had requested, with all the information about Skye Príosún. They had sat piled there, untouched, since she had brought them home two weeks ago. I'd been too much of a coward to open them, both eager to know more about the place Finn had been banished to and scared of what I would find out. If the Elemental was any indication of what Durupinen *príosúns* were like, I feared the details of Finn's new reality would be too much for my already crippling guilt to handle.

Even as I thought these things, half-curled under my comforter, I wanted to slap myself. I imagined Walking right then and there, slipping the bonds of my body, and turning to face the pathetic reality of post-heartbreak Jess. Is this seriously what I was turning into? Was this what happened when people decided to open up and love each other, or did I just particularly suck at it? I always thought I was stronger than this, that I was tougher than other people because I didn't need anyone. Now it was obvious that I avoided needing people because I would come to need them too much.

Where was my fight? Why was I letting this separation from Finn destroy me like this? Did I think I deserved it? Was I punishing myself for being foolish enough to let someone get past my guard? Probably. There's self-care, and then there's giving up on yourself, and I was forgetting the difference. I imagined Walker-Jess grabbing me by the shoulders and shaking me like a rag doll.

WAKE UP. SNAP OUT OF IT. DON'T WALLOW, FUCKING FIGHT!

I threw the blanket off myself. Finn needed my help. Something strange was happening at that *príosún* and he had risked serious trouble to find me and tell me about it. I might not be able to storm the place, or even pass his message along, but I could open those damn books and arm myself with knowledge, and that was a start. And then... my eyes lingered on my sketchbook, which I had barely touched in the last few weeks, except when a Visitation forced a pencil into my hand. I'd felt resentful of my artwork since it had become the wedge of evidence that had separated Finn and me.

Maybe it was also time to stop blaming the art and start using it to help myself move forward.

The Walker-Jess in my mind nodded her approval as I pulled the first dusty old volume toward myself and opened it. I wasn't done crying, but I sure as hell wasn't going to drown in the tears.

16

FALLEN

I WAS SO LOST in my reading that the buzz of my cell phone made me yelp in surprise. I glanced over at the clock and received a shock; I'd been reading, uninterrupted, for nearly four hours. Savvy's freckled face grinned up at me from my phone screen.

"On a scale of one to ten, how epically hungover are you?" I asked by way of greeting.

"Jess, something's wrong."

It was the tone of her voice, more than her words, that pulled me up short. Savvy's usually jovial sound was flat, scared. I sat up straight.

"Sav, what's going on?" I asked.

"I... well, I'm not really sure, but... we can't find Phoebe," she said.

"What do you mean, you can't find her?"

"I mean we can't bloody find her! We don't know where she is!" Savvy said. Her voice was rising now, a note of hysteria present in it.

"Sav, take a deep breath and walk me through it."

I heard Savvy pull in a long, slow breath and blow it out. "You remember I told you last night that she was supposed to come on the five o'clock train? Well, I figured she just forgot—I mean, she's not the brightest, you know that. I called her after you left this morning, but the phone just rang and rang. Then it just started going right to her voicemail, like someone had shut it off."

I frowned. "That's weird."

"That's what I thought, too," Savvy said. "So, then I rang Phoebe's mum, and she says Phoebe made the train. Said she drove her to the station herself and watched her get on!"

"Huh. Did she talk to her at all after that?"

"Yeah, she said that Phoebe rang her when she got to Paddington Station. She was complaining that Bertie couldn't pick her up like he usually does, and she said all the cabbies were rude and she didn't know how to work her rideshare app, even though we walked her through it a dozen times. Then she said something like, 'Oh this must be him,' and hung up. So, her mum assumed she got her ride, and that was the last she heard from her. That was a little before four o'clock yesterday afternoon."

"But then she never got to your flat," I said.

"That's right!" Savvy said. "She always comes by for dinner when she gets to the city. And I just keep thinking, what if she just got in some random bloke's car? I mean, she's just such a duffer, and I'm afraid someone a bit dodgy might have taken advantage of her, you know?"

"Okay, okay, let's not jump to conclusions," I said, as reasonably as I could, though my mind had made the very same leap as Savvy's. "There could still be a logical explanation for this. Does she stay with you when she comes to the city?"

"Nah, we can't stand each other, and anyway there's no room in my flat," Savvy said, dismissively. "She always takes a room at this little hotel in Mayfair, and we do the Crossing there. It's private, and there's no chance of getting interrupted by my sisters or my fool of a mum asking us if we want something to eat."

"Well, have you called the hotel?" I asked.

"Yeah, and the old biddy on the phone just keeps saying, 'I'm sorry but I can't reveal patron information, for privacy reasons,'" Savvy said, imitating the woman's snooty voice. "Won't even tell me if she's checked in or anything!"

"Is Bertie back? Have you told him?"

"Yeah, he got back not long after you left. He's headed to the hotel now, to see if he can get some more answers than I got," Savvy said.

"Well, there you go," I said, more confidently than I felt. It was Bertie, after all. "I'm sure he'll figure it out."

"I suppose, but... I just can't shake off this horrible feeling," Savvy said. "And Phoebe's mum is ringing me up every ten bloody minutes demanding to know if I've called the coppers yet, no matter how many times I try to tell her that we don't like to get the cops involved in Durupinen matters. I don't fancy getting the coppers involved in any matters, come to that."

186

"Don't worry about the cops," I said. "If Bertie can't figure it out on his own, the other Caomhnóir and the Trackers can help him. It'll be okay, Sav. Honestly, she probably just lost her phone or fell asleep at the hotel."

"In the meantime, what am I supposed to do about this Crossing?" Savvy asked, sounding exasperated. "I can't exactly do it myself, can I?"

"No, you can't," I agreed. "It's just one Crossing, Sav. I'm sure Hannah and I could come help, if you've got any spirits hanging around. But maybe you should call over to Fairhaven and see what Siobhán recommends, just in case? There might be a protocol for missing a Crossing. I'm not sure."

"Yeah, all right, then," Savvy said, still sounding exasperated. "There's at least one spirit who's been nagging me something awful the last few days. If we don't get this sorted by tonight, you think you and Hannah could come by and help me out?"

"No problem," I told her. "And keep me posted. I can put in a call to the Trackers' office if Bertie wants help."

"Yeah, all right," Savvy said. "Cheers, mate. I'll ring you later." She hung up before I could reply. Trying to shake off the uneasy feeling Savvy had left me with, I buried myself back in the book.

What felt like a moment later, a soft knock on my door jolted me from a doze. I glanced at the clock. It was almost three o'clock in the afternoon.

"Jess? Are you awake?" Hannah's gentle voice called.

"I am now," I said. "Come on in."

She peeked around the door, her expression contrite. "Sorry about that."

"No problem. I wasn't asleep on purpose. I just nodded off," I said, marking my place in the book and laying it aside.

Hannah looked down at the cover, which was written in Gaelic. She frowned. "I thought we agreed you weren't going to torture yourself with those?"

"I'm not torturing myself," I insisted. "I'm arming myself with knowledge. Finn asked for my help, and I want to be helpful. So, I'm going to learn as much about the *príosún* as I can, not to torture myself, but to hopefully be a better resource."

Hannah gave me a little smile and nodded. "That sounds... healthier."

I laughed. "Yup, that's me. The glowing picture of mental health."

"Hopefully Bertie will be able to help, too," Hannah said. "I wonder if Savvy's had a chance to talk to him yet."

"Oh, yeah, I talked to Savvy a little while ago," I said, suddenly remembering. I filled Hannah in on everything that Savvy had told me about the situation with Phoebe.

She furrowed her brow. "Hmmm. That is kind of odd, isn't it?"

I shrugged. "Phoebe is a bit... well..."

"Naïve?" Hannah suggested.

"You're a better person than I am. I was going to say dumb as a rock."

Hannah smacked me on the arm, which I allowed, because I deserved it.

"Well, I'm sure Bertie will track her down," Hannah said, though she didn't sound sure at all.

"Let's hope so," I said grimly.

"I was just checking to see if you were hungry. I made soup," Hannah said.

Although I hadn't thought about food even once since I'd started reading, my stomach suddenly snarled ferociously, and I realized just how hungry I was.

"Yeah, that sounds great," I told her gratefully.

Out in the living room, Tia was standing in front of Milo, who was circling her and looking thoughtful.

"Yes to the earrings, they are fierce, but only if you take your hair out of the braid and wear it down," he announced.

Tia bit her lip. "But the braid is..."

"Safe," Milo said bluntly. "The braid is safe. It's study-group safe. It's lab goggle safe. We're not going for safe. We're going for unforgettable. Hair. Down. Now."

He reached out and, with a grunt and a burst of energy, he popped the elastic at the bottom of Tia's braid. Her hair untwisted and twirled. Milo created a chilly breeze as he waved his hands around until Tia's hair fell, in shiny waves, onto her shoulders.

"What's going on?" I asked. "Is Tia joining the blog model crew?"

Tia looked horrified. "No! Milo's just helping me get ready. I'm meeting Charlie for a movie and then a bite to eat, neither of which involve a red carpet." She looked back at Milo with her eyebrows raised.

"Sweetness, everyone I style is paparazzi ready at all times," Milo said. "You can thank me later."

"I'll thank you now," Tia said, breaking into a grudging smile.

Milo gave an elaborate sort of twirling curtsey and sashayed back to the kitchen to hover over Hannah while she ladled soup into bowls.

"What time are you meeting him?" I asked Tia.

"In a few minutes. He's picking me up, actually," she said. She avoided my eyes as she said it, but I could see her cheeks rounded in a smile as she bent down to pick up her purse.

I could think of about a dozen things I wanted to say to her: that I loved seeing that smile on her face, that her happiness made me feel less empty, that Charlie couldn't possibly understand what a ridiculously sweet and wonderful person he now had the privilege to spend time with. But when she looked up at me, I just winked at her and said, "Have a great time."

My phone buzzed in my sweatshirt pocket, making me jump. I fished it out and saw that Savvy was calling me.

"Hey, Sav, what's—"

"I need your help, Jess." Her voice was tense, anxious.

"What's going on? Did Bertie find Phoebe yet?" I asked.

"I don't know. He was supposed to be heading over there when I talked to you. He promised to call me when he talked to the woman at the hotel, but I can't get ahold of him either now. It's been hours," she said. She sounded close to tears. I wasn't sure I'd ever heard her sound so close to losing it.

"Okay, okay, Sav, take a deep breath. I'm here, how can I help?" I said, in the calmest voice I could muster. From across the room, Hannah looked up, a bowl of soup in each hand and a frown of concern on her face.

"Can you come with me? I want to go over to that hotel myself and figure out what's going on, but I don't want to go alone," she said.

"Of course, I'll come with you," I said. "Just let me throw some clothes on, and I'll be right over."

"Do... do you think Ambrose could come, too?" Savvy asked. "I'm sorry. I wouldn't ask, I know he's a wanker, but... I have a really bad feeling about this whole thing, Jess. It just don't sit right."

"It's okay, Sav, don't apologize. This is exactly the kind of thing we have Caomhnóir for. Of course, I'll ask him. I'll be at your place as soon as I can."

"Cheers, mate," Savvy said, and hung up.

"What's going on with Savvy?" Hannah asked.

"Bertie went out to find Phoebe, but now Savvy can't get in touch with him, either," I told her, jumping up from the couch. "She asked if I would go over to Phoebe's hotel with her. She really sounds like she's freaking out."

"I'm coming, too," Hannah said, abandoning the soup bowls on the counter. "I want to help."

"Hey, if you two are going, I'm there, too," Milo said.

"Good. The more the better," I said. I had no objections. I could feel Savvy's nervousness seeping into my own thoughts, making them chase each other around inside my head as I groped for a logical explanation.

"What's going on?" Tia asked, looking from one of us to another.

"Hopefully nothing," I said over my shoulder as I jogged into my room to change. "Savvy's having trouble getting in touch with Phoebe. I'm sure it's just a miscommunication."

"Can I do anything to help?" Tia asked, twisting her hands together. She was too perceptive not to pick up on the fact that the situation was more serious than I was allowing.

"Yes, you can," I said, reemerging from my room, having swapped my sweatpants for a pair of tattered black jeans. "Have a fantastic time. We'll see you when you get back, by which time I'm sure everything will be completely sorted out."

Hannah hastily poured the soup back into the pot and shoved the pot into the refrigerator before saying to Tia, "Obviously, Charlie is welcome here any time, but do you think you could hold off on hanging out here tonight? It's the full moon, so..."

"Oh, right!" Tia said, nodding. "Your Crossing. No problem. I wasn't planning to bring him back here or... or anything." Her face went bright pink at all the unspoken implications.

"Great, well, tell him we said hi," I told her, sliding my feet into a pair of purple Converse sneakers and grabbing my keys and wallet out of the bowl on the entryway table.

"I will," Tia called after us. "Tell Savvy I said good luck! I'm sure everything will be fine!"

I gave Tia a quick wave and ushered Hannah and Milo out before pulling the door shut. I stopped in front of Ambrose's door and pounded on it.

"He's not home," Hannah said at once.

"He's not?" I asked. "Where the hell did he go?"

"Out for a run," Hannah said. "He stopped by on his way out, while you were sleeping. I figured it was fine, since we weren't supposed to be going anywhere."

I rolled my eyes. "Typical. Can't fucking escape him ninety-nine percent of the time, and the one time I actually need him for something, he's not here. Come on, then. We'll take the Tube and have him meet us."

I hurried down the stairs, pulled the door open, and walked smack into Charlie. He stumbled back and we both fell into the railing, catching hold of each other before we toppled off the front stoop.

"Jesus! Charlie, I'm so sorry, I didn't realize you were standing there!" I gasped as we righted ourselves.

"No worries, no worries," Charlie said with a laugh. "Although if you don't want me dating your flatmate, you needn't tackle me. I can take a hint."

I gave a half-hearted chuckle. "Yeah, I've never been known for my subtlety."

"Where are you off to in such a hurry, if it's not presumptuous to ask?" he asked, looking at Hannah and me curiously.

It *was* presumptuous to ask, but he couldn't possibly know that, the poor guy. "We're heading out to help a friend with something," I said. "Just going to catch the Tube."

"Would you like a lift to the station?" Charlie asked, hitching a thumb over his shoulder to a van parked right over his shoulder. It was black and had the museum logo painted on the side. "I realize it's not the most stylish ride, but it does the trick."

"That's really nice of you, thanks," I said. "But we can walk. Besides, four is a crowd on date night."

Charlie shrugged. "Suit yourselves, then." He stifled a yawn behind his hand.

"You sure you're going to be able to stay awake for a whole movie?" I asked him, giving him a skeptical look. "No offense, but you look more tired than I do."

"The study of medicine is not for the faint of heart or the lovers of sleep," Charlie said solemnly. "On the bright side, I've successfully memorized all the enzymes in the body."

"Good for you," I said, clapping him on the shoulder. "And there's coffee up there if you need it." I considered for a moment warning him that I'd murder him in his sleep if he treated the girl waiting for him upstairs with anything less than borderline religious reverence, but decided that might come off a tad overbearing. "Well, I hope you and Tia have a great night!" I said instead, and took off down the sidewalk before I said something that would get me in trouble with Tia.

I waited until we rounded the corner onto Portobello Road before I pulled out my phone and called Ambrose.

"Ambrose," he grunted, by way of greeting. He sounded winded. I must have caught him mid-run.

"Hey, Ambrose, it's Jess."

"I know that. What do you need?" he replied.

"Where are you right now?" I asked.

There was a pause. Then he said, "Abbotsbury Road, west side of Holland Park."

"How far away is that?" I asked.

"Mile and a half," Ambrose said.

"When you get back to the flat, I need you to bring the car and come meet us at a hotel in Hackney," I said.

"What on earth would you want to go to a hotel in Hackney for?" Ambrose asked, sounding truly mystified now.

"We promised Savvy we'd go with her. It's where her cousin Phoebe is supposed to be staying." Quickly, I filled him in on what was going on.

"Why hasn't the Council been notified?" Ambrose asked sharply. "A missing Durupinen is not a matter to be taken lightly."

"We don't know if she's missing or not," I snapped at him. "And we won't know until we can find out whether she's checked in to the hotel."

"Why don't you let the Trackers handle this?" Ambrose suggested.

"I am a Tracker," I practically yelled at him. "Do I need to get it tattooed on my forehead for you to remember that little detail?"

"I just meant... the full-time Trackers... the ones with more experience would be better suited to—"

"Look, if we get there and she's nowhere to be found, I'll bring in the entire Tracker department," I said waspishly. "But right now, it might just be a miscommunication, okay?"

"Yeah, yeah, all right then," Ambrose grumbled, finally admitting defeat. "I'm headed back to the flat now. Where is this hotel?"

"Savvy said it's just a few blocks from her flat. That's where we're meeting her. Just head toward Hackney and I'll text you the address when I get it from her," I told him.

"Right. Don't do anything stupid, all right? If anything seems dodgy, just wait until I get there."

"Yeah, yeah, the helpless females will just wring our hands until you arrive," I snapped, and hung up the phone. "He'll meet us there," I told Hannah and Milo, who were both trailing along in my wake as I continued to plow down the sidewalk.

"Do you think we should just wait for him, and we can all go over together?" Hannah asked, a bit breathless from walking so fast.

"No," I said bluntly. She didn't bother arguing with me—or maybe she just didn't have the extra breath to.

When we arrived at Savvy's building, she was already sitting outside on the stoop waiting for us, chain-smoking cigarettes.

"Cheers, you three," she said, standing up at once.

"No problem," I said. "Have you heard from Bertie?"

"No. Still not answering his mobile. I can't think of a single time he hasn't picked up on the first ring whenever I've needed a word."

"There's lots of good reasons not to answer a phone," Hannah said soothingly. "I'm sure everything's fine."

"Yeah, well, let's make sure, eh?" Savvy said.

"Ambrose is going to meet us at the hotel," I told her. "I've got to text him the address, though."

After sending Ambrose the information he needed, we set off down the street after Savvy. The shadows were getting longer as evening approached, and the sky was cloudless. I knew that soon the streets would be awash in moonlight as the full moon rose over the city. The nights of lunar Crossings had once filled me with trepidation. I had dreaded the flood of unfamiliar memories, the crowding in of anxious spirits preparing to Cross. I had worried that something might go wrong—that I would leave out a tiny detail or mispronounce a word, and be responsible for some terrible error—a Crossing gone awry. Time and practice had all but eliminated those fears, and now I actually looked forward to Crossings. The more I had explored my link to the spirit world, the more in tune I had become to the ebb and flow of energy. Now, when Hannah and I lit those candles and opened that ancient door, it felt like a release—like a great cosmic exhalation of a breath with which I'd filled my lungs gradually over the previous weeks, building it up, holding it in, until at last I could let it all go.

It was also a moment of validation—a reassuring answer to the hundred times every month I asked myself, "Why the hell am I doing this?" This, the Aether would whisper. This is why.

"This is it, just up here," Savvy said after a few minutes of brisk walking. She was pointing ahead to a dingy brick building with a sign on the front that read, "The Hotel Royal."

"Phoebe stays *here*?" I asked. I'd never seen a place so inappropriately named in my life.

"Yeah, I know, it's a bit seedy," Savvy said. "But it's also cheap, and Phoebe's a right old skinflint. It's also walking distance to my place and she flat out refuses to take the Tube. She says she's always afraid the tunnel's going to collapse and bury her alive." She rolled her eyes. "Bloody tunnels have been here since 1890, but she's sure the one time she rides one is the time the entire system crumbles to dust."

Savvy cocked her head toward the entrance, but I held her up. "Wait. What are we going to say when we go in there?" I asked.

Savvy spun around. "We ask for Phoebe's room number," she said.

"Yeah, but you already asked for it over the phone, didn't you?" I reminded her. "They said they didn't give out that kind of information." This made a little more sense now that I'd seen the place. I doubted many people checked in using their real names. Discretion was probably part of The Hotel Royal's dubious charm.

"I figured I could be a bit more persuasive in person," Savvy said darkly, and she was rubbing her fist, as though she were a cartoon mobster ready to give someone a knuckle-sandwich.

"No," Hannah said firmly. "I've got a better idea."

§

Inside the lobby of The Hotel Royal, its name grew exponentially more ironic. The wallpaper was faded and peeling in the corners. The furniture was threadbare. And the woman standing at the front desk had certainly never seen the inside of a castle. Her hair was teased to comical proportions, and her makeup looked as though it had been applied with a trowel. She barely glanced up from her gossip magazine as we approached the counter.

"Welcome to The Hotel Royal, how can I assist you today?" she droned between loud snaps of her gum. A cigarette dangled from between two of her brightly polished fingers. Before I could answer, a small, mousy-faced man and a woman in a mini skirt stumbled through the door behind us, laughing raucously and kissing each other.

"Oi, Dolores, number 12 free, then?" the man called over to the desk.

Dolores rolled her eyes, and drummed impatient fingers on the counter. "I better see some cash first, Tony, or you can see yourself out, you useless wanker."

The man called Tony muttered a stream of curses and reached into his trouser pockets, pulling out a roll of bills and peeling a few off the top. The woman beside him continued to laugh, snatching at the remaining cash and stuffing it down her cleavage.

Tony tossed the bills at Dolores, who pulled a key off a hook behind her and plunked it down on the countertop. "Number 12. TV ain't working."

Tony pocketed the key and he and his lady friend disappeared through a door and up a staircase. Dolores shook her head ruefully as she watched them go and then stared down again at her magazine, evidently having already forgotten we were standing there in front of her.

I cleared my throat. "Hi, we just had a few questions about your rates."

The woman looked up, slightly startled to see three young women standing there. "You what?"

"We had some questions. About your rates," I repeated.

"What for?" the woman shot back.

"Because we want to write a bleeding love ballad about it," Savvy snapped. "What, you've never had someone ask you about your rates before? We might want a room for the night. What are your rates?"

The woman chewed her tongue for a moment before answering stiffly, "What kind of room are you looking for?"

"Oh, I don't know," I said. "Something that will sleep all of us. What have you got?"

"Hourly or nightly?" Dolores asked, looking back and forth amongst the three of us, as if trying to decide if the question were even worth asking.

"Nightly," I said firmly, before Savvy could make what I knew would be a mouthy retort.

The woman heaved a sigh, as though it were the world's greatest inconvenience to have to actually do her job. She turned and picked up a large register book, which she lay open on the counter.

This was Milo's cue. Silent and invisible, he slipped behind the counter and materialized right beside the woman, peering over her shoulder down into the book. She was utterly oblivious, except for the fact that she gave a little shiver and started rubbing at her left arm as though it were going numb.

"I've got a single, that's £45 a night."

"She just said it's got to sleep all of us," Savvy said through gritted teeth. "You think the three of us want to squeeze into a single bed?"

"Well, I've got a suite, but... well, we try to keep it open, see?" Dolores whispered, leaning forward and tipping us a salacious wink.

I reached into my bag, pulled out three £100 notes, and slid them across the counter to her. "There. Is that enough to close it?"

Dolores raised her eyebrows, then looked up and smiled pleasantly. "It's all yours," she said, plucking the bills from the counter and pocketing them. Then she jotted something down in her register and reached behind her to grab the key, but Milo was shaking his head.

"I need a little more time here," he said, still frantically scanning the page in front of him. With a powerful little burst of energy, he caused the page to flip backward, so that he could scan the previous page.

Dolores turned again, holding the key out to us expectantly, but I didn't take it.

"Is that it? Don't you need our names or anything?" I asked her.

"You paid triple up front in cash," she said with a snorting laugh. "You can call yourself whatever you bloody well please. Ain't none of my concern."

I glanced at Milo, but he was still reading, so I fished wildly for another question. "Uh... is there a mini-fridge?" I asked her.

She snorted. "Nah. We don't have them in our rooms."

"I thought you said it was a suite," I pointed out.

"It's a suite without a refrigerator, that a problem?" she asked.

"No, it's fine," I said. "I was just... curious."

"Got it!" Milo crowed, soaring out from behind the desk and accidentally causing the register to blow shut with the force of his energy. "Phoebe Price, room twenty-six!"

Dolores stared at the register for a moment, unable to decide if something strange had just happened, but then made the conscious decision to ignore it instead. She pulled a phone out of her pocket, glanced at it, laid it down on the counter, and went right back to her fashion magazine. "Third floor. Last on the left. Lift is out of order, so you'll want the stairs," she mumbled.

"Pleasure doing business with you," I muttered to her, and we walked toward the same door Tony and his conquest had just taken.

"God, remind me to bathe in bleach when we get home," I said as we mounted the narrow staircase. The soles of my sneakers were sticking slightly to every stair tread.

"Since when do you walk around with hundreds of pounds in your pockets?" Savvy asked me.

"I was going to ask the same thing," Hannah added, panting a little.

"Catriona had all the paperwork for the Pickwick case couriered over to the flat the other day," I explained. "I swiped the cash from the per diem envelopes, just in case we needed it."

Savvy chuckled. "That was brilliant."

"I'm just glad I brought it, or we would have been pooling our cash for an hourly room next to Tony," I said with a shudder.

"Milo, did the register say anything else?" Hannah asked.

Milo shook his head. "The only information was the name, room number, and time of check in, which was 6:00 PM yesterday. The spot for check out was still blank."

"So, she checked in, but hasn't checked out yet," Savvy asked.

"According to the register, yes," Milo said.

"That's just so weird," Savvy muttered, speeding up.

Instead of going up two flights of stairs, we took the first door out onto the second floor corridor. Hannah peered at the number on the first door.

"This is the right floor!" she announced. "Number twenty. Phoebe's room should be just up here."

We all took care to tread quietly now, our tension mounting.

At last, we all came to a stop in front of room twenty-six. Savvy knocked smartly on the door.

There was no answer.

"Phoebe, you in there?" Savvy called. "It's Sav. Open up."

Still no answer.

Savvy looked at me, eyes wide and dark with anxiety. "What do you reckon?"

"Call her cell phone again," Hannah suggested.

Savvy pulled out her phone and hit redial. A moment later, a musical ring could be heard coming from the other side of the door. We all froze, listening to it repeat, until Savvy hung up.

"Now what?" Savvy hissed. "We can't just break the door down, but if she's in there and something's happened to her..."

"We don't have to wait for doors to open," Hannah said.

Savvy turned to her. "Huh?"

Hannah pointed to Milo. "Ghost, remember?"

Milo brightened at once, as though, in his nervousness, he had temporarily forgotten that he could walk through walls. "Oh yeah!" he said. Then, squaring his shoulders, he walked confidently at the door.

He flew back from it almost at once.

"What the hell—" he muttered and tried again. Again, he was unable to penetrate the barrier. "It's Warded!" he cried.

"Warded?" I repeated. "Are you sure? What in the world would she Ward it for?"

"I'm sure, look!" Milo said, and flew again at the door, which repelled him. He then tried the wall on either side of the door with the same result. Then he blinked out of sight.

"Milo, what are you—"

"Probably trying the rest of the perimeter of the room," Hannah said. "To see if there are any weak spots."

Sure enough, a minute or so later, Milo popped back into form beside me, looking both frustrated and a little pale. "It's no good, the whole room's been Warded," he announced. "The shades are drawn, and I can't find a weak spot, not even up through the floor."

Hannah frowned. "Did you try any of the other—"

"All of them," Milo said. "I think I flew straight through every room in this carnival sideshow of a hotel. Please excuse me as I gouge out my own eyes. Oh, and don't bother trying to knock on any other doors in this place. With the shit going on in here, no one is going to admit if they've heard or seen anything suspicious."

"Damn it," Savvy muttered, running her hands through her hair. "I don't like this. I don't like this at all."

A buzzing sound made us all jump. Ambrose was calling me.

"I'm outside. Where are you? I thought I told you not to do anything stupid until I got there?" Ambrose grunted at me when I answered the call.

"Oh, I'm sorry, was distracting the desk clerk so that Milo could swipe Phoebe's reservation information stupid?" I hissed at him. "Because that's what we've done so far."

A moment's silence, then, "Oh. No. That is—well done."

"Thanks for that ringing endorsement. Now, do you think you could find your way up to room twenty-six without drawing attention to yourself? We can hear Phoebe's phone ringing in there, but she's not coming to the door, and she's Warded the room for some reason."

"On my way," Ambrose said. "Don't open that door."

"What did he say?" Hannah, Milo, and Savvy all asked at once.

"He's on his way up," I said, pocketing my phone.

"What about Bertie?" Hannah asked suddenly. "Can you try him again?"

Savvy dialed Bertie's number. A ringing sound responded from inside the hotel room.

We all looked at each other, startled, listening to the ringing until it finally stopped.

"What in the world..." Savvy mumbled.

"This is just getting weirder by the minute," I said. "What in the world is Bertie doing here?"

Milo swallowed. "You... you don't think he and Phoebe are... like... *together*, do you?"

Savvy shuddered. "No. Abso-bloody-lutely not. Bertie would never dream of breaking the code of conduct like that. No offense to the bloke, but he just... doesn't have it in him."

I hadn't for a moment considered that we might be breaking up a lovers' tryst. But there was no time to even consider the unlikely possibility. The heavy thumping of footsteps behind us announced Ambrose's arrival.

"How did you get past the gremlin at the gate, then?" Savvy asked him.

"Called the hotel's main line and snuck past her when she turned to answer the phone," Ambrose said with a shrug. "This place is real dodgy. No security at all. What's the status?"

"No one is answering the door. It's completely Warded, and both Phoebe and Bertie's phones are ringing inside," I said.

Ambrose's eyebrows drew together into a deep, concerned "V." "Bertie's phone, you say?" He looked back at the door again, and this time his expression was alert, even wary.

"Is that bad?" Hannah whispered.

"It's not good," Ambrose countered. I saw his hand hovering near his belt, where a knife glinted from its holster.

"Let's get this over with then," I said. "Can you pick this lock?"

Ambrose nodded, reached into his pocket, and extracted a lock picking kit. I'd spent enough time around Caomhnóir by now to know that this was a standard part of their skill set. I was glad to see that Ambrose wasn't opposed to using it—he seemed the type who would prefer to just break a door off its hinges. Brute force now, ask questions later.

He worked for a minute, until we heard the lock click at last. He froze at the sound, listening for an answering noise from inside the room, but all was silence. Slipping the tools back into his pocket, he turned over his shoulder to us. "Step back," he ordered, and only when I glared at him did he grudgingly add, "Please."

We did as he asked. He twisted the knob slowly and pressed his shoulder against the door, easing it open just enough to peer through the crack.

"Jesus Christ," he whispered.

"What? What is it?" Savvy asked, her voice rising on a tide of hysteria.

Ambrose shook his head. "I don't think it's wise to—"

"Just let me in the bloody room!" Savvy was shouting now, shoving her way forward.

Ambrose turned to me, his expression grim. "We should get her out of here," he muttered to me.

"Oh, God," I murmured, my heart breaking into a gallop. "What is it, Ambrose?"

"Oh, for fuck's sake, just let me through!" Savvy bellowed, and barreled her way straight past Ambrose to the door, wrenching it open.

The light from the hallway flooded the dim room—someone had

drawn all the blinds. In the flickering, washed-out glow of the fluorescent light we saw a summoning circle painted upon the carpet. Inside it, Phoebe was tied to a chair, her entire body limp, her chin drooping down onto her chest. Runes had been scrawled all over the walls, the floor, and up and down Phoebe's arms and neck. There were signs of a struggle—a second chair lay overturned on the floor, a curl of rope still dangling from it. A number of candles had been scattered across the room, lying in dried pools of their own wax. One of the heavy drapes had been torn from the curtain rod and lay in a heap on the carpet.

"Phoebe! Oh, God. Oh, God, no, please, no, no, no," Savvy cried, rushing forward and falling to her knees beside the chair. She took Phoebe by the shoulders and shook her violently. To everyone's relief, Phoebe let out a muffled sort of groan. Savvy gave an answering cry and dropped her head onto Phoebe's lap, shaking with relieved sobs.

Ambrose followed Savvy into the room, knife drawn, peering first into the closet, and then the grubby bathroom, trying to ensure Phoebe's attacker wasn't hiding somewhere. I started forward, unable to bear seeing Savvy sobbing without trying to comfort her, but Hannah grabbed my arm.

"What?' I asked her, pulling my arm out of her grasp. "I want to help."

But Hannah didn't answer. She wasn't even looking at me. She was staring, wide-eyed, at something beyond me.

"What is it?" I asked her, and then, when she didn't answer, reached for her shoulder and shook her. "What is it, Hannah?"

But Hannah had no words. Her mouth opened and closed, and she looked up at me with an expression I could not even decipher, except that I knew, with every fiber of my being, that I never wanted to see it on her face again.

"*What is it, Hannah?*" I cried again.

She extended a violently trembling hand and pointed toward the corner furthest from the door. A single strangled word escaped her lips.

"Bertie."

I heard Milo cry out behind me. A molten wave of dread roiled in my stomach as I turned to look where Hannah was indicating. There, on the floor, crumpled in a heap, lay Bertie. His head lay in the middle of a pool of blood, which spread around him like a halo. His eyes stared directly at me, glassy and unseeing. One arm was bent at a strange angle and tucked beneath him. The other lay outstretched toward us, as though he were beckoning—begging us to reach out and pull him back from the place that he had gone.

But we couldn't. Where he had gone, we could not follow.

17

THE EYES ON THE WALLS

I N THE DAYS FOLLOWING, I would have only vague memories of what happened next. Hannah, slumping down in a faint in the doorway. Savvy, her gaze falling on Bertie's body for the first time. Ambrose, struggling to hold her back as she tried to crawl toward him, screaming his name over and over and over again.

Bertie.

It was all a blur. Sitting in the hallway, ignoring the stares of other hotel patrons who poked their heads out into the hallway to see what the commotion was all about. Waiting for the small army of Trackers and Caomhnóir to arrive, and watching as they swarmed over the room like efficient, stone-faced locusts. Watching Dolores disappear wide-eyed into her office, clutching enough bribery money to keep the police from being called. Riding to Fairhaven with Savvy in the back of a Caomhnóir SUV as she sobbed unrestrainedly into my shoulder. Pulling ourselves together just long enough to perform a hasty lunar Crossing as we waited for news of Phoebe's condition.

By morning, many pieces of the horrifying puzzle had fallen into place. Phoebe had been the victim of another attack, just like the one that had left Flavia unresponsive and blinded in the hospital bed beside her. Just like Flavia, Phoebe's eyes had turned a clouded silver color, and she seemed unable to recognize anyone, let alone communicate. Her Spirit Sight had been perversely twisted, so that she, too, was being forced to stare at her own soul trapped within the prison of her body. The attacker, whoever he or she may be, had either followed Phoebe to her hotel, or else lain there in wait for her to arrive. Unlike with Flavia, Phoebe had not been beaten, and the reason for this was soon discovered. A puncture mark from a needle indicated that the attacker had learned from previous mistakes, and drugged Phoebe with a powerful sedative rather than trying to force her cooperation. The attacker was still a mystery, as was the true purpose of the attack, which Bertie seemed to have interrupted. The Trackers and Scribes, try as they may, still had no idea what Castings had been used nor who had cast them. The Hotel Royal, due no doubt to its many illicit activities, didn't have working security cameras or reliable witnesses who could help shed light on who the attacker might have been.

Savvy did what she could to answer their questions, but she was an emotional wreck. I'd never seen her so shaken.

"It's my fault," she kept saying between shuddering breaths. "It's all my fault."

"Savvy, that doesn't even make sense," I told her. "What in the world could you have done?"

"I was terrible to them both," Savvy insisted, and each word sounded like a weapon she wanted to use on herself. "I was the one who kept suggesting a hotel every time Phoebe came out, instead of just letting her stay with me, like family's supposed to do. And I should have picked her up, instead of making her take a cab. She hated cabs. She hated this whole bloody city. I should have gone to the country once in a while, but I was too bloody stubborn. And I never should have asked Bertie to go check on her. I knew something was wrong, and I never should have... he couldn't handle..." She dissolved into inconsolable sobs again.

I tried to comfort her, but my words just bounced off the armor of guilt she'd hidden behind. Finally, I stopped talking and just let her cry it out. The armor would come down, eventually, and there was no use beating my fists against it in the meantime.

There were many unanswered questions, but Phoebe's attack seemed to lay one mystery to rest. When Flavia was attacked, there seemed a very real possibility that her assailants were members of the Traveler Clans, carrying out their own twisted version of justice for her unforgivable betrayal. But now that Phoebe had also been targeted, that possibility had been ruled out. There were enough similarities between the two attacks that the Trackers concluded they had been carried out by the same perpetrator.

Someone was hunting down the Durupinen of London. And that someone most likely had a connection to the Necromancers.

I should have felt afraid; logically, I knew that. But every time I tried to access that fear, I was met by a solid wall of flaming anger. This attacker, whoever they were, was a spineless coward. Flavia and Phoebe had something in common; they were both outsiders, vulnerable and essentially alone in an unfamiliar place. They were both without protection, cut off from the vast network of Durupinen who might have been able to protect them. This, I knew, was likely the reason the attacker had chosen them. I also knew—and the knowledge filled me with guilt—that my own reliable protection was likely the reason Hannah and I hadn't been targeted ourselves. Ambrose, as much as I detested him, was always, unflinchingly *there.*

"We're also enmeshed in clan life," Hannah pointed out, when I discussed my theory that night outside the hospital ward. Mrs. Mistlemoore had finally allowed Savvy in to visit Phoebe, and we decided to wait, to give her a bit of privacy.

"Enmeshed?" I asked.

"Well, yes, of course," Hannah said, looking surprised. "I'm a Council member. I'm back and forth to Fairhaven at least a couple of times a week. And you're still working as a Tracker. You're in constant contact with Catriona and other high-ranking Durupinen as a part of your work."

I considered this. I liked to think of myself as a rebel, bucking the Durupinen system and forging my own path. That perception was not exactly true—at least, not anymore. Somewhere along the line, I realized, we had gone from outcasts to insiders. I didn't know how to feel about this, except for confused and a bit resentful. It's not easy realizing you're a sell-out.

"You know what I just realized," Milo said with a grimace. "I mean, it's hardly the most important thing right now, with everything that's happening, but... well, Bertie was going to go to Seamus for you, right? With that information Finn passed to you."

My heart, already like lead in my feet, seemed to sink even lower. I had completely forgotten about that. Without Bertie, who could I trust to talk to the Caomhnóir leadership for me? How could I pass along Finn's concerns about Skye Príosún without incriminating both him and myself and getting us into even more trouble?

"Sorry to bring it up," Milo said, and I looked up to see him watching my face anxiously. "I just thought of it, so..."

"No, it's fine," I told him. "I'll just have to figure something else out."

Silence spiraled between the three of us, and the absence of

Bertie expanded even further—cut even deeper than it had a few moments before.

"Have you checked your phone lately?" Hannah asked me suddenly.

"What? No, why?" I asked. I reached for my back pocket, but the phone wasn't there. "Damn it, I think I left it in the car."

"Oh. Well, I've got about fifteen missed calls from Karen," she said with a grimace.

"What? Oh, great," I groaned. "Who told her?"

Hannah shrugged. "You know Karen. She's got connections. Something like this wasn't going to fly under her radar for long."

"This is true," Milo said. "She's practically psychic, when it comes to any trouble you two run into. Seriously, it's starting to feel like a sixth sense... well, seventh sense, I guess, if you count the whole ghost thing."

I groaned. This was literally the last thing we needed right now: our Aunt Karen piling her pseudo-parent anxiety on top of an already nerve-wracking situation.

"The longer we wait, the worse it will be," Hannah pointed out.

"Yeah, yeah, I know," I said. I held out a fist. "Best two out of three?"

She sighed. "Fine."

We played rock, paper, scissors. She totally cheated.

"Hi, Karen," I said two minutes later, when a frazzled Karen answered the phone.

"Jess, thank God! What took you so long? Are you all right? And Hannah? What the hell is going on over there?"

"Which of those questions do you want me to start with?" I asked, stifling a yawn. The adrenaline was finally wearing off, and I felt like I could have fallen asleep standing up.

Karen took a deep breath. "Let's start with the most important one. Are you okay?"

"Yes. I'm fine. Hannah's fine. We're both fine," I assured her.

"And I'm sure you'd tell me you were fine even if you weren't," Karen said with an exasperated sigh.

"Yes, you're probably right."

"I know you can take care of yourself, Jess, I promise, I do. But I just don't understand why you don't tell me when these things happen," Karen said. "I shouldn't have to hear about them two weeks after the fact from Celeste. You're halfway around the world. I just want to be kept in the loop."

"I know, I know," I said, rubbing my eyes. "I just know how you worry, and I don't want to alarm you over nothing."

"I think we can both agree this no longer qualifies as 'nothing,'" Karen said.

"Yes, we can," I said. "And I would have called you this time, I promise. But I probably would have slept first. And maybe waited until dawn in the US."

"Fair enough," Karen said. "I heard about Savannah's Caomhnóir, too. Oh, it's just terrible. How is she holding up?"

"She's a mess," I admitted. "She's blaming herself."

"What's the prognosis for her cousin?" Karen asked hesitantly, as though she'd almost rather not know the answer.

"No one knows," I said. "Without understanding what was done to her, they're not sure if they'll ever be able to reverse it, or what shape she'll be in if they do. It... it made me think of..." I trailed off, not sure if I wanted to bring up something so painful for Karen, but her mind had already gone down the same dark path.

"My dad," she finished for me. "I know. It's the first thing I thought of as well, when Celeste explained the condition."

"Do you think... is that what's going to happen to Flavia and Phoebe? I mean, will they spend the rest of their lives tortured by the fact that they're still alive?" I asked. I felt the tears in my voice, but I hoped that Karen couldn't hear them. It was hard enough convincing her I was fine without getting emotional.

"Oh, Jess, I have no idea," Karen said. "But there is one very important difference between my father and your friends, and that is the connection to the Gateway. It's in our blood, and it's meant to protect us from the pull and the lure of what lies beyond the Aether. We just have to hope that that protection is strong enough to help see them both through this Casting, whatever it may be."

I thought for a moment of my time in the Aether, when my connection to my calling and to my sister was powerful enough to close that door behind me. I never looked back, because I knew where I belonged. "It's got to be strong enough," I said, as though saying the words aloud were enough to make it solidly, incontrovertibly true. "It's just got to be. They'll come through this."

"I hope you're right," Karen said. "And in the meantime, while the Trackers figure out who's behind these attacks, I want you to be careful. I know Ambrose is... well, not your favorite person to be around, but listen to him. Trust him. He has been trained to protect you, and you need to let him do that, even if you don't think he's as good at his job as Finn was."

"Mm-hmm," I said. It was the only answer I felt safe giving. Karen had no idea about the truth behind Finn's reassignment, and I wasn't about to clue her in.

"Please don't go out alone in the city, all right? Especially at night. I know that you have a good head on your shoulders, and good instincts, but don't make yourself a target, please," Karen said fervently.

"Ambrose wouldn't let me even if I wanted to, so don't worry about that," I told her. It was true. Ambrose was going to be stuck to us like a mouth-breathing shadow everywhere we went from now on. I cringed just thinking about it.

Karen paused, and I could tell she was deciding whether or not to say something. Finally, it burst out of her. "Do you want me to come over there? I'm just going to come over there. I'll just reschedule some stuff and—"

"NO!" I barked at her. "You are not rearranging your life and your career so that you can hop a plane and hover over us for no good reason! We literally have a body guard 24/7. What can you do to protect us that he can't?"

"Okay, yes, I know, you're right. I'm being ridiculous now," Karen said. "I'm starting to rethink my question about why you don't call me when these things happen."

"It's fine, Karen," I said. "I appreciate the impulse, really. But we're good here. I'll—I'll call you more often, okay? Daily, if it will help keep you off a plane."

Karen laughed, and I could hear a modicum of relief in her voice. "Okay, okay. And I'll be grateful for the calls—and not just because I'm worried about you. I miss you girls, you know that."

"I do," I assured her. "And we miss you, too. And I promise that, when you have a break in your schedule later this summer, we'll plan a real trip for you. We'll go to Paris. We'll see some shows. Savvy will take you pub-hopping in Hackney. It will be great."

"You've got a deal," Karen said. "I love you girls. Take care of yourselves, all right?"

"We love you, too," I told her. "Talk soon."

I was still staring down at the phone screen, blinking the end of the call, when the doors to the hospital ward opened and Savvy slumped out. She was sniffling, and her eyes were red and swollen.

"I can't sit in there anymore," she exclaimed. "I'm just staring at her twitching and moaning, and I feel like I'm going mad. I'm sorry if that makes me a shit person, but I can't do it."

I stood up and threw an arm around her shoulder. "It does not make you a shit person," I told her. "It makes you a human with a heart and feelings who needs some rest."

"Why don't you go lie down, Sav?" Hannah suggested. "I'm sure they've gotten your room ready for you, just in case."

"Yeah. Yeah, I guess I'll do that," Savvy said, shrugging and looking around the hallway as though she had lost something important. "Don't reckon I'll do much sleeping, but it's better than sitting in there."

"Do you want us to stay?" I asked her. "We can stay the day with you, if you want some company."

"No," Savvy said, shaking her head vigorously. "That's right nice of you, but I'm not just staying the day. I might stay here until—until Phoebe's on the mend, you know?"

I nodded. If this was what she needed, to feel like she was helping or supporting Phoebe, then that was what she should do, no matter how long it took.

"Sounds like a good idea," Hannah said, obviously thinking along the same lines.

"And I can spend some time with Frankie," Savvy said, referring to her mentee, who was studying as a first-year Apprentice at Fairhaven. "Maybe I can be some use to her while I'm here."

"Sounds perfect," I said. "Did you happen to see Flavia while you were in there?"

"Yeah," Savvy said dully. "No change. They still don't know how to help her. And her friend—Jeta, was it? —she's gone home, back to the Traveler camp."

"Really?" I asked, surprised. "That's odd, I thought she was planning to stay."

"Only until the full moon, remember?" Hannah reminded me. "Then she said she would need to get back, to perform her lunar Crossing."

"Oh yeah, that's right," I said, as the memory floated vaguely to the surface of my sleep-deprived brain. "Well, I guess there's no reason for her to stay, now that we know the Travelers didn't attack Flavia. Our Council will finally be able to let the Traveler Council know what's going on. Maybe the Travelers will even want to help catch whoever did this."

"The more help we have, the better," Savvy said. "If I ever get my hands on whoever did that to Bertie…"

The memory of Bertie on that hotel room floor loomed over the rest of her thought, blotting it out, but there was no need to finish the sentence. I understood. It was same way I felt when Pierce was killed.

For some kinds of anger—the kind hollowed out by grief—there are no words, anyway.

§

It would have been easy to wallow in the anxiety and sadness left in the wake of the second attack, but luckily, preparing for the investigation at Pickwick's Museum didn't leave me much time for that. With only four days to prepare after returning from Fairhaven, I soon found myself too busy to dwell very much. While Savvy remained at Fairhaven, and the Trackers threw their full resources into apprehending Phoebe and Bertie's attacker, I arranged every detail of the trip for Pierce's team. By the time they arrived on a flight from Boston, I had their itinerary so jam-packed with haunted London locations that they'd hardly have time to eat—which was, of course, exactly how they liked it.

"Ghost Girl!" Iggy shouted as he jumped from the rental van in front of Pickwick's on Friday afternoon. He bounded across the cobblestones and swung me into a hug that lifted me off the ground and left me winded.

I laughed, massaging my ribs. "Good to see you, Iggy! I see you've thoroughly investigated all the haunted souvenir shops."

He was already wearing a t-shirt with a map of the London Underground on it, and a gap-toothed grin beneath an "I ♥ London" baseball cap.

"I bought 'em both at the airport!" Iggy said. "Couldn't resist."

"He's going to go broke on cheap tourist shit before we've even recorded a single hour of footage," Oscar grumbled, shutting the car door behind him and stepping forward to wring my hand forcefully. "Good to see you, girlie."

"And you," I told him. I gestured up grandly to the front of Pickwick's. "What do you think, on first glance? Did I do good?"

"Looks mighty haunted to me," Oscar said with an approving nod. "But you'd know better than me."

"You're going to have one hell of a night," I promised him.

Dan sidled up behind Oscar, setting a camera bag down on the street and framing the front of the shop between his hands, envisioning it on a screen. "This is going to make a great episode," he said enthusiastically. "I mean, the setting alone—the cobblestones, the storefront, the proximity to Fleet Street." He whistled. "The subscribers are going to eat this shit up. Nice one, Jess."

"Thanks," I replied. Dan had warmed up to me in the years since our first meeting, once I had proved my chops as a sensitive and promised not to touch his precious electronics, each of which he treated with the reverence one bestows upon a firstborn child.

"Hannah going to be joining us?" Iggy asked eagerly. His eyes lit up at the very thought, and I knew why. If I was Ghost Girl, Hannah was Super Ghost Girl. Her reputation for exciting paranormal events was legendary with the team, and so they always greeted her involvement with glee.

"Nope, not tonight," I told them, watching their faces fall just a little. "She got... uh... well, she's got to work tonight."

It was basically true. Hannah and Milo were headed back to Fairhaven for more Council meetings that evening. Ambrose had grunted and groaned about leaving me behind, but I had promised to be a good little girl and stay locked in the museum all night. He had dropped me off in front of the place with a suspicious expression, as though he thought I might immediately make a break for it, but it was hard to argue with me about my safety once I showed him a picture of Iggy. The dude was 6'4" at least and looked like a good-natured '80s wrestler. Finally Ambrose grudgingly agreed that, as long as I stuck close to Iggy, I would probably be fine. No need to tell him that Iggy was basically a giant bearded teddy bear.

"Come on in, you guys," I said. "I want to introduce you to the owner, Shriya, before she takes off for the weekend. Then we can unload and set everything up."

The team followed me into the museum, with all the reverence normal people might have when entering a church. They gazed around with a kind of wonder, senses tensed from the first moment for any unusual sight or sound that might present itself. They weren't always so sure of a haunting when they entered a space, but when I had vouched for the spirit activity, their confidence in the paranormal was definitely piqued.

"Shriya?" I called upon entering the lobby area. Almost at once, Shriya hurried out from the back room, beaming with excitement. Now that the day had come, she was as eager for results as the team was.

"Hiya," she said, shaking hands all around. "Pleasure to meet you all. Welcome to Pickwick's History of Photography, a hidden London treasure and, if your girl here is to be believed, a den of ghouls and ghosts."

"That's a pretty catchy slogan," Iggy said. "You ought to put that on the sign out front."

"I just may do that, when this whole investigation is complete," Shriya said with a laugh. "Let me show you around."

"Do you mind if I record this tour?" Dan asked, pulling out a small video camera.

Shriya reached up almost unconsciously to smooth her hair. "Eh, yeah, I reckon that's okay. Are you going to... that is... are you going to use it in your episode?"

"Not if you don't want us to," Dan said. "We've got releases for you to sign. You can opt out of being filmed, if you want to."

"Blimey," Shriya said with a nervous laugh. "I've never been on camera before. Well, go on then. I don't mind, if it gets customers through the door, in the end."

Shriya launched into a history of the museum and set off around the displays, with Dan, Iggy, and Oscar following her like eager tourists, posing questions as they went. I had promised the Trackers that I would appear in the episodes of the web series as little as possible, in the interest of secrecy, and so I decided to wait outside by the van until they had finished. As I made for the door, I saw Charlie waving cheerfully from outside.

"Hey Charlie," I said, pulling the door shut behind me and joining him on the sidewalk.

"Hello, Jess," Charlie said. "Have they started already?" He craned his neck, eager to get a peek at what was happening inside.

"Not the actual investigating," I told him. "They won't start that until tonight, when things have quieted down. Right now they're just getting the lay of the land from Shriya."

"Oh, right," Charlie said, looking a bit embarrassed. "I don't want to interrupt. I just wanted to stop by and give you this." He held out a slip of paper, which I took. "It's my cell phone number," he told me. "Since Shriya will be several hours away, she asked me to be on call, in case you and your team ran into any issues."

"Oh, great!" I said, pocketing the paper. "I appreciate that, Charlie. Thanks. But you know, I could have just gotten the number from Shriya. You didn't need to come all the way down here."

He grinned sheepishly. "You've found me out. I really just wanted a peek at all this. I must say, I'm rather intrigued about how it works. Are there Ouija boards involved? Crystal balls? Tarot cards?"

I laughed. "I think you'd be disappointed. It's decidedly more boring than that. Mostly we point cameras into the darkness and sit around waiting for nothing to happen. It's about ninety-nine percent patience and one percent action. But, with a little luck and a lot of persistence, we might just catch something interesting."

"I see," Charlie said. "Well, best of luck to you. Call my mobile, if you need anything."

"It could be the middle of the night," I warned him.

"Yes, Shriya told me. Let's be honest, I'll probably be up studying anyway. I have a little secret for you." He leaned in and whispered, "I'm a bit of a bore."

I threw back my head and laughed in earnest this time. It felt good, to really laugh. "Well, if we can liven things up for you, we certainly will."

"Brilliant," Charlie replied. "Well, have a good night. I look forward to seeing what you turn up in the old place."

"See you later," I said, and waved him off into the gathering darkness.

As I watched him go, the ghost of a small girl crept by me, peering warily into the museum and shaking her head.

"It's not what you're looking for," I told her. "I don't know what it is, exactly, but it's not what it appears to be."

She looked up at me, startled at being addressed by a living person. Her eyes, beneath a flowered kerchief, were wide and curious. "It's a trick," she whispered. "Isn't it?"

I shrugged helplessly. "I don't know. I guess so, in a way."

She gave me an appraising look, startling on such a young face. "Are you a trick, too?" she asked me.

"No," I said. "No, I'm not a trick."

She nodded, as though I had confirmed what she had suspected. Then she whispered. "Please fix it. They get stuck here. They get stuck and they can't find their way out."

I frowned at her. "Who gets stuck? What do you mean?"

"The ones like me," she replied solemnly. "They don't know any better. There will be no rest for them, if you can't fix it."

I thought of the spirits I'd seen inside, wandering back and forth, disoriented and wild with longing. "I promise I will try," I told the girl.

She turned her little head to the side, examining me quizzically, as though trying to decide if I was worthy of such responsibility. I never found out what she concluded, though, because she vanished on the spot as the front door opened and Shriya stepped out. She was smiling.

"Well, that's it I suppose. I'm handing over the keys to the kingdom," she said, dropping a ring of old-fashioned keys into my hands. "I've showed your team around, and they're already measuring and choosing positions to set up equipment. They seem like a good bunch of blokes."

"They are," I told her. "We'll take good care of the place, I promise."

"I'm not worried. In fact, I'm feeling hopeful for the first time since I inherited the museum," Shriya said, turning to look affectionately at the peeling old lettering across the front of the building. Then she sighed and turned back to me. "Right, well I've got quite a drive ahead of me, and the auction starts early tomorrow, so I'll be off. Here's the information about where I'll be staying."

She handed me a slip of paper, which I tucked into my pocket beside Charlie's phone number.

"You reckon you'll be in here all weekend?" Shriya asked.

I shook my head. "I don't think so. Typically for a place this size, one night should do the trick. I already talked to Charlie. I'll get the keys back over to him when we've finished, and I'll call you to let you know how it goes."

"Right, then," Shriya said. "Blimey, I hope you catch something interesting."

"Me, too," I said, though I had a feeling that our ideas of "something interesting" were vastly different. "Once the team has reviewed the footage, they'll sit down with you and show you all the pieces of evidence that point to spirit activity."

Shriya shivered. "I'm trying to decide if I even want to see it," she said with a chuckle. "How long do you think it will be until the episode is up on the website?"

"It usually takes them a couple of weeks to edit it all together. This place should be packed by the end of July."

"Excellent. Well, I'll leave you to it," Shriya said, giving me a little salute. "Can't believe I'm saying this, but I hope there are lots of bumps in the night."

I laughed. "Me, too. I'll call you in the morning."

I watched Shriya drive off, and then took a deep breath. *Here we go again*, I thought, feeling a bit nostalgic. Just like old times. I promised to enjoy myself, just a little.

Because Pierce would have wanted me to.

§

The anticipation was infectious as we prepared to begin. Dan was stationed, as usual, at command central, a long folding table that served as the hub of all the monitors, equipment chargers, and recording devices. The circuits for the building were woefully inadequate for the number of devices we needed to run, and so every gadget had been stocked with fresh batteries. Cameras and highly sensitive microphones had been set up on tripods in every corner of the main room, as well as one on the staircase leading to the second floor, and another tucked into the back office.

There was no shortage of spirit activity in the place that night, that was for sure. Whether the electronic equipment would pick it up, I couldn't be sure, but, in my experience, a location this packed with the dead was bound to produce enough tidbits of measurable activity to keep the team and their viewers happy. It didn't take much, bless them.

As for me, this was my chance to solve this mystery. If I succeeded, Pickwick's History of Photography wouldn't be haunted much longer. I didn't feel guilty about that fact. Just a reputation for ghosts would give Shriya the boost in attendance she needed to stay open—the overactive imaginations of the tourists would manufacture the paranormal encounters in the future. My biggest concern was locating the source of the spirits' fascination and removing it, so that they no longer chased after a Gateway that didn't exist. With any luck, Hannah and I would be able to Cross most of them before the weekend was over.

"Okay, kids," Oscar said, pulling me from my musings. "It's time to go lights out. Are you all ready?"

"Armed and dangerous!" Iggy replied, holding up an audio recorder in one hand and a thermal camera in the other.

"Locked and loaded," Dan called from the tech table.

"Let's rock and roll," I said, holding up my flashlight.

The lights went out with a pop. Slowly, my eyes adjusted to the darkness, which was tempered by the dull blue glow of the monitors on Dan's table.

"Holy *shit*," Iggy muttered. I could just make out his hulking form on the far side of the room, illuminated in multi-colored glow from his thermal camera.

"Already?" Oscar asked eagerly. "What is it?"

"Cold spots," Iggy hissed. "Cold spots *everywhere!*"

Oscar and I crept across the room to join him and peered around his massive forearms. The screen on the thermal camera showed changes in temperature in a spectrum of colors. All around the room, large blue, amorphous shapes were dotting the screen, some moving around, some stationary, some appearing and reappearing before our eyes.

Iggy looked up from the screen, mystified. "There's nothing out here to explain it," he said, wonder in his voice. "No air conditioners, no drafts, no cold temperature appliances. They're just... everywhere."

I looked up as well, the difference being, of course, that I could see about a dozen spirits flitting in and out of the space, leaving the frigid footprint of their presence lingering behind them.

Iggy turned to me and grinned broadly. "You weren't kidding! This joint is jumping!"

"Told ya," I whispered, winking. "Jackpot."

Iggy gave a whoop of glee and began circling the room, jotting down the locations of the stationary cold spots and marking them with "X's" made out of painter's tape on the floors and walls, so that they could be more closely investigated later. Oscar followed him with the camera, narrating in a whisper as he went.

"I'm going to try to get a feel for who's here," I called after them. Oscar waved a hand over his shoulder in response.

I pulled an audio recorder out of my pocket, flicked it on, and held it out in front of me. If I had been your average ghost hunter off the street, I would have asked questions aloud and hoped to capture intelligible answers on the recorders when I played them back, a practice called "electronic voice phenomena." But, since I would be able to hear the spirits clearly on my own, the device acted as a handy cover. I could carry on conversations, but still look to the others like I was simply using standard investigating practices.

I started in the opposite direction of Iggy and Oscar, so that I could speak more freely. The first spirit I approached was walking out through the back wall, and then in again, over and over. Each time she did it, she looked around her, as though expecting to find herself in a new place. Her expression was dazed, her eyes out of focus.

I watched her reappear three times before I spoke to her. She had a long white nightgown on, and her hair was wet and streaming down her back, as though she'd just stepped out of a bathtub.

"Hello," I said to her. "What are you doing?"

She jumped back from me, startled, as though she hadn't noticed me standing there until I had spoken. "What am I...?"

"What are you doing?" I repeated, more slowly.

"I..." The woman pointed to the wall behind her. "I'm trying to get through."

I frowned. "Through the wall?"

She shook her head, and if she had been more than a specter, I would have been spattered with water. "No, no, not through the wall. Just... just *through*."

I watched her again, disappear and reappear though the wall.

"Is... is this it?" she asked me, breathlessly. "Have I arrived? It... it doesn't feel different. I thought it would feel different, somehow."

Her eyes were wild and brimming with emotion. I didn't even know what to say to her.

"You've got to get out of here," I told her. "This place—it's not what you think it is. You're just torturing yourself."

"No, I... I can feel it. I know it's here. I've just got to get through it," she whispered, more to herself than to me. In fact, she seemed already to have forgotten that I was there, standing right beside her. I sighed resignedly and moved on.

"Jess, check this out! This cold spot on the wall looks just like a handprint! This is wild, man!" Iggy was saying from near the cash register. Then he gave a yelp as a curtain near his elbow fluttered and jerked, as though the invisible hand had tried to pull it back.

And so it went, for hours and hours; the team thoroughly delighted at every turn by some paranormal tidbit or another, and me, thoroughly frustrated by the spirits' lack of ability to overcome their own confusion to communicate effectively.

This was such a waste of time. I was never going to get any answers like this. The ghosts had no more idea of what was happening than I did. Right around one o'clock in the morning, I plopped down in a folding chair next to Dan and heaved a sigh of frustration.

"You tired, Jess?" he asked, looking at me through his black-framed glasses. "Want a Red Bull or something?"

"Dear God, no," I said, making a face. "Do you actually drink that shit?"

He shrugged. "Got to stay awake somehow."

"No, I'm not tired. I'm frustrated," I admitted.

"What? Why? This place is a hotbed of activity! This is going to be one of our best episodes yet!" Dan said.

"It's just... the spirit energy is so confusing," I said. "It's great that we're recording the activity for posterity, but I was kind of hoping to figure out exactly what it was about this place that was attracting so many ghosts."

"And you can't figure it out?"

I shook my head. "I've been trying to make contact over and over again, but they're all really confused—lost, almost. I can't get a straight answer."

"Do you think it's important to find out why they're here?" Dan asked, in a tone that suggested he hadn't even considered the idea.

"Yeah, I really do. They're not tied to the place, they're drawn to it. I need to figure out what's drawing them, because whatever it is, is making them too confused and disoriented to leave."

"Whoa," Dan said, eyes wide. "That's freaky."

"Yeah," I agreed. "And I don't like the idea of spirits being trapped anywhere, you know? If they want to hang around of their own free will, that's their choice. But that's not what's happening here."

"Hmm," Dan said, pulling off his glasses and rubbing at his eyes, thinking. "Why not use the footage?"

"Use it for what?" I asked.

"Well, if the spirits can't tell you what's drawing them, the footage might be able to," Dan replied.

I frowned. "I'm still not following you."

"It's like, if you look at one piece of a puzzle, you might have no idea what you're looking at. But if you step back and look at the whole design, then suddenly the individual pieces start to make sense," he explained.

"Okay," I said slowly. "I get the analogy, but how would that work?"

"Here, let me show you," Dan said. He swiveled his chair around and punched a few keys on his keyboard. The largest monitor right in front of us lit up with a camera shot of the first floor. "This camera angle is the widest one we've got," he said, turning and pointing to the furthest corner of the room, up near the ceiling. "We wanted to cover as much area as possible in a single shot. That way, if we catch a sound or a movement on a different camera or recorder, we can pinpoint it on the bigger image."

I watched for a few moments. I could see Iggy on one side of the room, Oscar on the other, along with a number of subtle disturbances in the air that I knew were all the others would be able to see of the spirits that wandered the space.

"Maybe, if you go back through the footage—you know, speed it up, slow it down, whatever—you might see a bigger pattern emerge," Dan suggested.

"Yeah," I said, nodding. "Yeah, that might help. Thanks, Dan."

"No problem," Dan said. "I'm going to take a break, stretch my legs. Are you good manning the table here for a few minutes?"

"Sure," I said, barely listening. I was already fiddling with the monitor. After trying a few knobs, I was able to figure out how to rewind the footage back to the beginning of the night. I started watching.

At first, nothing leapt out at me. I tried speeding the footage up, watching it at double, and then quadruple speed.

"Wait..." I muttered to myself. I rewound again, and restarted it, playing it as fast as it would go. It was then I realized that the spirits were not randomly wandering the room at all. They were wandering along very clearly defined paths, over and over again.

And what was more, I realized with a start, Iggy had inadvertently marked out the paths himself, when he put all his taped "X's" on the floor. I watched for a few more minutes just to be sure that I wasn't misreading the patterns, but the longer I watched, the clearer it became. I jumped up from the table and jogged over to Iggy, who was conducting a thermal sweep of the staircase.

"Iggy, can I borrow your roll of tape for a minute?" I asked him in a whisper.

"Sure kid, knock yourself out," he said, barely looking up from the screen. He reached down, unhooked the tape from a carabiner clip on his belt, and tossed it to me. I managed to catch it by the tips of my fingers.

Working quickly, I started in the middle of the room with the first "X" and taped a long, straight line right out to a stretch of wall between two display cases by the front door. Then I repeated the process, taping long lines out to the walls. After a few minutes, I stepped back to admire my handiwork. I had created what looked like a massive spider web that stretched over the entire space, so that we all appeared like insects caught in the threads.

Dan emerged from the bathroom and stopped dead in his tracks. "What the hell is this, arts and crafts time?" he asked, staring around in bewilderment.

"Shut up, I'm trying to figure something out here," I said, shooing him away. He shrugged and shuffled back to his table.

I stood at the spot in the middle of the room where the threads of the web converged, and stared down along the first tape line. At the end of it, hanging on the wall, were two portraits in small, glass cases. I turned a few degrees and looked down along the next line, and found myself looking at another portrait, similar in size, and also in a glass-fronted case. I turned again. And again. And again. And every time I turned, I followed the tape line to find myself staring at yet another portrait. I spun around again and counted them. There were fifteen of them in all.

I walked along the first tape line again and stopped right in front of the portraits, shining my flashlight upon them. A grim-faced man stared out from the glass, which made me feel like I was peeking through a window at him. He was dressed in a long black robe, like some kind of judge, and his hands were folded magisterially on his lap. I could see nothing unusual about him at all, until the glint of the flashlight shone upon his eyes.

His silvery eyes.

I leapt back from the picture with a gasp.

"Jess? You okay? You catch something over there?" Oscar asked.

"No, I... uh... no, it was nothing," I stammered. My heart was pounding so hard I could feel the beat of it against my ribcage. I took a tentative step back toward the picture, wondering—even hoping—that it had perhaps been a trick of the light. I looked at the portrait from every angle, shining the light at it, then across it, then shutting it off completely to squint at the image in the dull glow of the other equipment.

There was no doubt. The man in the portrait had silver eyes.

"Okay," I whispered under my breath. "Okay. It doesn't necessarily mean what you think it means. This picture is old and faded. Maybe there's a perfectly ordinary explanation here."

I followed the next tape line to the next stretch of wall, where two portraits hung side by side. I examined them quickly. Both men. Both in black robes. Both with silvery eyes. Line by line I followed the threads of my makeshift web and found silver-eyed portraits waiting for me at every turn. By the time I had finished, my breath was coming in sharp, frantic bursts. I felt trapped, caged in, surrounded.

"Jess? Are you all right?"

I whirled around to find Iggy standing right behind me. His face was full of concern.

"I... yeah... I just... I just realized something," I said between gasps.

"Do you want to get some air? You look kinda... green," he said.

"No, I don't need... I mean... I need to get out of here," I said.

"Yeah, that's what I just—"

"No, I mean I need to leave. These portraits... I've just realized... I need to show them to Shriya."

Iggy frowned. "Shriya? You mean the owner? But isn't she like, a hundred miles away by now at some auction?"

"Yeah. It doesn't matter. This is important. I'll just... I'm going to drive out there."

Iggy was protesting, but I wasn't listening. I was staring around for a box. My eyes fell on a stack of them sticking out of a shelf in the back room. I seized one and circled the room, carefully unhooking every silver-eyed portrait from the picture wire on the walls and laying them gingerly inside the box. As soon as I closed the lid I felt an almost seismic shift in the spirit energy in the room, like the twanging of the world's largest elastic band.

"What are you doing with those?" Iggy asked, utterly bewildered now.

I took a deep breath and faced him, trying to look and sound completely in control of the situation. "Shriya really wanted to know what was causing the hauntings. It's these portraits, I know it. So, I'm going to bring them to her so she can tell me everything she can about them."

"And you need to do that right now? In the middle of the night?" Iggy asked. "Why don't you just call her? Or wait until morning?"

"I... can't," I finished lamely. "It's, uh... a sensitive thing. I'm just picking up really bad vibes from these portraits. I want to get them out of here. You guys can hold down the fort for a couple more hours, right?"

"Yeah. Yeah, of course we can, but..." Iggy began, looking rather helpless.

"Great. I'll call you guys in a little bit," I said, pulling my jacket from the hook on the wall and tucking it under my arm with the box. "Have fun!"

And, leaving them all staring after me like I'd suddenly announced I was going to the moon, I shut the door behind me.

"Ouch!"

I looked up and realized with another jolt of surprise that I had walked right into Catriona.

"Catriona! What are you doing here?" I squeaked.

"Getting hip-checked into a wall, apparently," she replied dryly, rubbing at her shoulder. "Where the hell are you running off to?"

"I asked you first."

She sighed heavily. "I was in the city working a lead on Phoebe's attack, and I remembered this... uh... little project was going down tonight. Thought I'd stop by and see what it is that these cute little ghost hunters do."

"The cute ghost hunters are inside, but this little project has just turned into a full-blown, five-alarm emergency," I told her.

Her smirk slid off her face. "What do you mean? What's wrong?"

"If you want me to explain, I'll have to do it on the way," I said, fumbling with my cell phone. "I've got to convince a cab to drive me out into the middle of nowhere, so if you want to hear the story, you'll have to come along."

"But what story are you—" she began.

"Necromancers."

She stared at me, the color draining from her face. "Forget the cab," she said bluntly. "I'm driving."

18

A FAMILIAR FACE

C ATRIONA GUIDED ME through a short, slightly hysterical explanation of what I'd found. Her methodical questions seemed to bring some order to the chaos of my thoughts. I calmed down enough to text Hannah and update her on where I was going. After that, neither of us spoke much during the four-hour drive. I didn't mind the silence. I was too intent on getting where we needed to go. I clutched the shoebox full of photos tightly in my lap, as though it were a living creature that might, at any moment, make an attempt at a wild escape. Meanwhile, my mind was swimming, trying to make sense of what I had just discovered.

There was absolutely no doubt in my mind that the portraits were somehow linked to what had happened to Flavia and Phoebe. The men in the images had the exact same eyes—the same eyes, in fact, that I had seen on the Necromancers when they attacked us four years ago. The same eyes that taunted and haunted me out of Neil Caddigan's face. I knew that I was not making a mistake—I could not look into the faces of these portraits without feeling the same cold, creeping sense of dread. The men in these portraits were Necromancers. I knew it.

What I couldn't understand was how these portraits came to be in Pickwick's History of Photography, and how they could be connected to what was happening now. I had always known, from the moment I saw what had happened to Flavia, that there was a chance that the Necromancers were involved in her attack. The threat deepened, became more real, with Phoebe's attack and Bertie's death. But never, until this moment had I felt such tangible, physical fear.

What was the connection? What did Pickwick's, and these old photographs, and the recent spate of attacks have in common and what did it all mean?

Catriona's cool, unruffled voice broke into my thoughts. She may as well have been the voice of the GPS, so neutral was her tone. "Your museum owner may very well still be asleep. It's just barely seven o'clock. Do you know which building she's in?" she asked as we pulled into the parking lot of a quaint country bed and breakfast, which consisted of a farm house, several cottages, and a converted barn.

I squinted through the window and frowned. "No. But we might be able to... wait, I see her car right over there!"

I pointed frantically at a large blue van that was always parked in the narrow alleyway behind the museum. As Catriona swung the car around and drove toward it, Shriya appeared beside it, shifting a small cardboard box onto her hip so that she could pull the back door open.

Catriona steered our car smoothly into a spot between two trees, and I had the door open before she'd even thrown the thing into park.

"Shriya!" I called over to her. She pulled her head out of the back of the van, looked around curiously for a moment, and then spotted me jogging toward her. Her mouth fell open.

"Jess! What are you doing here? Did something... is everything all right at the museum?" Shriya asked, her voice sounding more panicked by the second.

"Don't worry, the museum is fine," I told her, crunching to a stop beside her on the gravel and trying to smile. "Sorry to surprise you like this. The investigation went great. Better than great, in fact: I think I've found the source of your haunting."

"That's brilliant, but... why did you have to come all this way out here just to tell me? I'd have been back tomorrow night. I hear these are pretty handy inventions as well," Shriya said, pulling the phone from her pocket and giving it a little shake.

Catriona arrived beside me just in time to chuckle at Shriya's joke. I opened my mouth to introduce her, casting around wildly for a false identity, when she stepped forward smoothly, putting out a hand and smiling in a much friendlier way than I'd ever seen her manage before.

"Hi, there," she said, in a perfect Boston accent. "Nice to meet you, my name is Susan Proctor. I'm one of Jess's producers. I help out with the narrating and the editing for the web series."

Shriya swallowed it hook, line, and sinker, thrusting out a hand

and shaking Catriona's without a moment's hesitation. "Nice to meet you," she said.

"And you," Catriona replied. "That's a great little museum you've got there. Should make for a fascinating episode."

"Thanks," Shriya said with a smile, before turning back to me. "So, what's this then, about finding the source of the haunting?"

"Can we find someplace to sit down?" I asked. "This will probably take a few minutes."

"Sure, let's head back to my room. We can talk there," Shriya said. She pushed the box she had been carrying further into the back of the van. I spotted a large framed portrait and a black metal contraption that looked like a movie camera.

"Good auction so far?" I asked her as we trudged up a walkway toward a small guest cottage with a blue door.

"Excellent," Shriya said. "My grandfather tried for years to get his hands on a portrait by Julia Margaret Cameron, but was always outbid. I won one in the first auction of the day today, so I'm chuffed. It was the whole reason I wanted to come. It will be a really important addition to the collection. It's likely people will visit the museum just to see it."

"That's great," I said, as enthusiastically as I could with my heart still pounding in my chest. I felt like every silvery pair of eyes in the box I was carrying was staring up at me like sentient things.

Shriya fumbled for a moment with the key in the lock, then opened the door and ushered us inside and over to a little sitting room. The place had all the charm of a classic English cottage, which on any other day I might have appreciated, but which now I ignored as I put the box down on the coffee table and took a seat.

"So, what's all this about, then?" Shriya asked, and she looked serious again. "What couldn't wait until tomorrow?"

"Do you remember me telling you, when we first discussed the possibility of ghosts, that the building itself could be the cause of the haunting?" I asked her.

"How could I forget?" Shriya half-laughed. "I thought I was going to have to burn the place to the ground, or else sell it."

"Well, the good news is that the building itself has nothing to do with it," I said.

Shriya raised her eyebrows, looking from me to Catriona and back again. "You're kidding! That's brilliant, then! Unless..." her eyes grew wide. "Oh bollocks, it's not me, is it? Did some ghost walk up to one of your microphones and tell you he was stalking me from the grave, or something like that?"

Catriona laughed, shaking her head. "We don't often get evidence like that," she said.

"No, don't worry, it's not you either," I told Shriya quickly. "Actually, after extensive... uh... analysis of the evidence, we were able to determine that the spirits were attracted to these."

I pushed the little box toward her and she opened it. She looked up, eyes wide. "The daguerreotypes?"

"The what?" The word sounded vaguely familiar, but I couldn't place it.

"Daguerreotypes. That's what these are."

"Oh. Well, yeah," I said. "You had them hung up all over the museum. For some reason, the spirits were drawn right to them, and were wandering all over the museum."

"You're joking!" Shriya whispered, looking down at the little portraits with a renewed curiosity. "How odd! What do you suppose they find so interesting about them?"

"I was hoping you would know the answer to that," I said. "What can you tell me about them?"

"Daguerreotypes were, for all intents and purposes, the earliest form of commercially available photography," Shriya said, holding one up and examining it. "Named for Louis Daguerre, the bloke who invented it. You see, photography wasn't done on paper, the way we think of photographs nowadays. It was a very delicate and complicated chemical process."

"What did they use then, if it's not paper?" I asked. "It looks like metal of some kind."

"It is metal," Shriya said, handing the little portrait to me and pointing out the features as she spoke. "Copper, to be more precise. You can see a bit of the copper color here at the edges of this one, where it's aged. It's a copper plate, coated in silver, and polished like hell until it was as smooth and reflective as a mirror. Then, the plate would be exposed to iodine or bromine fumes in a darkened room, which would make it light-sensitive. Then the plate was placed into a camera obscura—"

"A what?" I asked.

"It was the first camera," Shriya said. "We've got an original one back at the museum. Well, not an *actual* original one—not one of Daguerre's. But it's still a very early example, used by one of the first Englishmen to adopt the process. It's much less impressive-looking than you'd think—little more than a wooden box with a lens cap on it."

"That's right," I said, nodding. "I remember seeing it now."

"Anyway, the plate would be protected from the light until it was placed inside the camera obscura, see? Then, when the subject was ready, the photographer would remove the lens cap and expose the plate to the light. This could take a few seconds, or many minutes, depending on the brightness of the light. There would still be no image visible on the plate yet," Shriya said, her enthusiasm for the subject becoming clearer with every word, "until it was developed by exposing the plate to mercury fumes inside a specially made developing box."

"Mercury fumes?" I repeated, surprised. "I don't know a ton about chemistry, but isn't that... kind of..."

"Dangerous?" Shriya supplied, laughing. "Yeah, it is, and they weren't all that careful about it either. Nowadays, when people try to repeat the process, they are much more careful."

"People still make these?" I asked.

"Certainly. Not in any widespread sort of way. Just as a novelty, you understand," Shriya clarified.

I nodded. We still hadn't reached the really crucial part of the explanation, and I was eager to hear the rest.

"Anyway, once the plate was exposed to the mercury, the image, which had been invisible up until that point, is revealed on the silver surface. To set it, the plate was heated over a flame and treated with gold chloride. After that, the image was placed inside a protective casing, like this one. You'll rarely see a daguerreotype that isn't behind glass, because the images are so easily marred." Shriya shrugged. "And that's basically it. Daguerreotypes were only popular for a few decades, and then other, less expensive forms of photography took their place. These were always my favorite to look at, though. Just the way they glimmer, you know? If you get them at the right angle, it's almost like looking at a hologram. And the weight of them gives them real presence, too. It's almost like there's a real person inside there, somehow."

Her words sent a shiver up my spine that was not entirely unwarranted. "And what about the eyes?" I asked.

"The eyes?" Shriya repeated, looking puzzled.

"Yes. Is it normal for the subjects of these daguerreotypes to appear to have silvery eyes?" I handed the portrait back to her and she looked down at it.

"Well, no, not necessarily," Shriya said. "But as I said, the images were very delicate, and very easily discolored."

"But look at these, Shriya," I said, pushing the box toward her. "I took down every single daguerreotype hanging in the museum, and they all have the same discoloration in exactly the same spot."

Shriya reached into the box, a curious half-smile on her face, and began pulling out the daguerreotypes one by one to examine them. With each new portrait, her smile faded, until she was frowning with concentration.

"Huh," she said at last, laying the last of the daguerreotypes on the table. "That's a bit odd, isn't it?"

"That's what I thought," I told her.

"It doesn't look like tarnish, or a defect of the metal at all. I can't think what might have caused it," she said.

"Can you tell us anything about these particular daguerreotypes?" I asked her. "None of them had a name associated with them on display. Do you know anything else about them?"

"A bit, yeah," Shriya said. "They were the most recent acquisition to the museum, actually. According to the records, my grandfather bought them only three years ago."

Catriona caught my eye for the briefest of moments and then looked away, pretending to examine a daguerreotype. "Do you mind?" she asked Shriya, picking one up.

"Please, go right ahead," Shriya said. "Just handle it carefully."

"Oh, of course," Catriona said, nodding her head deferentially.

"Sorry, did you say all of them? All of these daguerreotypes belonged to the same person before your grandfather bought them?"

"Yes, that's right. And those are just the ones he chose to display. There are others as well, I think. Yeah, actually, hang on." Shriya stood up and disappeared around the corner into the bedroom of the little cottage.

As soon as she was out of sight, I turned to Catriona. "What do you think?"

Catriona was staring down at the portrait in her hand. "I think there's something really bloody strange going on here."

"Well, I know that," I hissed.

"No, I mean... have you had a real good look at these portraits?" Catriona asked. She was turning the one in her hand this way and that, observing it from different angles.

"Of course, I have! What do you mean?" I snapped.

"I'm no photographer, but I'm fairly sure that when you take a person's photo, the only image that should appear on it, is their own," she said quietly.

"What do you mean?" I picked up one of the portraits and stared down at it. "I only see one image."

"That's because you're looking straight down at it. Tilt it up to the light and look along the surface from the side, like this." She demonstrated, cocking her head to the side and looking along the portrait at eye level.

Mystified, I did the same. At first, all I could see was the image of a middle-aged man, his silvery eyes staring blankly up to the ceiling. But then, as I twisted my wrist just slightly, a second image appeared, popping from the silvery plate's surface like a hologram.

A woman, with long dark hair, trussed like an animal to a chair. Her face was twisted, her mouth open in a silent scream.

I gasped and fumbled the little case, nearly dropping it. I looked over at Catriona.

"What in the hell...?"

"Did you see her?" she asked.

I couldn't answer. I couldn't even nod. My heart seemed to have swollen and was constricting my windpipe. Slowly, half-convinced I had imagined it, I lifted the portrait in shaking fingers and again held it level with my eyes and turned it slowly. Again, as the light flashed across the surface, I saw her, as though in negative, and then, a moment later, her figure dissolved into that of the man, again, expressionless and stoic, eyes silver and blank.

"Who is she?" I breathed. In the next room, I could hear Shriya opening a closet door and muttering to herself.

"How the bloody hell would I know?" Catriona hissed. "But I've looked at three of these things since we sat down, and she's there—the same woman—on all three of them.

We stared at each other in horror for a long, silent moment, then, as though we had agreed aloud to do so, we both plunged our hands into the box of daguerreotypes and began to examine them one by one. It took less than a minute to confirm the awful truth: the same woman, whoever she was, was screaming up at us from all of the daguerreotypes in the box.

"Is that... I can't be sure... is she wearing a triskele brooch? There, at her throat?" Catriona hissed.

It took several attempts, turning and angling the portrait in my hand, before I caught a glimpse of what she was talking about. "Yes," I said firmly. "I'm sure of it."

"So, she's a Durupinen, then," Catriona murmured.

"Yes," I replied, feeling my horror mount by the minute. "But what does it mean?" I whispered.

Catriona shook her head. She looked as worried as I'd ever seen her.

Shriya emerged from the bedroom carrying a stack of leather-bound registers. "Here we are, then. These are my grandfather's records of the museum's artifacts. I brought them along to help me decide what to bid on and what to leave to the others to fight it out for." She took the topmost book and laid it open on the table. She licked her thumb and forefinger and began peeling the pages apart, running a finger down a list of dates until finally jabbing her finger at one. "Yup, here it is. 'Daguerreotype Collection, comprising some two hundred portraits, notes, sketches, and rudimentary photography equipment, and supplies.' Purchased by my grandfather for a sum of £10,000."

"Does it say who he purchased it from?" I asked.

"Yes. It was a private sale arranged through the Department of Theology at City University of London," Shriya said.

I could feel all the color draining from my face. Shriya, looking up, gave me a frightened look. "Jess! Are you quite well? You look like you're going to pass out."

I licked my lips, but my whole mouth had gone bone dry. "I... yeah, of course, I'm fine. Just tired. Long night at the museum."

Shriya nodded but did not look convinced, so I plowed on before she could question me further. "This, uh... collection that your grandfather bought. Do you still have the rest of it?"

"Of course," Shriya said. "The museum isn't big enough to house everything in my grandfather's collection, so we rotate things in and out of the exhibits, and store the rest in a storage facility in the city."

"Would you mind... do you think we could take a look at the rest of the collection?" I asked, trying to keep my voice calm and even.

"Sure, but... why?" Shriya asked, looking puzzled. "I'm not exactly fussed if the storage locker is haunted."

"A lot of times," I said, looking to Catriona for help, "knowing the history behind a haunted object can help to explain exactly why it's haunted."

"And by whom," Catriona added, jumping in. "It would make for an excellent follow up to the investigation, sort of like a little scavenger hunt for more clues. Audiences love that stuff—putting names and faces and historical contexts to hauntings. Makes it seem more tangible, you know?"

Shriya nodded. "I can see that," she said, smirking a bit. "You think more people will want to come see the museum if they can call out the spirits by name?"

"Exactly!" Catriona said. "Now you're catching on! Just think, you could brand merchandise specific to your haunting, and make the backstories part of your tour."

Shriya grinned. "That would be wicked!" she said enthusiastically. "And you're sure these daguerreotypes are the key to it?"

"Absolutely sure," I told her firmly. "So, what do you think? Can we check out the rest of that collection?"

"All right by me," Shriya said, but then her face fell. "I can't take you there now, though. I've got two more lots I've got to bid on today. Can it wait until tomorrow?"

"We'd love to take care of it while the team is still here, so that we can film their commentary. You know, make it all a part of the episode," Catriona said smoothly. "Is there any other way we could get over there?"

Shriya considered for a moment, then shrugged. "Look, if you don't mind digging through some boxes, why don't I just give you the address and you can have a poke around for yourselves?'

"We don't mind digging at all," I said quickly, "as long as it's okay with you."

"I already handed over the keys to the museum and let you have the run of the place; I think I can trust you with a few old boxes in a storage locker," Shriya said, winking. She ripped a blank page from the back of the register and started scribbling on it. "Right. This here is the address. Under that is the code for the padlock. And this here is the date that will be on the box. My grandfather organized everything chronologically."

I took the paper, folded it up, and put it in my back pocket. "Thanks, Shriya."

"You're welcome. Just handle everything carefully, and mind you lock it all up when you've finished," Shriya said. "And call me if you have any questions."

"Okay, we will," I said.

"And if you can't get me, call Charlie," Shriya said. "He knows that storage locker top to bottom. He should be able to help you if you need anything."

"That's a great idea," I said, standing up. "We don't want to bother you anymore, so we'll just get going. Sorry for descending on you like this."

"Yeah, she gets a bit excited when she solves a haunting. Just a regular Nancy Drew, aren't you?" Catriona said, smiling at me and giving me a gentle punch in the arm.

"Yup, you know me. I just get a bit carried away," I said, attempting a sheepish grin.

It was a pathetic attempt at camaraderie, but Shriya bought it. She stood up and walked us to the door. "Do you want to take these with you?" she asked, holding out the box of daguerreotypes.

I looked down at them. I didn't want to take them at all. I wanted to fling them across the room and break every single one of them, as though that might release the screaming woman inside, and somehow reverse whatever had been done to her. Instead, though, I tucked the box under my arm and smiled. "We'll let you know what we find."

19

PANDORA'S BOX

S AFELY BACK IN THE CAR, Catriona and I could finally speak freely.

"So, what fresh hell is this, then?" she exclaimed, as soon as we had peeled out of the driveway and onto the road.

"It's Neil," I said, and even his name in my mouth felt like acid. "Neil Caddigan."

Catriona gave a small gasp. "The head of the Necromancers? The one who turned Lucida? How do you figure that?"

"He worked for that college, in the department of theology. I tried to track him down when I first came to Fairhaven, when Pierce went missing, because I thought he might know where he'd gone. I emailed him at his faculty email address, and that was the college. I'm sure of it. It's the same college where my roommate goes to medical school."

"So, you think this collection might have belonged to him?" Catriona asked.

"It has to be his. It's too much of a coincidence," I said. "He probably kept it all cloaked under the guise of the college, to stop the Trackers from finding it."

Catriona muttered a stream of profanity under her breath. I knew this particular aspect of the situation would sting, as she was one of the Northern Clans' most prominent Trackers. If dangerous Necromancer artifacts had slipped through the cracks, she'd probably consider it her own personal failing.

"What I don't understand," I went on, ignoring the continued swearing, "is how these old portraits connect to what's happening now."

"Yeah, I'm trying to put those pieces together myself," Catriona said.

"I mean, this has to be connected to the attacks on Flavia and

Phoebe, doesn't it?" I asked. "It all fits together. They both had the same silvery eyes after they were attacked. And they had both been tied up, just like the woman in those daguerreotypes. Whatever happened to this Durupinen," I tapped my hand on the box, "someone is trying to replicate it."

"But why?" Catriona mused aloud. "What is the purpose of it? And who's doing it now?"

I shook my head. "I don't know. But it's somehow connected to the Necromancers. It has to be."

"And another thing that makes no bloody sense," Catriona said, pulling out her phone and dialing without so much as a glance at it, "is how the museum is involved. It seems like a hell of a coincidence, doesn't it?"

"Yeah, it does," I said softly, staring out the window. Had I really just stumbled upon a museum full of artifacts that came from the Necromancers? That seemed too far-fetched to be believed, even for someone like me, who had made stumbling into unlikely situations look like a lifestyle brand. "Maybe we'll understand it better when we see what else is in that collection in the storage locker."

"Oi!" Catriona said. I looked over at her, but apparently that was her way of answering the phone. She began relaying information about where we'd been and what we found, and so I knew she must have called someone at Fairhaven.

A moment later, my phone buzzed in my back pocket, startling the crap out of me, and causing me to lose my grip on the box in my lap, which clattered to the floor of the car. Cursing, I pulled my phone from my pocket and looked down at it. Iggy's face grinned up at me.

"What's good, Iggy?" I asked as I accepted the call.

"Hey, Ghost Girl. We're all wrapped up here. Just loading up the rest of the equipment into the van," he said blithely. "What a night! Can't wait to go through this footage!"

"Yeah, me too," I lied. "Are you headed back to the hotel?"

"Yep. We'll plan to sleep for a few hours, then start reviewing the audio and video," Iggy replied. "Did you find what you needed? You rushed out of here so fast. I was kind of worried."

"Yeah, everything is great. The owner is going to try to find some information for us on these portraits," I said, trying to keep my tone casual. "Might give us a nice backstory for the haunting."

"Great!" Iggy said. "Any idea when you might be back? We need to lock up, and we don't want to leave the place unsecured."

"Oh, shit!" I said with a groan. "I was in such a rush that I took the damn keys with me!"

"We can just hang around. How far out are you?" Iggy asked.

I looked down at the GPS. "Four hours," I said.

"Four hours?" Iggy cried. "Sam Hill, Jess, I didn't realize she was that far away!"

"I got a little caught up in the moment," I said. "Look, you don't need to wait for me. I'll call Charlie. He's the assistant at the museum. I'm sure he can come lock up for you guys."

"Yeah, let us know, would you?" Iggy said. It was hard to imagine anyone who'd been up all night sounding so amped up, but nothing got Iggy worked up like the possibility of truly irrefutable spirit evidence. And honestly, the museum had been so overrun with spirits the previous night, they were bound to have caught something impressive.

"I'll call him right now," I assured him, before hanging up and dialing Charlie's number. He picked up right away.

"Hiya, Jess," he said politely. "How's it going over there with the ghostbusting?" He chuckled good-naturedly at his own joke.

I forced a chuckle in return. "Oh, pretty good. We heard quite a few bumps in the night. Listen, could you do us a favor down at the museum?"

"Certainly," Charlie said. "What do you need?"

"Well, I had to head out, and forgot to leave the keys with Iggy," I said. "So silly of me. Would you mind popping over and locking up, so that the team can head back to their hotel?"

"Of course!" Charlie said. "No problem at all. I'm heading out in a few minutes anyway, to meet Tia for brunch."

"Oh, that's great!" I said, smiling in spite of my tension. At least something in the universe was going right at the moment. "This won't make you late, will it?"

"No worries at all," Charlie said. "I can manage it."

"Thanks," I said. "I really appreciate your help."

"Certainly. Out of curiosity, where was it you needed to go?" Charlie asked.

"Oh, uh, we figured out that the ghosts were attracted to some of the daguerreotypes in the museum. Shriya told us there are more of them, so we are just headed over to the storage locker to check them out," I said.

Charlie laughed again, sounding skeptical. "Daguerreotypes? Really? You're putting me on! What in the world would a ghost find interesting about a daguerreotype?"

"I'm not really sure yet," I said. "But we're going to try to find out."

"Well, listen, that storage locker is a bit of a death trap," Charlie said. "Why don't you let me go down there for you? I know it like the back of my hand, after all. I can find what you need and meet you back at the museum, if you like. It's no trouble."

"No!" I said, a little too quickly. "I mean, that's okay, really. Shriya gave us the address and the code. Go enjoy your brunch with Tia. We'll give you a call if we need anything."

"Fair enough," Charlie said. "Right when you walk into the storage locker, on the left, there's a step ladder you might find handy. Oh, and mind the back set of shelves. They're a bit wonky."

"Okay, thanks a lot, Charlie," I said. "And tell Tia I said hi."

"Will do. Ring me if you want a hand," Charlie said brightly, and hung up.

"Who were you talking to?" Catriona asked. She had finished her phone call and was now putting all her concentration into aggressively cutting people off on the motorway.

"First, Iggy called me," I said. "They can't lock up because I took the keys with me, like an idiot. But it's okay," I told her before she could agree with what an idiot I was. "I called Charlie, Shriya's assistant. He's going down there now to lock up so that we're free to head right over to the storage locker. He offered to meet us over there after he locked up, but I told him not to. We don't need him breathing down our necks while we try to figure this all out."

"Well played, that," Catriona agreed, nodding her approval. "If I have to keep putting on that buggering American accent, I'm going to bludgeon myself over the head just to stop the sound of my own voice."

"I'll be sure to sound extra-American, then," I muttered as I texted Iggy the update that Charlie was on his way to lock up.

The noise Catriona made in response might have been a laugh, but I couldn't be sure.

"Who did you call?" I asked her when I had finished my message and pocketed the phone again.

238

"Trackers," Catriona said bluntly. "They're going to pull up everything we have on Neil Caddigan, see if we can't connect him to this collection."

Hearing the name fall from her lips made me want to scream and throw things and punch my fists right through the windshield of the car. Somehow, no matter how hard I tried to put that man behind me, the effects of his machinations just seemed to rear their ugly heads again and again, dragging up every hateful, bitter, violent feeling I'd worked to leave in the rearview mirror. He may have Crossed forever on the day the Gateway reversed, but in many ways he was like a ghost, lingering in the dark corners of my life, finding little ways to let me know that he would always be there, whispering my name in quiet moments, breathing down my neck, appearing just in the corner of my eye.

You can't Cross a memory. Nightmares don't seek the Aether.

§

The storage facility was wedged between two grubby apartment buildings in a London neighborhood I'd never been to before, though it had the same air of neglect and run-down appearance as Savvy's neighborhood. The man working at the entrance pointed us toward the appropriate section without asking for any kind of identification or indeed looking up from his magazine at all.

"I'd say 'Securi-Tite' is a bit of a misnomer," I muttered as we walked through the warehouse. The ceilings were high and crisscrossed with pipes and flickering bays of fluorescent lights dangling from chains. The floors were bare, echoing concrete. Within the massive footprint of the facility were row after row of corrugated metal lockers of various sizes, some as large as shipping containers, others stacked on top of one another like gym lockers or safety deposit boxes. We couldn't hear a single sound in the place except for the hum of the ventilation system and our own footsteps. It seemed to be totally empty except for us.

"Here it is," Catriona announced after several long minutes of turning up and down narrow corridors. "Number 1502, is that right?"

"Yup," I said, handing her the paper. It was a large unit, with a metal door rather like a manual garage door, with a handle at the bottom, secured to a ring in the floor with a padlock. Catriona squatted down and fiddled with the padlock for a few seconds, before giving it a sharp tug and tossing it aside.

"Give us a hand here, will you?" she asked. Together we grabbed ahold of the handle and wrenched it upward. The door rose with a deafening, grating screech of metal on metal, sliding up and back along the track in the ceiling. Then Catriona groped around for a moment and found a light switch, which lit a single fluorescent tube set into the wall.

"Bloody hell," Catriona cursed, looking into the depths of the unit. It was packed full of boxes, piled onto shelving units and in stacks along the walls, with only narrow paths between them. "We're going to be here forever."

"Maybe we should have just let Charlie do it for us," I agreed. "But Shriya said the box would be labeled with the date, so let's start there. Charlie said there would be a step ladder... yup, here it is." I said, after a cursory glance into the corner, where the step ladder was revealed to be exactly where Charlie had said it would be.

We began the slow, tedious process of pulling down box after box to check the dates, which, unhelpfully, had been written on the tops of the boxes rather than on the fronts, where they might actually have done us some good. We'd been at it nearly an hour when Catriona cried out, "Ah-ha!" like a crime novel detective.

"You've got it?" I asked, excitedly.

"No, I shout 'ah-ha!' for laughs when I'm bored," Catriona said blandly. "Yes, of course I've got it, get your arse over here!"

I picked my way carefully through the box towers we'd dismantled until I came to crouch beside her in front of a large cardboard box with a tightly taped cover. Apart from the date printed on the top were the words, "Caution: Sensitive to Light. Handle with Care."

"Do you think we can open it?" I asked.

"Well we didn't come all this way to admire the box, did we now?" Catriona snapped.

"I know but... do you suppose the light will... damage anything?"

Catriona calmed her snark and considered the matter. "Shriya said that daguerreotype plates were light-sensitive. You never know, there may be some of those in there, never used. But the actual images themselves were hanging in the museum in broad daylight for years with no adverse effects. I think, for our purposes, a bit of dim fluorescent light won't hurt."

"Yeah, you're probably right," I said. "How do you want to—" But before I could even finish the question, Catriona had pulled a Swiss army knife from her pocket, flipped it effortlessly open, and run it along the edges of the box top, unsealing it in one smooth, fluid motion.

"Right. With your knife. Obviously," I said under my breath.

Catriona took a breath and then seemed to hold it as she prised the lid off the box. The inside of the box had been divided into compartments with cardboard partitions, neatly separating the contents. Three of the four quadrants were empty.

In the fourth quadrant was a stack of small squares, diligently wrapped in gauze and bubble wrap. Catriona pulled the first of them off the stack and unwrapped it. Out fell another daguerreotype in a polished wooden case. This portrait was also of a man, middle-aged, wearing a black robe.

"Well, isn't that bloody interesting," Catriona murmured, holding the portrait close to her face.

"What's bloody interesting?" I asked.

"It's new," she replied.

"What do you mean, new?" I asked. "How can you tell?"

"Well, to begin with, there's this," she said, turning the casing over and showing a tiny 'made in China' label that had been partially ripped off. "But that could simply mean that the casing itself has been replaced recently. But look at the plate. It's in pristine condition—none of the spotting or discoloration, like the ones we took from the museum."

"Maybe it was just stored more carefully?" I suggested.

"I don't think so, unless the subject is a bloody Time Lord," Catriona snorted. "Look closer at his left hand." She dropped the portrait into my hand.

I looked down at it. At first, I couldn't understand what Catriona was talking about. There didn't seem to be anything that suggested the image was any more modern than the others we had seen. Then the man's wrist caught my eye. A watch was peeking out from the robe.

It had a digital display.

"What the hell..." I muttered.

I flipped the casing over, but there was no date or name written upon it, nothing to suggest when it was taken, who had taken it, or who the subject was.

"The robe is a dead giveaway," Catriona said. "Ceremonial robes like those have been used by the Necromancers for centuries."

I vaguely remembered learning this information in Celeste's History and Lore class years ago, but had forgotten about it. Repressed was probably a better word. I tried to think about the Necromancers as little as possible.

"This man was a rank and file Necromancer," Catriona explained. "Those higher up in the Brotherhood wore stoles of various colors to denote their rank. Some even had medals. They liked to reward themselves based on the magnitude of their own crimes, naturally."

"So, do you think that all of these portraits are recent, like this one?" I asked.

"Only one way to find out," Catriona said.

We pulled out the other daguerreotypes one by one, unwrapping each and laying them out upon the floor in rows. Then, when only six of them remained in the box...

"Holy shit!" I cried, dropping the daguerreotype in my shock. It clattered against the cold, hard floor.

"What? What is it?" Catriona asked.

"Neil. It's Neil Caddigan. There, that's his photo," I whispered, at once embarrassed by my overwhelming fear and yet unable to shake it off. I felt tainted, like I'd just picked up something poisonous.

Catriona reached down and plucked the portrait from the ground, turning it over. The protective glass was now marred with a thin, jagged crack, but there was still no doubt about the face that stared out from beneath it. White hair, silvery eyes, and a smug, self-satisfied turn to his smirking lips—Neil looked just as I remembered him, just as he sometimes appeared in the twist or turn of a roiling nightmare. He looked so sure of himself, so confident as he posed, one hand upon his knee, the other resting on the arm of his chair. Several ornate rings adorned his fingers, and a wide stole lay draped over his robe, along with a large collection of medals and badges.

"He was really important in the Necromancer hierarchy, wasn't he?" I breathed as I stared down at him.

"The highest of the high," Catriona said, nodding. "Grand High Master, if I'm reading those medals right. None of the Necromancers who survived the attack on the castle would answer any questions about him, so I cannot say for sure, but based on our research and the evidence, he was the big boss."

"He's dead, though. What does it matter if they tell the Durupinen about him?" I asked.

"The Necromancers are notoriously tight-lipped, even under torture. It's one of the reasons they have proven so difficult to dismantle and destroy. Usually, in other criminal organizations, you can... erm... *persuade* one member to crack and provide you with the critical information you need to take down the whole bloody lot. Not the Necromancers, though. They choose death over betrayal every time."

"You mean we actually... kill people?" I asked.

Catriona looked at me sharply. "Do you think that a Necromancer would give even a moment's thought before taking your life?"

"No."

"The same is not true of us. Let's leave it at that," Catriona said curtly.

It was clear she didn't want to say any more on the subject, and I reluctantly swallowed about a hundred questions. Did the Caomhnóir do the torturing, or was that the Trackers' job? Had Catriona ever had to do it? Was this what lay ahead of me as a Tracker? Would I one day be asked to take part in something heinous like that? Then I thought of Neil and wondered if I wouldn't have happily turned some thumbscrews, or whatever outdated medieval torture methods existed in dank, *príosún* basements. Then I wondered what the hell this said about me, that I wanted to cause pain to someone else and promptly shut the whole train of thought down. There was no time for that kind of self-examination right now... or probably ever. So I changed the subject.

"So, these portraits—or whatever they are—someone is still making them?" I asked.

"Yes. Or were, up until a few years ago. How else could there be portraits of these more recent Necromancers?" Catriona said.

"But... are they just portraits?" I glanced uneasily down at the silvery eyes. "Or are they something more than that? I mean, spirits are actually drawn to them. There has to be a reason."

"I think the reason is in the other image," Catriona said, and her voice was deadly serious. "The one of the woman that we found overlaid on the portraits. We should see if the new ones have the same effect."

I held the daguerreotype of Neil level with my eyes and tilted it back and forth, trying to see if it had the same, strange image overlaid with it.

"The lighting is too dim in here," I said. "I can't tell if these ones have the image of the woman."

"Here, hand it over. I'll bring it out in the hallway where the light's better," Catriona said, holding out her hand and snapping her fingers impatiently.

I dropped the portrait into her hand and turned back to the box as she picked her way carefully through the maze of boxes and back to the storage locker door.

"What do you think happened to the rest of the stuff?" I asked her, over my shoulder.

"Can you be a bit more specific?" Catriona drawled.

"I'm talking about the rest of the stuff that's supposed to be in this box. This collection wasn't just daguerreotypes. There was supposed to be equipment and notes, too."

"Your guess is as good as mine," Catriona said. "Blast it!" she added as she tripped on the step ladder on her way out the door.

I pressed my hands against my head, which was starting to pound with the beginnings of a stress headache. I pushed my palms against my eyeballs, causing abstract shapes and colors to appear behind my eyelids. "Okay," I said letting out a slow, deep breath. "Think, Ballard. The portraits are of Necromancers. The portraits also have images of a Durupinen hidden in them. The men in the portraits have silvery eyes. Durupinen are being attacked and found with silvery eyes. This fits together somehow, but I just can't figure it out! *Think!*"

But my brain had officially ground to a halt.

"Catriona, you're the brilliant Tracker mystery solver. Can't you Poirot us out of this shit?" I called.

There was no answer.

"Cat?"

A strange muffled thump met my words, followed by a clatter.

"Cat? Are you still there?"

There was another sound, but I couldn't quite make it out. A moan? Heart pounding, I stood up too quickly, the blood rushing to my head, throwing me off balance so that I had to lean on the wall as I hurried through the maze of boxes. As I emerged around the last set of shelves, I saw Catriona lying on the ground just outside the storage unit, her blonde hair spilling across her face, one arm stretched out in front of her, as though reaching for the daguerreotype that now lay on the ground a few feet away.

"Oh my God! Catriona!"

As I started toward her, I had one last fleeting glimpse of her face. Her eyes were open, her mouth gaping. She seemed to be trying to say something to me. Her head shook "no."

Then, from behind me, an arm grabbed me around the shoulders. A hand clamped roughly over my mouth as a heavy blow struck the back of my head. Then a sharp pain shot through my neck, and everything went black.

20

BETRAYED

THERE WAS NO LIGHT. There was no sound save for my own ragged breathing. There was nothing. I shifted my body.

Oh God, except for pain. Blinding, sickening, agonizing pain.

I tried to think through the pain, to use my senses to figure out what the hell was going on, but every pulse of agony that shot through my head and down my body erased my capacity for rational thought anew. Fighting roiling waves of nausea, I held myself perfectly still, hoping and praying that it would pass. After a few moments, it dulled enough that the fog in my brain cleared, and I was able to begin to process my situation.

The room was so absolutely pitch black that I might have gone blind. I blinked around, straining to make out a single detail of the space, but nothing would resolve in the blackness. Someone had shoved a wad of fabric into my mouth. It tasted like dust and smelled of mildew. I gagged on it and retched, but my insides were empty—there was nothing to bring up. I felt hard cold stone against my cheek. A sharp twinge of pain up my arm made me realize that my hands were tied together behind my back. I didn't dare try to move them, for fear of bringing on another tidal wave of pain crashing down on me. After a heart-stopping moment of realization that I couldn't feel my feet, I realized they must be tied together too.

There was a muffled groan from somewhere to my left. It sounded like a woman's voice.

"Catriona?" I tried to say, but the gag rendered me unintelligible.

I tried to cry out for help. There was no response. I did not try again, realizing too late that my cries would be more likely to alert an attacker than a savior. I had to try to figure out where we were.

Steeling myself for more pain, I rolled myself over onto my back and then onto my side again, very nearly losing consciousness in the process. Then I stopped, gasping. It felt as though I had rolled through something sticky and wet. I could smell the tangy, musky scent of blood as my hair plastered itself to my face. That was how I discovered that the back of my head was bleeding. I could feel the dried film of it on the back of my neck and on my shoulders.

Swallowing back my desperation along with the bitter taste of bile, I began working my teeth and tongue against the gag that had been shoved into my mouth. It was slow and painful work—my jaw felt frozen and cramped from having been forced open for so long. Little by little, I felt the fabric giving way until finally, it fell to the floor.

"Catriona?" I whispered, or tried to. My mouth was so dry that no sound would come out, I swallowed a few times and tried again. "Catriona?"

A second sound, a sort of moan, came out of the darkness, but closer this time; I had rolled closer to her. Again, I fought through the waves of dizziness and pain to shift myself closer to the sound, propelling myself across the floor on nothing but whispered curses and grit, until my shoulder bumped up against another body.

"Catriona?" I whispered again.

She tried to answer me, but I could tell from the quality of the sound that she had been gagged as well. I stretched out my neck until my nose brushed against something—her chin. I lifted my face, found the gag in her mouth, and grasped onto it with my teeth, yanking it free.

Catriona wretched, sputtered, and coughed. "Bloody... bollocking... *hell*," she gasped at last. "What happened? Where are we? And why does my head feel like it's going to explode?"

"I have no idea where we are, but I think I know what happened," I replied in a hushed voice. "We were attacked in the storage locker. I saw you on the ground out in the hallway. The pain... I can't even..." My voice was lost, drowned in another wave of it.

"It's not just the blow to the head," Catriona said through gritted teeth. "We've been drugged."

"Drugged?" I hissed. "How do you... wait, I think I remember something. A stinging in my neck?" The memory was murky, covered in a hazy film of agony and confusion.

"I felt it, too. Just before I went down. A syringe in my neck, definitely. Must have been etorphine, or something similar," Catriona said.

"Why the hell do you know... actually, you know what? Forget it. I don't want to know why you know that," I said. Obviously, this was another one of those elements to Tracking I was better off being blissfully ignorant of.

"Do you have any idea where we are?" I asked her.

Catriona did not answer right away, but I didn't press her; I could practically hear her wheels turning. Finally she said, "Wherever we are, it's underground—that damp earthy smell."

I sniffed and noticed it immediately. "So, a basement?"

"Most likely," Catriona agreed. "Also, we're in the city."

"We are?" I asked. "How do you...?"

"Listen," Catriona said. "Can't you hear the traffic?"

Again, I fell into silence and concentrated. Sure enough, after a moment of two of hard listening, I heard the very faint sound of a horn blaring impatiently in the distance.

"Are we still in London?" I asked, frowning.

"I'm good, but I'm not that good, pet," Catriona said, with a touch of her usual asperity. "A city. Best I can do on that score."

"Anything else?" I asked.

"Yes, and it's arguably our most significant clue. This space is Warded," Catriona said.

And for the first time, she sounded frightened.

"Warded?" I asked, my panic much more pronounced. "You're sure?"

"Can't you feel it?" Catriona whispered. "Reach out!"

Though the darkness was pressing upon me like a weight, I closed my eyes and tried to focus my energies on locating a spirit presence. My efforts were met with a silence so deafening, so complete, as to only be explained by Wards. No natural place in the world was so devoid of the whisperings of life... or rather, afterlife.

"You're right."

"Too right, I am."

"What the hell does that mean? Durupinen did this? Why?" I hissed.

"Come on, love," Catriona said, managing to drench her voice in condescension even in this state. "I know you've been drugged, but for God's sake, you can't honestly have forgotten what we've been closing in on."

In my panic, I passed right over the opportunity to make a snarky remark about Catriona and her chronic need to insult me. The picture was resolving itself, growing clearer as I forced myself to focus. The daguerreotypes. Neil Caddigan.

I gasped. "Oh my God, of course! The Necromancers! It has to be!"

"I would venture to agree with you," she said, and I could almost hear the rueful smile in her voice. "If you recall, thanks to my darling cousin, the Durupinen aren't the only ones who know how to Ward spaces or perform Castings."

"They found out somehow," I said with a groan. "They found out that we discovered the daguerreotypes. They found out that we were investigating them."

"Right in one," Catriona agreed.

"But how?" I asked. "How did they find out?"

A man's voice came out of the darkness, quiet and calm.

"That's simply answered. I told them."

Catriona and I both froze. My heart thundered in my chest, and my body was tingling all over with the overwhelming panic that I could neither fly nor fight. It was Catriona who recovered herself first.

"Who are you, then?" she demanded, with a coolness that I admired even in my terror. "Show yourself."

A click, a pop, and the room was flooded with the wavering light of gas lamps. Involuntarily, I squeezed my eyes shut against it, dazzled after so long in utter blackness. Slowly I forced my eyelids to open a fraction of an inch, blinking away tears, until I could focus at last at the figure sitting casually in the corner.

"Hello, Jess," said Charlie Wright.

"Charlie?" I gasped. "What... what are you doing? What the hell is going on?"

"Oh, I'm quite sure you could figure that out if you tried," he said pleasantly, scratching at his chin, which was dark with stubble. "You're a clever girl, aren't you?"

I didn't respond. I was still trying to process my shock. I stared wildly around the room. Catriona had been right; it was definitely a basement. The walls were made of roughly hewn stones. Along the top, where the walls met the low, wood-beamed ceiling, black curtains had been drawn closed over small windows at what must have been the street-level. But perhaps the most significant—and most disturbing—element of the room was the vast collection of runes scrawled all over the surfaces. There were runes carved into the beams and planks of the ceiling, drawn onto the stones of the walls, and painted onto the floor beneath us. In the far corner of the room, tucked into the shadows, were several large shapes draped in lengths of black fabric. A gasp from beside me made me twist around to look at Catriona, who was staring down at the floor in alarm. We were lying right in the middle of a large Summoning Circle.

Charlie allowed us to take stock of our surroundings before sighing theatrically. "Oh, come now, Jess. It was your cleverness that got you into this mess, after all. Much too clever and much too nosy. You very nearly ruined everything."

I couldn't think. Charlie Wright? Sweet, nerdy Charlie? The world was upside down. Nothing made sense.

"Have I shocked you? I do hope so. Honestly, there have been days recently when I have quite shocked myself. I've done things I scarcely thought I had in me," he said.

"You're... you're a Necromancer?" I asked, though the answer to the question was obvious in the twist of his smiling lips. "But how did you... I don't..."

"It all seems terribly unlikely, doesn't it?" Charlie said, nodding his head sympathetically. "I never believed in spirits, you know. Well, honestly, I'm hardly the type. Spent my life studying science and math, deeply rooted in the firm basis of facts. Facts were safe. Facts were reliable. I had no need and no use for the supernatural in my life. It did not fit. Until about five years ago, when my parents were killed."

He was speaking in a bright, friendly voice, the very same tone I'd always heard from him, except that now, in juxtaposition with the circumstances, it set my teeth on edge and raised the hairs on the back of my neck. Alarm bells were going off inside me, clanging in discordant panic. This young man, despite every appearance of friendliness, was maybe the most dangerous individual I'd ever seen.

"Can you possibly understand what an event like that does to you?" Charlie asked. He looked from Catriona to me, waiting expectantly for an answer, like a teacher tossing out review questions. When we didn't oblige, he went on, "Oh, come now, Jess, you ought to. After all, you've lost nearly everyone dear to you, haven't you? Pity, that. The difference, of course, was that the answers to all your deepest questions came knocking on your door.

You didn't need to wonder what happened when someone dies. It was all explained to you, and you held the key to understanding it all, while the rest of us are left to wallow in our helplessness and our grief."

"I had been left with nothing. Every constant in my life stripped away, like that." He snapped his fingers. The sound echoed sharply around the room. "No answers to my questions. No explanations to ease my anguish. I'd spent my life solving problems and seeking logical explanations, and here I was, confronted with the first question to which I could not find an answer. I must admit it nearly broke me. Nearly. But then, I found Neil Caddigan."

I swallowed back the revulsion that name always brought flooding to the surface. "What do you mean, you found him? How?"

"Well, I suppose it was he who found me. I'm not one to believe in things like fate, but then... I was never one to believe in any of the things to which I now dedicate my life's work. I was already enrolled in one of Neil's seminars at City College of London when the accident happened. When I returned to classes he pulled me aside. He talked to me, asked me if I was all right. When it became clear that I was not all right, he asked me to lunch with him. 'I think I have some information that might help you,' he told me."

Anger boiled under my skin. Of course, Neil would never miss a chance to poison a mind, to recruit to his legion of followers. He had made a victim of Charlie as surely as he had made a victim of Lucida. Like any decent cult leader, sniffing out the vulnerable, pouncing on them in their moment of need, and offering to save them—a destructor in savior's clothing. However, as Charlie the victim had beaten, drugged, and kidnapped me, my sympathy for him was severely limited at that moment.

"In the corner booth of a nearly deserted pub, he told me about the Necromancers and the world they inhabited. 'With your extraordinary intelligence and your drive, you could be a valuable asset to our mission,' he told me. 'With your help, we could at last unlock the mystery, to take control of the forces that determine who lives and who dies. What mightn't you do to bring your family back, if that power was within your reach?' I did not believe him at first, of course. The fantastical does not so easily sink into a mind armored in the logical. I extricated myself as politely as I could from that luncheon and the next day, withdrew from the seminar.

The man was insane, I told myself, and I would have nothing else to do with him. Oh, how naïve I was."

Charlie laughed amusedly, as though he were simply reminiscing over a childhood anecdote. Beside me Catriona shifted uncomfortably. Her expression was warier than ever—clearly she thought, as I did, that Charlie was quite unhinged.

"Neil knew exactly what he was doing. He had planted the seeds; then, all he had to do was sit back and wait for them to take root. And take root they did. I lay awake, night after night, turning his words over and over again in my brain. What if—*just what if* what he said was the truth? What might I discover if I joined him? What if my loss—my pain—could be erased?"

"A fair question," Catriona said, interrupting for the first time. I thought I could hear the fear in her voice, well concealed beneath the contempt. "And one you ought to have seen through, if you're as clever as you seem to think you are. Neil Caddigan's ranks were swollen with those foolishly seeking a power to which they had no right."

Charlie's face hardened for a moment, then broke into a smile again. "Spoken like a true Durupinen, so confident in her own destiny, so sure she has the unalienable right to play God with the rest of us. I will not entertain your smugness. It is as Neil said. You are too weak, too limited, too afraid to use your power to its potential. And if you cannot wield it mightily, you do not deserve it."

"Our gift is not a weapon," I said, finding my voice for the first time. Perhaps it was hearing the echoes of Neil Caddigan in his words, but I felt an angry flame spark in my chest. "And the fact that you speak about it like it is one only proves you understand it no better than Neil did."

Charlie laughed. It wasn't his typical chuckle. There was a wild, unhinged quality to it, as though he were laughing to keep something darker and more dangerous at bay. Catriona heard it, too; I felt her stiffen slightly beside me.

"I will not waste your time or mine trying to convince you. Did Neil Caddigan manipulate me? Perhaps. But only to my benefit. Once his ideas took hold of me, I could not shake them. Two weeks later, I was back in his office, ready to assist him and the Necromancers in any way I could. I was determined to prove myself, to show them that I could be a valuable asset to them. It was perhaps the most exciting, most pivotal moment in the history of the Necromancers. They were poised, Neil told me, on the brink of a great coup that would bring the Gateways within their power at last. But before I could be fully inducted into the Brotherhood, all hell broke loose. And by 'all hell,' of course, I am referring to the Prophecy."

I recoiled as Charlie turned his gaze on me, a gaze that was full of undisguised loathing. "Just as I was poised to find the answers I needed, you and your sister tore our Brotherhood apart. Neil was dead, the upper ranks were captured or decimated. We were in shambles. The few who avoided capture went to ground, afraid to face a reckoning for their failure, and the rest of us were left to pick up the pieces of all that you destroyed."

"You can blame Hannah and me all you want," I said, "but the days of blaming ourselves are long gone. It was Neil's decisions—not ours—that led to your destruction."

"It does not matter, now," Charlie said with a wave of his hand. "Let the past molder where it lay. The damage you have done will be repaired."

"What do you mean?" I asked, my voice hoarse and dry.

He leaned forward conspiratorially. "We are rising, Jessica Ballard. We are rising again, and this time there will be no limit to the scope of our powers."

Catriona snorted. "You have risen before. And here you are, wallowing in the ashes of your failure yet again. A Brotherhood that cannot learn from its mistakes cannot succeed. You will be relegated to the gutters of the spirit world where you belong, make no mistake."

"Ah, but it is you who do not learn from your mistakes. You have underestimated the Necromancers time and again. Your arrogance will be your undoing, in the end. And the end approaches."

"You sound confident in that. Why should this time be any different? Why should this rising not end in a crashing fall, like all the others? Impress me," Catriona said.

Charlie leaned forward and whispered. "We have allies, now. Allies you have lost through your neglect and your arrogance and your ingratitude."

Catriona's voice shook. "What do you mean? What allies?"

"Soon your defenses shall be ours. And so shall your gifts," Charlie hissed.

"Our gifts?" I repeated, numb with fear.

Charlie did not answer. Instead, he stood up, careful to crouch slightly to avoid the nearest beam. He crossed the room to the corner where the fabric-draped shapes stood like a mockery of ghosts. He bent down, grasped one of them and, with a grunt, lifted it and carried it to the center of the room. He set it down carefully and then drew back the fabric with a flourish.

Beneath it was a lacquered wooden box, utterly unremarkable-looking.

"Ah, yes, the dreaded wooden box," Catriona said with a sardonic smirk. "Truly, I quiver with fright. Surely we cannot survive the wrath of the box."

I, however, did not scoff. I was too busy focusing my still blurry vision on several details of the box that stirred my memory. A metal circle on the front. A second, larger box that protruded from the first. A small metal plaque on the side. I struggled to tease the details out of the hazy fog of the drugs that still hung like a pall over my senses, dulling everything, making me feel like I was moving in slow motion.

"It's not a box," I said as the realization surfaced at last. "It's a camera."

"A what? Excuse me?" Catriona asked. I craned my neck to see her staring at me as though she feared I'd lost my mind.

"It's a camera obscura," I told her. "Shriya told us about them, remember? They were used to create daguerreotypes like the ones we found of Neil and the other Necromancers."

"Yes, very good, Jessica," Charlie said. "I'm pleased to see you're keeping up. When I first met Neil Caddigan, he had just risen to the highest ranks of the Necromancer hierarchy, due, in large part, to a monumental discovery. He had worked for many, many years on perfecting a process, a process that would change the Necromancers' relationship with the spirit world forever."

He paused, as though hoping one of us would encourage him to go on. When we didn't, he stroked the wooden box gently with a single finger, and sighed.

"Since the Necromancers were formed, they have been plagued by a single handicap that has impeded their advances more than any other. I am speaking of course, of the Sight, or lack thereof."

My heart sped up. Was he talking about being a Seer? How could he possibly know about my gift? No one knew, not even our own

Council. I swallowed hard and tried to sound clueless. "What are you talking about? What Sight?"

Charlie laughed, but it was cold, humorless. "My, my, those drugs have made you rather dull, haven't they? Your Spirit Sight, of course—the ability you each possess that allows you to see and interact with the spirits around you!"

I was so relieved that he wasn't referring to my role as a Seer that I did not at first notice or share in Catriona's sudden tenseness. After a few silent moments, though, during which Charlie seemed to be enjoying the effect of his words, I saw that Catriona was now staring at the camera obscura as though it were a dangerous weapon rather than a simple wooden box.

"Over the centuries we struggled to find a solution, to discover the secret of the Sight, so that we could imbue ourselves with it and strengthen our connection to the spirit world. With the Sight, what couldn't we learn and study about the Aether and beyond? What secrets mightn't we unlock?"

"The Sight cannot be put on or cast off like a piece of old clothing," Catriona spat at him. Her expression was twisted with disgust.

"Perhaps not," Charlie said. "But neither does it indelibly belong to the Durupinen. With the right understanding, the right science, and the right Castings, it can be replicated, and it can be bestowed upon others."

Catriona blinked. She seemed to be in shock. "That's not possible," she whispered.

"Wrong again," Charlie said, grinning. He seemed to be thoroughly enjoying himself now. Meanwhile, my arms were cramping horribly from being tied so tightly and I'd nearly lost all feeling in my feet. "Are you finally beginning to understand what Neil Caddigan and the rest of the Necromancers have been trying to tell you all along? Your view of the spirit world is blinded by your own arrogance. You have limited others by design, but by doing so, you have limited yourselves. But Neil dared to experiment—to push against those boundaries that you have so carefully built around yourselves. And at last, he succeeded." Charlie patted his hand on top of the box again, a fanatical gleam flashing behind his wire-rimmed glasses.

"Neil built that?" I asked.

"No," Charlie said. "I built it, based upon his designs. It is called the Camera Exspiravit. Take a good look at it. Remember it well, and fear it. It will be the end of Durupinen dominion as we've known it."

21

CAMERA EXSPIRAVIT

I LOOKED AT THE BOX AGAIN, and was visited by a wild desire to destroy it, though I was utterly helpless to do so in my current state.

"You see, when the Prophecy came to pass, Neil had already built a Camera Exspiravit, after decades of work and research. It wasn't a new idea. Necromancers had been working on it for centuries, experimenting with the idea since the advent of photography itself. You've found some of the attempts, I am sure, amongst the collection. Neil took up the work when he joined the Brotherhood. Many of his experiments went terribly wrong, but each taught him just a bit more, illuminating his path one step at a time until at last he reached his desired outcome. Perhaps you noticed, Jessica, during your tangles with the Necromancers, a certain odd quality to their eyes?"

"Yes," I said at once. "Their eyes looked almost silver." It had been one of the very first things I had noticed about Neil Caddigan when I had met him, years ago on that fateful night in Culver Library. And later, when the other Necromancers had attacked us and abducted Hannah, I had noticed it again in the eyes of our assailants.

"Yes, indeed," Charlie said, waggling his finger at me like I was a precocious child who had just amused him with my adroitness. "Every fully indoctrinated member of the Brotherhood was endowed with the Sight before carrying out the plan to kidnap your sister. It was the final step to full initiation into the Necromancers, a gift that had to be earned through dedication, perseverance, and commitment to our cause. The silver color is a side effect of the process."

"So that's the reason for the silvery eyes in daguerreotypes as well?" I asked breathlessly.

"That's right," Charlie said. "It was the gleam of Spirit Sight in their eyes, a gleam put there by this very invention."

"This isn't possible," Catriona murmured. "This just... isn't possible."

"Not only possible, Tracker. Actual. Surely you must have noticed during your interactions with the Necromancers that they could both see and interact with the spirits around them? Surely that did not escape your notice?"

"Yes, but I... I assumed it was a Casting. A bastardization of Melding, perhaps, or..." Catriona's voice trailed off as her mind groped about for any shred of logical explanation for the Necromancers' abilities. It was clear that she could find none.

"But your eyes are normal," I said to Charlie.

"I never made it to the final stage of my initiation," Charlie said, his expression darkening. "Neil had hand-picked me, with my proclivity toward research and science, to be his apprentice in this, his most important work. It was his intention to teach me all there was to know about the process of using the Camera Exspiravit, so that I could assist him in the complicated and arduous task of bestowing the Sight upon all new Brothers. But I had only just begun to embark on my studies when the Prophecy came to pass and the Brotherhood fell. We were decimated. The Candidates like me, who had not been at Fairhaven, went to ground. And with the identities of our senior members discovered, the Trackers located and confiscated or destroyed nearly all of our assets, properties, and artifacts."

"And we're bloody good at it," Catriona said. "I personally destroyed many of Neil Caddigan's belongings, and what we didn't destroy is kept under lock and key."

"You were thorough, yes," Charlie said. "But you didn't know about me, did you?"

Catriona didn't answer, but if looks could kill, Charlie would have dropped lifeless to the ground right there. He met the venomous glare with a smirk.

"The Necromancers were very careful to keep no records of Candidates, mostly to protect themselves, but in this case, I was the one who needed protection. For weeks I held my breath, sure that each new hour that passed would be the hour that brought the full might of the Durupinen thundering down on top of me. But weeks and then months passed, and at last I accepted that the Durupinen were not searching for me. I had fallen under their radar, a stroke of luck that I had not anticipated. At last, I felt safe to pursue my work again."

"But none of this makes sense," Catriona said, squeezing her eyes shut. "A wooden box cannot bestow Spirit Sight."

"Oh, not by itself," Charlie said. "You've got that right, if nothing else. The box itself cannot pluck Spirit Sight from the air, just as it cannot pluck a likeness or an image from the air. One with the Spirit Sight must be present, and then, her sight must be reflected onto the subject. Only then can the Spirit Sight be passed along, and bestowed upon another."

"One with the Spirit Sight," I repeated. "You mean a Durupinen."

"Yes."

I winced. "This still makes no sense."

"Yes, it is most complicated," Charlie said, a note of pity in his voice. "I cannot fault you for your lack of understanding, when I have just begun to understand it myself. First, the subject's image is taken with the camera obscura. They sit for the portrait, the lens cap is removed, and the plate is exposed to the light. Then, the lens cap is replaced. Then the Durupinen's image is taken on the same plate, the image captured directly on top of the first. Then the image is developed using chemicals, to produce the final daguerreotype, which is a melding of the two images."

"But," I sputtered. "That's just a photograph. A double exposure. Sunlight and a few chemicals can't magically make someone see spirits."

"No, indeed," Charlie said. "The key to the process are the many Castings involved. See for yourself."

He picked up the camera and slid the top of it off, revealing a hollow inside with a metal device for holding the plates. Then he walked a few steps closer to us, tilting the camera toward us, so that we could peer inside.

"Bloody hell," Catriona whispered.

The inside surfaces of the camera were carved with runes and markings—dozens of them. Round metal medallions had been hammered into the surfaces, gleaming like coins. There was also a strange scent of mingled herbs—I thought I could make out sage, lavender, and something that smelled like sulfur. There also appeared to be a set of prongs rising up in the center of the box, holding a large, multifaceted gemstone that might have been a diamond.

"What is this?" I whispered, more to myself than to Charlie. "What is all of this? This isn't how a camera obscura is supposed to work."

"Oh, no indeed," Charlie agreed. "We've quite reinvented it, it's true. And yet, when you see it... when you take a moment to appreciate this new incarnation... doesn't it become clear that this is what it was always meant to be? Its true form. Look at the way it all fits together, so beautifully, like it had simply fallen from the Aether in this very way."

Charlie looked down at the Camera Exspiravit with an affection usually reserved for offspring or small puppies in normal people. But I was quickly seeing that Charlie was not normal, and that this situation in which I now found myself was perhaps the most dangerous of my life.

"Your very own Castings, your very own system of magic, used to steal your gift and give it to the world," Charlie said, his voice full of wonder and something else less identifiable but far less stable. "I thought I knew what poetry was until I saw this."

Catriona seemed unable to respond. She was still staring at the inside of the box, trying desperately to fit together the pieces of what she could see, her overwrought, drug-dulled brain working furiously.

"The Castings capture the Spirit Sight, and the diamond refracts it—splits it—within the confines of the camera," Charlie said, an indecent enthusiasm in his voice. You would have thought Catriona and I were precocious students, eagerly engaged in his experiment, peppering him with questions and begging to be shown more, rather than two bound prisoners forced to listen to his ravings. Charlie, oblivious to the irony, went on, "Then the refracted components are focused onto the plate, and onto the image of the recipient."

He looked up from the camera eagerly, as though he expected to find us looking awed and impressed rather than horrified. He grinned, a bit manically, and continued. "Then the plate is removed and developed, and even during that stage, more Castings are required as part of the process. Once it has been completed, though, the resulting image, carefully encased, preserves the Sight for the subject."

262

"What do mean, the image preserves the Sight?" I asked, trying to think logically through my horror. If only we could just keep him talking long enough to come up with some kind of plan...

"The creation of the portrait is part of the Casting," Charlie said. "There are many examples in the history of mystical and religious culture that require the creation or use of an outside object to produce a result in the subject of the charm or spell. A needle in a voodoo doll, for example, will cause pain in the subject in whose likeness the doll has been created. The same is true of these portraits."

"And if the portraits were destroyed?" Catriona asked. "What then?"

"The Necromancer would lose the Sight," Charlie said solemnly. "That is why the portraits have been so carefully preserved."

"And what about the Durupinen used to create all of these?" I asked through gritted teeth. "No worries there about detriment to the subject, were there?"

"There was no detriment at all," Charlie said. "Not when Neil produced them, at any rate."

Catriona and I looked at each other. I could see a sudden dread in her eyes, as though she had just understood something that I did not.

"Neil had a willing participant," Charlie went on, looking directly at Catriona now and smiling blandly. "I am speaking of your cousin Lucida, of course, who was more than happy to assist. Through her generosity, Neil was able to bestow the Spirit Sight upon all of the upper ranks of the Necromancers. The gift they used to interact with the spirit world was connected to your very Gateway."

The muscles in Catriona's neck were working furiously, like she was fighting back the urge to vomit. "I don't believe you," she managed to hiss at last. "The woman we saw in those daguerreotypes wasn't Lucida. It was another Durupinen, one who was clearly being tortured."

"Well, Neil had to go through a few—ah—*volunteers* before he met Lucida. But if you'd kept looking through the collection you would have found a familiar face."

"I don't believe you," Catriona repeated weakly.

"But you don't need to believe me," Charlie said, pulling a daguerreotype from his pocket and holding it out for us to see. "The proof is right here, should you choose to acknowledge it."

Catriona was incapable of rebuffing the invitation. Unwillingly, she tilted her head, peering across the top of the portrait until the light shone off the image at just the right angle, morphing Neil's smug expression into Lucida's triumphant one.

I gasped as I glimpsed it, then tilted my head to try to catch it again. Beside me, Catriona was shaking with rage.

"I started with what little I had in my possession: a small notebook of Neil's, detailing the basic concept of the Sight and the theory that it could be imbued on a non-Durupinen by means of an instrument of photography and the correct combination of Castings. At the very back of the notebook was a rough drawing of a camera obscura, along with a few notes, and a crude list of musings. I knew that Neil's Camera Exspiravit, the one he had managed at last to build, had been destroyed along with all of the rest of his work files and the entire contents of our Grand Temple. If I was ever to help our Brotherhood to rebuild, I would be starting nearly from scratch.

"Bit by bit, I gathered the pieces. I interviewed the few high-ranking Brothers who had survived the purge. Only one remained who had been gifted with the Sight. He had been too old and in too frail of health at the time of the Prophecy to have been of any use in the storming of Fairhaven. It was his information that became the most valuable to me. He was able to walk me through certain parts of the process, to provide details that I could not find in any of Neil's written notes. And while there was much of the process he did not understand, the tidbits he provided me with were invaluable. He agreed to help me in my mission. Have you guessed yet to whom I am referring?"

I shook my head stiffly. I wasn't interested in playing a guessing game, not now that I was finally comprehending how much danger we were really in. I used Charlie's fixation on the camera to take in the room again, desperately searching for any possibility of escape.

"The gentleman in question had helped track down and provide many of the components Neil needed for his work. He was an expert, you see, in all forms of photography, both old and new. He had connections to antiques dealers and collectors, as well as a working knowledge of processes long out of date. It was his expertise that Neil relied on to begin his work, and so I knew that I would have to do the same. And so, I came to a quaint little museum tucked away in Old London Town."

I gasped as the pieces finally fell into place in my foggy brain. "Oh, my God. Mr. Pickwick. Shriya's grandfather."

"Correct again," Charlie said. "He was more than willing to help me, but his health was failing and his mind was not what it had been. He took me on as a shop assistant so that I could be close to him and his artifacts, many of which I would need to study to progress in my work. Under his tutelage, I was able to produce a working replica of a camera obscura and learn the traditional daguerreotype process, while helping him keep up the museum."

"But he died," I interrupted. "He died and left the museum to Shriya."

"A complication I had not anticipated," Charlie growled. "It was most inconvenient. How could I continue my work if I was separated from it? But luck smiled on me in this, at least. Shriya knew little about the day-to-day business of running the museum, and was therefore delighted to find her grandfather's young assistant to be so amiable and willing to help her keep things running."

This would have been a perfect moment in the conversation to hurl a snarky insult at him, but another nugget of information had floated to the surface of my memory. Shriya, arms full of boxes, cocking her head in the direction of a sealed basement door and saying, "I'm not allowed to open it. It's been sealed off. See? Black mold. It was all in the paperwork when I finally got the deed to the place. City health inspector would have to shut us down if we broke the seal. That stuff can kill you."

The sounds of the city... the smell and feel of a cellar...

"We're there," I said hoarsely. "We're there in the basement of Pickwick's right now, aren't we? This is the room that Shriya could never open. It wasn't sealed up because of black mold at all, was it? It was your fucked-up little laboratory all along."

"Tut, tut," Charlie said, clicking his tongue at me. "Language! Is that any way for a lady to talk?"

"Untie me and I'll show just how unladylike I can really be," I spat back.

I watched him roll my words around in his mind, twist them into something vulgar, then smirk and let them go. I saw it as clearly as the workings of a clock when the gears have been exposed. I wanted to spit at him, to claw his goddamn eyes out.

"At last I was ready to test my camera, but I had one, very crucial component missing from my experiment. In order to capture and reflect the Sight, I needed someone possessed of the Sight, which meant that I needed a Durupinen."

I tried to swallow again. My mouth was so dry that my throat felt lined in sandpaper.

"This was another great hurdle in my work. Neil had a willing participant in Lucida, who was eager to assist in his process, but I had no such accomplice waiting in the wings. And so, I would have to resort to other means to lay my hands upon the right person. I began my research into Durupinen living in the city of London and, lo, and behold, whose name should I stumble upon but yours?"

He smiled, rubbing his hands together enthusiastically, looking quite mad. "It was just so bloody poetic. The very woman who nearly destroyed us, used to restore us to power once again! I was giddy at the thought of it. But I tempered my excitement with caution. You had been through a great deal, and would not, I thought, be so easy to lure into a situation where I could carry out my plans. You were sure to be well-protected. I had to find an indirect means, a scenario that would make our crossing of paths seem a matter of coincidence rather than design. A little further digging into your life in London revealed the perfect avenue."

"Tia," I said through gritted teeth. "You were only using her to get to me."

"And I feel just terrible about it," Charlie said, with a theatrical pout. "Just desperately guilty, you know. She really is a very sweet girl, if somewhat naïve. However, I could not have been better placed to make her acquaintance, as she was taking classes at the very school in which I was already enrolled. A few quick phone calls, a heartfelt meeting with my adviser, and I found myself sitting right across the aisle from one Miss Tia Vezga, who fell almost at once for my unassuming brilliance and introverted charm. I took my time—I could tell that she was quite guarded, and she soon confided in me exactly why that was. She'd had her heart broken, poor dear. Well, I told myself, if it was already broken, what were a few more cracks?"

"You bastard," I hissed. "She trusted you."

"And still does," Charlie said, nodding solemnly. "A fact I will use to my advantage when this is all over. But enough with the tedious insults and the interruptions. You're ruining the climax of my story."

"Well, go on, then," Catriona sneered. "We can both see how dearly you enjoy the sound of your own voice." Her tone was mocking, but the energy beneath it was tense—jumpy. I knew that she, too, was using Charlie's long-winded explanation as a chance to figure a way out of this mess.

"Over time, I worked my way into that battered little heart, and soon she was telling me all manner of details about her life and, more importantly, her friends. At long last, she seemed ready to let our paths cross, and so I arranged for us to meet at the Portobello Market."

"And you knew that I would be intrigued by you at once because of the spirits," I said. "How could I resist getting to know more about the guy who attracted so many spirits? That's why you brought the Necromancer daguerreotype with you that day."

"Actually, there you are mistaken," Charlie said, shaking his head ruefully. "That was a misstep on my part. You forget, I have not been gifted with the Sight. While I knew the importance of the portraits, I did not realize that they attract spirit attention of their own accord. I did not realize that I had set myself up to catch your attention in such a manner. Imagine my panic when I arrived at the museum to discover you and Shriya, discussing your interest in conducting the paranormal investigation of the museum. I feared that my connection to the Necromancers would be discovered before I could perfect my process.

"Because, you see, I realized I wasn't content to simply experiment upon you. There were still questions in my process that needed to be answered, but I could not answer them without attempting the process and seeing what happened. This was risky, because for each attempt I made—"

"You would need a Durupinen to experiment on," Catriona snarled. Her brows had contracted together into a fierce line over her narrowed eyes. She looked angrier than I'd ever seen her. I felt like I could have spit flames myself.

"Flavia. Phoebe." I choked.

"Collateral damage," he said with a shrug. "It couldn't be helped."

"Couldn't be helped? Lucida went through the process with her Spirit Sight intact. Why, to this day, does her Spirit Sight remain unaffected while Phoebe and Flavia's have been twisted and destroyed, if not for your own incompetence?"

"Oh, well, as to that, I'm certainly not to blame," Charlie said, widening his eyes innocently. "I'm afraid you'll have to lay that blame at your own feet, Jessica."

I laughed, one sharp, short, mirthless bark of laughter. "You attacked two women, nearly destroyed them, and you're blaming one of the two women you currently have tied up? I can't fucking wait to hear the logic behind that conclusion."

"I had no intention of attacking anyone. Or at least, I had no intention of destroying anyone's gift. But, as I've just told you, there were still kinks to be worked out, and your discovery of the ghosts at the museum had tightened my timeline. I had no choice but to go forward, despite the gaps in my knowledge."

"How did you find them?" I asked through gritted teeth.

"I discovered them when I was searching for Durupinen in the area. There are many, you know, but not many that would make good choices for targets. As you know, most Durupinen are wealthy, well-connected, their lives heavily intertwined with other Durupinen. It would have been foolhardy in the extreme to attempt an abduction of any such Durupinen. But there were a few that might be described as black sheep. Your friend Savannah was one, but her frequent trips to Fairhaven meant that her cousin was really the easier target. A poor country bumpkin visiting the big city—it was so easy it almost wasn't sporting of me."

"And Flavia," I said. "She was a student at the university. You targeted her the same way you targeted Tia."

"She was a much feistier customer," Charlie said, a hand rising unconsciously to his bicep. "I thought she would be another easy target, cut off as she was from her clan, but I underestimated the fire of the gypsy spirit. But no matter. The effort was worth it, in the end. Through my experiments on Flavia and Phoebe, I was able to work out the final kinks of the Camera Exspiravit. It was ready for my real target."

"What about the other half of your experiments?" I asked.

Charlie looked genuinely perplexed. "What do you mean, the other half?"

"I mean, if you had a Durupinen, you must also have had someone who you were trying to gift the Sight to," I said. "Who did you use?"

"Oh," Charlie said, waving his hand dismissively. "It was easy to find a couple of willing volunteers amongst our Candidates."

"And what happened to them?" Catriona asked. "The Durupinen you discarded have been terribly affected. We do not know if we will ever be able to fully restore their gifts to working order."

"The Candidates, too, were afflicted with some rather... unfortunate side-effects," Charlie said with callous indifference. "But they, unlike the Durupinen, had at least volunteered willingly."

"You're sick," I blurted out, unable to help myself. "Those men are supposed to be your brothers, and you used them like lab rats."

Charlie's expression hardened as he surveyed me from behind his glasses. "I do not expect you to understand. There are things worth sacrificing for."

"Oh, yeah, real brave of you, sacrificing other people for your precious cause," I said, looking him up and down with disgust. "You're the one who doesn't understand sacrifice, or you would have offered yourself up, wouldn't you? Instead you let others suffer for your mistakes so you could benefit from their pain. You make me sick."

Something dark and violent shivered across his face, and for a moment I thought he was going to leap across the room and attack me. But as quickly as it appeared, it had gone, and his expression was mild once more.

"As I said," he replied softly. "I do not expect you to understand. But the days of dangerous experimentation have passed. My process has been perfected, the Camera Exspiravit is ready, and the guest of honor has arrived." He gestured to me.

Catriona looked at me, panic in her face, and then back at Charlie. "Leave her alone, will you? She's just a kid. Use me instead."

I stared at her, but Charlie was already shaking his head. "Oh, no, indeed," he said amusedly. "That won't do at all. If I'm going to be gifted with the Sight at last, I want to take it from her: the girl who nearly destroyed it all. I realize it isn't very scientific of me, but there's a touch of a romantic in here somewhere," he sighed, tapping his own chest. "I simply can't resist the sheer beauty of it, knowing that each time I gaze upon a spirit, I stole that very gaze right out of you, Jessica Ballard. As a matter of fact, I can't wait a moment longer."

He stood up and began to walk toward me. Catriona rolled

protectively toward me, but Charlie aimed a sharp kick at her, so that she rolled away from me with a cry of pain.

"I'm not going to be a party to this," I said through gritted teeth. "I will not assist in the rise of the Necromancers. I haven't been damaged like Hannah, or poisoned, like Lucida. There's nothing you can say to me that will force me to help you with this."

"Your words are highly amusing, given that you say them while trussed up and tied like a pig for slaughter," Charlie said wryly. "I know enough about you to know that you would never cooperate with me of your own free will. That is why I had to get you here the way that I did. And that is also why I've saved just a bit more of this, for when I've got you all set up and ready to take a pretty picture." He reached into his pocket and pulled out a syringe with a red plastic cap on it. He flashed it at me, then placed it between his teeth and bent down over me.

I shouted and struggled in vain as he hefted me easily from the floor and carried me over his shoulder across the room. He staggered and grunted as I flopped around, desperate to throw him off balance. As he shifted his position to lower me into a chair, I found his ear brushing against my cheek, and so, I used the only weapon available to me. I bit down on his ear until I tasted blood, until I felt the cartilage giving way.

Charlie shrieked, twisting violently away from me and dropping me onto the chair. My ribs collided with the arm rest, knocking the wind out of me. I heard the syringe hit the floor and roll away.

"You crazy bitch!" Charlie roared and, before I could recover my breath, he backhanded me across the face as hard as he could.

Catriona was shouting and Charlie was still swearing, but all I could see was blackness and then lights popping behind my eyelids like fireworks of agony. When I opened my eyes again, dizzy from the force of the blow, it was to see Charlie hunched over, both hands cradling the side of his head, which was covered in bright, wet blood. On the floor between us was the chunk of his ear I had just bitten clean off. I stared at it for a moment in macabre fascination.

"Jesus. JESUS," Charlie was half-sobbing. He shrugged out of his flannel shirt, and held it up to his ear to staunch the bleeding. I struggled against my bonds again, desperately hoping the struggle had loosened something, but my feet and hands were still bound impossibly tight. I stared wildly around the floor for the syringe, but it was nowhere to be found. Gradually, Charlie gained control of himself, slowing his breathing from agonized pants to long deep pulls of air. At last, he laughed.

The sick fuck actually laughed.

"That," he said softly, "was unbelievably stupid."

The adrenaline pumping through my veins was driving my heart rate up so that it felt like it was buzzing rather than beating, a mad swarm of bees let loose in my chest.

"What exactly did you hope to accomplish by pulling a stunt like that?" Charlie asked, still laughing. "You are still tied up. You can't possibly have thought you'd actually get free that way?"

"Guess I just wanted to give you a little something to remember me by," I said. Hannah once told me I would probably die one day from an overabundance of snark. Maybe she was the one who should be the Seer.

"Oh, I'll be taking something to remember you by, I assure you," Charlie replied. With a grunt he tore the sleeve from his shirt and tied it around his head as a makeshift bandage, freeing up his hands to set to work. As Catriona and I watched, he positioned several large lights on telescoping tripod stands around the room. Then, he rummaged around in a black canvas bag and produced a handful of white taper candles, which he fitted neatly into wall sconces around the room. Then he reached into the bag again and produced a small, shabby, but very familiar book.

"The *Book of Téigh Anonn*!" Catriona gasped. "Where did you get that?"

"I have my sources," Charlie said enigmatically.

He began wandering the room, muttering Castings under his breath. I could feel ripples of energy around the room, a trembling of the air as his words took their effect. As he worked, momentarily distracted from me, I closed my eyes, feeling out into my connection, desperate to get help, to connect with Milo, but the silence was deafening. Whatever Charlie had done to the room—or to me—had rendered the Spirit Guide bond useless.

His Castings complete, Charlie put the book aside and pulled something small from his pocket. For one panicked moment, I thought it was another syringe, but a moment later I watched as he pulled the cap off a permanent marker.

"Time for a bit of artwork," Charlie said with a smile that was really more of a leer. "Nothing you can't handle. I see you are sporting a bit of ink already."

He brushed one long, slender finger up the length of my arm, tracing a few of the lines of my sleeve tattoo. He followed the leaves up my shoulder to where they turned to birds, and brushed his hand gently across my collarbone, following their progress of flight. The feel of his touch made me want to leap out of my own skin. Then he moved his fingers up my neck, along my jawline, and cupped my cheek, his lips parted, and I thought for one wild moment that he was going to kiss me. He leaned in close to my face, so that his lips practically brushed against my ear.

"This won't hurt a bit," he whispered, pushing my head to the side, to expose the curve of my neck, and setting the tip of the marker against it.

And as my head was forced to the side, I could see past his shoulder, into the doorway of the basement. I could make out, through the slight haze of the sedative, a shape, a slightly blurred and yet familiar form, creeping stealthily toward us.

Her face was fierce—so fierce, so full of hatred, that I almost didn't recognize her. She caught my eye for just the briefest of moments, raising a finger to her lips. Then she raised her arm, and I glimpsed a flash of metal.

And then Tia Vezga plunged the syringe into Charlie's unsuspecting neck.

He fell forward on top of me with a cry of surprise and the chair toppled over. The back of my head struck the stone, and I felt one of my arms, still tied behind my back, twist at an impossible angle and snap. I think I might have cried out, but the shock and adrenaline had eradicated my senses. Charlie and Tia continued to struggle on top of me as Tia's thumb drove the plunger down through the barrel, driving the sedative down into his body. Charlie roared and flung his torso back, sending Tia tumbling off of him and across the floor. She leapt to her feet with surprising agility, arms up in a defensive pose even as she sobbed hysterically.

Charlie attempted to rise to his feet but lurched and fell on top of me and the chair once more. He raised his head, his glasses askew, saliva dripping from his mouth, to glare at Tia.

"You... you... how did..." he slurred.

Tia shook her head. "How dare you," she whispered. "How fucking dare you."

Charlie made one last, enormous effort to raise himself, to say something coherent, but he failed at both. With a gasping groaning sound, he collapsed on top of me and fell still.

There was a long, silent pause while we waited to see if he was really unconscious. Then Tia stumbled across the room, fell to her knees, and dissolved into uncontrollable tears.

"Oh, Jess! Oh, my goodness! Are... are you all right? Did he hurt you?" she was whimpering. Her hands hovered above Charlie's limp body, as though she were afraid to touch him now.

"I... I think my arm might be broken," I said through clenched teeth. "Can you help me get him off of me?"

Still heaving with sobs, Tia shoved Charlie's crushing weight off my chest and then, with a grunt of effort, righted the chair back onto its legs. Then she hurried around behind me to begin pulling at my bonds.

I jerked my head over my shoulder toward Catriona. "Untie her first," I said.

Catriona, still coughing from the kick to her midsection, called, "I'm fine, I'm fine. Get her untied first."

"Yeah, I know you're fine," I said. "At least, you're more fine than me, and more useful than me if he wakes up or if, God forbid, he's got any other Necromancers hanging around."

Catriona grunted her approval and rolled over onto her stomach so that Tia could reach her hands. Tia stumbled over to her and began working at the knots.

"Tia, how did you find us?" I asked.

"Charlie called me and cancelled our brunch date," Tia said between shuddering breaths. "He sounded... weird. He said he needed to do some stuff for Shriya, and that he was really sorry, and that he would call me later. I was already halfway to the restaurant when he called, so I just ate by myself and then decided to order him a meal and bring it to him, as a surprise. He had shut off his phone, though, so I didn't know where he was. I stopped by his flat, but he wasn't home. So, I took the chance that he might be down at the museum. You hadn't come home yet, so I thought you might be here, too. I saw that the van was gone, and the front door was locked. I tried your phone, but that went to voicemail, too. Then as I was leaving, I spotted the van in the alleyway. The side door was open. I... I heard voices coming from the basement, so I followed them."

The ropes slipped from Catriona's wrists and she gasped in relief.

Tia helped her sit up and reached for her ankles, but Catriona waved her away.

"I can get these," she said. "Go and help Jess."

Tia crossed back to me and knelt behind me. Her first attempt at the knot nudged my arm. I sucked in a shuddering breath and held it, trying not to cry out.

"Oh, J-Jess," she stammered. "It's b-broken for sure. The angle is so strange."

"It's okay, we'll get it taken care of," I told her. "Just get the ropes off. Where did you get the syringe?"

"I was wondering the same thing," Catriona said as she eased a foot through the loop of the loosened ropes.

"I was listening at the door and heard the struggle," Tia said. "I almost came in to try to help, but then the syringe rolled right out into the hallway, and I picked it up. I knew if I could just wait for the right moment, when he was distracted... oh, God, I just can't believe any of this."

The ropes fell away from my wrists as Tia dissolved once more into tears. Tucking my left arm against my side, I turned in the seat, stroking her hair with my good hand. "I'm so sorry, Tia. I'm so sorry. It's my fault. He was using you to get to me, and I didn't see it."

Tia wiped her eyes on her sleeves. "No, it's my fault. I should have realized. I should have known..."

"There was no way you could have known, Ti," I said. "Did you listen to him? He's a master manipulator. Well, he learned from the best."

Catriona had risen to her feet, looking surprisingly steady. She tucked one hand across her midsection, cradling her ribs. "We can discuss all of this later," she said curtly. "Tia, is it?"

"Y-yes," Tia replied.

"Did you see anyone else, Tia? Any other men in the vicinity? Any other cars parked nearby?"

Tia shook her head. "Everything was deserted except for the van in the alleyway."

"Right," Catriona patted her pockets. "Do you have a mobile on you that I can borrow?"

Tia nodded tearfully, reached into her back pocket, and tossed the phone to Catriona, who caught it deftly, despite the fact that her hands must surely be numb from being tied up.

"I'm calling for back up," Catriona said. "Don't move him, and don't touch anything."

"Does kicking him in the face count as moving him?" I asked politely.

Catriona cracked half a smile, but didn't reply. She turned without another word and ducked out through the narrow doorway. I could hear her footsteps all the way up the stairs and pacing around above our heads.

Tia was staring down at Charlie as though she had never seen anything like him in her life—an alien lifeform, inhuman and frightening.

"I didn't know," she whispered. "I can't believe that's what he was, all along, and I didn't know."

I reached out with my good hand, found hers, and squeezed it. "He's not the only one who surprised everyone."

Tia turned to me, face glazed with tears, and frowned. "What do you mean?"

"Busting in here like a superhero? Sticking him with a syringe like some kind of badass secret agent?" I said, nudging her with my shoulder.

She rolled her eyes. "Shut up, I did not."

"You were brilliant," I told her seriously. "Brave and amazing and brilliant. And you probably just saved my life."

Tia's face scrunched up, the bud of a smile unable to stem the tidal wave of crying that threatened to break forth. I pulled her in beside me and, holding her close, let the storm rage over the two of us. Moored to each other, I knew, we would weather it.

22

THE GATHERING STORM

"**T**HAT BASTARD! That treacherous, manipulative *bastard*," Milo whispered, shaking his head. "I swear on Chanel, if I had my way he'd never have two minutes of peace again in his life."

"Get in line," I told him.

"Yeah, right behind me," Savvy added.

"And me," Tia and Hannah said together.

They were all sitting in chairs around my bed in the Fairhaven hospital ward, where Mrs. Mistlemoore had set my arm and done what she could to counteract the nasty effects of the drugs. It had been nearly twenty-four hours since Tia had sprung us from the museum basement, but my head was still pounding and swimming with a dizziness that struck without warning. Mrs. Mistlemoore said the after effects were likely to last at least a week.

"I still can't believe this," Hannah whispered. "All those attacks."

"Have they made any progress yet? With Phoebe or Flavia?" Milo asked. Curtains had been drawn around both of the girls' bed spaces for privacy, and also to contain the Castings they had been using in their attempts to cure them.

"No, not yet," I said, reaching over and squeezing Savvy's hand as I did so; she was gazing guiltily over at where Phoebe lay hidden away. "But they are gathering all of Charlie's notes and equipment, and the Trackers took photos of the museum basement, and also his apartment, so they can try to piece it all together and reverse the Casting."

"They'd be able to piece it together a lot bloody faster if that bastard would cooperate," Savvy muttered, her nostrils flaring. "But they've been questioning him for hours now, and he won't say a word."

Tia stifled a sob behind her hand and lay her head on Hannah's shoulder. Hannah stroked her hair gently.

"Our Scribes are brilliant," Hannah told her. "They're like, our academics—our research librarians. They'll figure it all out and Flavia and Phoebe will be back to normal in no time, you'll see."

She said it confidently, to ease Tia's grief, but she looked me in the eye, and I could read her expression; it was brimming with doubt and worry.

Tia barely seemed to hear her. She was still looking around the place every now and then as though she'd woken to find herself landed in the middle of a fairytale gone terribly wrong. I remembered feeling the same way when I'd first arrived at Fairhaven—that sense of surrealness had taken a long time to fade. Tia had known only vaguely of the existence of Fairhaven—she had been allowed the general overview of the situation, but never the details, and it was never in the plans to actually let her see the place. In truth, I suspected only a handful of non-clan members had ever set foot in the castle. But after everything that had happened with Charlie—after everything she'd seen and heard in the museum basement—it was inevitable that Tia would need to be brought back with us, to be questioned and debriefed. I'd always done what I could to erect a sort of makeshift barrier between Tia and the Durupinen. I'd tried to shield her from the more frightening details of the world I inhabited. Charlie had blasted those barriers to the ground, destroyed any illusions of safety, and left her to fall, face-first, into the darkest pits of the spirit world. No wonder the poor girl looked like she'd been clubbed over the head.

"Of course, they will," I said, picking up Hannah's cue. "They'll make sure that Charlie's legacy in all of this is nothing but failure."

I swallowed back a lump in my throat and caught Savvy's eye. She knew it was a lie, because there was one act of Charlie's that no one would ever be able to undo, and the weight of it hung over Savvy like a shroud—slowing her steps, dulling her laugh, and snuffing out the trademark twinkle in her eye. There was no bringing back Bertie, no matter what the Trackers discovered of Charlie's plans. And there was also no amount of rationalization that could make any of us feel any less guilty about it.

If only we'd seen through Charlie sooner...

If only we'd gone to the hotel earlier...

If only someone had gone with Bertie, or called for back-up...

If, if, if... that word was a remorseless bastard, sometimes.

An idea seemed to have occurred to Tia. She sat up poker-straight, looking suddenly terrified. "He's not here, is he? They're not keeping him in the castle?"

It was Savvy who answered. "No. I may have... uh... roughed up a couple of Caomhnóir when I was trying to get access down to the dungeons. They told me he wasn't here, but I had to see it for myself. Lucky break for him, too," she added, with an ominous crack of her knuckles.

"You roughed up some Caomhnóir?" Hannah asked, looking alarmed.

"No need to look at me like that. I left them standing, didn't I?" Savvy said with an unconcerned shrug. "But actually, if you see a discipline report for me slide across your desk while you're in the next Council session, put in a good word for your girl, eh?"

Hannah's lips curved into a reluctant smile. "I think I know a few people who will vouch for you, in this situation."

"Yeah, you bloody well do," said a smooth, silky voice in reply. We all looked up to see Catriona strutting down the hospital ward toward us, looking grim. "Don't worry your head about it, Savvy. Consider it sorted."

"Cheers, Catriona," Savvy said with a wry smirk.

"How are you healing up, then?" Catriona asked me, looking me up and down appraisingly.

"Okay. How are you already up and about? And how the hell are you walking around in stilettos right now?" I asked her, pointing in horror at her feet.

Catriona shrugged. "I've had my fair share of bumps, bruises, and druggings in my time with the Trackers. I don't like to say you get used to it, but..." she shrugged. "Let's just say, at this point in my career, I don't often find an excuse not to look my best."

"Respect," Milo muttered under his breath in an awed voice. He was taking in every detail of Catriona's appearance with approval.

"Look, can you lot clear out for a few minutes?" Catriona said, looking at the others, grouped around my bed. "I've got to have a word with Jess. And Hannah, they want you to join them in the Grand Council Room. They're starting to review my report."

"Oh!" Hannah jumped up. "Of course. Jess, are you sure you're..." she gestured a little helplessly at me, her eyes lingering on my arm.

"Hannah, go," I said. "I'm good. Honestly, there's nothing you can do for me at this point but stare at me pityingly. I'll get by without it, I promise."

Hannah narrowed her eyes at me, but gave my good shoulder a squeeze. Savvy and Tia stood up, and Milo floated over to join them.

"Come on, love," Savvy said, throwing a friendly arm over Tia's shoulder. "I'll take you over to the dining room for a spot of tea, and then, let's go hang out with my mentee, Frankie. She's dying to meet you. She wants to go to medical school more than anything, and she wants to pick your brain."

"Oh!" Tia said, looking surprised, but pleased all the same. "Yes, all right. That sounds like a good distraction. Jess, is that okay with you?"

"Yes!" I said encouragingly. "Please, go get your mind off all of this."

"Oi," Catriona said, halting Tia with an outstretched hand.

Tia froze, looking terrified. "Um... what?" she squeaked.

"Just wanted to say thanks, again. It's not often I get myself into a situation that I can't get out of on my own. You saved our hides in there, and I don't mind admitting it," Catriona said, in a tone that suggested she did mind admitting it, just a little.

Tia gave her a tearful, fleeting smile, along with a nod of acknowledgment, but she didn't seem able to respond any further than that. Savvy threw an arm around her again, and they followed Hannah up the ward to the door. Milo, floating along in their wake, spun in the air, caught my eye and said, inside my head, "I got you, sweetness. I'm here in the shake of a tail feather if you need me."

"Thanks, Milo." I sent my reply thrumming along through our connection. "Get that tail feather out of here."

He grinned, gave a little shimmy purely for my amusement, and faded out of view.

"Well," Catriona said, perching herself on the edge of one of the chairs and tossing her hair back from her face. "Your knack for trouble really is uncanny, isn't it?"

I sighed. "Look, Catriona, if you're only here to give me shit, can we do it another time?"

"I'm not just here to 'give you shit,'" Catriona said, giving my phrase a slightly disgusted emphasis, as though the American-ness of it left a bad taste in her mouth. "I meant... you did well."

"How the hell is that what you meant?" I asked with a dry laugh.

"I mean, you sensed something wasn't right, and you took initiative. You went with your gut, and you uncovered what could have been a devastating plot, had it been allowed to run its course. We need that kind of initiative on the Trackers. You did well," Catriona said, looking at her own fingernails rather than at my face, lest we establish a meaningful moment of connection. "You know, despite overlooking the fact that the perpetrator was right under your nose."

I managed not to roll my eyes, but it was close. "I'm going to choose to take that as the compliment I think you implied somewhere in there," I told her. "And... thank you for your help, too. You... well, anyway, thank you." Part of me wanted to tell her that I'd appreciated the way she'd volunteered herself for Charlie's twisted experiment, offering to take my place, telling him I was just a kid. It was only much later, when the adrenaline of the situation had finally worn off, that I was able to fully appreciate what that gesture meant. But the other part of me knew that she'd either deny the whole thing, or else shrug it off as nothing. I decided not to give her the chance to do either.

"Do you really think they'll be able to help Flavia and Phoebe?" I asked quietly.

Catriona's face fell into serious, contemplative lines, an expression that looked utterly foreign on her features. "I don't know. I hope so. They've got a good shot at it, I think, but God knows how long it will take, or what shape those girls will be in by the time they've managed to do it. Staring at one's own soul... I can't imagine there won't be repercussions."

I shuddered. The silence spiraled. Catriona broke it with a sigh.

"Look, what I actually wanted to talk to you about is Charlie and what he said down in that cellar," she said.

"Which part?" I asked dryly. "The evil rambling is all blending together, to be honest."

"The part," Catriona said slowly, "when he insisted that the Necromancers would rise again."

I dug back through my tangle of memories, trying to remember exactly what Charlie had said. His words floated up to me, like bubbles to the surface of murky water.

"Let the past molder where it lay. The damage you have done will be repaired."

"We are rising, Jessica Ballard. We are rising again, and this time there will be no limit to the scope of our powers."

"We have allies, now. Allies you have lost through your neglect and

your arrogance and your ingratitude. Soon your defenses shall be ours. And so shall your gifts."

"They have allies now," I said slowly, turning the words over and over in my hand like a river stone: dark, smooth, and opaque. "What do you think that means?"

Catriona shook her head. "I don't know."

"Do you think there's a chance he was just bluffing?" I asked, and I could hear the plea in my own voice.

"Yes, I do," Catriona said. "But I don't think it's a good chance."

"So, what do we do?" I asked.

"The Trackers need to investigate it. And I want you to head up the investigation with me."

I blinked. "You want me to *what?*"

Catriona rolled her eyes. "You heard me. You broke your arm, not your ears. What do you say?"

"I... don't know what to say," I replied, my head reeling. "You... I mean, let's be honest, we've never been fond of each other, and I've barely even gotten started as a Tracker. Why would you want to consider me for something like this?"

Catriona appeared to be chewing the inside of her cheek, trying to decide how to phrase her answer. "It's true. I didn't like you at first. You're cocky and defiant, and you've got just a bit more attitude than I like."

When she didn't go on, I flopped back on my pillows. "Great, well, thanks for clearing that up."

"But, truth be told, I've had those very same things said about me," Catriona said, and I was surprised to hear a smile in her voice. By the time I looked up at her, though, it was gone. "We both play by our own rules. I think we are going to need that independence in this investigation."

"You don't think the Council is going to support it?" I asked. "I mean, you're on the Council."

"My voice may be on the Council, but that doesn't mean my voice will necessarily be heeded by the majority. Celeste certainly understands the threat of the Necromancers, I'll give her that, but she also cares about process and order. She will not underestimate the Necromancers, but she will still want to do things by the book. Look, what I'm saying is, I think the Council will approach this threat... carefully," Catriona said. "I'm not sure if we can afford to be careful."

We are rising, Jessica Ballard. We are rising again, and this time there will be no limit to the scope of our powers.

"We definitely can't afford to be careful," I agreed.

"Too right we can't," Catriona said. "The official investigation has already been opened, but we are going to expand it. It's going to take a lot of boots on the ground. You will likely be asked to do things you've never done before. It might require learning some new skills, ignoring a fair number of rules, and flying under the Council radar. What do you say?"

I didn't really have to think about it. Even if she hadn't been asking me to do everything I could to stop the Necromancers from gaining power again, wouldn't I have been doing it anyway?

"I'm in," I told her.

Catriona smiled. It was the first time she'd ever smiled at me without a trace of mockery behind her eyes. I wouldn't exactly call it "friendly"—I don't think Catriona was emotionally capable of "friendly." But there was definitely something there; it might even have been respect. "Excellent," she said, standing up. "I'll start the paperwork."

"My attitude will require its own paperwork," I called after her.

"That's for bloody sure," she replied, as the door swung shut behind her.

§

I woke to the sounds of muttering and scurrying feet. In my disorientation, the sound reminded me of mice and dark basements, and my heart began to pound as I scrambled up into a sitting position, blinking wildly around at me as my eyes adjusted to the dim half-light.

No basement.

No bonds.

I was at Fairhaven. Everything was fine.

I exhaled slowly, and made a conscious decision not to chide myself, as I might normally have done. It would take time, I reasoned, to move past the events at Pickwick's museum, and I needed to give myself that time.

I glanced over at the clock on the wall; it was just after two o'clock in the morning. Hannah, Milo, Savvy, and Tia had stayed with me until nearly eleven o'clock, until Tia quite literally nodded off onto Savvy's shoulder and I ordered them all to bed, grateful for an excuse to kick them all out without admitting to my own exhaustion, which I succumbed to almost at once. It felt like I'd only been asleep for moments, rather than hours. The sounds that had woken me had not been mice, but Mrs. Mistlemoore and the Scribes, who were moving around in the lamplight in Flavia's bed space, their forms silhouetted against the screen like a display of shadow puppetry.

I pulled my legs up in a crisscrossed posture and watched for several minutes. Once or twice, a little plume of smoke would rise like a smoke signal, and then, after a few moments, the scent would waft its way across the room and tickle my nostrils. Some scents were familiar—the warm, rich scent of sage, the heady perfume of lilac—but others were unidentifiable. At one point, I watched as a Scribe took a paint brush to the inside of the screen and painted a large, triskele upon the fabric. I stared at it and found myself praying and pleading—to whom, I wasn't entirely sure—that this Casting would work, and that Flavia would find her way out of the twisted prison Charlie had left her in.

Please. Please let her be all right. Please. Help her.

Suddenly there was a swell of excited murmuring, and a flurry of activity behind the screen. I watched, barely daring to breathe, as someone blew out a candle, and stepped around the metal frame of the partition.

It was Mrs. Mistlemoore. She looked exhausted, and was wiping a wad of white fabric across her forehead. She looked up and caught my eye from across the ward.

She smiled wanly. My heart lifted.

She shuffled across the stone floor, dabbing at her neck and face as she came. Finally, she sat herself heavily on the end of my bed.

"We've made some progress," she said.

"Really?" I felt the tears springing into my eyes. "You think she'll be okay?"

"There are hopeful signs," Mrs. Mistlemoore said cautiously. "We've released the hold of the original Casting, and the Sight has begun to... unravel itself. Flavia's body has relaxed, and she seems to be truly resting for the first time since you brought her here. You and Catriona brought us the missing piece of the puzzle."

"We did?" I asked.

"Oh, yes. We found this amongst Mr. Wright's possessions."

She held out a handkerchief, which had been balled up in her hand. As she opened her fingers, the edges of the handkerchief fell away like petals to reveal the charred remains of a daguerreotype in the center.

I backed away from the thing, as though it were poisonous, or about to explode. "Is... is that one of the portraits?" I asked, breathlessly.

"Oh, yes," Mrs. Mistlemoore said, and she gazed down at the thing with utter disgust. "It was discovered at Mr. Wright's apartment, protected in a glass display case. We were able to determine it was the portrait with which Flavia's gift was distorted by recognizing her image overlaid upon it."

When we had first arrived back at Fairhaven, Catriona and I had explained about the double images in the portraits even as I clenched my teeth through the agony of my arm being set. I shuddered to think what expression must have been captured upon Flavia's face, what pain had been memorialized upon the copper plate before the Scribes had burned it away. I decided I did not want to ask. But I did remember something that Charlie had told us, when Catriona asked what would happen if the portraits were destroyed:

"The Necromancer would lose the Sight. That is why the portraits have been so carefully preserved."

"So, somewhere some Necromancer guinea pig just lost the Sight, if he ever even possessed it," I said, digging deep through my anger to find half a smile.

"As to that, I cannot say," Mrs. Mistlemoore replied. "But with this portrait, we were able to work through the details of the Castings Mr. Wright concocted and devise a counter-Casting. Time will tell if it will restore Flavia completely, but, as I have said, there are good signs already."

"That's wonderful," I said earnestly. "Thank you so much for everything. Honestly, I don't know if anyone ever tells you this, but you are a rock star. I don't know what the Durupinen would do without you."

Mrs. Mistlemoore looked a bit flustered, and I realized, from her expression, that her work must go largely unacknowledged. "Well, now... I... I hardly think... that is to say... you are most welcome."

"Would it be okay for me to visit Flavia now?" I asked tentatively. "I don't want to mess up her recovery or anything, obviously. I just thought a familiar voice couldn't hurt."

Mrs. Mistlemoore considered this for a moment, then gave me a gentle smile. "Yes, of course you can. I think you may be right."

"Oh, wow, really?" I asked. I hadn't expected her to allow any such thing. "Thank you. I won't bother her. I just want to sit with her for a few minutes."

"Yes, I think I can allow that," Mrs. Mistlemoore said. "I've got a report to write up. Why don't you go sit with her now? But mind you, remember you've got your own healing to do," she said, with a sudden return to her brisk manner. "It's important for you to get your rest, so just a short visit. You can see her again after a good night's sleep."

"Absolutely," I assured her, in my most responsible voice. "I'll keep it quick."

She eyed me suspiciously, as though she thought I may be placating her just to get rid of her. I wasn't, but I could forgive the suspicion. Then she gave my dressings a quick look and then rose from my bed and headed off in the direction of her office in the far corner of the ward. Her steps looked weary.

I slid from my bed and padded across the room. The moonlight was still bright, though the full moon had passed a few days ago. Wide beams of it slanted across the floor and the walls, filtering in through the mullioned glass of the high, narrow windows and infusing the entire space with an unearthly glow. It would have been easy, standing silently in the swath of that moonlight, to believe that I was the only soul left alive in the universe.

I peered around the partition and released a breath I didn't realize I had been holding. It was a relief to see Flavia lying still and quiet, her hands folded together on her stomach, her face calm and peaceful as she slept.

I dragged a chair to the edge of her bed, wincing at the sound of the chair legs grating against the stone, but Flavia seemed undisturbed. I dropped onto it, realizing that even the short walk across the ward had worn me out. I took a moment to gather my thoughts, looking around the crowded space.

A lingering scent of herbs and candle wax hung around us like a curtain. The bedside table was crowded with scrolls, pencils, stubs of candles, a bowl full of amethyst and quartz crystals, and what looked like a long black feather. The runes Charlie had marked upon Flavia's skin were but faded shadows, having been scrubbed away to make space for new runes applied by the meticulous hands of the Scribes.

I looked across to the other partition. I knew that Phoebe lay behind it, still trapped in the torturous state Charlie had left her in. I wondered, once the Scribes had healed her, if she would ever be able to remember the attack—to tell us exactly what had happened. Then I wondered, with a lump in my throat, if she'd ever be able to tell anyone anything ever again.

I sniffed as the guilt began to creep in. They'd both been attacked as guinea pigs in a vicious experiment, but I was the real target. Would I have to walk around for the rest of my life with a bullseye on my back, endangering everyone who dared to get too close to me? And poor Tia. How presumptuous of me to drag her here, to pull her into my orbit for my own selfish reasons. I could reason with myself until I was blue in the face that I was trying to rescue her from her own heartbreak, but it was just as true that I wanted my best friend beside me to help me recover from mine. And now, instead of healing, her heart had been stomped to a pulp all over again. At this rate, she would never open up to another guy ever again, and it was entirely my fault.

I looked down at Flavia's slumbering face. "I'm sorry," I whispered to her, as quietly as I could. "I'm sorry I got you caught up in this mess."

She did not move. I hadn't expected her to. I wondered if she had heard a single word anyone had said to her since the attack. No one would know what she was experiencing until she came out of it—if she came out of it.

I reached my hand down and laid it on top of hers. It felt cool to the touch under mine.

"It's going to be okay," I whispered, praying it wasn't a lie. "You're going to be well soon. That bastard Charlie's been caught, and his whole plan has fallen apart. There's nothing else to worry ab—"

Flavia's hand twitched, flipped suddenly over, and clutched at my hand. I gasped, and tried instinctively to pull my hand away, but her grip was like stone, numbing my fingers.

"Flavia, can you hear—"

With a single flexing movement of her arm, Flavia yanked me toward her, so that my face was barely a few inches from hers when her eyes flew open. The silvery quality of them had faded, but they were still misted and strange, the colors swirling like clouds as she locked gazes with me.

And then I was falling—falling into her eyes like pits with no bottoms, and everything was darkness and howling and swirling, silvery clouds. I couldn't breathe. I couldn't see. I couldn't think through my panic. I lost all sense of time, of space, of everything.

And then it was over. I was staring down at Flavia, and her eyes were closed, her face peaceful. Her hand has folded over her chest again, utterly still. I blinked. Had I imagined it? Had I nodded off and had a crazy, drug-induced hallucination? I looked down at my own hand, which was throbbing. I could still see the white marks against my flesh where she had grasped my fingers, and the tiny crescent-shaped indentations—a few of them bleeding—where her fingernails had dug into my skin.

Then I felt a familiar aching sensation in my other hand—the hand which ought to have been in a sling, but which instead, I realized, was outstretched and reaching behind me. With a mounting sense of dread, I turned.

My sling lay discarded on the floor at my feet. My arm was extended, and little eddies of plaster dust were drifting down from my cast, which had crumbled to pieces at the end around my fingers—fingers that were still grasping the long black feather from Flavia's bedside table. Ink was dripping from the end of it onto the floor. Ink spattered my hand and the smooth white surface of my cast. An inkwell lay overturned on the stones, and a small puddle of black ink seeped from it, like blood from a wound.

"What the *hell*...?"

Slowly my eyes traveled up to the white screen of the partition, and for a fleeting moment, I knew what I would see before I actually saw it.

The stark outline of a prison fortress, perched upon a rocky seaside cliff like a crown upon a king. Waves crashed up around it, and ominous dark clouds swirled in the air high above. Rows of figures, with weapons raised, stood upon the battlements, crowded the ramparts, and stood sentinel before the doors. But the most chilling detail was in the air around the fortress: hundreds of spirits floated around it in formation—an army of the dead. All of this was glimpsed as though peering through the curving lines of the triskele the Scribe had drawn, as though the triskele itself were a camera lens through which the image must be filtered.

All the air seemed to have been sucked out of the room. I could not look away from the drawing on the partition, which I now realized I had created. Even as I stared at the place I had never seen before, had never even imagined before, the name of it rose to my lips as though I had always known it—as though it had been sitting, tucked away in my memory, a remnant of a past life or a forgotten dream.

"The Skye Príosún," I whispered.

It wasn't a question. I knew what I was looking at, as surely as I knew my own name. I also knew, as my eyes pored over the details of the figures with torches and fists and staffs raised, that something was terribly wrong. And then Charlie Wright's words echoed through my head again:

We have allies, now. Allies you have lost through your neglect and your arrogance and your ingratitude. Soon your defenses shall be ours. And so shall your gifts.

"This is a prophecy," I whispered. "This... is a prophecy!"

I whipped my head around and looked back at Flavia. She showed no signs of movement, no signs that she knew anything had just occurred.

My blood was thundering in my ears. My first, overwhelming thought was that I could not let anyone see this drawing. I must hide it—must get it out of here before someone discovered it.

I searched wildly around me and my eyes fell upon a pair of medical scissors. I snatched them up and lunged at the partition. The fabric was thin, and the point of the scissors pierced it easily. My hands shook like mad as I sliced in a downward motion, the taut fabric flapping free like a sail. In four swift cuts, all that was left of the partition was a metal frame and a few dangling tatters of cotton.

My first instinct was to crumple it into a tight ball and shove it out of sight under my sweatshirt, but I quashed that impulse at once. I couldn't run the risk of the ink smearing before it had dried and everything being ruined. As much as I wanted to keep it a secret, I did not want to destroy it. I would need more time to study it, to glean meaning from it, and I couldn't do that if it was nothing more than an inky blob. It was two thirty in the morning. The castle was surely nearly deserted. I would have to take the chance that I could move the drawing through the halls without running into anyone.

I glanced toward Mrs. Mistlemoore's office door. The strip of light was still visible beneath it. She was still awake. If she came out here and found the partition destroyed, and me gone, she would know instantly that something was wrong and probably put half the castle on high alert. I needed to hide what I'd done. I scanned the room and spotted the supply room door in the back corner. I lay my drawing gingerly across a nearby bed, like the world's most disturbing blanket. Then, as quickly as I dared, I wheeled the bare partition frame toward it, silently cursing every squeak of a wheel. Then I eased the door open and peered inside. It was a large space full of shelving stuffed with boxes and crates and cartons, all neatly labeled. In the back corner I found what I was looking for: a row of extra partitions. I steered the empty partition through the door and tucked it, as completely as I could, behind the other partitions. Then, I rolled an undamaged partition through the door, and, making sure Mrs. Mistlemoore was still safe in her office, wheeled it carefully into place around Flavia's bed space.

Throwing Flavia one last, anxious look, I gripped the corners of the drawing and swung it behind me, like a superhero donning a cape. Then, my heart still racing, I crept across the hospital ward and out the door.

The corridors were dark and deserted as I dashed through them, the drawing flying out behind me like the tail on a panicking comet. Occasionally, a floating form of a spirit drifted by me, but they took no more notice of me than I did of them as I pelted past door after door. I avoided the entrance hall, knowing there would be Caomhnóir guarding the front doors. I had to hide it. I had to get to my room where I could think, and...

I skidded to a halt, still two corridors away from my room, panting.

No.

It wasn't my own interpretation I needed now.

It was Fiona's. I needed Fiona.

I turned on my heel and fled back in the other direction, charging up staircase after staircase, full of a kind of manic energy I'd never felt before. It pulsed through me like electricity, charging my blood, clearing my head. I was running on pure adrenaline, letting my feet propel me forward without conscious directions from my brain, and all the while, the image of the drawing hung before my eyes, as though seared into the very air.

At last, I stumbled to a halt in front of Fiona's tower door. I raised my hand to pound upon it but, at that very moment, it flew open.

Fiona stood before me, her hair a tangled, disheveled mess, her eyes wild and dilated.

"Is it... did you...?" she breathed.

Without a word, I held the partition out to her. She reached a paint-spattered hand out for it, and held it up before her eyes, which went, if possible, still wider. She raked the image with her gaze, and then raised her eyes to stare at me.

"Just now?" she asked.

I nodded, feeling the dread creeping in upon me. "How did you know?"

Fiona shook her head. "No idea. Dreamed it, I suppose. Woke up, and knew you would be here."

I didn't question how this could be—it seemed, at this point, a natural part of this wholly unnatural event.

"I think... the Necromancers... Finn... please... you have to help me," I gasped.

I don't know what she saw in my face, but suddenly she reached out a hand and pulled me to her. I accepted the embrace gratefully, taking deep, heaving breaths, inhaling the scent of paint and turpentine and sweat like it was the very oxygen I desperately needed after half-drowning in my own terror.

A moment later, Fiona grabbed my shoulder roughly and pushed me back, so that we were face to face again. "There is work to be done," she said. "Get on in here."

I swallowed every doubt I had. I smothered every fear. I stared down at the image now dangling from Fiona's hands, an image I did not fully understand and yet which I was sure held the key to a dire warning.

Yes. There was work to be done. And it began now.

Acknowledgements

With gratitude to Andrew Hurlbut, whose fascinating daguerreotypes greatly inspired the twists and turns of this book.

Many thanks to James Egan at Bookfly Design for taking yet another of my vague, poorly explained ideas, and turning it into a masterpiece. Always delighted to have my books judged by your covers.

To my wonderful beta readers, Andrew, Becca, Missy, Nicole, and Danie, thank you for always eagerly accepting my pages, for your eagle eyes, and your helpful feedback!

To Joe, my partner in all things, thank you for taking another leap with me. What an adventure we're having.

And to you, fearless reader. If you've followed Jess and the gang this far, you have my eternal gratitude.

About the Author

E.E. Holmes is a writer, teacher, and actor living in central Massachusetts with her husband, two children, and a small, but surprisingly loud dog. When not writing, she enjoys performing, watching unhealthy amounts of British television, and reading with her children. Please visit www.eeholmes.com to learn more about E.E. Holmes and *The World of The Gateway*.

Made in United States
Orlando, FL
04 April 2022

16468670R00183